WITHDRAWN

PEPPERFISH KEYS

PEPPERFISH KEYS

A Detective Barrett Raines Mystery

DARRYL WIMBERLEY

Thomas Dunne Books

St. Martin's Minotaur ❦ New York

This is a work of fiction. All of the characters, organizations, and events portrayed in this novel are either products of the author's imagination or are used fictitiously.

THOMAS DUNNE BOOKS.
An imprint of St. Martin's Press.

www.thomasdunnebooks.com
www.minotaurbooks.com

Library of Congress Cataloging-in-Publication Data

Wimberley, Darryl.
    Pepperfish Keys : a Detective Barrett Raines mystery / Darryl Wimberley. — 1st ed.
      p. cm.
    ISBN-13: 978-0-312-36139-6
    ISBN-10: 0-312-36139-4
    1. African American police—Fiction. 2. African Americans—Fiction. 3. Florida—Fiction. I. Title.
    PS3573.I47844P47 2007
    813'.54—dc22

2007010838

First Edition: July 2007

10 9 8 7 6 5 4 3 2 1

Dedicated to Doris, Morgan, and Jack

Acknowledgments

I am pleased to thank the Live Oak Regional Office of the Florida Department of Law Enforcement for years of patient support. Thanks go as well to Captain Buddy Williams in Live Oak, to the sherrifs of Dixie, Taylor, and Lafayette Counties, and to retired lawman Russel Mobley. I owe heartfelt appreciation to longtime friend Ken Hewitt for helping me scout the locations upon which this fiction is based. Northing like strapping in with Ken on a rain-slick blacktop at eighty miles an hour. Makes you hungry for stop signs. Kudos to New York's Toni Plummer for helping market and push this novel. And I am always privileged to publicly acknowledge Ruth Cavin, the sharpest and most distinguished editor at a very distinguished house. Thanks for all your help, Ruth. Thanks to No-Neck and Rowdy. And thanks, finally, to my readers.

PEPPERFISH KEYS

The mise-en-scene ...

There is a Florida that has nothing to do with Disney World. Nothing to do with palm trees or Holiday Inns. Tourists are neither courted nor coddled in this Florida, and you can go a hundred miles and never find a golden arch.

1.

A stretched limousine sweltered in an Indian summer, a modern carriage on a rip of asphalt that terminated at a ragged border of grass and water. It would be inaccurate to call the place a beach. There was no strand to separate the saw grass from the bay beyond, no boundary of sand between the sammy earth and Pepperfish Keys.

Past the Keys beckoned the Gulf of Mexico, that place of pirates and privateers whose waters have for aeons lipped along the littoral of Florida's northwestern coast. A molten sun swelled over that wide bowl. It was only midafternoon and already a flight of pelicans glided off open water seeking an early roost ashore. Atop a cedar tree, perhaps, or perhaps in one of the beetle-ravaged pines that rose as solitary sentinels from the saw grass's damp pasture.

"I love this scene." A ponytailed Latino jabbed a remote at the DVD player installed in the cushion of his limo's rear-facing seat.

"You've seen it twice, for God's sake. . . ."

This protest from the twenty-something straddled over her

partner. Her belly rippled like a gymnast's beneath a halter top. Her legs strained tight against tie-dyed shorts. A mane of chestnut hair.

"Jussa minute, baby, this part—"

The heir apparent to Tom Cruise and Russell Crowe faced his nemesis on the limo's compact screen:

You tell them about me? You tell them anything at all? I'll pickle your fucking tongue—

" 'Pickle his tongue,' you hear that?"

"I heard."

"—I'll pickle it, I'll slice it, I'll feed it to your kids in a fucking hamburger—"

" 'Fucking hamburger'! I love it. Man takes no shit."

"Time for intermission?" She slid a hand inside his crotch.

He brushed her away. "Hit the rewind."

"Jesus Christ, Eddy, why don't we just go to a theater?"

"Not released yet. I told you."

"You also told me they were going to call it *Red Moon. Red,* you said. Not *Scarlet. Scarlet Moon*! Totally fag."

He shrugged.

"Movies. They change titles alla time."

"Lotta hype, you ask me."

"Bullshit!" He froze the DVD. "This hombre? Randall Damone? Has got legs. He's gonna be bigger than Brad Pitt. Bigger than Tom Cruise or that Australian. Anybody!"

She glanced to the car's small screen.

"He's that good, I wanta see him on something big and silver."

"You will."

"When?"

"Sometime."

"Eddy! I can't remember the last time we saw anything in a *real* theater."

"Whatchu talkin'? We got ourself a theater right here!"

"Oh, sure."

"And you the marquis, baby. You the star."

"I'm something, that's for sure."

"How 'bout a sneak preview? 'Coming Attractions'? Come on, baby. Make it hot."

"Okay."

She pulled the halter top over her head, licking a finger luxuriously to moisten one nipple—

"Here's 'Hot.' "

Then the other.

"Here's 'Bothered.' "

Her breasts firm as pears.

A smile split Eddy DeLeon's face to reveal a carcass of decayed teeth. No amount of money could renew the wreckage wrought in poorer years and poorer places to those mandibles. And Eddy would not consent to dentures or other, artificial reconstructions. He didn't need a pretty smile to get what he wanted.

He didn't need a pretty face.

Tokens of throwaway money could be noted at a glance. The ring binding his long ponytail of raven-black hair was bought in Mexico, beaten gold. A wide belt sported a pound of turquoise and silver. A single pierce of diamond. Rings of topaz or jade on the fingers of both hands.

Eddy bought a lot of junk at altitude. His fingernail clippers, for example. Eddy trimmed his nearly feminine nails with a silver-plated novelty bought on impulse on a flight from Mexico City to Miami. You might miss the cheap strand of cotton twine looped inside the collar of Eddy's Brooks Brothers shirt, but you could not miss the Etruscan design on the bling acquired at thirty thousand feet from some in-flight catalog.

Purchases made on solid ground tended to be less impulsive. Eddy loved the fawning attention to be had from a tailor in New York or Chicago. He bought two or three watches a year when earthbound at those cities, always from Govberg's. Always a Patek Phillipe. Occasionally he would pay too much for some vase or bronze at Christie's. Anything to show that Eduardo DeLeon was a man with money to toss.

He offered a snuffbox bought over Denver to his topless playmate. She took a hit. He took her pears into his hands.

"Am I staying home with you tonight, Princess? After the party?"

"Nothing at home we can't do here."

A certain cloud drifted over those flat, brown eyes.

"Man likes to mount his trophy on the wall, Beth Ann."

"I've never mounted on a wall."

The intercom cut off Eddy's reply.

"Boss?"

"What is it?"

A partition hissed down to reveal the driver in the front seat. "Crease" might be a tourist with his loud, Hawaiian shirt and baggy trousers. But there are scars old and ugly along his forearms.

"Orlando, boss. He's got your man."

"Tell him we're on our way."

DeLeon pulled from beneath his paramour.

"Eddy!"

"What?"

"You always do that. Get me tight. Make me wait!"

"Business before pleasure."

"Who is it this time?"

"Put on your top."

Ten minutes of blacktop later the Lincoln traded the sight of surf and sea for the breezeless shadows of the flatwoods. The hum of asphalt gave way to a sudden crunch of gravel and then a hiss of sand. Little to hear otherwise in this wilderness. Little to see. A pair of ruts snaked through bone-white loam. A monotony of pine and scrub oak and palmetto pressed in from either side, welcomed only for their meager shade of needles and moss and frond. But then a pair of headlights winked ahead. A low-slung sports car idling just off the primitive road.

"That's him."

The Lincoln pulled up to a Corvette glowing like kryptonite. Eddy lowered his honey's window with the tap of a nail; Beth Ann recoiled at the bloated face swelling suddenly before her own.

"Orlando. Welcome." Eddy leaned across the long back seat

to regard the blond-haired giant in jersey and slacks who waited outside. Orlando Fuqua had to bend deeply to peer into the limo's interior.

"And who is our guest?"

"It's Calhoun, Mr. DeLeon."

A black man the size of a child popped into view, his pitted face barely level with the Lincoln's rear window. Hair growing like lichen, patches of salt and pepper on a small, round skull.

"That's 'Taylor', sir—Senor. Taylor Calhoun."

"Looks like a fucking pygmy."

This from Beth Ann.

"Thass good," Eddy approved. "Thass real good, baby."

Most of Calhoun's clothing was grubbed, stolen, or, very occasionally, donated. A family from Jacksonville left the jeans that now bagged about his bandy legs like socks on a rooster. He'd fished his jacket from a Dumpster. The only scrap of his present ensemble actually purchased was a T-shirt featuring a buxom cheerleader above a logo for the Jacksonville Jaguars.

Taylor loved those Jaguars.

"I tole Orlando I watten finished with my work." The apple in the little man's throat bobbed like a cork. "I hatten change out the beer kegs. And Mama gave me some launderyin', too, but Orlando, he tole me you wanted me, so I come right along."

"I appreciate your consideration, senor." Eddy gestured magnanimously. "Join me, *por favor*. For conversation."

"And what am I 'sposed to do?" Beth Ann retreated from the window.

"Wait in Orlando's car."

"We'll be late for the party."

"No, no. This will only take—"

"A few minutes. Right."

A pair of rubies mounted on the gold-plated clasp of her purse. She clawed out a pack of cigarettes.

"This is fucked, Eddy."

"Help her out, Crease," DeLeon instructed his driver.

"Don't bother."

Beth Ann slid the length of the leather bench to exit the limo. Fuqua bundled Taylor in from the other side.

"Where to?" Crease inquired.

"The yard will do," Eddy told his driver.

The Lincoln's tires spun briefly before finding a purchase in the white, white sand to leave Beth Ann draped lasciviously across the hood of Orlando's 'Vette.

"So. Senor Taylor." Eddy turned attention to his new companion. "I interrupt your chores. My apologies."

"No problem. I just ditten expect Orlando is all."

"What, you expect me to do everything myself?"

"Oh, no! No, sir!"

"I can be everywhere, can I? Is why I keep people."

"Yessir. And I been a good man for you, Mr. DeLeon. Really!"

"I am glad to hear. You like Mama's?"

"It's not bad," Taylor hedged. "But a whorehouse for a man— Not much opportunity for advancement!"

"A sense of humor. I like."

"Where we goin', Mr. DeLeon?"

"Mmm?"

"Well, I hate thinkin' your ladyfriend's stuck back there by herself is all."

"Ah, well. Women, you know, they gossip."

"They do got themselfs a mouth." Taylor seemed relieved.

"*Muy grande,*" Eddy smiled encouragement. "And this will not take long. I hope there is no inconvenience."

"Oh, no! No, sir, senor. None at all."

A half mile later the limo emerged from the flatwood's cover to penetrate a palisade of corrugated tin. It was a junkyard. Spools of telephone cable stacked all over like checkers recently kinged on a cluttered board. Creosote posts piled beside pallets laden with fifty-gallon drums. A museum of antiquated trucks and cars oxidized in permanent retirement. Transmissions and engine blocks.

A BlueBird schoolbus rusted nearest to DeLeon's Lincoln. Its tires and wheels cannibalized, the bus bowed to Eddy's vehicle on brown axles. Inside the frigid limo, Taylor Calhoun sweated buckets as Eddy DeLeon applied his silver clippers to a fingernail sharp as a claw.

"So. You watch the cash at Mama's, don' you, Senor Taylor? Cash in. Cash out."

"An' I never took a dime, neither. Not even petty cash!"

"That is good," Eddy nodded. "That is very good. But I have something I want you to see."

Eddy palmed his clippers into his trousers and popped open an armrest to reveal a storage bin and video camera.

"I make videos. A hobby. These digital ones—so easy. See for yourself."

He displayed the viewfinder for Calhoun's inspection. A long lens captureed two African American men between a pair of columns on a terrace of marble steps. One man stode up the steps. The other edged painfully down.

"You know these two, amigo?"

"I . . . I doan think so."

"I can freeze the image. Now . . . Now you can see."

A pair of caryatids supported the entablature rising massively above the two videoed gentlemen. One of the actors on the stage beneath was easy to identify, a pygmy with patches of salt and pepper crabbing down the steps on arthritic knees.

"That is you, Senor Taylor? Is it not?"

"Mr. DeLeon, I can explain!"

"Do not insult my intelligence, senor."

Eddy punched "Play." The second player easily ascended the sloping steps. Long, powerful legs in pleated tans. The kind of physique that might have belonged to a professional athlete, a large-boned frame, powerful torso straining the limits of a navy blue blazer. A boulder-sized head. Clean shaven. Hair cut to the scalp. A black hand extended to accept Taylor Calhoun's limply offered grasp.

Eddy DeLeon froze the frame once again. Forced the viewfinder to Calhoun's reluctant attention.

"This nigger shaking your hand? Is Barrett Raines, is he not?

I should say, Special Agent Barrett Raines. Florida Department of fucking Law Enforcement!"

"But Mr. DeLeon, I known Bear awl my life! We used to fish when he was little. He lives on Deacon Beach, for God's sake. You know that!"

"I know that a courthouse is a curious place to fish. And the Suwannee County courthouse is sixty miles at least from Pepperfish Keys, senor. Sixty miles inland. What kind of fishing you doing over there?"

"I vote in Suwannee County."

"You vote."

"Right there in Live Oak. Always have, you can check and see."

"Election is not until November."

"Yes, sir, but they said they had to verify all the absentee voters; you know how it's been, all the problems they been havin'."

"And was there nothing else? No other—Opportunity?"

"No, sir! None. *Nada*!"

Calhoun now squirming on the limo's slick seat.

Orlando Fuqua laid a pale paw across the small man's chest.

"Don't make a problem."

"But Jesus, ain' a black man on the Keys don't know Bear Raines! I got cousins still sees him at church. We used to talk awl the time!"

"How 'bout movies, Taylor? You talk with this negro about my interest in *le cinema*?"

"I doan know nuthin' bout no movies, Mr. DeLeon. All I do is what Mama tells me; change out kegs, mop restrooms, that's *all*. Swear to God!"

"I see."

DeLeon dropped the videocam back into its plush bin.

"Orlando."

"Yes, sir?"

"Let him out."

"Thank you, Mr. DeLeon!"

Taylor's knees seemed uncertain as he followed Fuqua in a spill from the auto's interior.

"I been a good man for you, Mr. DeLeon! I always will!"

"Nevertheless, senor, I don' think I employ you any longer."

"No problem. I understand."

"Do you?"

"I do. Gracias."

"*De nada*," Eddy replied and Orlando Fuqua shot the runt through the knee.

Taylor Calhoun's scream cut the heavy air like a knife. They came over and over, his screamed imprecations. Agonized. Gut wrenching. Eddy DeLeon pocketed his nailclippers before stepping out of the car.

"Jesus!" Taylor screamed still. "Jesus God!"

Calhoun now clutching splinters of bone in a fetal collapse beside the schoolbus. DeLeon slipped his thumb beneath the loop of cotton twine disguised beneath the other necklace on his slender neck. Taylor struggling then to crawl beneath the rusting schoolbus.

"You don't need to do that, Mr. DeLeon! God! This here's enough! Oh God!"

A flick of the wrist. The string snapped, a pleasant "pop." A straight blade appeared, opened from the pearl handle in Eddy's hand.

"You Doan' Need To! You Doan'—!"

Eddy cut that squawk short. Ear to ear. The carotids sprayed the bus's yellow flank with an undeniable graffiti. The larnyx gaped open. A sucking sound, then. Like a baby gasping for wind.

"He still trying," Orlando grunted reluctant respect.

But then the head lolled obscenely to one side. The body relaxed. The legs twitched. A later examination would reveal the patched jeans to have been soiled.

Eddy repaired his blade on the dead man's trousers.

"Crease—" he spoke to his driver.

"Yes, boss."

"Before morning I want some other tires on the limo. Use Michelins, get rid of these others."

"An' what about Taylor?"

"Take him off the road someplace. Put on some dirt. And hurry. I don' wanta be late for the party."

2.

■ *It had already been a* long day by the time Special Agent Barrett Raines nursed his battered Whaler toward the pier extending like a pimp's pointed finger to Senator Baxter Stanton's decadently extravagant mansion. The senator's immaculately maintained residence and surrounding grounds looked over a well-dredged channel of silver water that cut through the saw grass off Pepperfish Keys, its attending pier propped on pilings set straight as a plumber's bob.

The dock was freshly painted, festooned with gaudy streamers, hung with lanterns and girandoles and otherwise accoutred to receive well-heeled guests, mostly out-of-towners whose launches berthed by the dozen, the ladies and their gentlemen being helped from runabouts and sleek-hulled watercraft by college boys in sweat-soaked cottons, or by coeds in skirts and blouses as diaphanous as the wings of mosquito hawks.

"Bear" Raines reflected that he was one of the few guests invited to this affair who was indigenous to the region. The Keys, after all, were part of Dixie County, just one county south of

Barrett's home on Deacon Beach. And if Bear was one of the few locals invited to Senator Stanton's party, he was certainly the only African American. Bear felt like a fieldhand calling on the Big House as he approached the pier in a boat camouflaged in a collage of paint and primer, sloughing over the twin wakes of a twenty-eight-foot Blackfin and some custom-built inboard that he could not identify, some sleek and timeless teardrop of mahogany and brass.

No natives owned boats like these. The lawman reached over to squeeze honey into a well-chipped mug. The caravansari of inboards and cruisers tied all about were the toys of folks who had come to the Keys from someplace else. These were the new-comers, both middle-incomers and millionaires, who had mi-grated to Florida's northwestern coast from places like Tampa or Miami or Orlando.

It wasn't the charm of local culture that lured this new gener-ation of residents to Florida's Big Bend, and the newly settled certainly did not come for the insects, snakes, and heat. What brought folks from south of Orlando to Florida's Big Bend was the press of population and money.

That and the promise of a hassle-free life.

For years northern Florida was neglected by real-estate mag-nates and developers. Who in his right mind, after all, would pay five or ten or twenty thousand dollars an acre for land infested with mosquitoes and moccasins, an abysmal school system, and a chronically underemployed population? But an ongoing flood of families to south Florida kept driving the cost of real estate to levels that had become unaffordable even for the well-to-do. Twenty thousand dollars won't buy you an outhouse in Coral Gables, even if outhouses were available to be bought, but you could get land between Tallahassee and Gainesville for five thou-sand dollars an acre and pastured lots along Florida's northwest-ern coast could be managed for a fraction of what a patch of grass would cost in Boca Raton or Naples.

The press of money drove folks north and so did the press of people. People relocated from south of Orlando to northwestern

Florida to escape the pressure of traffic, overcrowded schools, drugs, urban blight, and all the other things that plague a population bursting at the seams. But the first newcomers to Barrett's jurisdiction were not bringing families with them, not children anyway. These were self-styled entrepreneurs or retirees who despised taxes and shared driveways. It did not matter to these new citizens that the school systems were underfunded or that the dominant employers in the region were a pulpwood company and a prison. Certainly there was no concern for the festering poverty of black people or the newly entrenched slavery of Latin migrants.

Real-estate marketers and developers courted this largely libertarian population, promising both the retired manager from Wal-Mart and the stock broker from Melbourne a retreat from society replete with digital television, wireless Internet, and air-conditioning. Not to mention indoor plumbing. A fake pastorale free from urban obligation.

The first newcomer to Pepperfish Keys was transient, a weekend executive from Fort Meyers with a condominium near Steinhatchee. Within months a dozen other waterside retreats were erected on a variety of stilts, their owners following the waterline up and down the coast. Those first properties eventually were sold, and then resold to persons more interested in permanent residence. It was mostly in response to these transplants that tracts of tangled flatwoods were burned or bulldozed for re-landscaping into a faux wilderness dotted with EuroCracker architecture, tin roofs, and wraparound porches painted in bright pastels of exterior latex.

Then came the big money, St. Joe marketing thousands of formerly unproductive acres as the "Other Northwest," and before you knew it bonds were issued and taxes raised to pay for roads and bridges essential to accommodate an unsought colonization.

Some locals cooperated with the occupation more than others. Dixie County's elected commissioners were observed trading in their beat-up Fords and Chevys for Land Rovers and SUVs provided courtesy of investors pledging to "develop" the area.

One hand washing the other.

Oh, but the little man benefited, too, it was argued, and sure enough, within months, Piggly Wigglys and Stop n' Go's sprang up along arteries of asphalt cut through the flesh of sloughs and hammocks fashioned by the retreat of an ancient sea. You could rent videos, now, without driving to Cross City or Perry. You could buy beer, even on Sunday. And satellite dishes sprouted like lily pads from spec homes and doublewides that skirted the newly developed tracts like stained lace on a gaudy skirt.

Raines could still recall the unspoiled years on Pepperfish Keys, those boyhood days when that soggy extension of low-lands and sandbars had been no more than a backwater refuge south of Deacon Beach and Dead Man's Bay. You couldn't reach the Keys by land back then. Only local crackers or fishermen who knew the cypress poles that were in those years the only guides to navigation could get you into the place.

One of Barrett's first and unnerving experiences on open water came while still a boy, mercifully released from his father's rule for a weekend expedition with his mother's brothers who recruited their young nephew to load cane poles and canned bait into a flimsy outboard for a run down the coast. Bear could still recall the smell of briny water on that day of odyssey, a torch of sun burning mist off the saw grass. His uncle's flatbottomed johnny. The aroma of oil and gasoline. The feel of the cord that pulled the little two-stroke to life. A heron's startled flight. And then the journey over languid water. That had been frightening for Barrett, an apparently endless and disorienting wallow over oyster beds and turtle grass, pushing against a running tide, the sun a dull ball of sulphur. An eternity it had seemed, relieved only with a hard turn to port for Pepperfish Keys.

But once on firm land and his stomach settled the boy was en-chanted. The forests and fresh creeks bordering Pepperfish Keys were a paradise. A paradise, even then, though far from pristine. The vast tracts of tidewater cypress and loblolly pine indigenous to northern Florida had been clearcut in the twenties and thirties, leaving the earth to renew herself at random or to be cultivated at the stewardship of pulpwood companies whose hardhatted men reforested the spent sand with hybrid species of pine.

Even so, a few scraps of land close to the coast remained undisturbed, allowing a boy craving freedom to wander at will beneath shades of native oak and pine and cypress on a forest floor uncluttered with underbrush and sponged damply with a loess of moss and straw. There were no restrictions, no fences. No one bought or sold property along Pepperfish Keys in those years; land was acquired, if at all, by usucapion. It was a kingdom transgressed only by the capricious flights of birds.

Or perhaps the forays of fishermen.

Throughout a weekend mercifully free of beatings or humiliation, Barrett angled to his heart's content, catching with his kin enough mullet and snapper to fill a pair of Igloo coolers. Barrett's was not a boyhood littered with pleasant memories, which made the impressions of that solitary expedition all the more cherished: The breeze off briny water. The smell of a pine-knot fire. The pistol report of resin. Tangles of oily smoke working into your shirt, your trousers, your skin, your hair. Getting up early from the shelter of a tarpaulin tent. A bladder relieved over palmetto fronds. The morning's toilet accomplished with sand and saltwater.

Then to breakfast on grits and coffee dark and strong and sweetened with honey. Paddling out on water still as jello with your tackle, your water jug, your bait, to return with a setting sun to feast on the catch of the day, that bounty including an uncle's proudly displayed specimen—the elusive pepperfish for which the Keys were ostensibly named.

Now, there was a mystery. The pepperfish enjoyed an unchallenged if unsubstantiated status among natives. It was a fish whose name every local knew and pronounced but was officially listed nowhere. It would be many years before Raines prevailed upon a zoologist at Florida's Fish 'N Game Commission to locate the pepperfish in some more formal nomenclature, assuming then that "pepperfish" would be confirmed as a colloquial designation for some otherwise-identified species.

Barrett was disconcerted to discover that the pepperfish so puissant in memory was not listed in any officially sanctioned guide to saltwater life. Informal searches of cyber-sources failed similarly to situate the local creature within any phylum, genus, or species. Agent Raines even went so far as to visit the research station in Cedar Keys, seeking a scrap of information regarding a fish familiar from childhood. A sandy-haired researcher politely explained that no reference to the pepperfish could be found. There was nothing, in other words, to substantiate that anything called a pepperfish existed.

And yet people caught them. Not often, to be sure. But pepperfish were hooked or netted by folks all along the Keys. In fact, a whole apocrypha surrounded the pepperfish. He brought good luck. Caught on a full moon and prepared properly, he was an aphrodisiac.

Upon close query, however, Barrett began to notice that locals claiming to have caught or eaten a pepperfish were curiously vague as to its description. The few particularizations he ever heard seemed a poor match to the admittedly dimmed memory of Barrett's boyhood catch. No one, it seemed, recalled this fish in exactly the same way. The lawman began to suspect that any fish that could not be readily identified was christened a pepperfish on the spot. A moniker of last resort.

Nevertheless Barrett would himself insist if asked that of course he had caught and eaten pepperfish and, Damn, that was some of the sweetest eating he'd ever had! It was the memory of youth that kept the taste fresh in his mouth. The camp. The fire. What it was like as a boy to share a meal with grown men after a span of genial labor. To smell a breeze salted over water. Drink coffee down to the grounds.

And then to sleep untroubled by the prowl of panthers or the grunt of frogs and gators beneath an arbor of pine and cypress, separated from the Gulf of Mexico by a roost of heron and a border of stubborn grass.

The modern and moneyed men coming to Pepperfish Keys did not share those memories and were not inclined to care.

These men came to retreat, or debauch. They arrived from Jacksonville or Atlanta or Miami bearing trophy wives to their trophy homes and shoveling out the cash necessary to indulge in a second adolescence beside the sea, and they had nothing in common with the population they displaced.

The poor blacks and cracker whites whose families had fished and hunted the region for generations found themselves increasingly peripheral to life on Pepperfish Keys. Left to pick up the crumbs from wealthier tables, native-borns adopted that attitude so common among displaced persons, on the one hand hostile to anyone with means greater than their own and on the other positively sycophantic when it came to courting the jobs and money that outlanders brought to the region. Local whites and blacks and, to a much diminished extent, Latinos took the money offered to them resenting all the while the hands who doled it. Except for Baxter Stanton's hand. Of course.

Senator Stanton was well loved by his cracker constituency, a homegrown populist who declared often and publicly that he never forgot his roots. Here was a man who worked hard, beat the odds, got rich, and then had the good sense to come back home and build his Xanadu right on top of his granddaddy's homestead. Right on the swell of land that was the only high ground known on Pepperfish Keys.

Throttling back the single Evinrude driving his secondhand vessel, Barrett discerned the bulge of lawn rising beyond the dock and ascending in a gentle incline to the pier-and-beam foundation of Stanton's mansion and he felt the knot in his gut relax. The public ramp from where he launched at Deacon Beach was only fifteen miles or so from Baxter Stanton's private quay, but Bear remained afflicted with a fear of open water. People did get lost on the Gulf, even in good weather. And even after you got back within sight of land Senator Stanton's residence was not easy to find.

Deep inside Pepperfish Keys and secreted off a shallow bay the senator's mansion overlooked a featureless channel of water that snaked indistinguishably from a hundred others through a prairie of saw grass that split and split and split again before reaching the Gulf of Mexico. Oldtimers navigated to these invisible locations by instinct or the discernment of landmarks never certain in Barrett's eyes, and also by triangulating their position on the water from jerry-rigged buoys, cypress poles stuck at low tide by generations of local fishermen. Bear backed up his old Army lensatic compass with Loran, a handheld Magellan, a pair of marine-band radios, cell phone, and waterproofed charts. Not to mention life vests, fresh water, and flares. That and lots of coffee.

A modern navigator, if not intrepid.

Looking past the pier and grounds Raines could now see the porch swing that Senator Stanton insisted be prominent on his acre-sized veranda. An icon of earlier and rural architecture, the porch swing allowed native voters to imagine that the senator was still in touch with the common folk even though Baxter himself had long ago abjured porch swings and conversation for satellite TV and air-conditioning.

And other diversions.

The mansion's architecture jarred any tutored sensibility, a collision of gingerbread Victorian and art deco vying with plantation influences and scale. But it proved a source of pride for locals who, seeing the uninspired and stilted boxes of the newly rich, would smile knowingly and say, "Yeah, but you oughta see the *senator's* place."

Agent Raines was glad to be living in a modest Jim Walter ranch-style with jalouise windows. He was glad that his home was a spit off the Gulf on Deacon Beach, the beach itself a seaside village distant from any architecture worth mentioning. Barrett had always wanted to settle in his hometown, but was not exactly welcomed with open arms by the white community familiar with him from childhood. If it had not been for Ramona Walker, "Bear," as he was locally known, might never have got on the local police force.

Not easy to be a black cop in a white town. Many of the men, and women, whom The Bear nailed for drugs or theft or murder were people he had known since grade school. Some of the men he put in cuffs had at one time or another shoved him to the back of a schoolbus, or spilled his books in a hallway. Hard to keep a reputation for fairness or objectivity in that small society, and of course Barrett's family was not immune to the fallout.

A residue of resentment or bigotry affected Laura Anne and the boys in ways that had until fairly recently been subtle. Laura Anne, for instance, was an accomplished teacher and musician who could not get a permanent position at the local school. A written application was required of Barrett's sons before they could join the Boy Scouts.

And there were more quotidian prices exacted for living on the beach. It was impossible to get a plumber, carpenter, or electrician on time or sober for local repairs. There was no hospital, no clinic or EMS. Though the county subsidized a veterinarian, there was not a single doctor for human beings within twenty miles. The nearest supermarket was in Perry; Laura Anne spent half her free hours driving to get a pair of sneakers, a prescription filled. Everyday things.

Barrett drove an hour each day over two-lane blacktop just to get to his office. That trek took the lawman far inland to Suwannee County, a region where landowners hired immigrants to harvest their tobacco or rake their straw. The regional office of the Florida Department of Law Enforcement was installed in what used to be a redneck discotheque in the county seat at Live Oak; from that brick building beneath a generous grove of oak trees Agent Raines and a handful of colleagues coordinated criminal investigations ranging over seven counties and a hundred miles of coastline.

The FDLE's several regional offices took orders from a headquarters in Tallahassee, that bricked-in complex erected on the site of what had been, and still occasionally was described as, an asylum for the deranged. The mad hatters at Florida's Department of Law Enforcement had become indispensable to rural sheriffs in counties chronically short of cash and unable to afford the equipment, investigators, or forensic expertise necessary

21

to investigate sophisticated or extremely violent crimes. Special Agent Raines answered to Captain Henry Altmiller in Tallahassee, the near-Calvinist Altmiller famous for recruiting the best and most tenacious investigators in the Southeast. It was Henry Altmiller who recruited the department's first African-American investigator, and it was he who had assigned The Bear his present and dreaded task.

First thing, though, was to dock his boat without fouling on turtleweed or nicking some other craft or otherwise making a fool of himself. Barrett ran up the tilt trim as he glided toward an open berth on the pier. He killed the Evinrude, leaning starboard to bumper the hull before looping a nylon line about the brass lanyard that would secure his craft, the awkward wobble attending these chores easily blamed on the roll of his aging launch.

He could see that the pier was crowded with the kind of people not used to waiting in line, the men in tailored, linen suits, dressed as boys from Eton for croquet, their wives or mistresses in sheer, summer skirts and blouses got in Paris or New York. Bear felt like a hick in his off-the-shelf blazer, catalog shirt, and crisply pleated khaki slacks. He snugged a Christmas tie before mounting the gunwale, timing the roll of his boat to rise onto the senator's pier.

A few heads turned, the men scanning his boat and accoutrements, the battered hull, the ailing Evinrude, the Penn rod stuck in its ferrule, a lonely mast. The women who paused to note the latest arrival saw an African-American man just a smidgeon shorter than a coffin with boulder shoulders beneath an enormous skull. Hair cropped military short. Legs filling out slacks pleated and pressed to a knife's edge. They did not discern the bulge of a shoulder-holster hung inside the always-pressed blazer.

Barrett fished an envelope damp with perspiration from the breast of his Sears-bought blazer. Interesting that an agent from the FDLE was required to present in addition to his other credentials a manila invitation. A concern for security, he had been assured. The kids appointed to guard Baxter Stanton's sanctum were vetted by the senator's wife. Barbara Stanton selected the boys mostly on the basis of political connection, though she was always careful to include a token local at these affairs.

The coeds, on the other hand, were selected entirely on the basis of their social affiliations at FSU. They were all sorority girls, naturally, unanimously sweet magnolias from Mrs. Stanton's alma mater. Babs often mentioned her days at FSU. "It was the '60s, but we Tri Delts didn't do daisy chains," she'd wink. "We like our men one at a time."

A bevy of sorority sweethearts now fussed over the attendees, young girls, full of juice, with waists like wasps and breasts sworn to be natural. They floated up and down the pier, those ever-smiling coeds, ministering to the visitors' every need, every visitor except the single black man standing like a domestic in their midst.

Finally a burr-cut kid in brilliant, white cotton pressed through the crowd.

"Mr. Raines? Mr. Raines, have you been helped, sir?"

Scanning a clipboard, tall and tan and dressed like Gatsby. It took Bear a moment to place the young man.

"Tommy, is that you? Tom Slade?"

"Yes, sir."

Barrett knew Tommy, of course. Knew everyone in the Slade family. Tommy's uncle was a high-school classmate who ran a repair shop in Deacon Beach. Bear and Rolly sat two desks apart in Mr. Hilton's homeroom. More recently Barrett had been forced to put Rolly's son behind bars, the teenager's crime connected obliquely to a homicide that directly touched Bear's own family. It had been a terrible ordeal Laura Anne endured, a trial for which she had so far refused counsel.

Leaving her husband with a nameless burden.

"You up at Tallahassee, Tom?"

"No, sir. Gainesville. U of F. I'm a Gator."

"I won't tell. Need to see my invitation?"

"Oh, that's all right, Mr. Raines," the sophomore declined. "Tell you what, just follow me, I'll get you off this dock."

Heads turning, now, as the black man broke line.

Barrett offered eye contact casually with his better-dressed company. Heads snapped back to neutral as the grip of his handgun peeked briefly from its holster. Bear was returning the senator's crested card to the pocket of his Sears & Roebuck blazer when the question came.

"How's Miz Raines doin'?"

"We're good."

The reply came abruptly.

"Thanks for asking."

Agent Raines followed his escort off the crowded pier and onto Senator Stanton's regal grounds marveling at the ways a man could waste money. An enormous, ice-carved Aphrodite dominated the center of Stanton's lawn, that statued harlot melting over magnums of champagne. The barbeque pit was as long as a boat trailer, wafting mesquite that had been corded in Texas and trucked in for the occasion.

There were tables and tables of ribs and brisket and boiled shrimp. A twenty-piece band. A half dozen open bars. Lots of scenery.

"Get you anything, Mr. Raines?"

"I'm fine, Tommy. Thank you."

"Might keep your invitation handy. Just in case."

In case, what? That a badge and gun were not sufficient?

But Barrett kept that thought to himself as he plunged past the icy goddess of love into throngs of mortals come to worship a different sort of diety. He would estimate that a couple hundred of Baxter's closest friends were convened to mix and mingle, their money prominently displayed on a variety of necks and wrists and fingers, a bracelet of jade set in yellow gold from Bulgari, rings by Cartier or Vera Wang. The men favored watches with big faces and lots of hands, Hublot or Diesel or TagHeur.

They roamed the grounds as if they owned the place, in printed silks and cool linens got from some atelier in Miami or Paris, sampling liquor and brisket served by African Americans sweating over cole slaw and condiments in tuxedos of polyester. Many of the black people sweltering at their domestic labor were familiar to Barrett. Some were friends. Neighbors, even. But Barrett did not greet his community openly, not in this setting. Instead, there was an exchange of silent acknowledgment—a lifted chin, a smile—as though any other salutation were an offense to the Massuh or his guests.

Though there was one voice uncontained.

"That you, Bear?"

This bold query coming overtly from an aging black man in stained coveralls. Barrett knew Clarence Magrue, of course. Clarence was the nearest thing to a handyman you could find in Pepperfish Keys, a local scrounging jobs for half the wages anybody else would demand. The aging Magrue was also a first cousin to Corrie Jean Raines, the woman once married to Barrett's brother. Before all that business.

"Clarence, how you doin'?"

"Sweatin' like a fresh-fucked fox in a forest fire."

Bear smiled. "Hope they're paying you."

The older man settled a toolbox to the ground.

"Heard Corrie Jean got hersef a job," the older man volunteered that non sequitur. "Indoors. Wal-Mart. Over in Perry."

"That's good." Barrett felt a tug of guilt. Corrie Jean needed a job. She had two girls to think about.

"That's real good," Raines repeated.

"We been missin' Laura Anne." Clarence broached that topic with lowered voice. "Nobody at church kin play a piano like that girl."

"It's just the restaurant," Barrett lied. "Work and all. It'll smooth out."

"You be sure and tell her we thinkin' of her."

"Thank you, Clarence, I will."

"Reckon I better git back to work." The old man bent over stiffly to retrieve his tools. "House like that? But they ain't three pipes of plumbing you kin depend on. See you, Bear."

Barrett parted ways with the handyman to turn down the cobbled drive that had become a tarmac for a caravan of news vans sprouting masts and dishes on the far side of the grounds. Reporters from CNN and ABC and FOX scurried like rodents over cables and generators, urgent to interview Florida's favorite senator. Barrett was happy to pass unnoticed among these newshounds, the Invisible Man. But there was one reporter he could not avoid; he could see her now, even through the tangle of equipment and technicians. Head and shoulders above the rest.

"How much time, Dew Drop?"

Sharon Fowler juggled the feed-interrupt at her ear.

The pusselgutted techie who was engineer, cameraman, and flunkie for K-E-Y-S's Live News Van had enjoyed about as much of Ms. Fowler as he could stand. The Keys's local anchorperson had been determined to produce this show on her own, capturing the senator's triumphal return with two cameras while insisting that she be freed from the tether of a stick mike so that she might snag Senator Stanton before he reached his indoor retreat.

Dewey brushed aside bangs of dishwater hair spilling from the trap of his cheap bill cap. There were, Dew Drop estimated, at least a half-dozen other vans with talent determined to reach the senator's side. CNN even brought down a crew from Atlanta to cover the event. The thing was—those outfits had money to burn. Dew Drop was running cables and camera by himself, trying to pull off a live shoot shorthanded and armed with not much more than a screwdriver, gaff tape, and P.F.M.

"Dew Drop!"

Fucking demanding bitch.

"How goddamn much *time*, Dewey?"

"Five—make that four and a half minutes."

Sharon Fowler stood a fingernail over six feet tall even without heels and coordinated every aspect of her appearance to accentuate that fact. A strapless dress that might have been confused for lingerie showed off well-toned legs and a back muscled and broad from years of varsity volleyball.

Until her injury, Sharon had been tapped for Olympic competition. Enjoying a full ride at the University of Florida and majoring in sports journalism, the white-haired phenom seemed destined for twin careers in pro volleyball and network broadcasting until a game at Stanford and an injury at L-5/S-1 rendered her vertebrae unfit for the impact of moneyed play. It was a crushing blow for a small-town girl filled with ambition. Sharon Fowler went into her senior year expecting a gold medal, endorsements, and a gig at ESPN. Instead she was fitted with a back brace and forced to scrape for work at a backwater television station in Pepperfish Keys.

"Testing . . . Test . . . Goddammit, Dewey, this mike is dead!"

"I'll get it."

"Four minutes to show and I've got no mouth? Fuck."

"I said I'll get it!"

"You tired of this job, Dewey?"

"Gimme your mike."

" 'Cause there's people waiting in double lines'd do anything to have it."

Barrett steered a course toward Sharon and her frazzled engineer, avoiding cables and pop-out reflectors and Keno lights that you'd think were completely unnecessary at four in the afternoon. He noticed that a fair number of the out-of-town talent were checking out the Keys's local reporter. A bevy of Reese Witherspoon look-alikes all coveting ratings in lip gloss and highlighted hair.

Sharon wasn't that popular locally. She was distant with the native johnnies looking to fish, even disdainful, and her job did not merit celebrity status. Reporters, after all, were a dime a dozen. And nobody gave a damn about volleyball in Pepperfish Keys.

Agent Raines on the other hand had risen to notorious fame by the route of public humiliation when his widely publicized investigation of Senator Baxter Stanton completely and ignominiously tanked. Sharon Fowler had been only too happy to chronicle that debacle for the viewing public. She latched onto the Stanton investigation as though it were Watergate and never let go and now Barrett was summoned for what he knew could only be a televised spanking.

He had broken the pottery and was ten yards away from owning it when he was intercepted by a pinstriped prosecutor in wingtips and athletic socks.

"Anticipating your interview, Bear?"

State Attorney Roland Reed offering that jibe as he scribbled notes in the margin of a newspaper. "Fountain Pen" Reed was always scribbling notes or reminders on something not intended for the purpose, and never with a ballpoint. Always some instrument that required an ink well or cartridge. Mr. Reed was the senior prosecutor for the Third Judicial District, formally designated as a state attorney, an advocate for the state. He wore wool suits like hairshirts, even in summer, and defended the white socks as an essential guard against athlete's foot.

"You here for moral support, Roland?"

"Just get it over with, be my advice. In and out."

Barrett had known Fountain Pen from the first moment he stepped onto his high school's white-varnished basketball court. Roland lost his forward position to the colored boy and vowed never to lose another thing in his life. And he pretty much kept that oath, graduating from law school and going on to compile a winning record as a state's attorney, losing very seldom in his mission to convict druggies, pedophiles, and killers all over Florida's Third Judicial District.

The prosecutor displayed his paper.

"You've read *The Democrat*?"

"Who hasn't?" Bear allowed a smile.

"Libelous," Roland clucked. "Irresponsible. I sympathize."

"You should. You set me up."

Fountain Pen and his myrmidons occupied the back half and second floor of the American Bank building in Live Oak, a nondescript cream-and-coffee building of brick and glass smack downtown about a half mile from Barrett's own converted digs on U.S. Highway 129. Roland's office had the advantage of an upstairs view. You could see the courthouse out one side. The Dixie Grill out the other. Locals joked that they never had to worry about the bank being robbed 'till the state moved in.

Barrett sparred with Roland frequently while working homicides for Deacon Beach's municipal PD. And now, barely five years after Reed indicted Barrett's brother for murder, the newly minted state attorney and the newly promoted special agent were once again uneasy teammates.

Barrett's area of responsibility was a near-mirror of the Third District's, six of the counties assigned to the FDLE's regional office falling directly within Reed's aegis. The state attorney normally cooperated with local sheriffs, municipal authorities and the FDLE whose job it was to work the scene, canvass the evidence, and present the facts for prosecution. Reed ruffled feathers right away when he announced upon his hire that he intended to be a "proactive" prosecutor, which in plain English meant that Roland reserved the right to independently investigate any case with potential for a high profile.

Any potboiler that might draw the attorney general's attention would do. It was Reed himself, in fact, who persuaded the A.G. and the state's Republican governor to authorize an "Executive Investigation" of Democratic Senator Baxter Stanton.

"I'm surprised you got an invitation, Roland."

"You got one."

"I got ordered. You got invited."

"Baxter's not the man to hold a grudge."

"That's mighty white of him. Seeing that you were the man chomping to gnaw on his balls."

"Was your source convinced me," Reed returned.

"Tell you what, chief, why don't you do the interview with Sharon Fowler? I'm sure she'd love to hear that side of the story."

"The governor needs somebody to whip, Bear. You're it."

"I don't suppose you or the A.G. reminded the governor that I never wanted this investigation? Or that I told you both it was nuts to hang a case on a single source?"

"Too late now. I'm afraid you're the face on this thing, Bear. Nothing I can do about it."

Sharon Fowler extended a dead microphone to her engineer. "If you can't stand the heat, Dewey, I'll find somebody who can."

Dew Drop was pretty close to meltdown. The chaw of tobacco working beside the engineer's jaw had long gone sour. He spat, deliberately, virulently.

"You think I gotta put up with this?"

"You've got four minutes."

Dew Drop snatched the handheld away from his Amazon boss. God damn the woman, anyway! Ninety percent of the time things were pretty close to perfect. Ninety percent! And that was with equipment salvaged from the goddamn '80s! But tonight—of all nights!—the shit hit the fan. The compressor that should've raised the ENG's mast failed—for a while it looked as if he wouldn't even be able to sight the shot. Fixed that problem. Then the zebra on the roving camera, *his* camera, went south, so he had to eyeball the Sony, set it up as the static, and then take that TK-44 piece of shit and a ton of batteries to chase Sharon around.

So much for video. Audio had been a screamer all night. The IFB that hid behind Sharon's tone-deaf ear and allowed her to communicate with the producer back at the station kept cutting out; Almond Sinclair didn't know half the time if his on-site talent could hear what he was saying. So Almond's shitting bricks, relaying instructions to Dew Drop over the Motorola to Sharon. Sharon spitting back. Which meant, of course, that Dewey's ass was getting chewed from both ends.

And now the bitch wanted a wireless.

Had to be the wireless mike. After all, you couldn't look near as sexy sidling up to a U.S. senator if you were jerking around a tangle of cable. That wouldn't look good on the tape you were doctoring for NBC, or ABC, or ESPN or whoever the fuck you expected to kiss your ass at a million dollars a year.

Talent, Dewey shook his head. They were all the same.

"What's . . . keeping . . . my . . . *mike*?"

Dew Drop displayed the connectors that linked her handheld to the van's audio.

"It's your XLR. Pin's broke."

"Oh, great."

"I can fix it."

"I've seen better shit at Radio Shack."

"I got a spare cable." He scrambled to find one. "We'll just splice a three-way pin."

"Who's 'we', Kemo Sabe?" she snarled and Dewey was set to drive a screwdriver through her heart when a modulated voice intruded.

"You always treat your people like shit, Sharon?"

Barrett Raines turned sideways to squeeze past a perimeter of lights.

"Agent Raines. So you showed."

"Why wouldn't I? You planning an ambush?"

"Shit." She turned to her cameraman. "Dewey, I told you I wanted the pier and the porch in the *same* shot."

"The hell you think I'm doing?!"

"Over here, Agent Raines."

Barrett followed the reporter to her live mobile van. A detritus of soda cans and fast food littered the vehicle's interior. A compass dangled by its lanyard from a swivel chair bolted into the floorboard. Duct tape strapped a tin can to the arm of that chair; Barrett deduced the can's purpose when he spotted a package of Red Man wadded below. Otherwise the bay was jammed with electronics. Did not take a pro to see signs of cannibalized equipment. A pair of ancient Sony '75s. A switcher gutted alongside.

"You ever see a live feed, Bear?"

"I've seen a gator eat a calf."

"My raw tape." She popped in a blank cassette. "Everything I do on-camera will wind up on this. Our number *Two* . . ." she reached for another cassette, "I'll get with the spare recorder."

" 'Kind of tape you using?" Barrett inspected a bulky cassette.

"Beta," she replied, griping at the same time that KEYS TV, late to adopt the half-inch format, was nowhere near the digital age.

"And we still have a ton of three-quarter stacked in racks back at the station. Which means we have to keep equipment for both formats. Band-aid the old stuff. Bitch for new."

Sharon shook her head.

"Anyplace civilized I'd be using hard drives and disks. I'd have digital editing on site, state-of-the-art decks and switchers, and a *real* crew and back-ups out the ass."

"Doesn't look like you're set for an interview." Barrett tried not to sound hopeful.

"S'okay."

" 'Okay'?"

"I got what I need."

An alarm bell rang.

"From me? For the interview? When?"

"I can't hear a fucking . . ."

She slipped the feed-interrupt from behind her ear, tapped it sharply. Even Barrett could hear the distant rebuke which that check provoked.

"Suck it up, Almond," Sharon growled. "I've got my own problems."

She fumbled with the IFB.

"Make yourself useful?"

She pulled a bun of cornsilk aside and Barrett inhaled the perfume of her hair, an unfamiliar, uncomfortably stimulating nectar.

"I haven't got all day, Bear."

He slipped the feed behind her ear.

"And am I connected? On my hip? Make sure I'm plugged in."

A Marlboro-sized box of circuitry settled close to the small of a long, well-toned and well-tanned spine exposed by the cut of her gown. Barrett could see the peak of a scar down low. And another white line, higher and crossways, where the surgeon took a graft fom her ilium.

He jammed the feeder's male into the box's cold receptacle.

"Good." Sharon was already on her two-way, directing Dewey's camera from the van's monitor.

"Pan right a tad. There. That's it."

Barrett took a look. Dewey's stationary camera now framed the pier with its marina of expensive watercraft. Aphrodite melted in the foreground amid a promenade of sweat-free guests.

"I hate rich people."

Sharon ran her tongue over lips the consistency of plastic.

"When you're a reporter, you see rich people all the time. You can see the rich. Feel the rich. You can even screw the rich, sometimes. But you can never *be* 'The Rich'."

The radio squawked.

"Try your mike, Sharon."

"Test-Test . . . ," Sharon complied. "Okay, we're five-by."

"Pure fucking magic." Dewey gave a thumbs-up from his handheld camera.

"When was I ever on-camera with you, Sharon?" Barrett tried again.

"You had a ticket to get out of this place, Bear. A chance to move on, move up. Be somebody."

"Does that answer my question?"

"You had a U.S. senator dead in your sights. You had him tied to dirty money. Dirty people. But guess what?"

"You tell me."

"You blew it. You put blind trust in a completely unreliable source—"

"Not accurate."

"—you compromised your boss. You infuriated the attorney general, you embarassed the governor, and most important? You lost. Nobody can afford to lose to Baxter Stanton, Bear, but most especially not a black man working at the Florida Department of Law Enforcement."

"That the way you look at it, Sharon?"

"Doesn't matter how I look at it—"

"Four seconds," Dew Drop sang out. "Three . . . Two . . . !"

A wide smile displayed perfect teeth to the camera.

"That's the way it is."

3.

"*. . . You're hot,*" *Dew Drop warned* and Sharon took that cue.

"*Good evening. I'm Sharon Fowler, K-E-Y-S News Live. We come to you this evening from the home of Senator Baxter Stanton. You can see the gala celebration unfolding here. It's a celebration which from the senator's point of view is well deserved.*

"*For months Baxter Stanton's bid for re-election to the United States Senate has been tainted by allegations of criminal activity linking the senator with one Eddy DeLeon, a naturalized Honduran of uncertain means acquitted four years ago of a violent homicide committed in Miami.*

"*State attorneys from the Third Judicial Circuit in Live Oak began to acknowledge problems with their investigation this past July when in response to charges of harassment from Senator Stanton's attorney, State Attorney Roland Reed confirmed that a months-long probe by the Florida Department of Law Enforcement was based on accusations leveled by a single informant reporting to FDLE Special Agent Barrett Raines.*

"Agent Raines's undercover source insisted that Senator Stanton was using his legitimate and widely scattered businesses to launder cash raked in by DeLeon's unspecified but presumably illegal enterprises. On Wednesday in a stunning move from his bench Judge Randall Boatwright declared the state's entire case to be, quote, 'completely without merit.' In what has been described by those attending as a vitriolic hearing, the judge strictly ordered Special Agent Barrett Raines and the Third District's prosecutors to cease all probes of any kind into the senator's campaign or financial affairs. Senator Stanton in turn consented to withdraw a civil action against the Florida Department of Law Enforcement and State Attorney Roland Reed's Live Oak office."

Trapped on the sidelines, Barrett seethed. It was Roland Reed who jumped at the chance to investigate the money tree around Stanton's campaign. It was Fountain Pen Reed who bet the farm on a lone informer and against Barrett's counsel. But Sharon's next words put the real pepper in his chili.

"How did this mess get started? Earlier this month I conducted an interview with Agent Barrett Raines—"

An interview? *What* interview?

"—asking for the rationale which prompted what has been widely seen as a highly partisan attack on Senator Stanton."

"You're off-camera." Dew Drop opened his right hand wide and Barrett came storming over.

"What damn interview?"

Sharon's cheerleader smile switched off like a light.

"See for yourself."

The Sony monitor mounted in the live van's interior flickered with a new feed. Barrett recognized his own office on the tiny screen, a cubicle, really. There was the family photo, Barrett and Laura Anne, her own wide and remarkable shoulders bared in a baby-blue summer shift, sensual even in domestic pose, long chocolate arms draped about her husband and their fraternal twins. A mess everyplace else, folders in piles. A cheap radio, its antennae spliced with scotch tape.

All distorted by a fishbowl lens.

"What in the hell . . . ?"

Sharon smiled.

"Right after the judge's ruling, don't you remember? I asked for an interview."

Barrett felt a roar in his ears, like listening to a seashell.

"But there was no camera. You didn't *have* a camera."

"Never said I didn't. And you never asked."

Dew Drop cackled laughter and Barrett knew, then, that he had been truly ambushed.

She had deliberately chosen to nail him during lunch. Viewers would not see Barrett in the crisp and military presentation he assiduously cultivated. Instead, here was a large, black man sloppy with a loosened tie appropriate for a Shriner's convention spreading a cheap napkin over his chest to attack a cheeseburger, home fries, and a firkin of iced tea. But where was the camera?

Then he remembered. The briefcase. How Sharon had lifted her satchel off the floor and placed it on his desk. Placed it carefully. Wouldn't take much to hide a camera in a bag like that. And so now here he was, on tape, wiping mustard off his chin as Sharon remained behind her hidden pinhole lens.

"Maybe you could begin, Agent Raines, by telling me exactly how a criminal investigation came to be initiated against the senator?"

" 'Initiated'? Yes. Well, I guess I should say first off that this was not a vendetta."

"Was not a vendetta?"

"Not at all. The FDLE came into possession of information that we could not ignore. We shared that information with the county sheriff, the state's attorney, and attorney general. The information was taken very seriously."

"By that you mean, you took it seriously." Sharon's interjection came smoothly.

"I and others, yes."

That evasion punctuated with another slurp of tea.

"And this evidence, as it came to be called, came from—?"

"An informer, that's right," Barrett slurped.

"A paid informer?"

"We pay for information in some cases. When we have to."

Barrett winced to see his videoed response.

"Sometimes it's the only way we can get information, you know that, Sharon. And this particular source was felt to be reliable."

"You mean you believed the informer to be reliable."

"I had no reason to believe otherwise."

"But he, or she, was not in fact reliable at all."

"We don't know that."

Barrett more animated, now. Rising from his burger. Waving a pie-sized hand.

"Excuse me, Agent Raines. Are you saying that you continue to believe your source's allegations against Senator Stanton are accurate? That the charges have merit?"

Barrett wiped his hands of mustard and mayonnaise.

"I'm just saying that without further investigation we can't know for sure one way or the other."

A notepad floated briefly and out of focus before the camera.

"The presiding judge said that, quote, 'The persons charged to manage this case were apparently told what they wanted to hear'."

"What we believed to be true at the time."

"Which is to say," Sharon segued smoothly, "that Eduardo DeLeon was cleaning dirty cash through various businesses owned by Senator Stanton? That the senator was getting a cut of that money to finance his campaign?"

"Look at the public record, for God's sake! It wasn't three years ago Baxter Stanton was on the verge of declaring bankruptcy. Three years later and in a shaky economy he's seeking reelection with three and a half million of his own dollars in the kitty. Where'd that money come from?"

"Judge Boatwright found Stanton's financial disclosure to be fully in order," Sharon countered.

"That's true, but—"

"And isn't it also true that the Florida Department of Law Enforcement has formally ceased all investigations related to the senator?"

"As ordered, that's correct."

"So aren't you now admitting, Agent Raines, that the allegations you pressed this past summer, only months before a political campaign, were unfounded? *Are*, in fact, unfounded?"

"I wouldn't say unfounded, no."

Barrett saw himself squirming on camera.

"In fact, Agent Raines, isn't it true that you have no proof whatever that Senator Stanton was ever involved illegally or in any other way with Eddy DeLeon?"

"We felt we had," came the reply.

Sharon allowed the slightest hesitation.

"And based on that—what? Feeling? You risked a man's life? A man's reputation?"

"The case was handled fairly, Sharon."

"Apparently Judge Boatwright did not agree."

The station's feed ended with Barrett contemplating a bushwack of his own but Sharon had already left the van to resume her pose before Dew Drop and the ever-truthful camera, a vigilant journalist balanced and eager and gorgeous, even with the penalty of a tethered microphone.

"This investigation was quashed before it even reached a grand jury," Sharon played straight to Dewey's camera. *"That brought a sigh of relief, as you can imagine, from the Stanton campaign. The senator himself is due to arrive here at his home on Pepperfish Keys at any moment. I'll be back with an exclusive interview. But with the cloud of criminal allegations lifted, our very own Baxter Stanton now seems certain to remain Florida's favorite son.*

"I'm Sharon Fowler getting you the latest, first, from K-E-Y-S, Pepperfish Keys."

She held her onscreen smile, it seemed to Bear, way longer than was necessary.

"Off the air." Dew Drop heaved a sigh of relief.

Barrett reminded himself that this was a public place, with witnesses, before he strode forward to confront the local anchor.

"You didn't tell me we were on camera."

"That would be your word against mine, wouldn't it, Barrett?"

"Still not that smart an idea. Skewering an interviewee? Can't imagine that will make you look good in New York."

She smiled.

"It's already made me look good in New York."

Barrett fought the churn in his gut.

"Look, Barrett, you want to talk about this later, fine. But I still have to grab Stanton and then after that I've gotta run back to the station and edit the show."

Barrett found himself blocking her way.

"Don't come asking me for help again, Sharon. Not for a story. Not for a sandwich. Not for a transfusion of goddamn blood."

"No problem there, Bear."

She smiled.

"You're not my type."

An impulse to mayhem was saved by something clattering loudly up the senator's winding, gravel drive.

"There he is!" Dew Drop sang out.

Sharon was off as though to a starter's gun, sprinting to cut ahead of the other newshounds in a rush across the lawn.

"Dewey!"

Her cameraman scrambling to follow. Guests then joining the surge of journalists and technicians to converge at the mansion's wide, cattle-gapped gate.

At first all Barrett could make out was a pair of Suburbans tooling onto the cobbled drive, their tinted windows as impenetrable as tortoise shells. Then he saw horses, four of them, trailing the SUVs in expensive tack. Barrett hopped onto the news van's running board to better see what that pampered team pulled in its exorbitant train. "You have got to be shitting me."

A brace of broad-chested Morgans clattered up Stanton's winding drive pulling the most outrageous carriage Barrett had ever seen.

"It's Cinderella's coach!" a guest chortled.

And indeed it was. An orange pumpkin framed in fiberglass and complete with withered stem swayed on a snow-white chassis. A top-hatted driver beamed from its high seat, enjoying the penumbra of celebrity made possible by association with the passenger who, with his wife, waved to the crowd like visiting royalty from the comfort of their molded carriage. A pair of footmen in colonial garb threw baubles as if for Mardi Gras from a footboard on the rear of Senator Stanton's plastic coach.

Baxter and Babs waving out the window. Enjoying the effect of their fairytale arrival.

TV crews were fighting like cats in a sack to get the show on tape, Sharon and Dew Drop tumbling along with the rest, shoving through competing phalanxes of guests and domestics to reach the entourage. It was brilliant theater, Barrett allowed, and audacious. How many men would think to appropriate a fairytale coach to celebrate a miscarriage of justice? But of course in many ways the senator's was a Cinderella story. Rags to riches.

Or riches to rags?

The senator's carriage rattled past linened tables bent with the weight of beef and seafood before turning onto the circle of flagstone that fronted his famous porch. The well-heeled guests laughed hugely at the comedy ensuing, photographers and reporters shedding all dignity as they dodged horseshit in pursuit of the senator's outlandish carriage. Throwing elbows. Cursing to gain a favored angle.

Sharon pressed her advantage in that melee, using her tall, strong frame to shove aside more diminutive competitors. Baxter Stanton remained quite literally above the fray, but it was apparent that he relished the sight of the reporters now begging for audience, those same hounds who only days before called for their senator's resignation.

The Cinderella coach stopped below the short terrace of steps leading into Stanton's mansion, horses snorting indifference. The footmen dropped from their rearward perch to open the carriage's door and on that cue the band cut loose. Senator

Baxter Stanton emerged from his pumpkin coach to a spirited rendition of "Dixie." A black-tie tux hung on his scrawny frame like socks on a rooster. He was a prune of a man, a genuinely red neck prominent below dark hair cut to moderate length and parted left-to-right. Sharon Fowler shoved her stick-held microphone through the footmen's cordon.

"Good evening, Senator Stanton!"

Stanton ignored Sharon's mike even as he smiled directly into her camera.

"My wife first. If you please."

The guests roared approval. Barbara Stanton stepped febrile as an orchid from her carriage and into well-lubricated applause. Sharon extended her mike again.

"Mrs. Stanton! How does it feel to have the last six months behind you?"

"I'm just relieved," the former sorority girl smiled through layers of ceramic. "Relieved and grateful. It's been such a strain. You can't imagine!"

"But we were always confident, weren't we, dear?"

Stanton smiling broadly for his enthralled invitees.

"Always confident," Barbara bobbed in echolalia of her husband.

"And the people of Pepperfish Keys—"

Baxter commanded a stentorian voice, Bear had to admit that, a graveled baritone from a neck not much larger than a rooster's.

"—YOU GOOD PEOPLE! NEVER, *NEVER,* WAVERED!"

A cheer resounded for the homegrown boy. Sharon pressed in once again.

"Time for a few words, Senator?"

He palmed the mike discreetly.

"You just got a few, Miz Fowler."

"But, sir. You promised."

"Later. Shall we?"

"Of course, Senator. That would be fine."

Baxter waded into a picket of microphones, hands raised in evangelic fervor.

"We've weathered a hard storm! Fought a great fight, all of us! Time now to savor victory!"

Another cheer drowned the questions shouted from frustrated reporters. A rolling tide of The Rich swept that sorry estate aside. Baxter Stanton smiled broadly, arms opened wide, to be carried away on the hosannas of his muslin flock.

The cheers out front could be easily heard at the backside of Stanton's mansion. A rear gate admitted entrance to the pool secluded behind the four-story home. A wall of pyracantha rose to fence off the pool, its dense and spiked foliage a fiery hedge against prying eyes. Eddy DeLeon hunched his groin into Beth Ann's butt as she keyed digits into the pad that secured the rear gate's lock.

"Stop it."

"Won' be telling me to stop inna minute."

A buzz released a tempered bolt. DeLeon herded his honey to the pool. Another swell of adulation rising from out front.

"Somebody having a good time," Eddy smiled through his cataract of teeth.

"It's just noise."

Beth Ann pouting with that declaration.

"It doesn't mean anything," she went on. "They don't mean anything."

"You sure 'bout that, baby?"

" 'Course I am. You know I am."

He cupped her breasts like pears.

"Still hot and bothered?"

A platinum bracelet grazing the flesh of her breast.

"Eddy!"

"Come on."

"Not here." She tried to pull away.

"Why not?"

He slipped the golden ring that bound his ponytail. A raven fall of hair shook free.

"Somebody might come back here! Somebody's bound to!"

He shrugged off his tailored shirt.

"So let them."

"Eddy, please."

Her free hand fluttering to her small chest.

"Little rich girl getting cold feet. Is that it?"

"It's not that."

"You know, I notice things? Like—you don't mind screwing in the car, you know? But never *here*. And never for the night."

"Jesus Christ, Eddy, what do you expect? It's not my place! It's not my house!"

"If I was some hotshot from Washington that wouldn't matter. Would it? Or some Ivy League Boy Scout? No problem finding one of those in baby's bed. But not a greaser, is that it? Not some fucking spick!"

"Not so loud, Eddy. Please! Somebody could hear."

"You want me quiet?"

"Please!"

"So quiet me, baby. Settle me down."

He reached for the belt at his waist.

"Eddy!"

"You love me? Prove it. Right here. Right now."

She hesitated a moment. A moment only.

"Here."

She slipped the silver buckle free.

"Let me."

Night was well fallen before Senator Stanton negotiated the hundreds of congratulations and handshakes pressed between the floorboard of his carriage and the steps of his veranda. It took a determined forty-something to impede his progress along that gauntlet; Ruby Knowles slid well-kept arms through the senator's, a peacock feather bobby-pinned in auburn hair.

"When am I going to get my vic'try dance, Baxter?"

"Soon." He squeezed her arm.

"I'll look forward to it."

She let him go. Baxter flashed another brilliant smile, already loosening his cravat as he disappeared through wide, French doors.

"Senator, suh. It good to have you home."

A black woman of great girth bustled to receive the master of the house.

"Help me out of this straitjacket, will you, Wanda?"

"Yes, suh."

"Any calls from Tallahassee?"

"Naw. Just the woman."

"What woman?"

"She say you say meet her in the study."

Baxter frowned.

"You won' me have Clarence run her awf?"

"No, no. You say she's in the study?"

"She say you tole her."

"I'll take care of it. No one else inside the house, though, you hear?"

"Yassuh."

"And will you fetch an aspirin for Miz Barbara? It's her arthritis."

Baxter took the stairs two at a time. He hadn't authorized anyone to meet him in the study. Not that he could remember. But he was meeting so many women these days. Maybe he had promised somebody somethin'. Or maybe it was just Ruby.

He passed the second flight of stairs and was tackling the third. The study was not an easy niche to find in this labyrinth of oddly matched halls and decor. Up three stories to a round-about, cross a large foyer that allowed a view of the water, then up a half-flight to enter a space large enough for a small ballroom. A high ceiling, four walls, hardwood floors, completely unfurnished.

A narrow door on the sea side of the dining room would seem

to be no more than a niche for brooms. Stanton strode toward that closet. A brass knob presented. He turned it. Pushed. Pawed to find the light switch beside the door. A desk lamp snicked on, instead, to provide startling illumination.

"Hope you don't mind, Senator."

Sharon Fowler arranged a mile of well-toned leg on the chaise lounge opposite his cherrywood desk.

"On the contrary. I like a bold woman."

"Well, I knew if I waited in the cattle-call for my interview, I'd be waiting forever."

In marked contrast to the adjoining room's never-used space, the study was cramped and worn, knickknacks propped in niches of shelves sagging with books, trophies of all types mounted capriciously. Photographs took up the square inches that remained, a glossy documentary of colleagues, constituents, and celebrities.

All good, good friends of Baxter Stanton.

He closed the door, abjuring the recliner behind his desk to settle into a Chippendale more proximate to his unexpected guest.

"Sorry I couldn't spend more time with you out front, Sharon."

"Perfectly all right."

"Would have looked a bit too chummy."

"I'm just trying to do my job, Senator. And be fair about it."

"Fair to a fault, I would say."

"Sir?"

Stanton settled himself comfortably.

"Well, Sharon, every other media-mouth went after my ass with tooth and tong. Every bit of gossip unearthed, pursued. Every innuendo. But you didn't. Why?"

"I was never convinced that Barrett Raines had his heart in the case. Turned out I was right."

She paused.

"—Wasn't I?"

"I'll accept the people's verdict," Stanton smiled. Sharon swiveled her feet to the floor. "I'm no Girl Scout, Senator. If I thought I could substantiate some high-priced dirt on you, I'd run with it."

"So you want 'The Truth', is that it?"

"The truth pays. And the more somebody tries to hide the truth, especially somebody of influence, the more valuable 'The Truth' gets to be."

"Sounds like the workings of an ambitious mind."

"I don't plan to keep my light under a bushel, if that's what you mean."

"Mmm. Where you from, Sharon?"

"Appalachicola."

"Small-town, but nuthin' to be ashamed of. Puts sand in your shorts. Makes you want to go someplace else. Anyplace else. Doesn't do that for ever'body, of course. Some people like small. They like tidy. They like their coffee black ever' time and their eggs the same way ever' morning. Never had a dream in their lives. That's not me. And not you, either."

He smiled.

"Let's take us a walk."

She preceded the senator downstairs. A dog run off the bottom floor led past a sprawling kitchen. Sharon could see an aging black man kneeling in grease and filth beneath the kitchen's stainless steel sink.

"You checked that water heater, Clarence? That one upstairs?" Stanton called out.

"Yes suh."

"Well, is it gonna be fixed anytime 'fore Christmas?"

The coveralled caretaker lifted a stiff neck.

"I's tryin', Senator. But seem like you need a real plumber in here."

"Swear to damn God, people like Clarence—?"

Baxter now steering Sharon toward an exiting door.

"Confirm my theory there oughta be a law against the hourly wage."

A klieg light flashed as Sharon emerged with Stanton from the kitchen.

"Oh!" She ducked instinctively.

He smiled.

"Lights. For security. They're motion activated."

"I'm seeing spots."

"Sorta like havin' a camera shoved in your face?"

She did not reply.

"Come on."

Sharon followed his short stride along the hedged walkway. A muted cacophony of laughter and conversation spilled over from the party out front, along with sanitized rock 'n' roll.

"Louie, Louie" castrated for polite company.

"I take it you're looking to move on from the Keys," Baxter eyeing her openly now. "Big city? Bright lights?"

"I got a call from New York. ABC affiliate. WABC, actually."

"Job nailed down?"

"We've talked. But to get any further I'm gonna have to snag something big."

"I might could help."

"I'd be grateful."

"Anything for a constituent. You are my constituent—aren't you Miz Fowler?"

"Eddy—!"

A voice from the pool cut off her reply.

"Jesus, Eddy!"

A doll-baby voice filtered through the fiery shrubbery. Baxter seemed suddenly frozen to the warm ground.

"Senator?"

"Will you excuse me?"

"Sir?"

"Wait *here*."

Pool lights refracted through a disturbance of turquoise water to cast wavering, silver lines on the man and young woman coupled at its boundary. Beth Ann arched her back high over the tile's polished lip to accommodate her lover. Eddy DeLeon

48

stroking hard as he teased the aureoles of her breasts with his tongue.

"Beth Ann!"

Baxter Stanton livid across the pool.

"Jesus!" Beth Ann sliding into the cabana of Eddy's tattooed arms.

"Nice party, Baxter." Eddy bobbing lazily in the water. "Thanks for the invitation."

"Beth Ann get out of there!"

"No!"

"There are *people* here!"

"Oh, and I'm not one of your people? Daddy?"

"Don't you talk to me like that!"

Jabbing his finger like a dart.

"Not to *me,* young lady!"

"Go to hell."

Baxter striding over now in short, short steps.

"You put her up to this, DeLeon. You son of a bitch!"

"He didn't do anything!"

Beth Ann pulled herself away from DeLeon and out of the pool. She snatched up her skirt. Her top.

"Look. Hon. Come inside. No one's seen. No harm done."

"Thass one way to look at it," Eddy quipped.

"You keep out of this." Stanton was around the pool by now. "Come on inside, Beth Ann. Please!"

"I'm going home with Eddy."

DeLeon sliding from the pool like an otter.

"Hand me my slacks, baby."

"Jesus!"

Stanton's knuckles clenched white.

"Settle down, man," Eddy offered his broken teeth. "Iss not like you didn't know."

"She doesn't care about you. She doesn't give a shit about some wetback, you know that. This is all about me."

"Everything's about you, isn't it, Daddy? Everything!"

A sudden breeze. Her flesh in goosebumps.

She wrapped her arms tight.

"Let's go, Eddy."

"Get to your room, Beth Ann!" Baxter snarled.

"You can't make me."

"The hell you say!"

Baxter lunged to grab his daughter. A brown, scarred fist struck like a snake to intercept. Stanton winced to find his own arm trapped in Eddy DeLeon's wet grip.

"You wanna scene, Baxter? Hah? Right here? With me? At your . . . Coronation?"

Stanton tried to jerk free.

"Let me loose," he commanded coldly.

DeLeon complied. Stanton turned to his only child.

"Beth Ann, for God's sake!"

"I could talk, you know." She backed away. "If I really wanted to hurt you? All I'd have to do is talk!"

"No, senorita." Eddy paused over the zipper of his slacks. "You talk about your papa, you talk about *me. Comprende?* And Eddy DeLeon does not tolerate loose lips."

Stanton's red neck blanched.

"And now you're threatening my daughter? You son of a bitch!"

Stanton stepped between Beth Ann and DeLeon.

"We're finished, do you understand? You prick! This ends it. In fact—we never started!"

"Sure, man. You just give me whass mine and, you know, is cool."

"After the election," Baxter hissed. "That was our deal!"

"I got an obligation I cannot delay."

"Pull your head out of your ass. I can't do it right now. I can't!"

"That means I got to hang on to the collateral." Eddy side-stepped the senator to fondle his daugher's breasts.

That picket-fence smile.

"I wanted to do it in her room, you know? She been reluctant. But the pool? Man. This was pretty good."

"You fucking spick."

"Maybe I bring her back. Later, maybe. Mount my trophy on the wall."

Baxter raised a trembling finger to Beth Ann.

"You leave with this bastard, you're not coming back to this house. You hear me?"

"Oh, I hear you, Daddy. I hear real good." She took DeLeon's offered arm.

"You're not coming back. Goddammit, Beth Ann, not with this piece of shit!"

The rear gate banged aside on tempered hinges. Beth Ann stalked through; Eddy following. Baxter Stanton raging and impotent behind.

And Sharon Fowler there to see it all.

"Isn't that Eddy DeLeon?"

She caught the gate before it locked.

"Eddy and Beth Ann?"

He turned to her coldly. "I told you to wait."

"That was Eduardo DeLeon, Senator. With your daughter!"

"There's a time after which . . ."

Stanton raised his hands. Dropped them.

"After which a father can no longer tell his little one where to sleep."

"That's all this is, Senator?"

"That's all."

"I have to tell you that's not what it looked like. Or sounded like."

She remained at the gate. Baxter walked over.

"Few moments ago you said you wanted to get out of Pepperfish Keys. New York, wasn't it?"

"Yes."

"I know the folks at WABC. Know the news director, in fact."

"I'd rather know what happened here, at this moment," Sharon replied. "I'd like the truth."

"The truth?

Stanton barked laughter and light rippled from the pool's disturbed surface, refracted and uncertain.

"Well, Miz Fowler, the truth behind this little domestic squabble might get you fifteen minutes in a tabloid. Maybe. But if you're aiming for the networks, a modicum of discretion will get you a lot farther."

"I'll keep that in mind. Good evening, Senator."

She turned a long, bare back toward the gate.

"And congratulations."

Barrett Raines pushed off from the senator's gala affair well before the sun sank beneath the rim of a tequila horizon. All the charts and GPS and radios in the world were not enough to make Agent Raines fearless on the water after dark; he did not remain after his whipping at Sharon's hand to witness the adulation of Senator Stanton. Even so, by the time Bear tied off his Whaler on the familiar pier attached to his wife's waterside restaurant the tops of the pines were catching the day's last light.

The restaurant was tin-roofed, a single story of weathered cypress raised square as a box on dark pilings by Deacon Beach's grassy shore. Fifty millennia before Timucan and Muskogean and Creek Indians roamed freely and long before Andrew Jackson was chasing Seminoles, this entire region was submerged beneath a sea of saltwater. Paleontologists had unearthed the leavings of fishing huts established on a prehistoric coastline fifteen miles inland from modern shores. When those ancient waters receded they left a littoral verdant with arbors of hardwood, tidewater cypress, and loblolly pine. Parts of Pepperfish Keys survived the modern exploitation of that primitive largesse; Laura Anne's restaurant perched on the faultline of that topography, that boundary between the virgin and the forever corrupt.

It was not a fancy place. A rustic interior offered maybe thirty tables arranged casually about a central island and bar. Even from the tie-down out by the boardwalk you could see the naked and rare beams of tidewater cedar from which ceiling fans drooped like the petals of brown flowers on aluminum stems.

A great view. Cypress-framed windows with wide sills recessed beneath eaves of corrugated tin looking out to the Gulf of Mexico. The only ostentation allowed was the diner's original and entering door, a garishly painted portal salvaged from some sunken wreck during one of Ramona Walker's clandestine adventures. The shaded boardwalk and pier were not part of the restaurant's original architecture; these were Laura Anne's contribution. "No point in having a diner by the sea if people can't get outside and enjoy it," Mrs. Raines declared. So Ramona's old place got itself a walk and a quay and—

A piano.

Laura Anne won her baby grand while an undergraduate at a contest sponsored by Emory University. The Steinway was truly a grand prize and became over the years not only Laura Anne's instrument, but her retreat. She had always wanted to teach, to bring music to youngsters in middle and secondary school. Denied that chance in Deacon Beach, Laura Anne brought her music to Ramona's. The restaurant became a magnet for student-musicians, a place where diners were regular beneficiaries of Laura Anne's always-unscheduled performances.

Word got out that there was this dive on Deacon Beach where you could enjoy Rachmaninoff with your mullet or sea bass or shrimp. A coterie of musicians eager to perform descended on the restaurant, many of them remaining to bus tables or refill jelly caddies between turns at the piano or other chosen instrument. But it was Laura Anne's striking presence that was the big draw, this woman from out of Africa.

She was tall, was Barrett's wife. Nearly as tall as Sharon Fowler. High cheeks. Eyes wide as a deer's. Shoulders wide as a man's. Her skin was a deep complexion of coffee and cream that provoked unwanted conversation in some circles of the dominant and colorless community. Lots of speculation in those circles regarding the genealogy necessary to produce a color like

Laura Anne's. And she had a zest for life, an *elan vitale* that made the torches burn bright. The kind of woman who, Taylor Calhoun declared, "would make a train take a dirt road."

But not lately. As Barrett tied off his boat he strained to hear, hoped to hear . . . ? But, no. The baby grand was silent along with its mistress.

"Evenin', Mr. Raines."

Roy Folsom folded napkins at the host's podium near the door. He used a spoon to crease the edges, employing one of the diner's trademark hardwood platters as a blotter.

"Evening, Roy."

Roy had been with the restaurant when Ramona Walker still owned the place. He worked for that white woman to the day of her murder and was now as fiercely loyal to Barrett's wife as he had been to the Homecoming Queen of Deacon Beach.

"Should I tell Laura Anne you're here?"

"I'll find her."

The kiss of death for a restaurant is silence. In any vital eatery, knives and forks scrape noisily on plates and saucers. Spoons bang sugar into cups of coffee. In better days at Ramona's there would be a racket of blenders and barmaids and waiters singing the orders of snapper or shrimp or steak to the cooks out back. Suited sophisticates and local fishermen dining side by side in animated conversation. Families raucous after ball games. Kids running under tables. The only break in that welcome cacophony being the solos rendered impromptu on Laura Anne's Steinway.

But tonight there was no music and no conversation. Only the whispered pump of ceiling fans. The lazy swing of the steward's door. The muted swirl of cubed ice in tea already sweetened. The soundless travel of a spoon along the crease of a paper napkin.

Barrett found his wife with a platter of shrimp untouched below the slow paddle of a ceiling fan.

"Hey, baby."

"Hey."

Her smile was wan. Her hair, coarse and resentful of domestication, tumbled unbraided. Eyes large as a deer's. High cheeks. Full lips. A flat belly beneath firm breasts. These were normally the gifts sufficient to fuel a steady churn of desire.

Instead he asked—

"How's business?"

"Air-conditioning's broke."

"We'll fix it."

"Got to pay for it."

"I'll talk to Rolly. He'll cut us a deal."

She shook her head.

"Business is bad."

"It'll turn around." He slid in beside her. Offered his hand.

She took a butter knife, instead. Sampled the tartar sauce wasted on her plate.

"Needs something. Cumin, maybe."

"Laura Anne—"

"How was the senator's party?"

"Terrible." He placed his hands on the table. "I got roasted."

"That Fowler woman?"

"Yeah. Set myself up for it, too. Should have known better."

"You've been scapegoated, Bear, that's all. Hadn't been her, it'd have been somebody else."

"Well, it's over, anyway. The senator's off the hook. Everybody's thrilled he's headed for reelection. Couple of months nobody's going to remember any of it."

"Stanton will remember," she sniffed. "That's a man holds grudges. Kidding yourself you think he won't."

He tried again to take her hand.

"Why don't we go home, hon? You can have Roy close up."

The brilloed tangle of her hair barely moved as she shook her head.

"I'll just stay. You go on."

Barrett glanced at his watch.

"You could put the boys to bed," he suggested.

That seemed to rouse her a moment. She even seemed about to respond when—

"Miz Raines?"

Roy approached their booth.

"Yes, Roy?"

"Mr. Slade's here. About the air-conditioning?"

"I'll be right there."

Barrett felt himself sliding out of the booth to accommodate his wife.

"I can help Rolly with the air conditioner," he offered.

"No," she declined. "You go home. Tell the boys 'night for me."

Her broad shoulders slumped as she followed her employee back toward the kitchen.

"Tell 'em Mama's fine."

4.

Senator Stanton's party did not wane until the wee hours. The senator and his wife had excused themselves a little after midnight, but the guests did not take that cue. There was still way too much brisket to be gorged, too much shrimp, and magnums of champagne yet uncorked. And unlike Bear Raines, these partygoers had no fear of boating beneath a rind's peel of moon. Either that, or they were too drunk to care.

Virtually the only early departures, in fact, aside from Agent Raines, were the band and the news crews scrambling to meet their ten o'clock obligations. It was near to dawn before the remaining guests could be persuaded to leave, college kids themselves exhausted, herding recalcitrant adults to their tony boats. There were the inevitable frayed tempers as revelers overwrought or inebriated squabbled with a spouse or escort. Women lost earrings, or husbands.

Stanton's domestic staff remained to clean up the detritus left behind by the visiting rich. A fog rolling in off the Keys soaked a lawn littered with plastic cups, plastic plates. Black men and women bent to the trampled Saint Augustine lawn, policing Styrofoam cups and paper plates from the damp, like field hands picking cotton. It was not difficult in that confusion for a patient visitor to linger at the foot of the stairs until the foyer was momentarily cleared of prying eyes, and then to ascend.

Anyone reaching the second room to the right off the third-floor landing would find that Beth Ann was safely returned home. As her father's hired help policed the grounds below, the daughter stretched naked and satisfied on a silk-sheeted bed in that upstairs room. It was actually more a suite than a bedroom. A separate dressing room and bath attached to a bedroom the size of a small loft. French doors opening from a high-ceilinged interior to a balcony with a view over the Keys.

A breeze from offshore stirred linen curtains; Beth Ann rolled over to face that fresh stimulation, a recent perspiration still clinging to her belly, her breasts.

Tendrils of incense rising from a joint to disperse in the circuit of her ceiling fan.

"Round and round." She flopped over the side of her mattress to retrieve the roach. A deep drag. A knock at the door.

"Mmmmhmmm," Beth Ann exhaled with the summons.

Another knock. Just one.

"Jussa minute." She rose from the bed, wrapping the sheet about her waist like a sarong, her upper torso toned and tanned and shining with sweat. The joint glowing like a cigarette or sparkler in her hand.

Crossing the floor in bare feet. Opening the door a crack.

"Ohhhh."

A smile opened petulant lips. She took another hit. Held it.

"I knew you'd be back."

"God damn it."

"Baxter. Must you?"

Barbara Stanton nursed her coffee and hangover in the midst of a morning-after kitchen. A row of garishly painted cookie jars flanked a cuckoo clock standing sentinel above a formica counter littered with evidence of the previous evening's gala, bottles of booze crowding platters of barbequed scraps. Babs freed a hand to massage her temple. "Goddamm it to hell."

Her husband traipsing in unshaven, unwashed, and unhappy, his rooster neck rising like a pipe from a terry cloth robe.

"You need a shower, Baxter."

"The hell you think I've been? There's no goddamn hot water."

"It's that thermostat."

"Barbara, you don't have the foggiest goddamn idea what it is."

"It just needs a tap."

"A 'tap'?"

"What Clarence says."

"Clarence can't find his ass with both hands."

"Then call somebody that can."

"Could run a campaign on what we spend for goddamn plumbing."

"You've got to bathe, Baxter."

"I 'spose I could skinny dip in the Gulf of damn Mexico."

"I still think it's the thermostat. Why couldn't it be the thermostat?"

"Well, why don't you go see, then? Bang it with a hammer, you think it'll do any good."

"Beats complaining."

Stanton watched his wife knead her scalp as she stumped out of the kitchen. He could hear the stairs squeak in protest as she grumbled upstairs. That's where the hot-water heater was located. Upstairs. Left more room in the kitchen, their architect had insisted. Plus there was additional floorspace on the third floor that was ideally suited to accommodate a larger tank.

Barbara hated stairs. She hated Baxter goading her into a chore that made her climb the rigid steps. There was nothing wrong with *his* knees. The master bedroom had been mercifully located on the ground floor. The six bedroom suites occupying the third floor were foreign country, so far as Mrs. Stanton was concerned, a domain set aside for whatever constituent wrangled an invitation to visit. And for Beth Ann, of course. Beth Ann had one of the suites all to herself, the best in Babs's opinion, with a view over the water. Her daughter treasured that lofty retreat. She even liked the stairs, the little goat. They guaranteed a certain isolation.

Each of the upstairs bedrooms had its own bath and shower. That had been a luxury upon which Baxter insisted. Raised poor himself, Stanton grew up sharing sinks and shitters. Not in this house, he had insisted. Stanton wanted a house where you got your own bathroom and lots of hot water in which to luxuriate. To that end a hot-water heater with a tank six feet tall and a couple in diameter was installed on the third floor.

It had been a fine solution, everyone agreed. Everyone except Beth Ann. That's because it was Beth Ann's bathroom that was best suited to hangar the monster heater. And from her nearby bed Beth Ann complained that she could hear the propane burner each time it fired to heat the heater's oversized cylinder.

Barbara paused at the landing before her daughter's bedroom. Surprise. A rapper's muted garbage spilled from inside, the bass and lyrics thumping in muted percussion.

"Beth Ann?"

She had not seen Beth Ann the previous evening. She did not expect to find her home come morning.

"Beth Ann!"

No reply. Only lyrics pumped out like shells from a shotgun.

. . . You talk like apple pie
It's all a fucking lie!
Eat your shit and die . . . !

Barbara frowned. How on earth was she to make herself heard above that raucous filth?

"Beth Ann, open this door!"

Little pig, little pig.

"I'm coming in!"

Barbara stepped into a suite that looked to have been sacked by Huns. A chest of drawers was spilled onto the floor, panties and bras and other unmentionables. A cabinet of CDs and DVDs littered a carpet stained with cigarettes and beer and another odor familiar from college days. Shoes and soiled jeans scattered randomly. Skirts and cutoffs kicked into piles.

"This room is a mess!"

Barbara weakly announced her presence.

Not a single photograph of family or friends on the walls. Instead, posters of rock and rap groups adorned the interior, including a print of Madonna draped barebreasted and ecstatic over the haunches of a Negro.

Barbara skirted that uncomfortable image.

But it was the bed that stopped Babs in her painful tracks. There were no sheets on Beth Ann's bed. No blanket or pillow. Had Wanda already come for the linen?

And what was that, nail polish? That sprayed dull and dark across the cherry headboard? And on the burgundy mattress was another stain, some unfamiliar dampness seeped into wine-dark matting.

. . . You life's a fucking sty
You got no reason why
Eat your shit and die . . . !

Trash. Barbara stepped to the boombox beside the bed, pawed at the brightly colored knobs and buttons before giving up and yanking the plug from its socket. The racket cut off with a squawk. What she heard then was the steady drum of water onto Mexican tile.

The shower? Of course.

A wide door segregated her daughter's bedroom from the bathroom and shower beyond. The hardwood floor between bed and loo was curiously free of obstacles, but streaked darkly as if a mop had been hastily applied through a puddle of syrup.

Those stains, did they match the headboard's? The mattress?

"Beth Ann—?"

Still no reply. Barbara found herself panting now. Light-headed. She was getting too old for this, for the mess, the stairs. She edged around a pair of panties on her way to the bathroom's closed door.

She turned a chromed latch, pulled.

Steam gushed out as if from a sauna.

No wonder there was no hot water!

"Beth Ann, you need to get out of that shower!"

There was no reply to her shouted request. No movement inside, either. Nothing from the daughter to acknowledge her mother's presence.

Babs entered Beth Ann's outsized bathroom.

A panel of mirrors, completely fogged over, hung above an enormous valet unit. A toilet and bidet were situated opposite. Two walk-in closets were visible as if through clouds beyond these. And then on the bath's far side drummed the shower. Bricks of frosted glass and a mottled, aluminum-framed door provided a degree of privacy. Steam cloaked the skylight that normally illuminated the shower's spacious stall.

"Goodness!"

Something was hanging from the showerhead. Something shrouded in superheated mist. Barbara edged forward waving a drawn hand as if to dispel that warm vapor.

"What in heaven's name—?"

She reached forward tentatively. Then yanked the framed door open—

A basket stuffed with shampoo and conditioner dangled from the shower's brass head.

"Lord!" Barbara soaked her arms reaching in to twist off the faucet.

Her husband's voice piped in over an intercom.

"We gonna have water anytime soon?"

She ducked out of the shower.

"I doubt it."

"What was that? Barbara?"

"Never mind. I'll check the heater."

She turned to the bathroom's walk-in closets. One ample cupboard, Barbara knew, provided tiers of brightly colored towels. The other set of louvered doors concealed the hot-water heater.

"Checking right now."

She tugged on a child-sized knob and the flimsy doors jammed in their frame, swollen, probably, with humidity accumulated equally from inadequate ventilation and overzealous hygiene. Babs tried again. Her hand slipped off the steam-slicked knob.

"Oh, bother!"

She considered a moment. Pulled a towel off its rack.

"Let's just see."

Barbara wrapped the heavy, cotton fabric about the closet's small purchase. Gave a jerk. The louvered wings bounced open.

"Oh—! Oh, Jesus! Jesus God!"

Beth Ann Stanton coupled the hot-water heater like a lover. Her supple, sinuous body looked bullwhipped. Deep cuts slashing her torso. Her legs. Bloody sheets bound her wrists and ankles to embrace the heater's steel shaft. Her eyes were glazed and open, her throat slit ear-to-ear. But it was the final, unnatural insult that recoiled Barbara through the closet doors.

A tangle of thin, metallic tape spilled like worms from her daughter's broken mouth.

"Baxter!"

The mother's scream shrieked over the intercom.

"Oh, God! Baaaaaxxxterrrrr!"

5.

Barrett Raines woke in his Jim Walter home the next morning to the aroma of bacon and coffee. He reached over sheets heavy with humidity hoping to find his wife's flank. Not there. It was getting more common, waking in the morning to find his wife not in their shared bed. Laura Anne had taken, when coming home late from work, to sleeping on the foldout in the den. On one occasion Bear even found his wife curled on a cot beneath the unwalled shelter of what passed for the Raines's garage. Right there by the Malibu.

"Why're you out here?" he had asked.

"I didn't want to wake you," came the reply.

And so it had been, off and on, since the occasion of her trauma.

He slid out of the sterile bed, grabbed shorts and slacks.

"Laura Anne?"

"She up awready," a warbled reply filtered in from the kitchen.

That would be Aunt Thelma. Laura Anne's aunt. The sinews on those scrawny arms wrapped about her bones like dark twine on a ball of cord. An ancient woman, Thelma had moved into a house trailer beside the Raines's as a convenience before becoming indispensable.

But Saturday was Thelma's day off. It used to be an inviolable routine, Ben and Tyndall, twins now in their sixth year of school, scrambling Saturday morning to thier fold-down table as Barrett made pancakes from scratch. Laura Anne enjoying relief from kitchen duty. The easy conversation that would invariably ensue. Teasing back and forth. Sometimes a wink from Mom to Dad that the boys were supposed to be unable to interpret.

That was the way it used to be. Pancakes and orange juice. Coffee and honey. And laughter. Just a normal family on a Saturday morning.

"They's you paper." Thelma nodded to a copy of the *Tallahassee Democrat.*

The paper. At least that had not changed. But Barrett's initial sense of comfort dissolved with the headline: "FDLE Agent Leads Flawed Investigation."

Barrett tore through the flimsy pages.

"Somethin' wrong?"

"It's nothing, Thelma."

The coffee went cold in its cup as Bear scanned the various and several columns related to his role in the investigation of Senator Stanton's alleged improprieties, the *Democrat* citing commentary from Tallahassee to Key West to conclude that Special Agent Raines was an incompetent if not vindictive fuckup. Republicans ripping Agent Raines as the pointman for an outright calumny of the state's most popular politician. To read the rag in his hands, you'd think Bear had gone after Baxter Stanton with bulldogs and billy clubs.

Some of the same pundits who only months before were calling for Stanton's resignation now leaped through their asses to demand Agent Raines's, those stalwarts of the fourth estate falling over themselves to appease the senator they had themselves hounded all summer.

As if.

Barrett left the paper and his coffee on the table. Where was it mentioned that the charges leveled against Baxter Stanton were not initiated by the FDLE, but were undertaken at the order of the governor? What columnist explained that the executive investigation into Senator Stanton's affairs was urged by an ambitious prosecutor in Live Oak by the name of Roland Reed?

"Fountain Pen. You son of a bitch."

"Whatchu say?"

"Nothing, Thelma."

"Din sound like nuthin'."

"It's nothing."

Barrett brushed past his wife's kin to stuff the paper into the trash.

"Aren't Ben and Tyndall supposed to be having breakfast?"

"Boys got up wit Laura Anne."

The old woman pouring bacon drippings into a skillet already spitting lard.

"Somethin' 'bout badges or somethin'."

Barrett felt his stomach knot.

"Did you mean Cub Scouts, Thelma? Where Laura Anne took the boys?"

Thelma slapped her spatula into spitting grease.

"Laura Anne took 'em is all I know."

Laura Anne had taken them, yes. Without so much as a Post-it on the refrigerator to remind her husband.

"It's probably 'Scouts," Barrett feigned competent knowledge. "Boys must be getting their merit badges."

An occasion for which a father ought to be present. Barrett glanced at his watch. The lodge was practically around the corner, a spartan butler building erected right behind Deacon Beach's Police Department.

"Maybe I'll just get a refill on that coffee." Barrett was about to amend his schedule when the phone rang.

"Could be Laura Anne, theah," the old crone suggested.

He hoped it was. But the moment Barrett scanned the number displayed on his cell phone he knew that it was not.

Barrett tuned in a Steve Miller song sliding from soft sand to asphalt on the single road out of Deacon Beach. Took an hour at reckless speed before he reached the cattlegap that allowed a land-side entry to the Stanton estate. A state trooper waved him through. There was already a posse of lawmen on the scene: Highway Patrol at the perimeter, deputies from the Sheriff's Department on the grounds, plus a brace of crime scene investigators from the FDLE. The department had diverted a mobile crime lab from a double homicide in Cross City in order to have its personnel at the sheriff's disposal. Looking toward the water Barrett could also see a twenty-four-foot Vaha with state seal and insignia, the craft indicating the assistance of what used to be called Florida's Marine Patrol.

Bear scanned the grounds looking for a windbreaker stenciled "FBI," but there was no sign of a federal presence. No FBI. No Secret Service, either, but Bear was not surprised. There was a lot of bullshit about cooperation and sharing information and similar rhetoric since 9/11, but in Florida the county sheriff ran the show and Smoot Rawlings did not trust the feds and was paranoid with regard to the FDLE.

Toward Agent Raines he was merely bigoted.

Doesn't matter, Barrett tried to tell himself. It's just another crime scene. Just another killing. But of course, it wasn't.

A county deputy confirmed Bear's identity before directing him to park at a spot outside the familiar yellow tape. Pulling himself out of his unmarked, Bear spotted a dimunitive, slump-shouldered woman in a nylon 'breaker.

"Morning, Midge."

"Agent Raines."

"Nice to see a friendly face."

"Wouldn't go that far."

She replied, penning a careful note onto her legal pad. Barrett did not press any further courtesy. A persistent rumor would have you believe that Midge Holloway had been demoted to a field assignment for lack of what was euphemistically labeled "team spirit." And it was true that the humpbacked investigator was a licensed medical examiner who had until recently been the Chief Forensics Investigator at the FDLE morgue in Jacksonville.

But Midge never liked The Dungeon. She liked being outside, liked seeing the evidence firsthand. She liked working the scene. So it was Midge herself who took a cut in pay and a transfer to Mobile where her formidable skills could once again be appreciated up close and personal.

"Took you long enough to get here," she accused.

"Didn't get the call till after eight. Got a time of death?"

"Nothing I'd sign off."

Barrett hated wasting time. The first forty-eight hours following any homicide were crucial, each passing hour giving the killer or killers time to destroy or hide evidence. Or to run. Homicides in rural areas presented special challenges in this regard. A body found in Miami or Tampa could be on an autopsy table within an hour of its discovery. In another hour or two a medical examiner could in most cases give investigators a time and cause of death and be well on the way to analyses of prints, hair, fiber, and blood. You could begin analysis of any DNA material collected.

But rural settings slowed things down. It would take three hours at least to transport Beth Ann's corpse from her father's home to the regional morgue in Jacksonville. And this was a high-profile case, which meant the ME was going to cover his or her ass every way he or she could. Which meant that even with luck Barrett would not have any sanctioned forensics before nightfall.

Time keeps on slippin', slippin', slippin', Into the future . . .

"Have you seen her, Midge?"

"Seen her? Sure."

"I'd like to have your opinion."

"My opinion you wait for the medical examiner in Jacksonville to give *his* opinion."

"Well, if it's too much to ask."

"God damn impertinent," Midge said, but then she shoved her legal pad into a clipboard.

It was a very large, very complicated scene, four or five acres trampled by hundreds of guests. An untrained eye would see people in uniform or out swarming about apparently at random, other persons standing about with no obvious purpose at all. But for Barrett Raines this was an ordered and predictable landscape. Breathing hard as he followed Holloway up Stanton's winding stairs, Barrett recognized on the railings a smudged detritus of the graphite-based talcum used to lift fingerprints. Climbing on, he passed one of Midge's people teasing a fiber from the carpet, as earnest in her work as an anthropologist on some ancient dig.

And in fact the work was similar. The entire scene was gridded off, every artifact photographed, stained, lifted, or extracted from the scene given a precise location, description, and time of discovery. In addition, Midge was responsible for maintaining a minute-by-minute log establishing a chain of custody for the gathered evidence, a narrative detailing every hand touching the material from the moment of its discovery to its presentation in a court of law.

Glancing out a window Barrett spotted a team of divers on the pier. There were chemists on site, botanists, photographers. Everyone here had a role to play in this theater of death. Everyone except, ironically, the prosecutor who palmed his ridiculous pen on Senator Stanton's third-story landing.

"'Lo, Barrett," Roland Reed preened. "Glad you could make it."

"The hell—?"

Barrett hated gasping for breath before Fountain Pen Reed.

"Who invited you, Roland?"

"Our governor."

"Doesn't he trust the FDLE?"

"You'd have to ask."

"Jesus. Does the sheriff know you're here?"

"He's glad I'm here. Well, 'glad' is probably too strong a word. More welcome than you are, certainly. Took some wrangling to convince Sheriff Rawlings he oughta bring in The Bear. There's baggage there to sort out. For sure. But in the end I just pointed out that Smoot did not want to put himself in the position of having to take responsibility for this crapshoot all by himself."

A crapshoot, for sure. With baggage. Dixie County's first-term sheriff had once been Barrett's boss on Deacon Beach. That was before Bear got promoted to the prestigious fold of the FDLE. Smoot left the Beach to run for sheriff in neighboring Dixie County. Rawlings was barely halfway through his first term when Bear coaxed his old boss into backing the FDLE's fight with Baxter Stanton.

Now, the FDLE was running off with its tail between its legs, Senator Stanton was more powerful than ever, and Sheriff Rawlings was pretty damn sure his first term in office was going to be his last.

"Where is Smoot?" Barrett inquired.

"Kitchen. With the senator and Barbara."

Barrett nodded to an open door.

"This Beth Ann's bedroom?"

"It is."

"Sign in, first," Midge ordered. "And grab some slippers over those shoes. I don't want anybody trashing my scene."

The first impression Bear got when entering Beth Ann's bedroom was that he had blundered onto the scene of a burglary. Posters of rap artists and movie stars thumbtacked securely onto unscathed walls, but everything else in the bedroom was ripped up and tossed, drawers pulled from their chests, underwear mingled with jeans and socks and CDs. A Ziplock bag was sliced from end to end, its cache scattered pungent on the floor. Barrett could see the remains of a roach.

But of course this was no burglary. The odor of blood permeated the place, that treacle aromatic commingling with an acrid residue of marijuana. There was blood everywhere, on the bed, on the floor. A geyser of blood had arced up precipitously over the headboard of Beth Ann's bed and onto the wall above, a dark, coagulated corona over sunny sheets. Barrett took a moment to regard the significance embued in that congealed pattern before turning to the trail of platelets leading from the bed to the bathroom.

"I see a shoe print. Woman's."

"Her mother," Roland spoke up authoritatively. "Traipsed right through."

"Was it Barbara discovered the body?"

"Yes."

Midge Holloway followed Roland and Barrett into the bathroom.

"Where's the water heater?"

"In there," Midge nodded. "Behind the linen closet."

The louvered doors beckoned. Barrett paused just a moment before brushing those barriers aside. A mechanic's lamp threw garish shadows onto the gruesome portrait before him. What had once been a living, willful being was now a carcass mated cruelly to a metal shaft.

Beth Ann's small, sinuous body, so supple while alive, drew up now like a string of gut. Barrett could almost taste the sweet, coppery scent of her blood. It dyed her skin burgundy and mingled on the floor with a void of feces and urine. Bear felt his chest go tight. That had not happened in a while, the tightened chest, the sudden shortness of breath. The closet was cramped, of course, and cloying.

"You all right? Barrett?"

"Missed breakfast is all."

He leaned over to inspect the curling, narrow mess that tangled like worms in her mouth.

"Some kind of tape, you think, Midge? Like from a cassette? An audio cassette?"

"Have to take it out to ascertain that, wouldn't we?"

Roland Reed craned for a better view.

"Can't you just pull it out?"

"Can. Won't." Midge shook her head.

"Why not?

"Because I've got shit for brains."

"Ms. Holloway—"

"Doctor Holloway, actually, and there's no way I'm going to break a jaw and teeth to fish out whatever's lodged in that victim. Plus, there's no way I'm going to risk contaminating whatever DNA's down her throat. Or do you typically go to court with trashed evidence?"

"I was just suggesting . . ."

As Midge and Roland sparred, Barrett felt an unexpected clutch in his gut. It was not the scent of death that triggered this nausea, not the smell of death. It was rather a persistent if perverted sense of life. There was something vital and lascivious in the way Beth Ann hunched the heater's cylindrical phallus. Bound tightly. Head thrown back in an awful, silent passion.

It was a Caligari cabinet, the victim elaborately displayed in a way calculated to stir a sexual urge.

"Should have told me you was here," a voice that could have come from a pit of gravel filled the linen closet. Barrett turned then to acknowledge the arrival of Dixie County's sheriff.

Sheriff Rawlings's voice was more dramatic than his presence. Unlike most sheriffs, Smoot was downright sloppy in appearance and attire. He didn't wear a uniform. A pair of drip-dry slacks, invariably wrinkled, draped over badly bowed legs. Short-sleeved shirt with a breast pocket. Tony Lima boots, scuffed as if he'd been roping calves, which he probably had been.

He had a cowboy's frame, short and compact. Big hands, though. And a vice's grip, like a jockey. He kept a pack of Big Red chewing gum to ward off the temptation of cigarettes. Had a wad going now in cheeks as full as a chipmunk's. Was hard to look directly at Smoot's eyes, a pair of gelid orbs so protuberant they seemed likely to pop out of his head.

Everything else was bottled pretty much like you'd expect for an Appalachian transplanted to the New Northwest. A wide, plain face below a thick tangle of iron-gray hair pressed at the temple by the press of a flat-brimmed straw hat stenciled on its cheap band with the insignia of his office.

"Heard you were with the senator, Sheriff," Barrett greeted his old boss with deference. "Didn't want to interrupt."

Smoot refreshed his stick of gum by plugging in a second.

"Goddamn slaughter, what this is."

Barrett nodded. "Pretty elaborate."

Sheriff Rawlings pointed his trigger finger at the victim.

"Kind of crap is that stuffed in her mouth?"

"We're thinking audio tape," Barrett answered. "Roland was just trying to talk Midge into retrieving it for us."

Smoot nodded. "Be nice to find a confession, wouldn't it? Some psycho spillin' his guts? Be too damn easy."

"Too easy," Barrett agreed. "Whoever organized this scene isn't interested in confession."

"Prolly not." The sheriff worked his gum before turning to Midge. "Was she raped?"

"Traces of semen on her inner thighs," Midge replied. "But I can't really check for signs of entry till we get her off the heater."

"An' what'd he cut her with, Midge? Should we be lookin' for a switch blade? Butcher knife?"

"A straight razor, I'd say."

"Or something very similar," Barrett seconded that assessment. "Looks like the perp is right-handed, for what that's worth. Got her from above and behind, looks like."

"Agreed," Midge seconded tersely.

"Time of death?" Smoot growled.

"I've taken an anal reading," the hunchback shook her head. "But the water heater complicates things. There is a roughly predictable drop in body temperature following mortis, as you know. But a host of factors can speed up or slow down that rate and here we've got a low-mass body strapped around eighty gallons of hot water. Makes it hard to gauge lividity, too. She could have died anytime from three in the morning till breakfast, I just can't tell with certainty."

Smoot frowned. "Her mother wanted to know if it was quick. I didn't know what to tell her."

"Beth Ann was dead before she got to the bathroom," Bear declared with certainty.

"The hell do you figure that?" the sheriff demanded.

"The splatter pattern at her bed," Barrett replied. "You see that high arc of blood? Had to be arterial, ejected at that pressure, and consistent with the slashed carotid and jugular on the victim.

"And I doubt there was much struggle; I don't see any defensive wounds. Do you, Midge?"

"None that are obvious," Midge confirmed. "No bruises consistent with a fist or blunt object. Nothing beneath her nails. The ligatures you see are postmortem."

Barrett fought another surge of nausea.

"Most probably this attack was not even anticipated," Midge went on. "Sheriff Rawlings, can you get in here?"

Barrett and Roland Reed squeezed aside to allow Smoot into the closet. Midge directed Rawlings's attention to Beth Ann's body.

"You've got the very deep laceration at the neck. And then see this deep cut through the trapezoid? And working down on her back? Her legs? Tells me something. 'Cause when you get cut, if you see it coming, your muscles go rigid as hell. A blade, even a sharp blade, does not leave the same wound in taut muscle as it will in tissue that is relaxed and pliable. We won't know for sure till we check serotonin levels, but the wounds I see suggest that the surrounding tissue was flaccid. Very pliable."

Midge peered up from her camel's hump.

"So concurring with Agent Raines, it is my opinion that you can tell the mother her daughter died quickly, probably with little anticipation, certainly before any mutilation occurred."

A scowl threatened to warp the round pie of Smoot's face.

"Okay, so the perpetrator catches her off guard. He slits her throat and kills her. But why'd he strap her to the heater? Why cut her up? And what the hell's the point of stuffing tape down her throat?"

"Could simply be rage," Midge offered. "Though most likely the tape is meant to demonstrate the perpetrator's dominance of the victim, in one way or another. A sign of control. Certainly this is the kind of signature commonly inflicted by psychopaths on their victims."

Smoot rolled twin sticks of gum into the pouch of his cheek.

"So we're lookin' for a psycho? Serial killer, maybe?"

"We need to be cautious." Barrett mopped his forehead with a broad black hand. "Displays like this are not uncommon to serial homicides, particularly when committed by organized killers. On the other hand, we can't count out the other possibility."

"What other possibility?" Smoot growled.

"That our perp is not an outsider. Not crazy. That Beth Ann knew her killer, and that this whole exhibition has been staged to throw us off, to send us looking for a transient or out-of-towner when we ought to be . . . Ought to be . . ."

"Barrett?"

"Make a hole!" Barrett barely made the commode before he was heaving bile.

"Thought you'd be used to a crime scene by now, Bear," Roland Reed taking pleasure in the spectacle.

Barrett thinking of no riposte that would not accent his humiliation.

"You all right, Barrett?"

Smoot Rawlings's concern was unexpected.

"Be fine, thanks." Raines flushed the commode.

The water swirled. An initial maelstrom seemed promising. But then the vomit began to rise in its bowl. "Shit!" Barrett scrambled back as Reed chortled derision.

"Somebody get a mop!" Smoot called out.

The toilet filling now to the very brim.

"Need a plumber's friend, Bear?" Reed stepped gingerly to safety.

"Needs a damn plumber," Rawlings growled.

"You all right, Bear?" Midge queried.

"Be fine," Barrett replied and was rising from the toilet when—

"Hello. What's this?"

He leaned close to the floor.

"Something here."

A slip of paper pressed damply to the toilet's wide base.

"It's a receipt. Credit card, looks like. Midge?"

"I've got it."

The snap of a Latex glove.

"Prob'ly Beth Ann's." Smoot offered that surmise. "She never bought anything with cash I don't imagine. Can you make it out, Bear?"

"Water's bleached it pretty badly."

"We'll pull it up," Midge assured him. "But right now, gentlemen, if you don't mind and before anybody else pukes on my scene, I'd appreciate it if you'd pursue your separate duties someplace else."

6.

Thing the driver really liked about his route around LA were the billboards. You got billboards in LA like no place else. The outsized marquees on Sunset or Hollywood Drive were, like, 3D real. So big you could be driving down 101 and it was like you could reach out and touch them. Touch the harlot's breast. Draw blood with the gladiator's sword. And then there were the curtain marquees, those fabric advertisements lowered like enormous flags to flutter like lingerie over whole sides of buildings. Shimmering lifelike in the perpetual haze.

There was a new one, this morning, he saw it heading west toward Burbank. Some new starlet laid out at least twelve stories high. Tits ten feet across. "*Scarlet Moon,*" the title was lettered tall as a tree. Some new guy was getting hyped for the lead, but it was the chick who kept your attention, that bared belly and swelling breasts fluttering in whatever breeze stirred the fronds on the palm trees beneath.

Normally, the driver would slow down to ogle the skyscraping teaser. But the traffic this morning had been slow, even by

Los Angeles standards. He'd had to make a run by Village Roadshow, first, all the way over on the Burbank side, before turning his turd-brown delivery van back across town to some start-up in Santa Monica.

Usually, the service designed their routes more efficiently. But the driver was just as happy, on this occasion, for the lapse. It helped that he had a regular stop that fit in well with the morning's additional demands.

The Lava Java was a coffeehouse shoehorned into an island set between rows of townhouses and apartments common to the state-named streets running west of 405. A California kind of place. Caffeine and vitamins and smoothies churned with exotic ingredients from Malaysia or Mexico, the various herbs and spices combining with your common yogurt and yeast to blend a concoction cool as a cucumber and thick as cum. Powerstrips along the floor for your laptop or other electronic diversion.

Lots of skin showing on the customers perusing their websites and email this morning. Lots of legs and bellies. Tits implanted firm as polyester inside haltertops above anorexic abs. Chicks hoping to get noticed by somebody in The Bizz. They lounged, these wanna-bes, on furniture that looked salvaged from St. Vincent's. Kind of a seedy interior, really. But clean. And bright— Californians had to have their sunshine, the windows looking out onto the street shaded by a perfect row of eucalyptus.

The driver entered unremarked. Functionaries were ubiquitously ignored in LA, and besides, the cafe was routine on his list of deliveries. Another case of protein and carbs from Champion Nutrition, or EAS, or MetRx. He looked at his knockoff watch; the drive across town had put him late, and he hated being late. So the driver was more than usually glad to see his coming appointment lounging, unconcerned, with a mug of steaming java.

Talk about a character. Dude looked like a pimp, all that bling. The ponytail! And, Jesus, guy, when you gonna do something about those teeth? Wonder where he was from? Probably the barrio, the driver decided. Some local mule for some higher-up with real class.

Eddy DeLeon glanced up from his coffee.

"Got my package?"

"In the van."

"I'll take it outside."

"Let me drop this shit, first, I'll meet you," the driver replied.

The cafe's manager signed for the six buckets of glutamine-enriched protein that were the driver's legitimate delivery. By the time the delivery boy got back to his van DeLeon was waiting in the passenger's seat.

"I wish you wouldn't do that."

"Do what, senor?"

"Break into my van. Every time we do this, I tell you I'll be right out; by the time I drop my stuff you're in my space."

Eddy's clippers snicked through a healthy sliver of nail in reply.

"I just wish you'd let me unlock it for you is all," the driver groused.

"You got my package or what?"

"You got my money?"

DeLeon nodded to an envelope on the console between them.

"Five thousand."

"I wanted to talk about that, the money."

The ponytailed Latin with bad teeth seemed completely unperturbed.

"We can talk, sure."

"It's just that five thousand—I mean, I don't know exactly what's *in* these packages, but I'm not stupid. Like when I pick up at Golden Circle and then drop off at some post-production on some lot at Paramount, I know it ain't chocolates. Am I right?"

"Is not chocolates," DeLeon confirmed thoughtfully. "Very good."

"So if it's what I'm thinking, maybe I need more than five thousand yam per load."

DeLeon paused over his cuticles.

"How much you make off me last year? Come on, how much?"

"I don't know. Forty thousand. Fifty?"

"Forty-five," DeLeon confirmed. "Forty-five large for nine deliveries and five minutes work. And no risk. I take all the risk. But a man gets greedy? He becomes a risk."

"Not greedy. Just wanted to see what the traffic will bear."

"Lemme put it to you this way, *compadre*. You—? are the least important link in this operation. I can buy drivers like whores. The good ones, I keep. The bad ones? Use once and unload. But the greedy ones, you know what I do with them?"

"The fuck, man?"

"I pickle your tongue."

"Pickle my—?"

"Tongue," Eddy reiterated patiently. "Cut it out, first. Then pickle it."

"Oh, *then* pickle it—?"

"*Si.* And then I make you eat."

"Hey, look, buddy—"

"I'm not your fucking buddy," DeLeon replied and the driver noticed the extra loop of twine that ran beneath the gilded necklace looped onto the spick's neck.

"All right, you know what?" The driver displayed open hands. "Fuck it. Five thousand is fine."

"Is better than fine. Is *bueno*." DeLeon exposed a feral rot of incisor.

"Okay." The driver reached past Eddy to retrieve an aluminum container. "But you need to hurry. Thing's supposed to be delivered by one."

DeLeon glanced at the address above the bar code on the service-wrapped delivery.

"At Universal? For Lieberman?"

"Yeah."

"They renumber his bungalow again?"

"The hell do you know these things?"

DeLeon tucked the cannister beneath his slender arm.

"I have it back by noon. Meet me on Lankershim. Same joint."

"Okay."

"And amigo—no more talk about money. All right? I hate to see you in a pickle."

It didn't take long for Barrett Raines to conclude that Sheriff Rawlings was totally unprepared to tackle the logistics necessary to conduct an investigation of Beth Ann Stanton's homicide. There were many ducks that needed lining up, but the biggest challenge, intially, was to find investigators in sufficient numbers to interview the hundreds of guests, staff, and media who were known to be at or near the scene of the crime.

Bear broached that problem carefully as he trailed Dixie County's straw-hatted sheriff down the stairway that led to Beth Ann's bedroom.

"What kind of support are you going to need, Smoot?"

"Support?"

"Getting statements," Bear nodded. "Christ, there must have been over two hundred people on the scene."

"Not at three in the morning," the Sheriff rebuffed.

"We don't know the time of death for sure, Sheriff. And even if we did, we'd still need to interview everyone present."

"I could bring in some of my people," Roland Reed offered tentatively. "That is, if you didn't want the FDLE involved."

The sheriff stopped so abruptly on the stairs that Barrett almost stumbled into his backside.

"The last thing, and I mean the very last damn thing, I need from you two turkeys is advice. You got that?"

"Yes, sir," Roland retreated. "Absolutely, Smoot. You are the commander in the field."

Smoot took a wad of gum from his mouth and stabbed it onto the railing of the stairway.

"I need your help, either of you, I'll goddamn ask for it."

Barrett did not press the issue. Sheriff Rawlings had already paid a huge political price for cooperating with the FDLE's investigation of Senator Stanton. He did not trust the FDLE. He did not trust Barrett. And in any case Smoot Rawlings was elected to his office; he was in no way obliged to defer to the department or to the Third Judicial District. Time was wasting, but Barrett knew his old boss well enough to know that this was not the point to press for concessions. He'd give Smoot the night to cool off, to face facts. A night to face reality.

He drove back to Deacon Beach. Made sure the boys were doing their homework. Ate some mullet Laura Anne brought home from the restaurant. Watched his wife watch the evening news without comment.

"Your day go all right?" Barrett inquired.

She nodded. "Fine."

Some story droning on CNN about the woes of Hollywood. Kids downloading feature films off the Net. Crooks pirating DVDs.

"People rationalize stealing easier than anything," Laura Anne commented listlessly.

The next morning he rose early and headed south for Cross City. Sheriff Rawlings's office was installed in what looked like a warehouse, the Dixie County Courthouse, a construction of cement blocks draped around a steel skeleton. Hardly any windows, a few vertical slits, glassed in. The roof was metal and blue and topped the whitewashed blocks below like some outsized Butler building. Did not strike the casual observer as a seat of justice. More like the kind of place you'd find the Fed Ex man.

Barrett entered the undecorated shed from the street, ignoring a metal-detector never in repair to pass the Tax Assessor's Office and Supervisor of Elections before reaching a cipher-guarded lobby looking into an open bay busy with clerks and supervisors and deputies. Somewhere behind that bunch was Sheriff Rawlings's modest niche.

An unfamiliar clerk out front seemed surprised to see a black man displaying an FDLE ID.

"Agent Raines for Sheriff Rawlings."

She frowned.

"Do you have an appointment?"

"God's sake, Cindy," the sheriff bellowed false gallantry from some rook beyond the bay. "Let the man in."

"I know the way," Barrett assured her.

On his way across the cube of desks and workstations Bear observed in-boxes sloppy with paperwork. He heard the warble of phones, heard radios breaking static like the calls of crows to the reply of sleep-deprived deputies. Post-its fluttered in pastel colors like prayer wheels. All the signs of an office under stress and underfunded.

It never ceased to gall Bear that the same county commissioners who passed bonds for roads or real-estate developers couldn't find a dime for schools or law enforcement. Teachers were actually paid better than deputies in Dixie County, not that it meant much. Smoot's uniformed officers were paid twenty-three thousand dollars a year and were forbidden by statute to take overtime.

The county's elected officials were not, in fairness, solely to blame. Voters got the law they wanted and there remained in public perception a Barney Fife stereotype of rural law enforcement that did not square with reality. Florida's rural counties were petri dishes for big-city crime. Methamphetamine labs rose like mushrooms beneath the cover of pine trees and trailer homes. Bales of marijuana washed ashore to be retrieved on unprotected coasts. Shrimp boats hauled cocaine beneath their nets and the homicide rate for cash-strapped counties was way above the national average.

It was a TV culture. Turn on the tube and you'd typically see a pair of uniformed blues lounging unmoved on a city street as a pair of weary if well-dressed detectives gumshoed over a corpse. Drifting in and out of the scene would be a photographer and at least one sexy forensic specialist. Maybe a social worker on the side to console the victim's wife or husband or parent.

In rural areas a solitary man or woman was the Initial Responder, the Crime Scene Investigator, the Evidence Technician, and the Follow-up Investigator. Get done with those chores you got called to court on your own time for trials, depositions, and hearings. Maybe hold a widow's hand on the side. This for twenty-three thousand dollars a year.

And rural law enforcement was rarely anonymous. Deputies often knew the folks that they found shot, clubbed, or gutted. Their children played on football fields or basketball courts with the survivors of violent crime. Deputies could be related to the victims of homicide that they found in a ditch or double-wide. It could be your cousin got killed or raped. Bear Raines once investigated his own brother for the homicide of his closest friend on Deacon Beach. There just wasn't another body around to do the job.

Sheriff Rawlings had twelve men and four women to cover the entire county, killings to stray cats, twenty-four hours a day. Bear knew that sixteen people weren't sufficient to work the normal load in Dixie County, let alone the burden dumped with Beth Ann Stanton's homicide.

"Get in here, Bear."

Barrett squeezed through a metal doorframe to enter an office about the size of a large closet. A GI desk was cluttered with files, phone, and a Mr. Coffee. Photos from bygone days took their place with plaques from the Optimist Club. The Rotary Club. A grainy black and white was more prominently displayed, its young cowboy at full gallop in pursuit of a calf. "Smoot Rawlings—Senior Cowboy '89" read the caption.

The familiar straw hat plopped on the pommel of a saddle stowed beside the state flag and filing cabinets bent with the weight of three-ring binders, unfiled regulations, and back issues of *Law and Order*.

Smoot stabbed the keyboard of his computer to dissolve the thumbnail of some country diva.

"What can I do you for?"

"How about the interviews?" Barrett raised the issue right away. "We need statements from everybody who was at Stanton's party; that's the immediate priority. Seems like we've got only about twenty turned in so far and some of those look pretty sketchy."

"I got people calling every day, Bear."

"You're busting your ass, Sheriff, I know. But it's not going to hack it. We're over forty-eight hours into this investigation and we need those interviews *now*."

Smoot stabbed a finger at the files on his desk.

"There's a hundred and seventy-eight folks on the guest list. Not counting cooks, waiters, the band. God knows who all else."

"You need bodies and I can get 'em," Barrett replied. "I have ten agents already tapped in Tallahassee. The department's got other folks all over the state which is important because as you know most of the folks we need to interview aren't local. They are high rollers, though, which means they ain't gonna be eager to get involved with a murder investigation."

"I thought about that." The sheriff pulled out a stick of gum. "Thought maybe the senator could make it plain people need to cooperate. Call in some chips, if he has to."

"Good idea," Barrett agreed. "But until we can complete the initial statements and triage the whole mess, we can't tell the wheat from the chaff. That's your call, obviously. What to run with, what to drop."

Rawlings's jaw worked with his gum.

"Don't seem like I got a lot of choice," the sheriff said finally. "But I want a copy of every statement that's taken, you hear me, Bear? Every damn one."

"Certainly. I'll get you hard copy plus tapes if we interview over the phone."

"Other thing. The senator's awready told me he doesn't want the FBI involved and neither do I. And nothing goes to Roland Reed, I mean *nothing,* without me signin' off."

"It's your investigation, Sheriff. Now, if you don't mind what have we got from Jacksonville?"

"Couple things. Midge's take on the scene was on the money. Somebody slit Beth Ann's throat from behind. Abuse was all postmortem. Got about a million prints and partials to check out, of course. That's gonna take awhile. Be two weeks at least before all the DNA gets sorted. There was a lot of blood in that room."

"A lot of everything in that room," Barrett agreed. "Including a wad of tape stuffed down her throat."

"Got the word on that, too. Gimme a minute—"

The sheriff shuffling notes from beneath the pile on his desk.

"Lessee. Here it is. It was an audio tape, just like we thought. Some rock group in South Florida. Night Fog they called themselves."

"Named after the film," Barrett recalled. "Group actually had quite a following at one point. Part of that Goth thing. Fascination with body parts and Nazis. Very exploitative lyrics. Very violent."

"So they ain't Garth Brooks?"

"Not hardly."

"How they connect to Beth Ann?"

"Have no idea. Concert? We could check for that. See if she was a groupie, maybe."

"I'll take that one." Smoot jotted a note. "Something for you, that credit card receipt? The one by the commode?"

"You mean the one I puked on?"

Rawlings allowed a smile.

"Turns out it traces to a Barnes and Noble in Fort Myers. We found about forty receipts in the room altogether, by the way. Some local, others from malls or stores or bars scattered all over the state. Looks like the senator's little girl partied as wide as she did hard."

Barrett made his own note. "I'll get somebody checking out the stores that aren't local. See what we can turn up."

"All right." Rawlings slipped his ballpoint into his shirt pocket. "There be anything else?"

"One item, yes."

"And that would be?"

"I need to interview Senator Stanton."

Rawlings scowled.

"I already talked to Stanton, Barrett. Sat him down the very first day. Didn't you read my report?"

"I read it, yes."

Smoot's jaw clamped over a wad of Big Red.

"There some question you think I left out, Bear, just tell me. I don't mind goin' back out."

"We both need to get back out there, Sheriff. But I need to be the one interviewing."

" 'Makes you think Stanton'll talk to you? Hell, you just tried to put the man in jail!"

"Getting full credit for it, too."

Smoot spit his gum into a trashcan. Peeled out another from a pack on his desk.

"I'll see what I can do. But if Stanton starts rippin' you a new asshole, don't look to me for help."

"Don't worry, Sheriff. I'd never put you in that position."

Smoot snorted.

"You already fucking have."

Barrett Raines and Smoot Rawlings arrived at Senator Stanton's mansion and found the newshounds waiting. Barrett scanned the small sea of microphones. No sign of Sharon Fowler in the kennel.

"No statement, boys," Smoot growled, ignoring with Barrett the volley of queries and imprecations that chased them both to the porch.

Miss Wanda waited at the wide front doors, bags sagging darkly beneath damp eyes. Ushered inside, Bear soon found himself perched on the edge of a wickerwork chair positioned almost directly beneath a parakeet's cage. The senator had been careful to keep his inquisitor at a remove in an uncomfortable seat safely distant from his own padded lounger. Smoot Rawlings occupied one of a pair of rocking chairs nearer to the aggrieved father. A coffee table fortified with oatmeal cookies and sweet tea shielded the senator from his unwelcome guests.

The senator had received the lawmen in his lanai, a sunroom extending off the kitchen on the ground floor and exposed through generous glassed panes to the grounds outside. Barrett noticed Clarence Magrue clipping a bristling hedge of pyracantha. Barrett recalled from Smoot's report that the hedge ringed Stanton's well-kept pool. He considered briefly stripping naked, rushing from his catbird seat to a self-inflicted drowning.

The opening remarks were not salutary.

"Well, now, Agent Raines, are you still tryin' to nail my hide to a wall?"

That challenge rendered in furious detachment.

"The allegations were not brought by the FDLE, Senator. The governor initiated our investigation."

"And what did you find for the governor? A paid snitch?"

"Senator, that case as you know is no longer before our department. Judge Boatwright has made certain it will never even come before a grand jury. That's old business. New business: Somebody's murdered your daughter. I am here to help Sheriff Rawlings find the killer and put him in a gurney. That's why I'm before you now, sir."

Sheriff Rawlings placed his tea carefully onto a felt coaster.

"I can throw Agent Raines off the case, if you like, Senator Stanton. 'Fact, I can tell the whole bunch not to show their sorry asses inside the county if that's what you want, but I gotta tell you, Senator, I could use the extra hands."

"You still trust this son of a bitch?" The senator cast his insult as if Barrett were not even in the room.

"Come to killings I do, yessir. He's got a knack."

"Well, I hope so. Because Agent Raines and his department have a record with regard to my affairs that does not inspire confidence."

"Had some dealings along that line myself, Senator."

"As I say. Does not inspire confidence."

Barrett cleared his throat.

"Senator, do you want to find the bastard who killed Beth Ann?"

"That's a hell of an impertinent question."

"Nevertheless. Do you?"

"Of course I do. I want to strangle the son of a bitch with my bare hands."

"Yessir. So what say we get started?"

Baxter Stanton pressed his fingertips together in an incongruously Buddhist pose. A lounger barely squeaking with his bantam weight. A decision was being weighed, Barrett knew, and divining the senator's intentions in the creekbed of his face it seemed to Bear that the call was going against his involvement.

"All right," Stanton broke the silence abruptly. "If Sheriff Rawlings thinks you can be of some use, fine by me. But tell your chickenshit boss that the FDLE is *not* going to use my daughter's killing as a pry bar to reopen any kind of investigation into my campaign or my affairs. Is that clear?"

"Crystal clear, Senator."

"This is Sheriff Rawlings's case."

"Absolutely."

"You serve at his pleasure."

The senator did not have to say, "And mine."

"Yes, sir," Barrett swallowed crow.

"Go on, then."

Stanton did not offer Agent Raines any tea as he leaned forward to refill his own.

"First off, Senator Stanton, I'd like to talk about the last time you saw your daughter."

"It was sometime after eight. She was in the pool; I already told the sheriff."

"Yes, I was just wondering what brought you out to the pool in the first place."

"What 'brought' me?"

"Well, Senator, with a couple of hundred high-rollers at your door and media all over, I'd expect you to be mixing and mingling."

"I did mix. I was tired. I repaired to my study."

"Pool's a long way from your study, Senator. The only obvious exit out back that I could see was through the kitchen over there."

Stanton paused a moment.

"Clarence was working in the kitchen. We've had a problem with plumbing. I just dropped by to see if he'd got it fixed is all."

"And you can see the pool from the kitchen?"

Stanton sipped his tea.

"Like I say, I was tired. I just stepped out back, is all."

"And according to the statement you gave Sheriff Rawlings you saw your daughter swimming in the pool?"

"Yes," Stanton replied and immediately knew he'd made a mistake.

Barrett nodded past the parakeet's cage to the wall of pyracantha outside.

"Pretty obvious you didn't see anything through that hedge, Senator. Pretty obvious, in fact, that the reason you put in that shrubbery was to keep the pool private."

"I say I 'saw' her," Stanton waved it off. "By that I mean I discerned her presence. Her voice."

"Voice? So she was talking?"

"Yes, and I heard her."

"And was she talking to herself, Senator Stanton?"

A flush spread like crimson over that scrawny neck and for a moment Barrett figured he'd pushed too quickly.

"No. No, she was not talking to herself."

"So it was voices you heard. A pair? Two or three?"

"Two voices, yes."

"Senator, if Beth Ann wasn't alone in the pool, I need to know who she was with. If you could just help us with that."

Stanton placed his sweating glass very deliberately on the hardwood table.

"I came outside. I heard voices. I found Beth Ann in the pool with Eddy DeLeon."

The parakeet shrieked. Smoot Rawlings choked on his tea.

The senator, Barrett noted, kept a poker face.

Bear left his basket seat to take a place nearer the senator. He wasn't satisfied that Stanton was supplying the entire truth. But right now he'd settle for what he could get.

"Was this a one-shot deal, Senator?"

"What do you mean?"

"Was Beth Ann seeing Eddy regularly?"

"Have no idea."

The reply came too quickly.

"Pretty hard for me to understand why you didn't tell the sheriff about DeLeon right off the bat, sir. Regardless of whether you were specifically asked."

"First place, DeLeon's about the last person I'd suspect of killing Beth Ann. If you saw them, well—you'd know. But I suppose the real reason I didn't want to tell you, or anyone, about my daughter being with Eduardo DeLeon is that it's an embarrassment."

"Embarrassment?"

"You have children, Mr. Raines?"

"Twins. Boys."

"They can do crazy things, can't they?"

"Yes, they can."

"Beth was the kind of girl'd do anything to get attention. She got older, it got less and less cute. She began to look for ways to embarrass her mother. Or me. Some of the goddamnedest things. But she always comes—she always *came* home."

The eyes suddenly bright as dimes.

"You feel like Beth Ann was just usin' Eddie to pull your chain?"

This from Sheriff Rawlings.

"I hope that was the case." Stanton's reply was hoarse. "I can't imagine the little bastard being brazen enough to come back after I saw him with her myself. To kill Beth Ann in her own room!"

He paused.

"But the only thing I can say for sure is that the last time I saw my daughter alive she was with that spick son of a bitch."

Barrett Raines and Smoot Rawlings left the senator's home to find a swell of curiosity seekers joined to the press of microphones and cameras that already crowded the scene's taped and fragile boundary.

This was a big story, Barrett mused. And getting bigger by the minute.

He spotted Sharon in the crowd then, taller than most of her male competitors. A head taller than any other female present.

Looking good.

Smoot nodded to a nearby deputy. "Frank, I want you and Tyler to move the locals back off the tape. Be nice about it."

"Yes, sir. You wanta say somethin'?"

"Agent Raines will handle the media. He's a well-known expert."

The whir of cameras as the two men approached. Microphones extending on rigged booms and slender hands. Barrett took a deep breath, exhaled, and then with what he hoped was a clear, casual voice smiled to the milling press.

"Okay, folks. Let's have a press conference."

Some confusion, then, as recorders and microphones thrust like spears into Barrett's face. "Here's what we've got," he began, and summarized the findings so far garnered, holding back any information which would be known only to the killer.

No mention of the tape stuffed down the victim's throat. No mention of mutilation. Most importantly, no mention of Eddy DeLeon; the last thing in the world Raines wanted to do in front of these sharks was chum with that bait.

". . . That's about all I can tell you at this time," Barrett concluded. "A word regarding protocol. I am sure ya'll know there are several law enforcement agencies supporting this investigation. But it's important to reiterate that Sheriff Rawlings is in charge of this case. So any further questions from the press should be directed to Sheriff Rawlings or his office."

Smoot's jaw clamping down on his chewing gum.

Barrett kept a pleasant smile. "I reiterate that we are in the very early stages of this investigation. We have no evidence of facts pointing us to a suspect at this time. Now, if ya'll will excuse me—"

Sharon Fowler extended her long arm.

"Agent Raines, is it true that Beth Ann Stanton was seen hours before her murder at her father's residence in the company of Eddy DeLeon?"

A hammer came from somewhere to fall on the anvil of Barrett's heart. Smoot Rawlings paled to the pallor of ash. A feral growl rose from the gathered newshounds.

They loved an ambush, Barrett knew.

And knew he had to break out.

"Do you have some information related to this brutal killing that you'd like to share with our investigators, Ms. Fowler?"

"Excuse me. I asked a question."

"I heard your question. Now you hear this: If you or anyone hearing my voice has a source which places Mr. DeLeon on this premises at *any* time proximate to the homicide in question you are obligated legally and ethically, if not by the canon of your profession, to turn that information over to authorities.

"If on the other hand you are simply fishing, Sharon, then I have to say your question is irresponsible and I am in no way obliged to respond. I believe that concludes our business for the day, ladies and gentlemen. Thank you all."

It took a pair of deputies to break the phalanx of mikes and cameras barring the way to Barrett's cruiser.

"God dammit!" Smoot wrenched the passenger door to the limit of its hinges. "God damn, how'd she know that?"

"She could have seen them herself," Barrett replied tight-lipped. "She was at the party. She knows the house."

"More likely one of the help was back there an' saw 'em,"

Smoot cursed. "Some damn local playing barkeep or waiter saw and then went yakkin' to Sharon. 'Course if we ask who she'll just say it's her goddamn 'source'."

"There were lots of eyeballs at that party, Sheriff. And we haven't interviewed half of 'em."

"Then I guess we better get you back to work."

Within moments Rawlings was gunning his Crown Vic over the senator's cattlegap and onto the county-owned blacktop. Barrett steadied himself on the stock of the shotgun mounted between them.

"You think DeLeon could of killed Beth Ann?" Rawlings checking the rearview as he snapped a pair of Ray Bans from his pocket-planner.

"Be a stupid thing to do." Bear shook his head.

"What I hear he keeps a razor," Smoot countered.

"A razor."

"What I hear."

Barrett let go of the shotgun.

"You read the paper last Saturday, Sheriff? The *Democrat*?"

"Gave you a pretty good whipping. Deserved, in my opinion."

"That being said, you can understand why I don't want to announce Eddy DeLeon as a suspect in this case till I get evidence a little more substantial than what he uses to shave."

"I'll get your evidence." The sheriff's promise was terse. "There's something on that crime scene's gonna tie Eddy to Beth Ann and I'll find it. Yes, Miss Mary. And when I do I'm ramming it up that cocksucker's well-oiled ass."

7.

■ *If you're working for the* FDLE anywhere in northern Florida, chances are you're going to spend a lot of time driving. Not counting the miles racked up on the morning's drive to Sheriff Rawlings's Dixie County office, Bear Raines rolled up fifty-three miles on the odometer on the way from Smoot's roost to the FDLE Regional Office in Live Oak.

And it wasn't like fifty-three miles of interstate. The drive from Cross City to Live Oak required Bear to pick up Route 349 for a run roughly parallel to the Suwannee River until reaching Branford where a jog to Highway 27 connected to US-129, then northeast on 129 the rest of the way in. With the commute home Agent Raines would log a hundred sixty miles behind the wheel.

Of course, there was work in between. Roland Reed was anxious for a formal report summarizing Bear's interview with Senator Baxter Stanton. Eddy DeLeon's involvement with Beth Ann was going to hit like a bombshell; Barrett had already e-mailed that warning to the state's advocate. Roland was just covering his ass with the demand for additional paperwork, requiring Bear to waste an hour of precious time.

The rest of his time was spent lining up bodies to assist Sheriff Rawlings's overtaxed deputies. It was past five o'clock before Bear took a call not related to homicide or bureaucracy. Blackshear's Auto Repair phoned in to say that his personal car was ready to roll. Jim Blackshear brought the vehicle to Bear's office himself, meeting the lawman outside the ciphered door to present the keys.

"She's ready to go."

Barrett had to smile. The restoration, or resurrection as the twins deemed it, of his Malibu SuperSport was always a work in progress. The interior still needed help, but at least the guts were finally in place. New ball joints, tie rods, and idler arm for the front end. New tires. New clutch for the four-speed tranny linked to a pistol-grip shifter. He'd had the original block rebuilt at a speedshop in Gainesville. Three hundred ninety-six cubic inches running cool and a four-barrel carb that snorted gas like a coke addict.

One by one over the years Barrett had restored every mechanical system on the car. Except for the air-conditioning. Would take another fifteen or sixteen hundred dollars at least to upgrade the Malibu's a/c, which meant that Bear was going to be driving windows down on the way home.

He took the usual route on Highway 51, that boiling blacktop running south and west from Live Oak all the way to Steinhatchee. The Suwannee River divided Suwannee from Lafayette County at the Hal W. Adams Bridge. Took around ten minutes to reach that cabled span, the river below churning brown and untamed and ancient. It was a straight shot past the bridge to the small town of Mayo. Barrett eased by the courthouse and through a solitary traffic light before picking up speed on the blacktop heading west.

It was miserably hot. The sun baked his face through the Malibu's windshield like a microwave. The asphalt beneath his car sizzled like steak. Lazy johns boiled off the blacktop to a point past perception and the highway was a claustrophobe's nightmare, palmettos girding a wall of pine trees pressing in from either side of a shoulderless road. A zipper of sky overhead.

Barrett could not wait to shed his tie, shirt, and sweat-stained blazer and jump naked under a cold-water shower. Then collapse on his La-Z-Boy beneath a fountain of frigid air for a reprise of *Star Trek* or volleyball—anything unrelated to cops or corpses. Or reporters.

Or maybe he'd stop by the restaurant, see if he could get a smile back on Laura Anne's face. Coax her to the piano, maybe. At least begin to roll back the clock to the way things had been before his wife plummeted into her depressing spiral, back to those shared intimacies that used to sustain them both through torrid days. But competing with those desires on the long drive home was a gnawing anxiety.

It had to do with Taylor Calhoun. Barrett hadn't heard a peep from Taylor in over two weeks. Under normal circumstances that wouldn't be worrisome; Calhoun never contacted Bear on a predictable schedule. But once Senator Stanton's triumph over the FDLE had been made public, Barrett expected to hear from Taylor, if not for money at least for a repeated guarantee of protection and security.

"Nobody knows you're working for the FDLE," Raines constantly assured his diminutive snitch, by which Bear meant that only a strictly limited list of persons in law enforcement were trusted with the black man's identity. Captain Altmiller at FDLE Regional was required to be apprised of all informants. Judge Boatwright had to be trusted. Selected attorneys at the Third District knew. Roland Reed knew.

Did anyone else know?

And if Taylor's cover had been compromised, was there any chance that the entire investigation of Senator Stanton had been sabotaged? Looking back, it seemed to Barrett that the senator's lawyers had seemed uncannily prescient of his intentions. In one instance, a proposed wiretap was challenged by Stanton's team even before the warrant was approved. In another case, auditors sent by the FDLE in pursuit of suspicious transactions arrived to find businesses that had been rushed offshore or dissolved entirely. It was as though someone had given Baxter Stanton the FDLE's playbook.

Of course, there was always the chance of an inadvertent betrayal, Taylor Calhoun's identity revealed on a note or instruction mingled among the hundreds of files and dozens of depositions that were finally turned over to the senator's lawyers at Judge Boatwright's stern direction.

Could be that, and nothing more.

Barrett recalled that the last time he'd spoken with Taylor was at the Suwannee County Courthouse. Talk about a breach of security! From the get-go, Barrett had absolutely ruled out face-to-face meetings with his informant. When Taylor had information he was to relay it by landline or slow-mail. Never e-mail. Never cell phone. And *never* in person.

Similarly, Taylor was never paid in person, always by direct deposit and always through a laundered source. Those were the rules and up to their last communication Taylor had never, ever, violated the firewall separating him from Barrett Raines. Until a little more than two weeks earlier when Bear looked up to see Taylor Calhoun crabbing down the steps of the Suwannee County Courthouse.

"Bear, I got somethin'."

"Taylor, the hell are you doing here?"

"Got you somethin', Bear. Izzfor real!"

Taylor always thought he had something for real.

"Let's get inside."

"Eddy's messin' around in the movie business!" Taylor offered that ambiguous pronouncement before he and Barrett were yet behind doors.

"The movie business."

Taylor's larynx bobbed in his scrawny neck. "Yup. He just got back from Los Angeleez last week. Been goin' least once a month."

"Eddy hits Vegas most every month, too, Taylor. That mean he runs a casino?"

"But ever time he comes back from LA he's got these DVDs, Bear. I'm talkin' movies ain't yet made it to Blockbuster!"

"Folks do it all the time, Taylor. They rob 'em off the Internet."

"Stuff I saw ain't off no Net."

"And how would you know that?

"I just *know,* dammit!"

"You 'just know'?"

"Come own, Bear! Let me dig around! They's a pile of shit right there at Mama's—"

"No," Bear had cut him off. "I do *not* want you poking around Mama's."

"Ain't whores enough in three counties could make the cash runnin' through that cathouse," Calhoun persisted.

"Just work the bar, Taylor. You see a car isn't local, jot down the tag. You see a meeting listen in. Hear a name pass it along. That's *all.*"

"Bear, I'm tellin' you they's big bucks goin' through that place. In *cash.*"

"We know where DeLeon gets his cash," Barrett replied with superior patience.

Which was a lie. No one knew for certain where DeLeon got his money. An incarcerated felon who claimed to be familiar with Eddy's enterprises told FDLE investigators that the Honduran native derived most of his take from drugs pushed all over the state. Methamphetamines, mostly, had come word from the prison rat.

Similar stories drifted in from mules or middlemen. There was plenty of smoke linking Eddy to traffic, but no fire, certainly never a bust. And DeLeon's other sources of income, though shaded, were not jailable. Barrett knew, as an example, that Eddy bankrolled Mama's seaside brothel, but he could not prove that DeLeon received profits from that prostituting enterprise.

A sheet-metal business was entirely legit. So was income derived from Internet porn.

Barrett voiced the idea that pornography might be Eddy's bread and butter.

"Dirty pictures? Ain't a drop in the bucket." Calhoun wagged his round head. "Tellin' you, Bear, you get me a thousand dollars, I'll get you the real skinny."

"You're going to get yourself in trouble, is what you're going to get. Now, goddamn it, Taylor, you get information of any kind, you relay it by phone or mail. If Eddy's got something illegal in the film business we'll find it and you'll get your compensation. Though I can't promise anything like a thousand dollars."

"Fuck you, then!" Taylor bowed up. "Think you're King Shit? I'll just call the feds, is what I'll do. Call the fuckin' federales!"

Taylor had huffed away and Bear had not heard from him since. Neither had anybody else. The little fart was just sulking, Raines told himself. Pissed off that he couldn't shill Bear for more easy cash.

The movies! Unless it was blow jobs or bondage Bear could not imagine anything that would connect Eddy DeLeon to the film industry. Even so, it'd be reassuring to hear from Taylor Calhoun.

As if on cue, his cell phone warbled for attention. Bear snapped it open.

"Raines here."

"It's Roland."

About the last damn person in the world Bear wanted to hear from was Fountain Pen Reed.

"Bear, I know you're headed home, but I need to see you. Just a few minutes."

"You expect me to turn around and drive back to Live Oak?"

"No, as a matter of fact I'm pulling in to your wife's restaurant as we speak. Thought I'd grab a bite while we talk. Won't take any time."

Barrett cursed silently.

"All right. Tell Laura Anne I'll be in."

Roland Reed was halfway into a crossword puzzle and a seafood plate by the time Barrett passed through the salvaged doors admitting entry to his wife's restaurant. A local station broadcast the news from a television set above the diner's island bar. Bear spotted a waiter.

"Roy, is Laura Anne around?"

"In the kitchen, Mr. Raines. Won't me to get her?"

"Just tell her I'm here, would you?"

"Bring you something to eat, sir?"

"Coffee'll do. I'll be joining Mr. Reed."

Roy nodded understanding.

"I'll get it right out."

Fountain Pen made no effort to stand as Bear approached his table, gesturing instead to the hardwood platter set before him.

"Sit down, Bear. The mullet's good."

"Roland, if you want to talk, let's talk. Otherwise I can eat at home."

"Fair enough."

The prosecutor paused for a sip of iced tea.

"What's on my mind is that right now we are relying solely on Senator Stanton to establish that Eddy DeLeon was *in flagrato* with Beth Ann the night she was killed."

"He saw them in the pool. You read my report."

"Not your report I'm worried about." Roland jabbed a remote at the TV mounted above the bar.

A backdrop of Pepperfish Keys framed Sharon Fowler for her evening anchor. A high-collared jacket made respectable the silk and sheer blouse that clung to her skin like lingerie beneath. Her hair was pulled back straight as a Puritan's and tucked.

Eyes leveled on the camera like a crossbow.

"Good evening, I'm Sharon Fowler. The investigation into the murder of Senator Baxter Stanton's daughter took a bizarre twist today when information obtained by this reporter established that Beth Ann Stanton was last seen alive with Eddy DeLeon, the crime figure whom Senator Stanton has consistently claimed never to have met . . ."

"Never met him!" Roland capped his pen.

". . . DeLeon was seen in the company of Stanton's daughter Sunday night at the senator's well-publicized celebration. Sources close to this reporter say that Beth Ann herself invited Eddy to the Stanton residence."

"Beth Ann invited him?" Roland looked to Barrett for confirmation.

"News to me," Bear replied tersely.

"The link between DeLeon and Beth Ann Stanton complicates an already delicate investigation," Sharon went on. *"Special Agent Barrett Raines was clearly not eager to respond to any new information that might require a fresh look into the relationship between Eddy DeLeon and Senator Stanton or his family."*

Barrett slapped his cup into its saucer. "That's bullshit!"

"Barrett—?"

Laura Anne frowned at her husband's shoulder.

"I'm sorry, hon. It was nothing."

"Well, you could hear that nothing all the way to the kitchen."

"Said I'm sorry."

She turned to Roland Reed.

"You need anything, Mr. Reed?"

"Roy's fixed me up fine, thank you, Laura Anne."

Barrett regarded the woman who sank spent and passive into a wooden chair. Where was that full, vital wife he knew? His rock. His salvation. Laura Anne ran an absent hand through disheveled coils of hair, her blouse riding up her hip.

"The boys eaten?" she asked her husband.

"I haven't been home yet."

"They need to eat."

"The boys are fine, Laura Anne. Thelma's not going to let them starve."

"Shouldn't depend on Thelma," Laura Anne mumbled and then turned to her head waiter. "I'm through for the day. Roy."

"Yes, ma'am. But we're short in the kitchen."

"Shut down some tables. If it gets real slow, close up early."

Roy glanced to Barrett.

"Yes, ma'am."

"Let me drive you home, babe," Barrett offered.

Laura Anne declined, that tall, strong stature bent and slow. That enviable complexion gone brown and sullen.

"No, I'll be fine."

Barrett watched the steward's door swing closed on his wife's long, stiff back.

"I'm sorry, Bear."

This from Roland Reed.

"But we need to talk. This thing with Sharon Fowler—"

"Nothing we can do about her."

"Find her source, we can help ourselves plenty," the state's attorney replied.

"We can't make Sharon give up a source, Roland."

"A journalist's privilege isn't unlimited, especially where a homicide is involved. I could find a judge."

Bear shook his head. "The only way we're going to get Sharon off our ass is to make the news for a change instead of chasing it."

Roland tugged at the napkin in his vest. "I just don't want to look like I'm trying to put Eddy DeLeon into the senator's bed as well as his daughter's."

"Who said anything about that?"

"Can't ever tell what we'll uncover, Bear."

"The evidence leads where it leads, Roland; there's nothing I can do about that."

"I understand, but bear in mind we've got a federal judge

strictly admonishing us from *any* kind of investigation that gets into the senator's campaign arrangements, his finances, phone records. Anything like that."

"What's that go to do with the fact that Eddy DeLeon was screwing his daughter?"

"Be nice if somebody saw 'em besides the senator, is all I'm saying. Be prudent if we could get ourselves an independent source for that information."

"Somebody like Sharon Fowler?"

"Her source, at least." Roland pocketed his pen.

"You just want to keep your nose clean, Roland; that's your real priority."

"I'm just saying if we can get some witness other than Baxter Stanton to substantiate DeLeon's involvement with Beth Ann, we should do it. Another source. That's all I'm saying."

"Well, speaking of sources—"

Barrett leaned forward on large arms.

"Have you heard from Taylor Calhoun? A call? A note? Anything?"

Roland frowned. "No."

Bear settled back.

"Taylor came to me couple of weeks ago. Claimed to know where Eddy gets his bankroll."

"That crap about movies?"

"He told you, too?"

"After he tried selling you, apparently. The movies! Right. Eddy DeLeon and Julia Roberts. Honestly? I'm beginning to think Taylor was blowing smoke from the beginning."

"You weren't of that opinion this summer."

"Changed my mind. In light of evidence. Like you said, it leads where it leads."

"That's self-serving coming from you, Roland."

"Fuck you. For a hundred bucks a month—? Calhoun would tell us anything he thought we wanted to hear."

"You wanta talk money? In the last two months alone Baxter Stanton has paid off something like two million dollars of debt.

On top of that he's declared over a million in profits to the IRS. Where's Stanton's cash coming from?"

"Not from Eddy DeLeon. At least, not according to Judge Boatwright. According to the judge, Senator Stanton derives his income from his twenty-seven legitimately held businesses."

Barrett pushed his chair away from the table.

"Laundromats and car-washes? A bowling alley? You don't believe that any more than I do."

"Doesn't matter what I believe, Bear. Doesn't matter what you believe. Only thing that matters is what we can prove and, to return to the matter at hand, if we're going to *prove* that Eddy DeLeon was screwing Beth Ann Stanton the night of her murder it would be nice to have somebody other than her daddy for a witness. We need another set of eyeballs, Bear. Another source. Which leads me back to Sharon Fowler."

"What do you want me to do?"

"Talk to her."

The state attorney dropped a pair of bills onto his plate.

"Meet privately. Off the record. Explain why we need to know where she's getting her information. And tell her not to worry. After all . . . we protect sources all the time."

8.

■ *Sharon Fowler leaned in her* silk blouse over a digital editor. It was an obsolete deck, an old BVW75. KEYS TV maintained machines for both half- and three-quarter-inch formats in bins jerry-rigged in what used to be a hallway. The station's computers were almost as antediluvian as the editing equipment. One machine cannibalized to keep another running. Every chair, stool, and desk was got from some store in liquidation. The building was falling apart, acoustic tiles drooping from a drop-down ceiling to reveal ducts heavy with mold.

But Sharon Fowler was insensible to those distractions. The tapes had her attention, the disparate footage that when edited and synchronized would introduce Sharon Fowler to the boys in New York. The first cut wouldn't do at all; it had been rushed to make her ten o'clock show. Sharon had already spent hours cutting and re-cutting that footage. Hours sweating in the bin. But it was worth it. This story was her resume, her audition. It had to be right.

The process was nearly complete. Sharon had long ago established "In & Out" points for each edit. The audio was laid down and synchronized. Now came the fun part, shuttling back and forth between two decks and two tapes to cut-and-paste a final product.

The "Play" and "Record" decks each held a half-inch tape, one of raw footage, the other tape containing previously edited footage. The tapes plugged into separate monitors, those two screens mounted side by side for Sharon's inspection. She was working on "Preview" mode, a working edit that would not yet commit her to a final product. There were still a few enhancements that needed to be included before Fowler mailed her show to WNABC.

The raw footage of Senator Stanton's triumphal arrival reeled off on one small screen while the edited footage froze on the other. No distraction was permitted as Sharon scrolled through the virgin images on her left-hand deck:

FOLLOWING SHARON: *Sharon pushes through a press of cameras and competing REPORTERS to reach Senator Stanton's Cinderella coach. She offers the senator her hastily repaired microphone.*

"Good evening, Senator."
Stanton ignores her. Smiles over Sharon's head to the CROWD beyond.

"My wife, first, if you please."

Sharon shuttled the tape further into Dew Drop's captured footage. Back and forth to find the right spot.

"Yes. There you are," her voice soft in the bin.

Another snatch of cinema verité, Baxter Stanton's practiced smile caught in Dew Drop's camera.

The pumpkin coach FRAMES SENATOR STANTON and his wife. BARBARA STANTON beams a Tri-Delt smile to the CROWD.

WIDEN SHOT *to include Sharon's approach, tall and toned in a bareback gown.*

"Time for a few words, Senator?"

"You just got a few, Miz Fowler."

"But, sir, the interview . . ."

Sharon froze the monitored frame to cut off Stanton's reply. She then shuttled ahead once again, ahead in sequence, ahead in time.

Far enough?

"Not quite . . ."

Sharon muttered and jogged a few frames forward. Just a few.

"There."

MEDIUM SHOT: *Senator Stanton smiles with his wife beside their Cinderella coach. Sharon extends her microphone like a bouquet of roses.*

Sharon paused the tape on the Medium Shot. She then culled a closeup of Baxter Stanton, easy enough to patch that mug in. Now, for a digitized splice and dice.

"Okay."

The resulting edit created a revised sequence, a fabricated continuity linking Sharon's handheld microphone with Stanton's broadly smiling face. All that remained was to match up the scene's audio with Sharon's digitally manipulated visuals.

"See how you look *now.*"

"Time for a few words, Senator?"

The Senator smiles graciously.

"We were always confident."

OVER SHARON'S SHOULDER.

"And the people of Pepperfish Keys—YOU GOOD PEOPLE! YOU NEVER, NEVER WAVERED!"

"That's not how I remember it."

Barrett Raines's ursine frame filled up the editing bin's door.

"Or is this an abridged version?"

"You've had your interview, Barrett."

She didn't even bother to turn around.

"Isn't that fiction you just created, Sharon? Make believe? Or is this what journalists call license?"

She swiveled on her second-hand chair to face him.

"If I'd cut it straight, Stanton would have come off as a rude, chauvinist prick."

Barrett nodded. "You, on the other hand, would have looked ridiculous."

"But not now," she smiled. "I'd call that a win-win, wouldn't you?"

"I'd call it a lie."

A frost hardened.

"What can I do for you, Agent Raines?"

"For starters, you could tell me how you knew that Eduardo DeLeon was with Beth Ann Stanton in the hours before her murder."

"Are you confirming that he *was*?"

She chuckled deprecation.

"Let's get something straight, okay, Sharon? A little quid pro quo? Why don't you try being straight with me. I'll do the same for you. Now. How'd you know Eddy was with Beth Ann?"

"I was there."

" 'There'?"

"With Senator Stanton, at the pool. Didn't he tell you?"

Barrett measured his words. "The senator didn't say anything about you, no. Any idea why?"

She shrugged.

"I could conjecture he's hoping I'd bury the story on his daughter's involvement with Eddy."

"Did he make you an offer you couldn't refuse?"

"Apparently not."

She smiled.

"So exactly how would you characterize their involvement?

Beth Ann and Eddy? In other words, what exactly did you see?"

"I saw them screwing."

"Uh huh. And Stanton saw 'em as well?"

"Of course. There were some heated words, I couldn't make it out, exactly. I was stuck on the far side of the action."

"Must have been frustrating for you."

"I don't mind a little frustration."

Barrett fought a sudden urge to scratch his balls.

"Okay, so there were words. What then?"

"Beth Ann left with DeLeon. Stanton asked me to go easy. I left the party."

"For where?"

"Back here. I had a ten o'clock broadcast to get ready and after that I pulled an all-nighter on this sucks-ass editor."

Barrett leaned on the door's metal frame.

"You've covered the Stantons for a while, now, haven't you, Sharon?"

"Six years, about."

"So what's your take on Beth Ann?"

"She was the kind of bitch would drop a match into a room filled with gasoline."

"Ouch."

"She had her reasons, I guess."

"Anything I should know?"

"I've been pretty helpful, don't you think, Barrett? So when do I get a turn at the blender?"

"I'm just trying to get at the truth, Sharon."

"Oh, bullshit!"

She laughed outright.

"Excuse me?"

"Bullshit, Bear. Oh, you'd love to know who killed Beth Ann Stanton, sure you would. But it doesn't have anything to do with The Truth! Or even less, The Law! Give me a break."

"All right, then. What is it about? You tell me."

She pushed up from her chair to approach him.

"It's about revenge, Bear. Can't you admit that? A way to

screw your enemies and redeem yourself in the eyes of your department. A way to tell Roland Reed to go fuck himself. That's what it's about."

"Only partly. And I've got rules, Sharon. I play by the rules."

"Of course you do. So do I."

Sharon stretched stiffly, her hand a knot at the base of that long spine.

"I've got work to do."

"One more question."

"If it's quick."

"I don't need a name; I don't expect you to expose a source. But did you have somebody inside the FDLE during the period of time that we were actively investigating Baxter Stanton? Or at the Third Judicial Circuit?"

Her eyes never left the editor.

"What in hell makes you think I'd ever answer a question like that?"

"What if I told you there was a life at stake?"

She shrugged. "There's always a life at stake, Bear. Everything touches everything else. You know that, don't you? From personal experience."

He felt something like iced water in his stomach.

"Goddammit, Sharon—"

"If you don't mind, Bear, I need to finish this tape."

Sharon Fowler closed up the editing bin barely fifteen minutes before her ten P.M. gig. The later broadcast wasn't much more than a replay of the six o'clock fare, really, but Almond Sinclair gushed accolades anyway.

"Terrific show, Sharon! Just dynamite!"

The news director beaming as he bounced right by Dew Drop and the station's other supporting players, his hands turning one over the other as if washing dishes. Other congratulations were scattered and tepid. Dew Drop ducked out to avoid Sharon altogether.

"Beth Ann and Eddy having *sex*?" Almond rattled on oblivious. "Talk about the inside scoop. Talk about getting the dirt!"

Sharon retrieved a backpack off her desk.

"Almond, if you don't mind I'm cratered. I'm going home."

"Oh, certainly, certainly. Get some rest," Sinclair cooed. "Stay close to your pager, though. Story like this can break any time."

Sharon swung the backpack over her jacket without reply. This story was way past breaking and the only call she cared about was the one that would take her away from Pepperfish Keys.

She left by the rear door. Stepping from the station's erratically cooled interior into its parking lot was like stepping from a freezer into a steambath. A dark steambath. There was no moon out. Sentinels of pine and cypress shrouding the lot. The hell was her car?

It took a second for her night vision to kick in.

Ah. There you are.

Sharon took a crow's line toward her BMW two-seater, snapping her car keys off the backpack. She'd bought the car used. Figured a used Beemer conveyed a better statement than a brand-new Mitsubishi. More in line with where Sharon meant to be.

She was reaching to open the driver-side door when the cool, once-experienced-never-forgotten impression of a gun barrel came bluntly to rest at the base of her skull.

"Don't get frisky."

Sharon stifled a sudden urge to scream, to urinate. She'd seen a million PSA's coaching responses to just this situation. What did they say? Rule One—Don't panic. Rule Two—Don't get in a car. Scream or run or defend, if you have to, even if it means you get shot.

All she needed was his instep. A spike to the instep of his sandaled foot and half a second to break free—

"Don't even consider it."

A tap to her spine sent a spike of pain down her back, her legs.

"Okay!" she gasped. "Okay, you're the boss."

"No, I ain't. But the boss is exactly who you gonna see."

The gun's impression was suddenly lifted. Sharon turned

warily to see a doughboy with scarred forearms bared in a loud Hawaiian shirt.

Behind her abductor, not twenty yards away, was a long Lincoln limousine.

Sharon stiffened.

"You might as well shoot me here. I'm not going anyplace."

Crease smiled.

"Eddy said you'd be like that."

"Eddy—? DeLeon?"

"That's the boss."

Crease stuffed the revolver beneath the stained band of his shorts.

"So I'm 'sposed to tell you Eddy's got a story. One hell of a story. But you got to come to him to get it."

"Tell Mr. DeLeon he can come to me."

Crease wagged his head.

"Naw. Play or fold. Get in your car and follow me, or lose the story. Your deal."

Sharon Fowler was pretty sure if DeLeon meant to kill her, he'd have done it in the deserted shadows of the parking lot. There were even less pleasant options to be endured, of course. But the moment Crease allowed Sharon access to her own car those scenarios seemed improbable.

Eddy said he had a story. Well and good. She'd see. Sharon followed Crease past Ocean and away from Deacon Beach onto the Oldtown Road before turning sharply onto an unfamiliar and unpaved feeder that snaked off into a tract of pine and palmetto. It was dark as the inside of a cow. Her headlights bored a wavering cone of light into a blizzard of sand kicked up by the Lincoln's steel-plied tires. Sharon switched to low beams, keeping her low-slung car as close to the limo's taillights as she could manage.

A railroad track came out of nowhere.

"Shit!"

Her two-seater bottomed out following the Lincoln over the rails. A hard turn on the far side almost sent her into the ditch. Sharon fishtailed dangerously before settling again behind the limousine. They were traveling parallel to the railroad's bed on a sand-rutted track.

The headlights ruined whatever night purple might have allowed her to take in of the surrounding terrain. Sharon had no idea where she was. She almost missed the warehouse that materialized abruptly out of the gloom. The limo's bright braking lights warned her. Sharon downshifted and dropped back. Her earlier confidence was by now diminished. This place was definitely off any beaten track. She was only slightly relieved to see the reflected taillights of a pickup nestled distant from the warehouse's high, cyclone fence in a dark stand of indistinguishable trees.

Kids, probably, she told herself. Necking. Maybe there was a lover's lane nearby. Maybe. Somebody who could hear her scream.

A cantilever gate swung open to allow easy entry through a razored fence.

"Nice garage." Sharon's voice sounded hoarse.

The Lincoln's headlights cut twin swaths through an atmosphere heavy with humidity and dust, pulling the car as if by twin cables into the warehouse's cluttered yard. Sharon stopped her car at the gate, buzzed down a window.

Crease left his vehicle to stroll back, smiling in the limn of her dimmed lights.

"Why can't we talk out here?" Sharon's hands remained at ten and two on her wheel.

"What? Don't you trust us?"

"I don't trust anybody who puts a gun to my head."

"That was me," Crease pointed out. "Don't hold it against Eddy."

Sharon wondered briefly what valence bound this piece of work to Eduardo DeLeon.

"All right." She killed her lights and grabbed her backpack. "But I'm leaving my car out here. And I want the gate left open."

Crease shrugged. "Why not?"

Sharon swung out of her bucket seat and followed Eddy's pale ferryman through the boundary of the high fence to a kind of breezeway or portico that extended from the warehouse's larger structure. A door barred the way. Metal. Double-hinged. A couple of lightbulbs swayed on a naked cord to illuminate the lock.

Crease juggled a handful of keys from his shorts. He selected a Yale, slipped it in. A deadbolt shot aside. Sharon followed Eddy's man on in.

A very dim interior. Shadows indistinct against an ambiance of dull light, red, like the inside of a submarine. Tangled contortions of dull-finished metal stacked in piles on either side. A narrow alley in between. "Ouch!"

Sharon's hand jerked of its own volition to find her leg. When she brought her palm to her face she could see the smear of blood.

"Hope you got yer shots," Crease chuckled and led her on, deeper into the guts of the place.

It had been a manufacturing facility of some sort, Sharon could divine that. The labyrinth of ductwork, vents, and grilles filling some steel-beamed space, the razor edges of metal exposed to cut her passage. Sharon followed Crease into the warehouse's gloomy interior, stanching with her fist the fresh blood that wept from her recent wound. She almost ran into Eddy's driver when Crease abruptly pulled to a halt before a conveyor belt that fed what looked like a guillotine.

"We call it 'the Cutter'," an accented voice floated from behind.

Sharon jumped as if stung to find Eddy DeLeon smiling in shadows from a kind of den cleared in the middle of his rough-hewn house.

" 'The Cutter'—because he cuts metal," DeLeon repeated helpfully, his face pulsing with the varied illumination of a TV screen.

"Sheet metal, that is. Mostly."

Eddy was lounging in a papa-san, one of those round bowls of bamboo that GIs bring back from Thailand or the Philippines, this one as big as a bed and cushioned with a burgundy futon and foot pillows. The papa-san and flat-screen TV were themselves part of a living space improvised in the sheet metal shop's angled interior.

There were amenities. Besides the television, there was a bar, its cheap finish an inadequate mirror for the surrounding reflections of metal and ductwork. An open kitchen, more like a galley, hinged onto a cinderblock wall extending at right angles to the bar. A series of jagged trails wandered off from the remaining and unsegregated space, haphazard hallways winding between stacks of metal leading to—where?

Sharon could not see. She did not care to see.

"Before business went bust we got contracts all over," Eddy smiled apologies for his dormant facility. "Business is good we make ducts for air-conditioning, panels for equipment, road signs, you name it.

"But is hard work, sheet metal. You get cut easy; I see you have discovered for yourself."

Stepping carefully into Eddy's lair Sharon noted that the television was part of an entire entertainment unit. She saw a video camera. A DVD player.

"You like movies?" He waved her over.

Something like pornography glowed from Eddy's flat, wide screen. A tangle of limbs. Bellies and breasts. Heavy breathing.

Time to cut this off, Sharon decided quickly and was about to announce her intention to leave when an onscreen lover lifted her face to the camera.

It was Beth Ann Stanton.

"Ah, yes," Eddy smiled. "The star of the show!"

Her tiny legs and back glistened with sweat. She bent down. The image jiggled, abruptly. Rookie cameraman. But then things steadied and Sharon recognized the setting for this staged encounter. The Cutter's conveyor served as the bed for the torrid scene, Beth Ann straddling a lover atop that wide, leather belt. Riding him like a pony.

Back and forth. Back and forth.

A pair of well-manicured hands reached from below to frenzy the hardened nipples of her breasts.

"Rock a bye, baby," a little-girl voice on the audio, Beth Ann panting as if run through a steeplechase.

"Rock a bye!"

Reaching then for her partner's hair. Eddy's head lifted by a ponytail. Beth Ann reining on that raven mane as if hauling in a runaway stud. Naked. Abandoned. Heels slipping on the sweat-slick leather.

"Nothing better than a nice girl gone bad." Eddy aimed his remote at the television. "You know what I mean?"

"Click" the scene dissolved in a crackle of static.

"What do you want with me, Mr. DeLeon?"

"I want to be your source."

"—I beg your pardon?"

"Your source, senorita. I can provide information you may obtain in no other way. From no other person."

"Information comes to me all the time, Mr. DeLeon. Usually without the prelude of a kidnap or tetanus shot."

"No worries there. Is a clean cut."

"I'm reassured."

"Crease, bring her something."

Eddy's man waddled in the direction of the galley. She heard a cabinet door squeak open. The run of a tap.

"So what do you have that is so valuable, Mr. DeLeon?" She eased her backpack to the floor. "Other than pornography?"

"Prophecy. The future."

"Like a horoscope?"

"My moon in your house? I could dig that."

"You're digging yourself into a hole."

She pressed the damp towel offered by his henchman onto her bleeding and bared thigh.

Eddy smiled.

"You not into astrology? The signs from the heavens? All right, how 'bout something more substantial? More like—well. How's this? Within the week Special Agent Barrett Raines will make an arrest related to the murder of Beth Ann Stanton. He will have a strong suspect. A known killer."

"Who?"

"Me," Eddy replied.

Toying with the loop beneath the bling on his neck.

"May I record this conversation?"

"Knock yourself out, baby."

Sharon fished her Sony portable from the backpack. Popped in a fresh cassette. Fast-forwarded it just a tad. There. Now to "Record."

A ruby light winked confirmation.

"Okay, it's Monday, approximately 11 P.M. This is Sharon Fowler. I have identified myself as a reporter from K-E-Y-S television. I'm with Eduardo DeLeon. You all right for some questions, Mr. DeLeon?"

"Call me Eddy." DeLeon grabbed what might be an erection. Sharon elected to ignore the display.

"All right, Eddy. Tell me this: Did you kill Beth Ann Stanton?"

"No." He seemed unperturbed. "But someone very, very clever has. And now they intend to hang it around my neck."

"Can you prove that?"

"No. But you can."

"Excuse me?"

"Turn off your machine."

When Sharon complied Eddy raised himself Indian fashion inside his bamboo bowl.

"You want dirt, senorita? I got dirt by the landfill. I got politicians from Tallahassee to Key Fucking West. I got city councilmen. Cops. Commissioners. I got facts and figures—

"You want the *big story*? I got dozens. And they can all be yours, Sharon. Exclusive. But you want it, *concita,* you gotta do this one thing: You gotta find out who killed my girl. Find the shithead who slit her throat."

DeLeon rolled off the papa-san to approach her. Sharon clutched her recorder as though it were a lifeline.

"That's crazy," she said finally.

"Is this crazy?"

He displayed a hand of thousand dollar bills as though they were playing cards.

"For research."

"Mr. DeLeon—"

"Eddy. And don' tell me you can't take it."

"I'm a journalist, I can't take money. Not from anyone."

"Why not? Is not like I'm paying you to lie. Believe me, I am a man in sore need of truth. And you need the truth, too, Ms. Fowler. For your story, your big story. You need it bad."

He stuffed the wad inside her pack.

She could see his teeth. Smell his feral breath.

"I really can't."

His face inches from her own. Flat brown eyes.

"I can be an extremely valuable source, senorita. Or a very serious enemy. You choose."

Sharon counted ten hammered beats of her heart.

"I won't guarantee anything."

"No guarantees in life, mama." Eddy's hand strayed to idle on her hip before he turned back to his flat-screened TV.

"Whoever killed a senator's daughter is bound to be ruthless." His warning came casually. "You must trust no one. No one."

Eddy stabbed the remote. There it was again. Beth Ann and Eddy, released from their frozen frame.

Back and forth. Back and forth.

"Nothing better."

DeLeon wasted not a second glance in her direction. Crease took the bloody towel before guiding Sharon back to the shop's dead-bolted door. She was careful to avoid the many sharp edges that lined the way.

9.

9. *Barrett Raines woke up in* bed beside his somnolent wife unsatiated, unrefreshed, and still worried about Taylor Calhoun. The conversation with Sharon Fowler only added grist to those disparate mills. As he scrambled eggs for his twin sons, Bear put in a call to Sheriff Rawlings's office. "Tell Smoot I need to see him. Be in soon as I drop the boys off."

He was driving Ben and Tyndall to school regularly these days, letting Laura Anne sleep to a decadent hour. It had got to the point that the morning drive was about the only relief Bear got from concerns over his wife or work, a few minutes' respite to be found in the uncensored chatter of sixth graders.

Typically he'd leave the Malibu at home, the twins preferring the Crown Vic. Mostly because it had air-conditioning. On this morning's drive Barrett got to hear about the test Ben and Tyndall took for their Swimming Badge ("Ben was afraid of the water." "Was *not*."), and their First Aid Badge ("They had this dummy, you had to blow in his mouth." "It's called resuscitation," Ben amended precociously. "And you blow *into* its mouth."). Turned out there was a newcomer to the boys' troop. "His name's Lamont; he's not from around here," Tyndall supplied. "Said he came from Orlando. Near Disney World. So that's three of us they got."

"They *have*," Ben corrected, but his father noted the larger distinction—

Three of us. That "they" have.

"Pretty soon we'll be integrated," Ben the Precocious quipped and Barrett was glad to have an excuse to laugh.

"Do good boys," he said, depositing the twins outside their windowless school. Pulling away he tuned in a Perry station. "Another beautiful September day," came the Chamber of Commerce forecast even though it was hot as grits and goddamn gravy.

It was an easy half hour from Deacon Beach to Smoot Rawlings's office. The old Dixie Highway that used to offer a precarious blacktop for traffic skirting Florida's western coast had long been broadened to four lanes of thoroughfare creasing a wilderness of pine, panthers, and palmetto. The old road had been a conduit for timber barons of a bygone age.

Barrett noted the recently renovated Putnam Lodge, once the inn of choice for timber barons eager to show off chandeliers and an interior of peckywood cypress. The restored lodge was guestless now, a museum sharing the highway with a sprawl of low-rent motels catering to a bonanza of lawmen brought in from all over the state to find Beth Ann Stanton's killer.

He cruised past the Dixie County High School and its unchallenged Confederate flag, past the Carriage Inn and a score of small dilapidated shops or curios on the way to the blue-topped county courthouse. Smoot ushered Barrett brusquely into his cube of an office.

"Pretty early in the day for a sitdown, Bear. Got somethin' on your mind?"

"I do, but let's start with the interviews. How we doing?"

"Seeing the light. Probably a hundred and fifty complete, including most of the out-of-towners. My one detective's got statements from nearly all the locals; he says by this time next week we oughta be done. But you didn't drive down here just for that. Did you, Bear?"

"No."

Barrett hesitated.

"Well? What is it?"

"I'm worried I've got a man in trouble."

"Man would that be?"

"A source we had inside the Stanton investigation."

"Ain't no 'we', here, Kemo Sabe. Are you talking about a snitch? Your snitch?"

Barrett nodded. "Resides in Dixie County."

"Makes you think he's in trouble?"

"Hasn't checked in, for one thing. Not even for money. I've worried awhile over the possibility there was a leak from inside the Stanton investigation. Just last night I was talking with Sharon Fowler; I was trying to find out how she knew Beth Ann was involved with Eddy DeLeon."

"Trying to smoke out her snitch?"

"Turns out Sharon was the source. She witnessed Eddy DeLeon and Beth Ann in Stanton's pool, and they weren't swimming."

"What was Sharon doing out by the pool?"

"She was with Stanton."

"Ah. And how exclusive was that interview?"

"Didn't ask. But I did ask Sharon point-blank if she was tapping a source inside the FDLE or in Roland's office. I didn't push for a name. Just wanted to know if there was a leak from our side."

"You said you've been worried awhile."

"By mid-summer I was wondering if Stanton's lawyers had my playbook. Tried to tell myself I was just paranoid, but I couldn't kill the worry that somebody on our side might be talking out of school."

"Nobody in my shop," Smoot bridled. "Don't go up that tree."

"Sheriff, I didn't ask Sharon if she had a source in your office. I didn't even allude to it. You can trust me there."

"Trust?"

The sheriff's jaws worked hard on his gum.

"You told me Baxter Stanton was taking dirty money. You told me the attorney general would back me up. The goddamn governor! Now, I got an election comin' up that I am probably going to lose, and you set there telling me I can trust you? You, of all goddamn people?!"

Barrett took a long, slow count to a neutral corner.

"Sheriff, I didn't come here to piss up a rope. I came here because I'm concerned about a man's life. That's why I'm here."

Rawlings peeled out a fresh stick of Big Red. "Sure you're not lookin' for a backdoor to Baxter Stanton?"

"All I'm concerned about is finding my man."

Smoot slipped the wrapper off his gum.

"Cain't find a man without a name."

"It's Taylor Calhoun."

"Taylor?"

Smoot seemed genuinely surprised.

"Sumbitch, that peckerwood? Over at the whorehouse?"

"Have you seen Taylor, Sheriff? Anywhere at all?"

"Nope, an' now you mention it, I don't think he's been out at Mama's, either."

Barrett did not ask what business took Smoot to Mama's house.

"Taylor was keeping an eye out for us," he told the sheriff. "Who came in. Who went out. That sort of thing."

"Nothing at Mama's but bitches and beers."

"Taylor seemed to think there was a lot more," Barrett replied, but did not elaborate.

Rawlings grunted, "Little fucker. You check his house? He's got a trailer in Strawman's Hammock."

"No," Barrett replied stiffly.

Smoot paused.

"You been back out there at all, Bear? To the Hammock?"

"Not really."

"Understandable."

"Just haven't had a reason is all."

"Not pushin'. We have our differences but I wouldn't see a hair harmed on Laura Anne, you know that."

"I believe I do, but right now Taylor's on my mind."

"Awright, then." Smoot snaked a legal pad from under the mess on his desk. "I'll send somebody out to the Hammock. If Taylor's home, that ends it. But long as you're here you might as well tell me the last you saw him."

"Not since before Beth Ann was killed. That would be, what, two, two and a half weeks? Was in Live Oak."

"This was a planned meeting?"

"Not even. Little fart ambushed me in broad daylight on the courthouse steps just to tell he'd figured out where Eddy DeLeon got his money."

"Which was?"

"From feature films. Little jughead's got this notion that Eddy is pirating movies out of Los Angeles. Crazy idea, I know, but then if it wasn't for Taylor neither of us would know that Eddy's using Mama to launder his money."

"Taylor got you that?"

Barrett affirmed with a nod. "Some good eyes in that round head. Good ears, too. But that day he jumped me in Live Oak I chewed Taylor's ass. Then I paid him some pocket money and sent him home. Days later Beth Ann was murdered and I haven't heard a word since."

"There a line connecting these dots, Bear?"

"I don't even know if there are any dots to connect."

A rap at the door interrupted their conversation.

"What is it, Cindy?"

"That cable man, Sheriff. He called again."

"Hell with him, we're gonna go to satellite."

"No, not that one. The Mexican. The one called in yesterday? From the junkyard?"

"Didn't Jody go out?"

"I left him your note," she pouted.

"Got a call from a fellah yesterday morning," Rawlings explained for Barrett's benefit. "Apparently he's been usin' the yard to secure his equipment. Cable spools, trucks, that sort of thing. Anyway he saw something spooked him. You know these Hispanics, they get excited."

Barrett elected to let that pass.

"We talking the Cross City junkyard?" he inquired neutrally.

"Not the town's, no," Smoot shook his head. "Rolly's yard."

"Rolly Slade's? Out near Steinhatchee?"

"Yeah. Why?"

Barrett felt a crawl of hair.

"Sheriff—isn't Slade's Salvage right down the road from Mama's?"

The pattern of blood splattered across the BlueBird chassis that kneeled like a camel in Rolly Slade's salvage yard was a twin to the design sprayed onto Beth Ann Stanton's headboard.

"Tell me that ain't a slit throat?" Smoot Rawlings eyed the coagulated calligraphy.

"Don't get ahead of yourself, Sheriff."

This from Midge Holloway. For the second time in as many weeks, Midge came with her team to sample a murder's signature. Doc Holloway had already taken samples of the blood; she squatted now with an honest-to-god magnifying glass to inspect a flattened tire.

"Lucky you haven't had any rain." Midge polished her glass on her sleeve.

"Any idea how long the blood's been here?" Barrett asked.

"Days, surely. Couple of weeks, perhaps. Doubt much longer."

"About the time Beth Ann was killed, then?"

This from Smoot Rawlings.

Midge shrugged. "Could be. Could also be earlier or later; I can't be that precise."

"I called the county clinic to see if they had anything we

could use to DNA Taylor Calhoun." Barrett pocketed his cell phone. "He was in for some tests a while back. Diabetes."

Midge nodded. "If it matches what's on the bus you got your man."

"Wouldn't think the little fart had that much blood in him," Rawlings spat.

"It's arterial, same pattern as we saw at the other scene." Midge pocketed her glass in her windbreaker. "Except here there are signs of a real struggle. See these gouges in the sand? The victim crawling, kicking, maybe."

"I'd kick, too, somebody was slitting my throat," Smoot grunted.

"Possibly, Sheriff. But I'm betting there was something else going on."

Midge pointed to the tire.

"We got a slug out of that tire."

She displayed a bullet tagged inside a Ziplock bag.

"Nine millimeter. I'm guessing a ricochet."

"Why a ricochet?" Barrett asked.

"Slug didn't puncture the tire's ply, for one thing," Midge replied. "And you can see the slug's deformed—see here? Could have been anything deflected it, of course, but I won't be surprised to find some blood or tissue on the slug."

"Couldn't there have been separate incidents here, Midge? A knifing and a shooting?"

"I doubt it." She craned from the hump on her shoulder. "I'd say there's a high probability the slug got lodged in this tire during the same basic time frame as blood was splattered onto the bus."

"You casting any footprints? Tire tracks?" The sheriff pulled himself erect.

"Too many. We're interviewing the cable man now, but it looks like any number of vehicles and people have been in and out of this yard over the last couple of weeks. If our Latin friend hadn't offloaded his spool right beside the bus, this crime scene could have been missed altogether."

Smoot peeled off a stick of gum.

"Be nice to know if Taylor Calhoun was here."

"Won't be long before we know," Midge replied. "As Dr. Pound would say, dead men do tell tales."

Smoot Rawlings grunted. "With apologies to Dr. Pound, I ain't ever had a dead man tell me anything."

Rawlings nodded to Barrett. "We need to get out to Taylor's trailer right away. We don't find him there or at Mama's or drunk some damn place I'm gettin' out the dogs. Get out the damn Coast Guard, I have to."

"Thank you, Sheriff."

"He could still be alive, Bear. Might not be his blood at all."

"Not what my gut's telling me."

"Then let's hope your gut's goddamn wrong."

By noon a score of paid law enforcers from various agencies were gathered with volunteering civilians to look for Taylor Calhoun. A systematic search began, with canines leading men and women on the ground. Deputies from Taylor and Lafayette County augmented Smoot's people on ATVs and horses to comb the flatwoods bordering Rolly Slade's salvage yard. Florida's Marine Patrol trolled offshore; it would not be the first time a floater was found dismembered by gators or sharks, or even birds. The sun burned like a keg of sulphur. There was no wildlife stirring, not a squirrel, not a crow. You could see resin drawn from the bark of pines by the September sun and the smell of pine cones and conifers scented the air in a sultry incense. Barrett Raines was down to shirt and slacks. He'd swapped street shoes for a pair of brogans and borrowed Smoot Rawlings's twelve-gauge to accompany the nine millimeter always holstered at his shoulder.

"Gonna get heavy carryin' all that artillery."

That remark coming from a plainclothed lawman paired with Barrett for the search. Barrett knew Sheriff Rawlings's solitary detective, but only by reputation. First impression was of a big-boned, lazy kind of dude. A pale and loose-fleshed giant.

"Sidearm be easier than a shotgun." Orlando Fuqua cleared the chamber of a lightly handled Glock.

"Better to have it and not need it, than need it and not have it," Barrett returned with as much good humor as he could muster. He knew that some agents in the Live Oak office thought Orlando was a scumbag. Agents groused that the detective had a lifestyle out of line with his county salary. Orlando drove a Corvette, usually a new one, which raised a few eyebrows. But as Barrett pointed out to his colleagues, Fuqua was single, lived in a trailer, and had no obvious debt. His car was his castle.

But everyone agreed that Sheriff Rawlings's detective was not a stellar performer; most of the cases the pale giant pushed were low-level drug dealers, always poor, usually black. Barrett was unwilling to attribute racial bias to the plainclothesman; most of the men and women who Fuqua busted were convicted, after all. And Orlando had his sheriff's confidence.

"Orlando can be a slacker, sure," Rawlings often declared. "But be damn if he don't have a handle on everything goin' down in Dixie County. Best I ever saw on that score."

The sheriff's confidence notwithstanding, Detective Fuqua would not have been Barrett's choice for a partner with whom to spend hours in tropical misery. It was a miracle the pale and bloated son of a bitch could stand the heat.

"I could take the radio," Orlando offered.

"Fair enough." Barrett handed Orlando the two-way and offered his canteen.

"Water?"

"Naw."

Was that a curl of distaste in the detective's reply?

"Waste of time, beatin' these goddamn woods." Fuqua adjusted the Motorola's squawk. "The fuck do we expect to find?"

"Why don't we check our grid?" Bear responded and unfolded a topographical map.

Each team on the ground was assigned a grid to comb. Handheld GPS units and mobile communication enabled lawmen and volunteers to report the exact coordinates of their position. Even so, Barrett found his GI-issue Lensatic indispensable. He'd humped many miles over all types of terrain with a magnetic compass; no new technology would completely replace it.

"Okay, we're two clicks south of the junkyard." Barrett jabbed a finger. "We'll be walking this line for another click or so, basically parallel to the road and just this side of Strawman's Hammock."

"Waste of time," Orlando repeated. "Somebody killed Taylor in the junkyard, they wouldn't take time to drag him in here."

"No?"

"Hell, no. They'd just dump him in the water. Someplace off the Keys."

"A rookie might do that," Barrett agreed. "But an experienced killer would know better. Bodies float. They get caught in shrimp nets and anchor lines or wash ashore. Whoever got killed in Rolly's yard, would be smarter and easier to bury 'em in the flatwoods. Either that or let the predators pick him clean."

"So how damn much territory are we talkin'?"

"Not going to be easy," Barrett allowed. "But if there is a body I doubt it's far off the road. We're only covering a hundred meters on either side. If that search doesn't turn up anything, we might widen it another hundred, but not more than that. Sure you won't have some water?"

Orlando spit.

"No."

"Suit yourself."

Pushing through the flatwoods is a sentence of hard labor. That was not always the case. There had been a time when the forests of northern Florida were carpeted in a loess unruffled by brambles or stinging nettles or other noxious undergrowth. The leavings of acorns and straw were the principal ground cover in those years, an understory unobstructed by tangles of thorn and lush with copses of fairy wand or toothache grass. Deer tongue.

Perfect for barefoot boys with fishing poles.

But what was once easy walking had grown into a virtually unbroken and variegated thicket. A gauntlet of briars and brambles drew blood from Barrett's arms as he pressed over the tangled terrain. Poison oak brushed his face, his hands. The silence broken as the men pushed off road and into a torment of insects. Already Barrett could see his pale-skinned partner feeding the mosquitoes. Orlando Fuqua was pouring sweat and cursing, slapping at skeeters and hacking into revetments of kudzu and grapevine as though killing snakes.

"This is fucked up beyond all goddamn recognition." Fuqua swatted a mosquito sucking blood.

It was hard terrain, but at least it was familiar. Bear could tolerate heat and insects as long as he had solid ground, a map, and a compass.

And a weapon, of course. Be silly to be in the flatwoods without protection.

But even armed and equipped Bear felt squeamish as he skirted the stand of native yellowheart pine that marked the boundary of Strawman's Hammock. It was as though there existed a malicious and impermeable border at the hammock's edge that he could not cross. The stand of native timber once comforting to roam was now a nest of nightmares. Barrett felt a sense of foreboding coming so close to that bogeyman's domain, a vice closing on his chest, the sensation of sucking air from a vacuum.

If Taylor Calhoun was dumped in Strawman's Hammock, someone else would have to find him.

Bear was about to take an angle pushing away from the hammock when he realized he'd lost track of Orlando Fuqua. "Orlando?"

He turned around. Slowly. There he was, Smoot Rawlings's favored detective directly at six o'clock. Orlando entertained his machete in one hand. In the other hand Barrett saw a nine-millimeter Glock.

The safety snicked on. Then off. Then on.

Bear felt the barrel of the shotgun on his shoulder.

"The hell, Orlando? We hunting squirrels?"

Some decision seemed to being weighed behind that bloated face. A pallor of sweat glistening on the blond forehead.

"Orlando? There a problem?"

The gunhand rose slowly—to wipe a path through the perspiration soaking Fuqua's wide forehead.

"Tell you the truth I ain't feeling so good."

This given in a voice devoid of inflection.

Barrett kept a grip on his scattergun.

"Maybe you'd better take a break."

"Mebbe I better."

Orlando reseated his handgun's safety and holstered it before sheathing the machete in a scabbard of nettles. Barrett felt his bowels involuntarily relax.

Crazy fucking white man.

"You have to hydrate, Detective. Can't expect to hump these woods without water."

"You're right, you're right. Tell you what, the road's, what? Due west from here?"

"Correct."

Barrett was surprised Orlando was aware of that orientation. He sure as hell hadn't been paying much attention to the map.

"Why don't I just hook out?" Fuqua suggested. "I'll get some ice on my neck. Water down. Come back with a couple canteens of water."

"We shouldn't split up," Barrett demurred.

"Won't take long—like you said we're only a hundred yards off the road."

Barrett felt the sting of sweat in his eyes. "You bring a cell phone?"

"Yep. Got your number on the speed-dial."

"Then go ahead. When you're ready, call and I'll give you coordinates to my position."

"That'll work." Orlando checked his GPS as he retrieved the machete.

"Just make sure you hydrate."

"Right."

The bloated face bobbed.

"I won't make that mistake twice."

Within seconds the plainly clothed giant was invisible, swallowed up by slash pine and stinging nettle.

10.

Barrett Raines dismissed concerns for Orlando Fuqua as he pushed on alone through the undergrowth scanning for signs of Taylor Calhoun. The undergrowth had become spectacularly dense, briars sliced through the fabric of Barrett's shirt and trousers. Sand seeped into his brogans, his socks. The attack of yellow flies added to the mosquitoes' assault.

The heat was unremitting. The shotgun's barrel weighed hot as a poker on the trap of Bear's shoulder and he'd neglected to bring a hat. He tested his canteen. Nearly empty. In boyhood years you could safely refill your jug off most any running stream. And then something intruded on the odor of heat and resin and pine straw. A dank, almost fetid odor.

"Water," Bear mouthed silently, but the slough ahead was not a tributary. It was still. It was green. It was covered in a film of scum coursed by waterstriders and thin-limbed spiders. Even so, Barrett was glad to find something to soak his shirt, even if stagnant—

Even if barricaded by a hazard of cypress knees.

Of course, cypress knees weren't knees at all; they were extensions of a root system thrust up through the water, a grove of javelins slick with mold and bacteria. A filthy impalation. Barrett picked his way carefully through those spears, his brogans slipping on roots slick with sammy. He was already unbuttoning his shirt and was set to scoop off an icing of algae for the water beneath when he heard the welcome sound of a running stream.

The slough and its cypress knees stopped on a gentle swale that embanked a spring-fed stream. Barrett secured his map and arms and other gear and sloshed into that freezing bath, squatting like an Indian as he scooped ice-cold water onto his face, his neck. Barrett remained in that numbing luxury a full minute before getting back to work. He checked his map and weapons and walked across the stream, pausing to fill his canteen.

That's when he saw the curved tines of a rib cage.

It came out of the ground like fingers half-clenched, a chest full of bones reaching up like a curled hand from a shallow grave in the clearing that spread before the stream. Barrett froze a moment in the register of unexpected discovery. But then he left the stream with deliberate caution, water sloshing in his shoes as he approached bones not yet yellow with age.

He could not examine his discovery too closely; he did not want to disturb the site. He tried to tell himself that he wasn't even sure that these were the remains of a human carcass. It could be a calf, Bear told himself. A large dog, even.

He did not see a skull, anywhere. Were there legs? Arms? The ribs looked torn clean away from the rest of the body.

What kind of predator could do that? A gator?

That could be it, a calf or deer coming to water. The gator striking.

But then Bear saw something else, some sort of fabric caught several yards from the bleaching cage. A couple of scraps of material hung up on a mulberry bush. Barrett circled carefully to inspect, his footgear sucking water. A woman's face stared out from one silk-printed rag, you could make out the eyes. Most of a face. A separate flutter of fabric displayed what appeared to be a breast straining to burst a haltertop above a portion of text printed in bright team colors.

Barrett knew in his gut that he had found what was left of Taylor Calhoun's shirt. Probably the only shirt the little man ever bought with his own money. Which meant that barring a miracle the rib cage he saw before him was once Taylor's, too.

"Shit." Barrett punched the butt of his shotgun into the ground.

This should not have happened. Should not have.

Bear fumbled for the cell phone clipped at his belt. His hand trembled as he stabbed in the quick-dial to Smoot Rawlings's mobile. An apologetic bleep prefaced the always-annoying, "Your call cannot be completed as dialed."

He tried again and got a different message:

"Out of area."

He reached on instinct for the radio.

"Well, shit."

Orlando had the radio; Bear let him walk out with it.

"Don't panic, Janet," Barrett admonished aloud.

There really was no problem. All he had to do was fix the site with his handheld GPS, jot the coordinates on his map, and hike out to the road where the sheriff had his command post. Once Rawlings contacted Midge Holloway and her team, Barrett would guide them back to the site.

More hassle than was necessary, sure. But no cause for concern. Barrett propped his shotgun on a mayhaw's sandpaper trunk. He pocketed his compass and broke out his global finder. Spread his map.

That's when he heard the hogs.

Not every hog herded in the days of Florida's open range made it to market and not every Poland China nurtured in some modern cracker's pen gets turned into sausage. The animals rooting across the clearing from Barrett were a long way from any sort of domestication. These were hogs gone wild.

Wild. And mean.

The dominant boar emerged first, large for an undomesticated male, a couple of hundred pounds at least. He burst from a fan of palmetto nosing what looked like a coconut along the ground, the snout lowered in that erratic dribble, a pair of tusks, nasty scimitars.

And then a pair of sows burst from the undergrowth in apparent contest for their leader's makeshift ball, the females followed by a litter of pigs. Must have been a dozen of the little ones, their hides ragged with russet hair stiff as the quills on a porcupine. A short melee became complicated with the thrash of other hogs emerging from the palmettos, perhaps thirty full-grown animals, a sounder of swine rooting now to dispute the dominant male for possession of his plaything.

The snort and slash of tusks marked their contest. That and the high-pitched squeal of piglets. The ball disappeared briefly in a tangle of hooves but Barrett could see in patches of white and black hair all that remained of Taylor Calhoun's scalp.

A boyhood recollection was triggered by the sight, Bear climbing the split-rail fence of a muddy pen to slop his neighbor's hogs. But the animals ignored the boy that morning, occupied furiously opposite the trough. Bear remembered hesitating before his daily chore—Had the swine already been fed?

A churning frenzy in that pen. And then he spotted the rubber boot, one of the pair of overshoes that Mr. Henderson always wore in the pen. And then Bear saw the pale, white stump of a foot, a boar and a sow contesting possession for that unsocked meal.

Barrett tried to ease the sudden hammer in his chest. He knew better than to dispute territory with hogs, especially wild hogs. Best course would be to retreat. Get back across the stream. Trick would be to make that exit without drawing the hogs' attention.

And he just about made it. He had backed calf-deep into the moving stream and was halfway across without incident. But then a piercing scream rose from the clearing's competition and a young male burst in a beeline for the running water. You could see the recent wound, the gut opened by some razor sharp tusk. The young male plunged into the water panicked, strings of gut hanging. Barrett stopped cold. And for a moment it seemed the junior boar's distress would call no attention at all.

But then Bear saw a sow's snout jerk straight up and a snort of alarm milled suddenly through the sounder.

The skull was forgotten abruptly, the lead boar following his sow straight and stiff-legged toward the new scent, a flare of nostrils sampling the air, nearsighted eyes casting to find the source. Then the boar stopped rigid as a statue and Bear knew he'd been discovered.

He knew what the boar could do if provoked. He'd seen the work of boars. But the real danger now was the sow.

The boar has been feared primevally in forests from Europe to Asia. Even the diminutive javelina is a chainsaw on hooves. But the male hog's reputation for vicious behavior pales beside that of the female, especially a sow protecting her litter. Certainly in the wilderness of northern Florida a hunter would much rather encounter a boar than an irascible sow. A sow backing her pigs is fearless, intelligent. And she is aggressive.

Barrett was glad he had a shotgun. Great thing about a twelve-gauge besides its stopping power was its noise. A shotgun was a cannon compared to a rifle or sidearm, and fortunately even sows in herd tended to follow their boar's lead so there was a good chance that if Bear shotgunned the dominant boar the attending shock and racket would disperse the remaining animals. But if he killed the boar and the sow didn't run he could have a problem.

Smoot had specified that his shotgun was loaded with four shells of Number One buckshot. If Bear took out the boar with a single shot he'd be down to three rounds, which raised an interesting question: How d'you divide three shells into thirty hogs and have one black man left over?

The boar lowered his snout at the edge of the cold-running stream and Barrett pulled the pump's stock firmly against his shoulder, braced for the recoil, and pulled the trigger.

And then nothing. No cannon. No recoil. No acrid odor of powder or smoke. Nothing but the fall of a firing pin.

"The fuck?"

Barrett worked the pump on his shotgun.

Rack-rack.

Nothing in the chamber.

Rack-rack, rack-rack.

Nothing. Not a single round.

Son of a bitch, here he was with thirty mad hogs and an unloaded shotgun.

That left his sidearm. A nine-millimeter Smith & Wesson can stop a man. If you're an excellent shot it can even stop a moving man. But Bear knew there was no way in hell he was going to hold off a charge of wild hogs with a nine-millimeter handgun.

But it wasn't like he had much choice in the matter. Bear reached over to unholster his remaining weapon. The ambidextrous safety was familiar; he planed his thumb along a travel of cool metal until he felt a serrated edge and flicked it down. The boar was already advertising a charge by now, damp scoops of earth tossed into the air by pawing hooves. The rest of the sounder milled along the water's frigid boundary, their tails stiff as broom handles.

The boar came first. And then a sow.

On open ground Bear wouldn't have stood a chance. It is hard to imagine how fast hogs can move. Even through water the animals charging were a streak of hide, and they were smart, the sow swerving to take his flank as the boar charged head-on. Bear held a Weaver stance and put two rounds into the charging male. One of 'em must have stung—the boar pulled up short squealing fury. That left the sow. Barrett swiveled and fired twice. He missed with the first shot; it took a second round to break the female's charge.

Four slugs gone from a clip of nine, not a single animal killed and the herd was going crazy, boars and sows snorting and squealing, their pigs feeding the frenzy. And now the animals displayed a feral intelligence, a cohort of hogs plunging upstream and down to hem their new meat in a circle of teeth and tusks.

Best chance was to reach the cypress knees. If he could get back to the slough's barricade of knife-sharp roots, he might have a chance. Better for sure to fight in that hedge than ankle-deep in an open stream. Barrett committed to that course of action and was edging backwards to quit the stream when the boar charged again.

Like a bolt from a crossbow he came. A blur of hide in a spray of water.

No time to sight. Just point and pull. Two rounds. Two short, sharp reports.

The boar shrugged the slugs off like bee stings.

Bear fired twice more, the handgun bucking in pie-sized hands. The boar was not ten feet away when the fourth shot broke his rush, but it had taken half a clip of ammunition to turn the bastard and this animal wasn't giving up, not by a long shot. And neither was his herd.

They had him encircled, now. They could come from anywhere, all points of the compass. Thirty hogs closing a net and Bear with one round in the chamber.

He was scared and the hogs smelled it.

"Come on you sons of fucking bitches!"

Bear reached the slough brandishing his shotgun like a club.

"Come on, you bastards! Let's get this over with!"

But then something like thunder exploded over the slough. Thunder and a fall of heavy rain.

"Go on hogs!"

Sheriff Smoot Rawlings burst from the understory on horseback pumping a well-loaded shotgun.

Two more explosions. Two wads of buckshot into the maelstrom of hogs and a pair of sows rolled belly-up.

The lead boar's first instinct was to attack. The alpha male went straight for Smoot's horse. No hesitation. No fear. Smoot retired the shotgun for a carbine and shucked off three rounds as calm as cancer. Took three rounds from a 30/30 to take that boar down.

And then a posse of ATVs and deputies came pouring into the clearing firing shotguns and revolvers into the furious hogs. Whooping like cowboys. The boars and their sows milled in mass confusion under that riot. A frenzy of pork running pell-mell.

But then a snort from a single sow brought her piglets to the cover of brambles and vines and with that defection the rest of the cohort bolted for the cover of undergrowth, hastened on their way by the percussion of curses and gunfire and the terrified squeals of pigs.

"Hold up!"

It took a few moments for Smoot to rein in his men, the incongruous straw hat perfectly in place, the shotgun quiet across the pommel, the carbine returned to its saddle holster.

"I said hold up, dammit!"

Smoot made sure his deputies were held in check before he cantered back to reach the FDLE agent collapsed now at the edge of the slough.

"Damn, if you cain't get yourself into some fixes, Bear."

"Some fixes," Barrett acknowledged weakly. "But I found Taylor Calhoun, Sheriff. What's left of him, anyway."

"Cheese and crackers. You sure?"

"Scraps of his shirt in that dogwood by the creek. Right over there's his skull."

"Shit fire. Boys—"

Rawlings wheeled his mount to address his deputies. "Listen up. We found our man, gentlemen, which means we got us a crime scene chewed to shit. So back off with the vehicles an' let's try and not fuck this puppy more than we already have."

Midge Holloway was not happy to see "her" crime scene "compromised beyond imagination," but managed to recover virtually all of Taylor Calhoun's scattered remains. A pelvis was unearthed within minutes of her team's arrival. Wasn't long before they produced a humerus and a kneecap. A shattered kneecap.

They put Taylor together one bone at a time. Sometimes in splinters. Midge confirmed that Calhoun's throat had been cut.

"Same as Beth Ann's?" Smoot asked.

"Similar if not the same," Midge replied.

"I told Taylor he'd be safe," Barrett declared woodenly. "Told him I'd look after him."

"Ain't your fault, Bear." Rawlings shook his head. "Just be glad it ain't your bones we're pickin' up out here."

"Thanks to you, Sheriff. I do thank you for that. And your men."

"Nuthin' to it."

Barrett took a swig of water through his chewing gum. "Guess I ought to thank Orlando, too."

"Orlando?"

"Well, if he hadn't told you where to find me I'd be hog-meat, wouldn't I?"

"Orlando didn't tell me where to find anything," the Sheriff retorted.

"Didn't he?"

"No, I was comin' back along the road when I saw him by the truck with a canteen and a cell phone. I asked him where the hell were you? Told him he shouldn't of left you in the woods by yourself."

"My fault, not his." Barrett shook his head. "My fault for not having a radio, too. And there's no excuse for not checking the shotgun."

"Shotgun? You mean my shotgun?"

"One I borrowed, right."

"What's wrong with my gun?"

"Wasn't loaded."

"Bullshit."

"Believe me, Sheriff, there'd been shells in this weapon I'd have been pumping 'em."

"Lemme see." He reached past Barrett to take his Remington pump.

Bear watching Midge bag bones.

"I told him I'd take care of him," Bear said again.

"Cain't blame yourself for Taylor," Smoot frowned over his shotgun. "You didn't kill him. What you can do is find the sumbitch did."

"But Beth Ann Stanton's murder has to be the priority," Barrett replied tiredly. "I can't forget that."

"The hell, Bear, we got two victims both connected to Eddy DeLeon, both with their throats slit. And 'cording to the girls at Mama's, Eddy carries a razor. That puzzle ain't hard to put together."

"Maybe," Barrett allowed. "But what if there's a piece we've missed?"

"Got a place you'd like to look?"

It was ten o'clock the next morning when the Dixie County Sheriff and the FDLE's Agent Raines stumped up the broad steps of Senator Stanton's generous porch. Smoot had told his detective to meet them; they found Orlando lounging in the porch swing and sipping iced tea. He rose in deference to Rawlings's approach.

"You tell the senator we were coming?" Smoot asked his detective as Barrett wiped the soles of his feet on an astroturf mat.

"Not exactly." Fuqua shook his head and before that response could get clarified the front door opened wide to frame a woman well into her forties.

She stretched beneath the door's high-placed lintel in a tanktop and split skirt. Nice legs for a woman over forty. Carried everything else nicely, too. In fact, not many women in their twenties could display a top and bottom better than Ruby Knowles.

Orlando scanned her body like a bar code.

"Why, hello, gentlemen. And you must be Sheriff Rawlings?"

"County Sheriff, yes, ma'am."

"And you are—?"

"Special Agent Barrett Raines." Bear displayed his ID. "Florida Department of Law Enforcement."

"Oh, yes," Ruby Knowles smiled sweet as saccharine. "I remember your picture. From the papers."

"Yes, ma'am. And you are—?"

"Ruby Knowles. Fort Meyers. And ya'll call me *ma'am* one more time I'll skin you alive."

A bright laugh to accompany the brittle smile. Eyes languid beneath a pound of mascara.

"Is Mrs. Stanton at home?" Barrett inquired with the subtlety of a sledge hammer.

"Out of town," Ruby's reply came airily. "Truth is, I think she just wanted to get out of the house. Can you blame her? Baxter left just minutes ago. Fundraiser, or some such thing. But he said to make you-all welcome."

"Sorry for any trouble." Rawlings followed her through the door.

"No trouble," she smiled over a well-toned shoulder. And then, turning for the stairs, "I assume we're headed for the bedroom?"

An interesting assumption, Barrett noted to himself, and allowed Ruby to lead him as if on a leash up the stairs. The suite was still taped off. Rawlings directed Orlando Fuqua to keep a running chronology of their return to the scene. Anything pertinent to the room's examination had to be documented. Barrett was glad Ruby Knowles was present to witness his activity; the last thing he wanted was for some Johnny Cochran manque to sell theories of planted evidence or conspiracy to a jury jaded by Kenneth Starr and talk-show radio.

"Ms. Knowles—"

"Ruby, please."

"Ruby, yes. Do you mind remaining in the room with us?"

"Delighted to," she smiled.

By now the room's ransack was not obvious, virtually everything moveable having been taken for prints or other forensic sifting. The bedframe remained, its headboard stained darkly, but the mattress was gone, having been transported to Jacksonville for extended analysis. Nothing left to sleep on, now, but boxsprings onto whose unquilted suspension Ruby Knowles now settled without permission or apparent qualm.

A heavy-metal poster tacked overhead featured a leather-clad blond handcuffed to a bed of nails.

"Go girl," Ruby purred.

Barrett nodded to the poster. "Would you say this was typical of Beth Ann's taste? This kind of music?"

"She wasn't into Glenn Miller, if that's what you mean."

"You know the Stantons pretty well?"

"Never made a secret of my long friendship with Baxter," she replied. "Or with Babs, for that matter. You can ask Detective Fuqua."

"Orlando conducted our initial interview with Ms. Knowles," Sheriff Rawlings confirmed.

"It was lengthy," Ruby purred. "But not tiresome."

"There's a transcript at County," Fuqua offered belligerently.

"I'll need to take a look at that," Barrett responded.

Ruby inspected a fingernail.

"Detective Fuqua said I should call if I had any new information. I don't."

Bear smiled pleasantly to the senator's mistress. "Why don't you just catch me up, now? If you don't mind."

She shrugged consent.

"So when did you arrive at Pepperfish Keys?"

"Saturday," Ruby replied shortly. "Flew to Gainesville from Fort Meyers. Drove up from there."

"And you're staying—?"

"Here, at present. Townhouse before the party. SeaShore Drive. New place. I can show you."

"That's all right. Did you see Beth Ann at any time Sunday evening or early Monday morning?"

"No."

She leaned back on the protesting springs. Stretched luxuriously.

"Makes me feel funny. Bein' on her bed."

"It's never easy when somebody you know dies."

"That depends on the somebody."

"Bad, isn't it? To speak ill of the dead?"

Ruby displayed a wide sorority-girl smile. "Beth Ann Stanton was spoiled rotten. She was dishonest. Disloyal. And a sinkhole for her daddy's attention."

"Seems like you might require a good deal of attention yourself, Ms. Knowles."

She pulled her torso from the springs with a magnificent crunch of abdominals.

"I put my life on a shelf for fifteen years married to a man who never touched me. Now he's dead. I'm rich! I want to make up for lost time. What's wrong with that?"

"Not a thing."

"Sheriff?" she appealed.

" 'Course not. You got a life to live."

Rawlings stirring uncomfortably. Orlando preoccupied with the postered bondage on the wall.

Barrett crossed from his seat to a desk beside the bed.

"Don't believe I saw this before."

It was a photograph, the kind of family snapshot conspicuously absent when Barrett first viewed the room. Beth Ann's smile was innocent in this Kodak moment, a young girl happy in her father's arms.

"I let Barbara bring it in," Smoot apologized.

The mother needed a shrine for her daughter. Something to bind the wound of that loss. Or perhaps the photograph was a bandaid to cover something less innocent. Barrett bent over to read a scrawl of text penned in the margin.

" 'To Peaches from Cream'?"

Ruby sniffed.

"Anybody's cream, what I could tell. Anybody her daddy despised."

"That include Eddy DeLeon?"

"Rumor has it."

"I can't use rumor, Ruby."

Her eyes glittered below the mascara.

"Then I 'spose I'm no use to you at all."

A commode flushed in the joining bathroom.

"Goddammit!"

Barrett turned with Smoot Rawlings to see Fuqua duckwalking out of the loo.

"Son of a bitch!"

"What's your problem?" Rawlings challenged his detective.

"Damn john's stopped up," Orlando cursed over the cuffs of his slacks.

"Happens all the time," Ruby clucked sympathy.

Barrett was thinking it was nice to see Fuqua nonplussed, for any reason, when something clicked—

"Wait a minute. Wait just a minute—Sheriff, we need a plumber."

"It's not a crisis," Ruby drolled.

"Orlando, get a plumber."

"Sheriff?" Orlando turned to his boss.

"It's all right," Rawlings waved him off. "Man wants a plumber, what the hell. Get him a plumber."

"Fine, then." Orlando dipped his head to squeeze out of the room.

Rawlings turned to Bear Raines.

"What's bit you, Bear?"

"What have we got right now that ties Eddy DeLeon to this scene?"

"Well, Sharon Fowler. She saw him. So did the senator."

"They saw him at the pool. With Beth Ann. But then they saw him leave and that's Eddy's alibi. Nobody can put him back on the premises."

"Beth Ann came back," Rawlings pointed out.

"Doesn't mean she came back with DeLeon. We can only speculate right now how Beth Ann got back to her daddy's house, but what if we had concrete evidence that Eduardo was in her *room*?"

"We'd have a suspect," Rawlings nodded. "But what in hell's that got to do with the commode?"

"Ruby—"

"Yes?"

"Suppose you're going out for a party. Big time. Hot date. You carry a purse?"

"Can't do without."

"What's in it—quick! Don't think."

"Cash, credit card. Compact."

"How about a condom?"

Ruby smiled.

"Ask Detective Fuqua."

11.

A solitary golfer and his caddy paused midway on a perfect, green fairway like dabs of paint on a distant canvas. A groundsman purred his cart to a quiet stop alongside. Jamey Patterson took great pride in the sculpted topography that he had raised from a drained swamp to fashion Pepperfish Keys' only golf course. The links' eighteen holes snugged like a shoehorn into a natural boundary of slash pine and water hazards. A corridor of dogwood and rosewood trees mingled with the hybrid arbor and natural wetland to frame fairways that in springtime blossomed spectacularly in white and pink and scarlet.

Summers were the challenge. Summers were brutal. It had been Jamey's idea to route unpotable water off nearby sloughs to irrigate the course. Even so it had taken a while for the '419 turf to take on the course's talcum powder drives. Jamey selected a hardy sod for his greens, the Tif Dwarf distinguished both by its texture and by its stamina in the face of northern Florida's molten, summer heat.

Visiting professionals regularly praised the course, something that gave Patterson near infinite pride. It was understandable, therefore, that Jamey took personal insult to Eddy DeLeon's grinding a cigarette into the carefully cultured par four whose traps bracketed the pin on the final hole.

"Mr. DeLeon," the groundsman spoke up quietly. "Can you just use the receptacle on your cart, sir?"

Eddy smiled through broken teeth. A pair of gold bracelets bound his neck inside the collar of his Izod shirt. A silver keeper snugged the hair that hung in a raven ponytail down his back.

"No problem."

DeLeon twisted his spikes once more into the smoldering butt. Then, still smiling, Eddy took the iron whose titanium shaft seemed a straw in Crease's palmy hand. He addressed the ball. A perfect shot dropped a shoelace from the flag.

The prick smiled.

"Gonna be a nice day."

The golf course was part of a faux country club, a hangout for the new immigrants to Pepperfish Keys, those travelers from Saint Augustine or Fort Myers or Atlanta who demanded tennis courts and saunas and poolside margaritas. A place for dot-commers and retirees.

Idle husbands. Idle wives.

The club's architecture was dictated by the climate and the recreational activities profitably milking its members. The golf course required a pro shop, of course, and a bar. You had your pool, your tennis court. A sauna rarely used. There was the usual country-club etiquette. You could dress casually, as long as it cost a lot, and conversation around the bar, if not civilized, was to remain low-key.

Teenagers at the Pepperfish Keys Country Club were discouraged from wearing baseball caps indoors, though adults were not so chided. Indolent wives or golf widows could be found smiling from beneath billcaps over hands of bridge or Yahtzee, their men pretending to ignore a hit parade of younger women showing off bronzed legs and bellies beneath white, cotton tops and skirts. Local boys pretending to be occupied at bussing tables, or icing beer, jobs that for the most part demanded little attention and earned meager pay.

It was not clear to most of its paying clientele how Mr. DeLeon had acquired membership in their club. Eddy was not subdued in conversation. He was not likely to relax at a table with "The Journal" pondering with some heavy-jowled banker the merits of the Chrysler merger with Daimler-Benz. You didn't see DeLeon in quiet consultation with some investment broker regarding opportunities at Google or Microsoft. In fact, Eddy never sat with anyone aside from his chauffeur. He ordered the waiters about as if they were stableboys, and smothered coeds fetching drinks and sandwiches with unwelcome innuendo.

His play outside now finished, Eddy entered the clubhouse alone as usual, ordering a tuna fish sandwich and a vodka collins on his way to a table overlooking the club's well-populated pool. The sandwich was delivered and wolfed down in two bites.

Eddy lingered over the scenery, switching to a second and third and then a fourth Bacardi and Coke received, as the sandwich, without a tip or other expression of appreciation. Sitting alone and shunned, clipping his raptor-like fingernails into a crystal ashtray intended for other refuse. His eyes blinking occasionally and slowly, like one of those lizards in *National Geographic*.

He was on his fourth or fifth drink, was Eddy, his back to the club's entering doors and engaged by the bevy of girls or young women displayed invitingly around the pool. Those factors taken together might account for his indifference to the cordon of lawmen converging on his table.

"Eduardo DeLeon."

Eddy turned languidly to find Barrett Raines standing with the sheriff and a posse of deputies.

"Bear. You got somethin' for me?"

"Matter of fact, I believe I have."

Barrett Raines dangled the bagged prophylactic clearly and publicly over Eddy's table.

Shocked gasps, or twitters, all around. Everyone in the club turning to see.

Eddy tossed down the last of his rum and coke.

"I see a sock. Doesn't mean it's mine."

"Oh, it's yours, Eddy," Barrett assured the man. "We can match the DNA to your blood, or even—"

Midge Holloway leaned in to gather the crystal ashtray.

"—Even your fingernails."

DeLeon's scarred fists clenching white around his finished drink.

"The fuck is this?"

Sheriff Rawlings twisted the cuffs off his cowboy belt.

"You are under arrest, Ed-Ward-O DeLeon, for the murder of Beth Ann Stanton."

"You son of a bitch." Eddy spat at Bear's feet.

"Everything you say can and will be held against you in a court of—"

"Son of a bitch!"

Eddy launched himself from the table. Barrett met that charge chest high and late. He lost his feet. His head snapped back. A table was in the way. A chop of hardwood to the back of the head. Stars swimming.

And then claws. DeLeon's honed nails driving into Barrett's neck. Closing. But then the claws retracted, a momentary release. Bear's vision cleared to see Eddy's free hand fumbling beneath his goldplated bracelet. Looking for the simple string that secured the razor beneath.

Barrett brought up a knee, hard. A grunt, then DeLeon rolling sideways. But he had the razor! Bear could see the pearl handle popped free of its feeble leash.

"Freeze."

Smoot Rawlings directed DeLeon's attention to the cavity of his .357 magnum.

"Drop that blade or you'll be dead before you hit the goddamn ground."

DeLeon's eyes glazed, breath labored.

"Drop it, Eddy."

The razor clattered to the tile like silverware. Rawlings had

DeLeon cuffed and on his feet before Bear could pull himself fully erect from the floor.

"Mothafuckah!" DeLeon lunged at Bear again but the heavy barrel in the sheriff's hand whipped down and dropped the little prick like a sack of wet cowshit to the unforgiving floor.

It had been a long time since Barrett Raines had experienced anything like the ovation he received in his Live Oak office following the arrest of Eddy DeLeon. Cricket Bonet, Barrett's frequent partner, called in congratulations from Tallahassee. Roland Reed made sure he was there to play cheerleader.

"Atta boy, Bear. Way to be."

More sincere congratulations came over by phone or email from all over the state, a network of agents and state's attorneys thrilled to have Eddy DeLeon behind bars.

"We even got a fax from Captain Altmiller." Glenda Starling was pleased to be the one who gave Bear that news.

The fax from Barrett's boss was followed by an email from the attorney general, all very open and public displays of support for the district's calumniated agent, but it was Barrett's peers whose esteem he most appreciated, the half-dozen other agents with whom he worked in the regional office, their administrative personnel.

"Speech!" somebody yelled. And then again, "Speech!"

Barrett acknowledged that request with a grin so wide it hurt his face.

"Thank you-all. Many thanks. We've got a suspect, a strong suspect, and that's good. We've got the newshounds off our backs. That's *really* good."

Hoots all around to second that emotion.

"But Eddy DeLeon is not convicted. He's not even indicted, which means we've got plenty of work left to do. And not just for Beth Ann Stanton. Most of you know by now that Taylor Calhoun was under this office's protection. I'm not about to forget Taylor. I know you won't either."

Solid applause for that sentiment.

That was about it. Barrett was already installed in his cubicle savoring the moment when Glenda Starling peeked in.

"Way to go, Bear."

"Thanks, Glenda."

"Roland Reed asked if he could have a few minutes."

"He asked? Now, there's a change in weather."

Roland Reed breezed into Bear's cube, the attaboy smile still plastered over his face.

"Congratulations, Bear."

"Thank you, Roland."

"Knew you'd bounce back."

Bear let that passive jibe slide.

"Heard you got Eddy to lose his cool, too." Reed robbed a fold-out chair from an adjoining cubicle.

"Wasn't entirely planned," Bear averred. "By the time we got the warrant, Eddy was on the links. Smoot decided to make the arrest at the club. Figured Eddy'd be less likely to do something stupid in front of witnesses who already despise him."

"Smoot didn't exactly get that one right, did he? But hey—all's well that ends well. I'll take a count of homicide any day."

"Two counts," Barrett reminded him. "Don't forget Taylor Calhoun."

"Oh, sure, Taylor. 'Course not."

Checking his watch.

"Can't linger, Bear. You've given me some work to do."

"It's not a lock yet, Roland."

"Hell it's not. Eddy DeLeon is headed to a gurney."

With that the state attorney for the Third Judicial District rose from his pilfered seat and came face-to-breast with Sharon Fowler.

"Ms. Fowler."

"Mr. Reed." Sharon occupied her hands so that she wouldn't have to take Roland's. "Hello, Barrett. Hope I'm not intruding."

"Not at all." Barrett allowed her to see the faxes piled on his desk.

"Why the visit, Sharon?" Roland apparently could not resist sarcasm. "Victory interview?"

"I'm here to talk about Eddy DeLeon."

"Here's a headline: 'Latin Lover Kills Senator's Daughter'."

"Go with that one and next year you boys'll be selling real estate."

Barrett leaned forward.

"You have something to say, Sharon?"

"Yes. You got the wrong guy."

"Wrong guy."

"Eddy DeLeon did not kill Beth Ann Stanton."

"And do you have a reliable source to back that claim, Ms. Fowler?"

"I believe so, yes, Mr. Raines."

"I don't suppose you'd give us a name? Somebody we can actually talk to?"

"You know I can't do that."

"Then why don't you shove your source up your ass?" Roland suggested. Barrett raised a hand.

"Take it easy, Roland."

"We don't owe this smear-artist the time of day."

"We're not talking about time," Bear replied. "We're talking about a homicide."

Returning to the local anchor.

"If you can't give up a name, Sharon, why come at all?"

"Because I can help you find Beth Ann's killer."

Barrett glanced to Roland. Considered a moment. Reached down to get Glenda on his in-house line.

"Glenda—Hold my calls till I tell you, okay? Thanks."

And then, to Sharon.

"Take Roland's chair."

She sat nearly as tall in the state attorney's surrendered seat as Roland managed standing. Her hair was pulled back simply and caught with the same barrette she'd worn the night of Stanton's party. A dark, gray jacket matched a pleated skirt. Bear noted the small, Sony recorder that she placed on his desk. So did Roland Reed.

"Thought you wanted this off the record," Reed objected.

"Entirely," she affirmed. "I've turned off my recorder. As you can now verify for yourself."

"How about hidden cameras?" Bear inquired. "Peepholes? Wires?"

"Nothing like that."

Roland Reed leaned against the wall to one side of the seated anchorwoman. Barrett faced her across his desk from the more comfortable seat of his roll-around.

"Now, exactly what are you offering?"

"To help you find a killer."

"We've got a killer."

"Not Beth Ann Stanton's," she shook her head.

"You have a source on this, Sharon? Or is this something you cooked up for ratings?"

"Eduardo DeLeon did not kill Beth Ann Stanton," she repeated evenly. "He may be a thief. He may even be in bed with Baxter Stanton, something that thanks to you two we may never know. But he didn't kill Beth Ann Stanton. I am confident he did not."

"Confident enough to, say, supply us a witness?"

"I never reveal my sources, Bear. You know that."

"You've ambushed a few."

"My privilege. More than that—my right."

Roland Reed turned to Bear.

"The hell are we doing even listening to this crap? She comes in here with some two-headed calf claiming special insight into our case. But she won't divulge."

"I'll divulge information," Sharon corrected him. "But not sources."

"Thanks loads."

She leaned toward Barrett, her skirt edging higher over rock-hard thighs.

"I could go on the air with this." Sharon fixed him with jade eyes. "I could broadcast a story that would make you people look like redneck idiots. Condoms at a country club! But I didn't do that. I came here to inform you. To cooperate. But if all I'm going to get in return is attitude—"

I'm pretty sure we know who's got the attitude, here," Roland returned tightly.

Barrett rocked back in his chair.

"You two finished? Because if you are, I've got to decide what to do with this information."

"It's not information. It's bullshit."

"Use it or lose it," Sharon shot back.

"I'm pretty sure I can find a commode somewhere that works."

Sharon turned her attention to Barrett.

"Prediction for you, Bear. Sooner or later a jury's going to look past the smoke of circumstance you're calling evidence and they're going to ask—'Why?' Why would Eddy DeLeon, street-smart Eddy, hard case, kill a senator's daughter, in her bed, with potential witnesses all over the place?"

"Same reason he went for me at the clubhouse," Barrett returned. "Because he's a sociopath. Because once you push the right buttons, Eddy DeLeon is capable of anything. Any kind of violence you can imagine."

"That won't do for a jury."

"We'll find something that will."

"You'll find something, sure."

She palmed her pocket-sized recorder.

"But will it be the truth?"

When Sharon rose from her chair she towered over them both.

"Don't say I didn't warn you."

She left, then, striding like a jock, confident, unhurried. Heads whipped around from computers and phones to follow Sharon Fowler all the way to the door.

"Seems pretty sure of herself, doesn't she?" Roland's laugh was hollow.

"She's fishing," Barrett dismissed the meeting.

"Could have done that without driving to Live Oak," Roland mused. "She could have fished over the phone."

Bear shook his round head. "If Sharon wanted to help, all she had to do was give us a name."

"She's never going to give up a source." Roland tapped his pen like a telegrapher. "Even so does that mean she can't help us? Does that mean we can't use *her*?"

"The hell you getting at, Roland?"

"Journalists don't need search warrants, Bear. They aren't hindered by due process or privacy. They get information routinely in ways we are prohibited from even trying. But here Sharon drives all the way in to Live Oak just to offer us help. Now, why would she do that?"

"To fuck us to the wall. Again."

"Maybe. Or maybe we've got something she wants."

"I don't care; I don't trust the woman."

"You can always trust Sharon Fowler to look out for Number One," Roland declared. "So let's suppose, just suppose for argument's sake that Ms. Fowler is not so much interested in helping us as she is in helping herself.

"Two questions occur to me off the bat: One, what could a television reporter possibly gain from defending Eddy DeLeon? And two, what's Sharon got to gain from allying herself with you and me? It sure as hell isn't because she admires the FDLE or the Third District."

Barrett shook his head.

"She wants to be in the loop, that's all."

"We could use that motivation to our advantage."

"Or we could tell her to piss up a rope."

Reed capped his fountain pen. "Look, Bear. Either we buy the notion that a smalltown and narcissistic bitch has suddenly converted to Concerned Citizen coming here on behalf of poor, misunderstood Eduardo DeLeon, or we figure Sharon came here looking to advance her own agenda.

"Now, I have no idea what could make Sharon believe that

Eddy DeLeon is innocent of Beth Ann's murder, or even if she actually believes it, but we absolutely know she can't prove Eddy's innocent, because if she could you can bet your ass it'd be the top story on the six o'clock news. She's hit a wall, Bear. I'd lay money on it."

Bear stared at the faxes on his desk.

"If I were Sharon," he mulled it over, "and I had a stand-alone source telling me that Eddy DeLeon was innocent of murder, I would want a way to confirm it."

Reed shrugged. "Or rule it out. Either way, Sharon needs our help. Which gives us some leverage we weren't even looking for, because while Sharon's digging into Beth Ann's murder she'll be looking for links between DeLeon and Baxter Stanton. What if she finds something we missed?"

"No way!" Barrett shoved back from his desk. "Is *that* why you're greasing me to take this bait? To take another crack at Senator Stanton?"

"I'm just saying . . ."

"Bullshit, Roland. I followed you through that door once already, remember? Smoot Rawlings doesn't believe I ever gave it up."

"Bear, you know there's some kind of connection between the senator and Eddy DeLeon. And you know it's criminal."

"I know my hands are tied, too."

"Your hands, yes. And mine. But not Sharon's."

Bear regarded the kudos still warm on his desk.

"It's risky."

"Costs nothing to talk," Roland persisted. "Besides—what've you got to lose?"

"A lot, judging from past performance."

"Call Sharon tomorrow," Roland urged. "No commitments. Just see where it leads."

"I don't like the idea of getting in bed with a journalist."

Roland slipped his pen into his vest.

"Would not be a problem for me."

12.

Mr. Lee Thiet was cleared by Control for final approach on Three-Five Left at Austin/Bergstrom International Airport. It was the second time within the month that the veteran pilot had landed at Bergstrom, this time to meet Eddy DeLeon on neutral ground, and the flight from California to Texas generated omens that were not encouraging.

The weather was spotty all the way in from the Texas panhandle, anvils of thunderclouds hammering the atmosphere. He was forced to divert way north of the preferred route to Austin, finally got into local traffic only to spend a half hour boring holes in the sky before getting clearance to land.

Other pilots might grouse over such inconvenience, not Lee Thiet. Mr. Thiet was a balanced man. In fact, he craved equilibrium. He did not curse the weather or the traffic or the incompetent controller. He did not complain. Lee touched down a few minutes past noon and tied off perfectly composed to take his scheduled appointment.

But when he entered the lounge of Trajen Flight Support, Eduardo DeLeon was nowhere to be seen.

Mr. Thiet stopped at the desk to check for messages. Nothing. No message by phone, no email.

"Will you be needing fuel, sir?"

"Yes, please."

He was flying a Cessna 210, his own aircraft. Nothing fancy, just a normally aspirated Lycoming driving a constant-speed prop. It was a fine aircraft, of course. Good at altitude and cross-country and rugged for unimproved fields. But importantly for Mr. Thiet the 210 was also pedestrian, ordinary, unremarkable. The last thing Lee wanted to be was conspicuous. You showed off your Hawker or your Velocity or your Starduster in retirement. Not when you were in the midst of transactions.

Lee learned early to favor a low profile. He was only an infant when his father left South Vietnam's ancient city of Hue to liaison with American advisors in Saigon. Lee kept the last photograph his father ever took. In that snapshot an overloaded helicopter rotored heavily from the roof of the American embassy. A Vietnamese woman clung for her life to the chopper's skid. Lee remembered her skirt, how the silk blossomed like a parachute beneath the churning rotors. Even in that terror he was ashamed to see his mother so exposed.

Lee kept his own exposure to a minimum. There were no security guards checking Trajen's clients. No metal detectors. No wands. The runway-facing entry at the Austin FBO was unsecured and unobstructed, a wall of glass from floor to ceiling looking directly out onto the tarmac. Every imaginable kind of aircraft tied off at Trajen's fixed based operation and every imaginable client could be found at one time or another killing time in the lounge, high-roller lawyers and lobbyists sharing coffee with local Bubbas or the occasional celebrity. Operations ran around the clock, which was useful. The employees were polite and deferential and devoid of curiosity.

"And will you be staying overnight, sir?"

"No."

"Very well."

Mr. Thiet paused on his way to the pilot's lounge to check the weather. A kiosk of computers allowed pilots to file flight plans electronically and you could get forecasts for any region. Lee moused through windows of weather reports, killing time as he scanned the lounge for his Florida connection. The omens were not improving. Whole regions of instability threatened the local area, a series of dopplered splotches marking thunderstorms and hail. There was a serious depression brewing in the Gulf, a long trough in a falling barometer heading for Florida's northwestern coast.

And still no sign of Eddy DeLeon.

Mr. Thiet retired to the pilot's lounge, a well-fixed niche set apart for "Flyers Only." Lee could normally find a sense of center in that eddy of leather and industrial carpet. The amenities included a sleep room and shower. The lounge itself arranged a hemisphere of reclining loungers to face a TV screen as wide as a fireplace. You could get free coffee all the time, and popcorn. Lee especially liked that, the popcorn. Take a bag of popcorn into the lounge and settle yourself before that enormous screen and you could almost imagine you were at the movies.

Mr. Thiet loved the movies. For a number of weeks and over a number of flights he had enthusiastically followed a retrospective of Mr. Hitchcock's ouvre. He saw *The Thirty-Nine Steps* in Seattle. Caught most of *The Birds* in Boston. And now in Austin he was installed with a fresh bag of popped corn as Jimmy Stewart hung terrified and disoriented on the fragile steps of a staircase stretching dizzily into the screen.

Vertigo. Every pilot was familiar with that sensation, the sudden, irrational sense of disorientation that made you fly straight into the ground. It started in the clouds, usually, a place where the evidence of mind and senses were totally at odds with the instruments you had to trust, that place where a flyer could not be convinced he was flying upside down or into a mountainside.

There were many ways a man could lose his orientation. The present threat to Lee's sense of equilibrium began weeks earlier when Eddy DeLeon called to say that their shared enterprise required additional capital, that the planned supply of product would be crippled without an added investment of half a million dollars U.S.

Mr. Thiet doubted whether this dire assessment was true, but had nevertheless deposited the half-million as a loan to be remanded with interest in an offshore account in return for guarantees of fifteen million pristine DVDs of Randall Damone's latest film. *Scarlet Moon,* everyone agreed, was destined to be the box-office hit of the coming season and there was plenty of room for bootleg distribution.

Lee's first experience with pirated DVDs came in Beijing where along with roasted duck or Russian vodka customers were enticed to purchase the latest Hollywood releases on copycat DVDs. Lee recalled buying *A Beautiful Mind* for less than a dollar. That DVD, however, was a so-called "first-edition," a poor-quality copy taken from a videocamera filming a movie screen. A year later, however, Lee saw near-perfect fidelity on a DVD of *The Sorcerer's Stone*, that disc acquired from a street vendor hawking his wares costumed as Harry Potter.

Piracy was blatant. And rampant. In Malaysia alone, government officials estimated that underground factories exported 360 million unlicensed video discs each year to China, South America, not to mention Switzerland. The one-dollar sales hawked on street corners in Bern or Beijing and ignored by executives in Burbank and Beverly Hills began to constitute serious erosions of profit. Industry sources in Los Angeles claimed losses of $8 billion a year on a variety of balance sheets, those numbers rising near-exponentially as sophisticated cartels globalized their control of pirated product.

The entertainment industry fought back against Lee's and other such organizations, belatedly, with a variety of security and encryption systems. Most were woefully inadequate. The Content Scrambling System, long the dominant protective shield for movies and video games, could be hacked with a seven-line code churned out by students at MIT. A bewildering variety of firewalled product was coded to protect films released by Paramount, or Universal, or Disney, only to be castrated or circumvented by online hackers in Boston, New Delhi, and Denmark.

Lee himself had no technical expertise. He had no interest in the bits or bytes of digitally mastered movies. He had only a businessman's notion of how DVDs were created or cloned. Lee was a middleman and as a middleman he retooled connections derived from years trading heroin and weapons and stolen merchandise to meet the new opportunity, delivering very high-quality DVDs of American films to underground distributors scattered from Singapore to Prague. To that end, Mr. Thiet needed dependable sources who could bribe or steal original material from Hollywood insiders and technicians. Eddy DeLeon had been extremely successful in this regard. Within five years, Eddy's sources had provided material for over one hundred titles reproduced on 100 million unlicensed DVDs, most of the originating material obtained by bribe or theft from movie insiders in the United States.

It took money to finance that kind of enterprise, of course, and in this regard Mr. Thiet was not stingy; he had paid $2 million in the last year alone to his Florida-based source, a heavy investment to be trusted to any single man in the movie business. But Eddy DeLeon always delivered the latest films and the hottest so when the Honduran called to say he needed another half-million Lee laundered the cash and sent it in.

Then came more unwelcome news. There would be a month's delay with the product. Eddy relayed that information over the phone to his Asian partner. Unavoidable, but not to worry, Eddy declared, adding that the promised product would be delivered no later than Memorial Day.

Lee was furious. The whole point for sinking added money into the pirated copy of *Scarlet Moon* was to release the product before its Hollywood premiere. Lee reminded his distant supplier that he had just advanced over $2 million to ensure that 15 million discs of *Scarlet Moon* would be in the hands of his underground distributors no later than mid-August.

DeLeon explained with obsequious apology that the delay was not his fault, but that it would take an additional month to obtain the digitized linear tape that would guarantee a perfect replication of *Scarlet Moon*. Of course this meant that production of the pirate DVD would be concomitantly delayed resulting in additional expenses, by the way, so sorry, of $640,000.

Mr. Thiet told DeLeon that his wholesalers were voicing concerns and that these were men with long memories, long reaches, and long knives. Eddy assured him that there was still time to beat the film's Memorial Day debut.

"I already know where to intercept the tape; I got the driver," Eddy told his backer. "Gonna be cherry. Unfucking believable quality. I even got masters of the artwork for your jacket. *¿Comprende? Ende problema.*"

No problem? Mr. Thiet was beginning to wonder. He had extended credit before to proven sources promising outstanding product. Not often. But you had to take a chance now and then, otherwise the supplier would simply run his wares to another cartel. You could kill the man, of course, but that would be a little like killing the goose with golden eggs. The trick was to balance opportunity against risk and in matters involving equilibrium Thiet Lee was a master.

"You have a partner, Mr. DeLeon, your guarantor. I want to meet him. Face to face."

"No can do, Mr. Thiet." Eddy's voice had been high and thin over the phone. "My partner insists on remaining silent. Silent and invisible."

"Senator Baxter Stanton is far from invisible."

Lee might have enjoyed seeing the effect of that intelligence on the Honduran's face.

"Did you actually suppose you could keep your partner's identity from me, Mr. DeLeon?"

The spick's cocksure voice hesitated.

"You doan need to see the senator."

"I do indeed."

"Why?"

"So that I can look him in the eye when I tell him that if you fail to meet your obligations, I will make sure he never returns to Washington."

Lee recalled Eddy's response to that ultimatum.

"*Bien.*" There was something like admiration in that ghetto voice. "I like."

Mr. Thiet flew to Austin to meet Senator Stanton a couple of weeks later. Baxter Stanton arrived in the height of scandal, his battle with Florida's attorney general still unresolved. He landed in a Lear that invited attention, leaving his pilot in the cockpit to cross the tarmac incognito and ridiculous in a baseball cap, Eddie Bauer boots, and wraparound sunglasses. A cross between Bono and Pete Rose.

"Let's get this over with," the rooster was terse. "I intend to fly back to Tallahassee tonight."

Lee delivered his terms with alacrity. The honorable gentleman from Florida would agree to cover Mr. Thiet's extended loan to Mr. DeLeon *and* any additional expenses. With interest. A deadline for delivery was set for the twentieth of September.

"If I do not receive product as specified by that date you will immediately refund all investment that I have contributed to this project."

"And how much is that?" the senator rasped.

"Two million six hundred forty thousand dollars, U.S.," Lee replied. "Which taken with other incentives that I have already made clear should provide ample inducement to deliver 15 million DVDs of *Scarlet Moon* as required."

Baxter Stanton assured Mr. Thiet that the promised product would be delivered by Fed Ex to Lee's Hong Kong warehouse no later than the third Saturday of September, concluding with the complaint that there was "no need for threats."

"Tell Mr. DeLeon I will need a progress report," Mr. Thiet dismissed the United States senator like an errand boy. "Tell him to meet me here, in Texas, in four weeks' time. Noon."

The command was conveyed, the appointment confirmed, and four weeks scrolled by. Mr. Thiet returned to Texas. But Eddy DeLeon was nowhere to be seen.

Vertigo is a terrifying sensation. Lee Thiet cringed to see Jimmy Stewart teeter disoriented and nauseous on the faulty balustrade of Hitchcock's set. Mr. Thiet saw parallels between his dilemma and that of the film's protagonist. A risk was taken, instability endured, and all for a feckless partner.

Balance needed to be restored, Lee knew that. He would not ignore his instruments. He would not fly in the clouds. He would find the horizon and land on solid ground even if it meant cutting his losses.

Even if it meant cutting them to the bone.

The woman in Hitchcock's film was breathless and blond, a siren to Stewart's tormented character. Mr. Thiet had never seen the movie through to its conclusion and had given himself up to savor the climax, to surrender fully to the last few frames of Hitchcock's masterpiece—

But then a short-sleeved rent-a-pilot hooted over his laptop.

"They got 'im! They got the sumbitch!"

"Excuse me," Mr. Thiet challenged the disturbance.

"Oh, sorry there. But they got the guy killed the senator's daughter. The one in Florida?"

Mr. Thiet gathered the remote carefully.

"Perhaps I can find a broadcast," he offered politely and trolled the remote to reach CNN's Headline News.

"... *the arrest was made in Pepperfish Keys, one of those unlikely spots attracting new money to Florida's Big Bend,*" an Atlanta anchor spoke before a backdrop of local footage. "*Mr. Eduardo DeLeon, you can see him there, the man in the pony-tail cuffed between a pair of deputies, has now been formally charged for the brutal murder of the daughter of Baxter Stanton, the United States senator who only days ago seemed to have defeated every distraction threatening his bid for another consecutive term in office.*"

"Bastard's hit himself a bad stretch, ain't he?"

"Yes," Mr. Thiet agreed. "A very bad stretch."

It was obvious he would not be meeting Eddy DeLeon on this day. Obvious as well that Eddy DeLeon and Senator Baxter had got themselves into an imbroglio threatening much more than a single movie.

Mr. Thiet consulted his cellular phone, selected a number.

"Excuse me."

He left the lounge. Waited for the connection to be made.

"I need a message delivered privately to our Florida supplier."

He spoke with forced composure.

"A private delivery, yes. Inform our supplier that the circumstance presently existing between him and his elder partner dangerously compromises his relationship with me. Tell the gentleman I shall reschedule a meeting when circumstances permit. And be advised we may have a conflict of interest impossible to resolve without direct intervention."

Mr. Thiet pocketed his portable and hurried back to experience the resolution of Hitchcock's thriller, but he was too late. The narrative had reached its climax in his absence and the moment was lost, that ecstasy ineffable and sexual squandered for a phone call.

Mr. Thiet stabbed the remote to find The Weather Channel. A full-blown tropical depression now pushed through the Gulf. A younger pilot might try an end-run around that mercurial line, but not Mr. Thiet. A real aviator does not lose his sense of equilibrium, Lee reminded himself. He does not fight the weather. He does not fly blind. Lee settled into his luxurious recliner, ignoring his popcorn, seeking a balance.

Planning the flight to Florida.

Barrett Raines searched for a centerline through the slap of windshield wipers and sheets of rain. The AM radio's forecast ripped with static warned of severe thunderstorms and hail. You could smell ozone even through the vents of the a/c and lightning forked to the ground in blue-green bolts. The road was perilous. Petroleum that had been begged to the surface with the day's earlier heat now mixed with rain to make the road slick as snot on a doorknob.

Barrett was actually slowing his car when something sounding like a grenade exploded and his hand twitched on the steering wheel, not much, just a twitch. But then the car turned sideways and he was sailing into a wall of hybrid pine.

Foot off the gas. Countersteer.

Keep her in the road!

The yellow line straightened and the rational part of Barrett's brain explained that a bolt of lightning had hit a pine along the narrow shoulder and the tree's resin, expanding with that sudden and solar heat, simply exploded.

That and nothing more. Motherfuck, Elinore.

Barrett exhaled a bellows of air. He could barely make out the forecast crackling over the AM station, "... *a big blow brewing ... the Gulf ... tropical depress ... tornado alert from Cedar Keys to ...*"

When he was a boy Bear used to cheer the arrival of hurricane season. In those days the autumn storms provided just about the only respite from dog days made intolerable by landlocked heat and humidity. By September any relief was welcome. It probably wasn't righteous to pray for floods, cyclones, and wind, but when you were baking in some tobacco field or sweating in a classroom with nothing but a box fan and Mrs. Hicks, you didn't care. You got a break from school or you got a break from the heat. It was all good.

But if Bear were to pray for anything at present it would be sunshine. The blacktop taking him to Deacon Beach was now white with water, the sky above a matte of black so deep and dark as to seem artificial. Bolts of lightning splintered both sides of the road; he could feel the concussion, even inside the cruiser. And then came the hail, golf balls of ice exploding on the Ford's sheet-metal roof and hood like shells of artillery.

Made for an exciting combination of hazards—water and

wind, lightning and hail, and a ribbon of road flooding silver. It almost made Bear miss his turnoff. Even in good weather the narrow macadam snaking off Highway 51 to Harvey's Marina was easy to miss; Barrett eased down that narrow road toward a modest but welcome harbor.

Bear knew Harvey Sykes well, had cropped tobacco side by side with Harvey when they were boys. Sykes went on to become one of the few locals showing any entrepreneurial energy or sense, one of the very few able to capitalize in any significant way on the influx of outsiders to Pepperfish Keys. Originally a fishing camp, Harvey's Marina and its related concerns faced a canal dredged into a crescent of cypress and saw grass. An ideal place to have a boat repaired, to put out for a day of fishing or skiing. Close enough to the Keys for an out-of-towner to claim residence, but far enough away, at least for the present, to be affordable.

Contiguous with the marina were Harvey's drydock and icehouse, a well-stocked baitshop, and a convenience store stacked with carousels of computer games and movies. The drydock serviced commercial fisherman, shrimpers in particular, as well as the sleek-hulled pleasure craft of those part-timers bringing new money to Pepperfish Keys. A modest cafe was always busy and Harvey had recently tacked on a bar that offered frigid air-conditioning and ice-cold beer to locals and out-of-towners weary from work or play.

Probably eighty boats of various description were sheltered at Harvey's, inboards mostly. But fully a dozen slips at the marina's unsheltered extremity offered power and sewage for a colony of floating homes that had become an affordable option for folks wanting a place on the water.

It was still hailing when Barrett Raines pulled onto the marina's gravel lot; every car or truck standing in the open looked like it was hit with birdshot. Would be some busy folks at State-Farm tomorrow. But Bear's immediate problem was to get out of his own dimpled vehicle without being pummeled senseless.

He eased his cruiser as far beneath the marina's metal bib as he could manage. The slips' awning cut off the falling hail like a light switch, but anything moored on open water was taking a beating, wads of ice slamming into the fiberglass shells of ski-boats and runabouts and sailing vessels.

Buckyballs of ice bounced off a catamaran's Dacron deck as though from a trampoline. Harvey had tried to sell Barrett a Hogey on one occasion, doing his best to coax Bear out of his ailing Whaler and into a sexier boat. But there was only one vessel this afternoon in which Agent Raines had any interest. Bear shoved open the door of his Crown Vic and was immediately challenged.

"Hot damn, Bear!"

Harvey himself emerging in a sou'wester shouting above the hail that pounded his aluminum-roofed slips.

"Looks like you gone be filin' some *in*surance." Harvey seemed happy to appraise Bear's riddled cruiser.

"State will, at least." Barrett shivered involuntarily as ice slipped inside his collar.

Harvey jerked a finger toward the screen door of his cafe.

"Inside. Make you some coffee."

The cafe was roofed in metal, as the marina, with cin-derblock walls. By the time Harvey got a fresh pot of java the hail had begun to wane, but not the rain. Harvey pressed a warm mug into Barrett's hand along with a squeezer of honey.

"Brings you out in this shit, Bear?"

"Fishing," the agent replied, which was close to the truth.

"How're your boys?"

"Field trip. Silver Springs."

"Gives you and Laura Anne some quiet time, I guess."

"Oh, yeah. Sure."

In fact, Barrett had phoned his wife as he left Live Oak to check out that possibility.

"Boys are away," he reminded Laura Anne. "I could pick you up early from the restaurant, if you like. We can go do something."

A hesitation.

"No. . . . Things might get busy."

"Laura Anne, it's raining frogs."

"We're shorthanded. I better prep."

"You sure?"

"I'll be fine."

It had become a pattern since her trauma, avoiding intimacy of any kind. In some ways Barrett was glad to have the excuse to stay away from his empty home. Work was a harbor, too, wasn't it?

"You still got that Whaler, Bear?"

This from Harvey Sykes.

"I do."

Bear scanning the vehicles scattered about Harvey's parking lot. There was one car virtually untouched by the storm, a BMW sheltered beneath the spread of a magnificent magnolia tree.

"Still puttin' in at the public ramp?" Harvey inquired.

Bear nodded absently. "I am."

"You oughta get yourself a slip, Bear."

Barrett smiled to decline and then a thought occurred. An excuse for his inclement visit.

"What d'you think about a houseboat, Harvey?"

"Well, sure. I can fix you up."

A burst of lightning lit the interior like the flashbulb of some giant camera. Walls trembling with a concussion of thunder. Harvey sipped his coffee carefully. "Hellacious weather to go shopping."

"Weather hit on my way in," Bear replied lamely. "But what the hell, long as I'm here."

" 'Least let me get you something for the wet."

Moments later, Barrett was huddled inside a puny poncho. A spray of saltwater mixed with the rain to rake the marina. Barrett felt a sting on his face, his hands. Whitecaps were breaking onto the slips, banging boats against bumpers jerry-rigged from styrofoam or automobile tires. The houseboats occupying the most distant slips were not sheltered. Barrett pulled his poncho tight on a slip 'n slide to Sharon Fowler's waterborne home. Good damn thing the slips were numbered. There she was. No. 61.

Christ. What a boat.

Rolling slowly before him in its padded slip was a seventy-seven foot Summerset. Hail was gathered like peas in a pan on the tight canvas covering her jacuzzi. The upper deck was covered tight and shipshape. There were two small craft moored beside the houseboat, a jet ski bumpered on the starboard side of Sharon's numbered residence, and a twenty-foot runabout.

A satellite dish aimed starward off the Summerset's bow.

Bear knew that Sharon could not possibly afford this boat on the salary she garnered at KEYS TV. Sharon's daddy had bought the vessel. In fact, he bragged loudly that he paid cash for it. Mr. Fowler was close to losing his dairy near Appalachicola when a company laying pipeline through his pasture unearthed a rich vein of dolomite. That natural cache made the family cash-rich, if not financially astute. Daddy immediately got himself a cluster of expensive toys, one of which was a trophy-home for his good-looking daughter. And what a nice home it was. A hardwood deck. Lots of teak and chrome. Barrett glanced back toward the parking lot. Sharon's BMW was still there, garlanded with a bruise of blossoms, but that didn't ensure she was home. He edged onto the catwalk linking the pier to Sharon's houseboat, testing the redwood slats against the slick purchase of his leather-soled shoes.

He got to Sharon's boat without making a complete fool of himself, but now what? The houseboat's domestic cabin was entered through a custom-made door that was not a hatch. There was no doorbell. Should he knock? Hail the captain? Would anybody hear?

He pounded a metal postern twice. Then again, tepidly.

"Shit!"

The poncho whipped off his shoulders with a sudden gust and Bear was left to soak in his slacks and blazer.

Goddammit, was she home? If he could just get a look inside.

There were windows looking out to the deck, real windows, not portholes. Barrett leaned past the door to peer into the cabin's interior. It was like looking through the bottom of a glass of water. What was that, a liquor cabinet? Yes. And mounted on the wall behind—?

Bear could make out a shark's dorsal fin and then a swordfish. Both stuffed and mounted. But where was Sharon? Barrett wiped the glass with the soggy sleeve of his blazer.

There she was.

It was difficult at first to discern what the volleyballer was doing in view of her deep-sea trophies. Bear's own breath clouded the window. He pulled away, briefly. Then back. Jesus.

Sharon was stripped to a pair of running shorts, and stretched as if for some medieval interrogation across a large ball, canary yellow, couple of feet at least in diameter. It took Raines a moment to realize that Sharon was working to maintain a balance atop the ball, the long, strong body arched to the floor at head and foot, her breasts rising perfect with each deep inhalation, her abdomen scooped like a bowl.

Straining to balance on the ball's unstable center of gravity.

A sheen of perspiration to accompany that effort. Her hair falling *sans barrette* to the boat's hardwood floor. A clap of thunder startled Barrett from his sloppy espionage. A bolt of lightning striking. Barrett slipped on the rain-slick deck, falling heavily against Sharon's sternside door.

So much for stealth. Barrett scrambled to regain his feet.

What should he do? Should he leave? Get off the boat? Would he have time to negotiate that awkward retreat, reach the marina's shelter and turn if caught with a polite salutation to say, Ah, Sharon! Happened to be in the neighborhood.

A bell of thunder opened the door, Sharon Fowler draped casually in the frame, a T-shirt dimpled by the nipples of her breasts and clinging damply to her back, to the muscled bed of her abdomen. Long legs reaching bare feet.

"Agent Raines," a smile tugged on moist lips. "Please do come in."

She set him on a beanbag thoughtfully placed before a radiant heater at the border of the houseboat's well-fixed galley.

The heater's tungsten elements buzzing orange coils of comfort. Steam coming off his blazer and slacks.

"Here."

She place a cup of coffee within reach.

"Instant. That's all I have. Sorry."

"It's fine. Thanks."

The floor shifting subtly with the churn of saltwater outside. The yellow ball bouncing sleepily across the parqueted floor—*poing, poing*—Sharon extended a long leg to intercept.

"Whole bunch of things you can do on this thing. You can work glutes and abs. And erectors. That what you got working, Bear?"

"Cheap shot."

"I wasn't peeping at *your* door."

"I couldn't tell if you were home."

"Bullshit, you were watching."

"Roland sent me out here fishing, Sharon, I admit that straight out. But I didn't intend to invade your privacy."

"How long were you at the door?"

"I tried to knock," Barrett protested. "I yelled a couple of times. Not like there's a bell."

She laughed and it surprised him.

"A doorbell, sure! What every home on the water needs."

Sharon rose without effort from the floor.

"You're soaked." She padded over to a louvered closet. "I've got some sweats here somewhere might fit. Old boyfriend. Extra-extra large."

"Don't want to put you to any trouble."

"Can change in the bathroom if it makes you feel more comfortable."

"Not sure anything's going to make me comfortable at this point."

"Bathroom's just past the bar, Agent Raines." she tossed him a set of sweats big enough for a linebacker. "Leave your things outside and I'll pop 'em in the dryer."

He changed in the loo, dropped his wets outside. He hesitated to include his shorts with the socks, slacks, shirt, and blazer but commonsense overcame embarrassment. He wasn't going to put on wet underwear inside dry pullovers.

By the time he was changed Sharon was installed at her galley's marble-topped counter.

"So you came to ambush me."

"I did *not*," he said firmly and she smiled.

"It's all right, Bear. Not like I can hold it against you, is it? Not after the way I bushwacked you. And by the way I apologize for that; I shouldn't have brought a camera into your office without your permission. Aside from the ethics, it wasn't smart. It worked for me in the short run, sure, but now I need your help. I do, really. I admit it. And you need mine."

The bail shifted again on the unstable floor.

"It's for my back, really, mostly." She nudged the ball with her toe. "There's this series of exercises I have to do. Because of my surgery?"

"I don't think I realized it was that much a problem."

"Take a look."

She turned her back to him, pulled up the still-damp T-shirt.

"Down low. Around L-5 and the sacrum. See it?"

Barrett saw a zipper running between the well-defined muscles of her back and torso and below the line of her shorts. He felt something stir that he didn't want stirring. She swiveled back Indian-fashion to face him.

"They cut a chunk from my hip, too? For the graft? From the ilium—?"

Barrett noticed that in casual conversation Sharon sometimes exhibited that smalltown and southern tendency to end declarative statements as interrogatives.

"The surgeon who did me called it a 'transverse process'? It didn't take."

"Sounds like an ordeal."

"Was. Still is, sometimes. But the ball's good therapy."

Barrett found himself searching for something to look at that wasn't tall, damp, and sexy. He nodded to the trophies above her bar.

"The swordfish. Shark. Where'd you get those?"

"I caught 'em."

"You're kidding."

"Was on the Atlantic side when I hooked the swordfish. Must have been three miles out. Got the shark in the Gulf. Brought in a marlin, one time. In Hawaii? Four hundred pounds of pelagic. That was before I hurt my back. Worked that bad boy for an hour and a half. I couldn't afford to have him mounted, though."

Barrett glanced outside. He could see a break in the clouds. The therapy ball, he noticed, was steady on the houseboat's hard floor. Remaining now at a comfortable if not temptless remove.

"Bear, you mind a personal question?"

He grunted. "Does it matter if I mind?"

"Everybody around here knows your story, Bear. You grew up in a Jim Crow pocket of Florida with an abusive father and a crazy mother. Your brother was a sorry son of a bitch, by your own account, and yet you shed all that baggage to get yourself an ROTC scholarship and majored in, what was it—? Criminal justice?"

"Classical studies. C.J. was a minor."

"So you finish that business and five years after leaving the Army you are the number one draft for the FDLE. You are free. Totally. Your pick of assignments anywhere in the state and you came back to this redneck place? I don't get it."

Barrett shrugged. "Sometimes the shittier the place, the harder it is to let go."

"Not for me," she shook her head. "Quick as I can I am outta here."

She was close beside him, now. Only two rags of cotton between their skins.

"I'm a dreamer, Bear. I dream big. I dream for the future. And I'm betting somewhere, someplace deep inside, you do, too."

"That have anything to do with your offer to help us, Sharon?"

"Help you," she corrected. "I came to offer *you* a proposition, and yes, of course, I think I'll benefit. I never made any bones about that. But I think you'll come out ahead, too, Bear."

"What precisely do you have in mind?"

She looked him directly in the eye.

"I want to go undercover on Eddy DeLeon."

13.

The line of storms breaking an hour to the south did not reach Tallahassee and for that Midge Holloway was grateful. Even in good weather it would take a couple of hours to make the run from the state capital to Sheriff Rawlings's evidence room, and Barrett's favorite crime scene investigator had not looked forward to transporting her cache of evidence down rain-slick blacktops in a hailstorm.

Midge was logging out a variety of evidence for delivery to Cross City, but it was the material related to Beth Ann Stanton's case that demanded extra attention. Roland Reed had insisted that all analyzed material germane to Beth Ann's homicide be delivered by ground transport. Captain Altmiller authorized a reinforced van from the motor pool for that purpose, not exactly an armored van, but caged and plated with a heavy duty chassis and a big V-10. It was one of the vehicles normally used to transport violent offenders.

Not all transfers of evidence warranted such trouble, or expense. The Putrid Room in Tallahassee displayed shelf after shelf of fingers, thumbs, and more tender parts that were amputated from their bulky owners and shipped piecemeal by Federal Express for identification. Registered mail was commonly used to return small samples of fiber or other evidence to prosecutors in Mayo or Cross City or Live Oak. But Roland Reed said he'd be damned if he'd jeopardize the prosecution of Eddy DeLeon by depending on the U.S. mail and so after some discussion Midge agreed to personally supervise the transfer of all evidence related to *State of Florida* v. *DeLeon* from Tallahassee to Dixie County's jurisdiction.

"At least that way," the gnome-like specialist declared, "I'll know for sure it's done right."

A break in the weather did not, unfortunately, bring a respite from paperwork. There were dozens of smudges, stains, prints, fibers, and samples that had to be accounted for, nearly all of which had undergone multiple analyses by any number of technicians working at a variety of laboratories. It was essential to establish a chain of custody for every scrap of that material, beginning with the moment of its recovery and extending to every lab where it was swabbed, sampled, dusted, daubed, or photographed. Midge Holloway knew that the evidence she'd be transporting was critical for the state's case against Beth Ann Stanton's alleged killer. It was an important task, but, as Midge reminded herself, it was also not rocket science.

She'd been assigned a driver, for which she was grateful as Midge never liked to drive. Special Agent Jack Sandstrom was a team captain and wide receiver at Florida State before the FDLE sent him south to Palatka and St. Augustine and then to Miami. It had taken Jack twelve years to get back to the capital where he now captained the FDLE's small-bore sharpshooters. "First thing I did when I got back was grab season tickets for the Seminoles," he reported happily.

Sheriff Rawlings assigned Midge one of his own men, both for added security and to co-sign the relevant records related to custody. Midge had worked a couple of scenes with Orlando Fuqua, most recently when she was called to collect Taylor Calhoun's bones in the flatwoods east of Pepperfish Keys. They had barely started work when Orlando repeated one of those downhome, corn-liquor jokes that inevitably purchased its humor at the expense of blacks, or Latins, or Jews.

"Not on my crew," she had admonished the detective.

"The fuck you talking to?"

"You heard me. I've got all kinds of people on my team. Last thing they need is the benefit of your wisdom."

He didn't like it, she could tell. And so perhaps it wasn't so surprising that in Midge's company Orlando tended to be reserved. He floated at her side now like some kind of outsized apparition, a pale man with pale, giant hands, casual in a sports shirt and wrinkled slacks, his weapon secured at the hip in a holster never oiled or maintained as he dragged tar from an unfiltered Camel into his lungs.

A veteran clerk singing out evidentiary items like an auctioneer.

"State vee Mariott, Eight-Nine Baker. One each Marlin shotgun. Twenty-gauge."

"Check." Orlando scrawled his signature beneath Midge's, jotted down the date and time.

The clipboard dipping with the impact of his hand.

"State vee Lagrange," the clerk droned again. "Seventeen, Eighteen, and . . . Nineteen Bravo. Rifle shells, twenty-two shorts. How we looking?"

"Signed off," Orlando mumbled past his cigarette.

"Received," Midge affirmed.

A cardboard box was then opened for inspection. Three bags and fifteen pounds of cocaine.

"Blow a lot of noses with that shit," Fuqua seemed to rouse.

"Proba blee," their sharpshooting driver agreed pleasantly.

The clerk scanned the final two items.

"State vee DeLeon."

Orlando glanced to Midge.

She straightened painfully.

"Make damn sure we get this one right."

"Lessee," the clerk scanned the description, "one each bag of fingernail clippings. Forty-nine milligrams. Number Seven-One-Six. . . ."

"Check," Midge received and signed.

". . . and one well-used prophylactic. Trojan. Number Seven-One-Seven. I authorize transfer."

"I receive." Midge signed and passed the clipboard to Fuqua.

"Is that it?" Orlando scrawled his receipt.

"If it sends his ass to the electric chair," the clerk replied, "I'd say it's enough."

U.S. 90 offered four wide lanes due south as far as Perry, a road inviting fast travel. Midge was pleased to see Jack Sandstrom driving their reinforced van cautiously. There were intermittent showers, still, the moon breaking through scuds of cloud heavy with humidity. Took roughly an hour to reach Taylor County.

"How far to Cross City?" Jack inquired.

"Another hour, I'd guess, in this weather," Midge answered.

Orlando rousing himself on the bench seat behind Midge and Jack. Might have been asleep back there, for all Midge could tell.

"Mind if I smoke?"

"Yes," Midge answered shortly.

Fuqua stuffing his Camels back in his shirt pocket.

They turned off Highway 90 for Highway 19, two narrow strips of blacktop frequently punctuated by repairs. The van was barely through town when a lane of orange cones detoured them. Agent Sandstrom slowed the vehicle to a crawl. A quarter mile of construction later the road resumed, a mere hump of asphalt raised from a swamp. Deep ditches on either side. The road to Cross City was swallowed in a vast forest of hybrid pine destined for pulp and paper. The smell of the Perry mill invading the van's interior through the vents of its air-conditioning.

A stench of sulphur. Like rotten eggs.

No habitation along this stretch. No friendly farm off to the side. No cultivated fields of any kind. You could see at intervals where a dirt road snaked off to the side, occasionally an asphalt feeder. Just a pig trail disappearing into a maze of hybrid pine.

Lightning broke briefly and unexpected to strobe the van's interior, startling Midge in her highbacked seat. She was glad to have the van's shotgun seat, and reluctantly grateful to Orlando for surrendering it. It was cramped on the benchseat behind her for a man Fuqua's size, but he'd insisted on Midge's sitting up front and she had not objected.

The weather was what had Midge on edge, more accurately the road conditions arising from unpredictable weather. She was not concerned for her security. After all, in addition to a van modified for the transport of angry felons Midge had two lawmen on board, both well armed. Orlando brought a modified M-16 to complement his nine-millimeter Glock. Her driver was a sharpshooter carrying two handguns, a .357 magnum in a side holster, and a snub-nosed .38 down low. Even Midge knew how to use the twelve-gauge racked to the dashboard up front.

Midge was more worried about flat tires than gunfights.

Jack Sandstrom nodded to a ditch turgid with water.

"Must have rained like hell through here."

"Like a two-cunted cow pissing on a flat rock," Orlando quipped, that unexpected contribution getting nervous chuckles from his companions.

"Hellacious storms we been havin'," Orlando turning suddenly loquacious. "Nights like this my old man used to say the Devil was beatin' his wife with a broomstick."

He released the strap securing his handgun in its holster.

Casually. In plain view. Inclining those pale eyes to the driver.

"Myself, I think the Devil'd be tempted to stay home on a night like this. How about you, Jack?"

"Oh, yeah."

"Devil tempt any man. With the right incentive."

Midge turned in her comfortable seat.

"What's got you chatty, Orlando?"

"I'm sitting back here with fifteen pounds of snort."

"That's a temptation?" Midge smiled.

182

"That's retirement," Orlando retorted. "Hell, all three of us could retire."

"Making the Devil happy in his work," Midge observed drily.

"I could stand it."

"Making the Devil happy?"

"Retirement. Get me a place on the water. Bet you we could get us 'prolly seven, eight million dollars off what we got in here."

Fuqua turning then, to their driver.

"What about it, Jack? Even split three ways that's—Two? Three million? Tell me you couldn't stand that?"

But Jack was watching the road.

"Ah, shit."

Easing off the accelerator.

"What?"

Midge turning her attention back to the road.

"Looks like a washout."

"No, wait." Orlando leaned forward. "It's not washed out. No, it's just a low-water crossing. County put it in couple of months back."

Jack slowed his van to a crawl. A pole candycaned in black and white registered the depth of passing water, the road dipping into a virtual culvert, rising immediately on the other side. To complicate matters, an intersecting county road was blocked with those damned orange cones. Stop signs sandbagged at all approaches.

"Had lots of wrecks along here," Fuqua remarked. "County decided they'd stopsign the low-water mark as well as the County crossing till they get the road raised up."

"The road's under water."

"Looks like," Orlando agreed.

"Is it running?" Jack inquired. "If it's still we can try crossing. But if the water's moving . . ."

"No need to take chances," Midge approved her driver's caution.

Only a fool drove through running water.

"See, here we are, stuck on some country-ass road—"

Orlando snapping his clip back into its magazine. "—when we could take what we got and be on the beach."

"Now, Detective Fuqua." Jack wiped the windshield with his sleeve. "You know you aren't doing anything with that cocaine."

"Midge, what about you? You wanta retire?"

"I'm just gonna check this water."

"Suit yourself," Orlando replied and smashed his handgun into her skull.

Midge's head snapped forward into the dash. Jack moving, then, more quickly than Orlando would have expected, his right hand leaving the steering wheel for the .357 at his hip.

Orlando fired his Glock through the seat. A pair of explosions ringing then in the van's steel interior.

"Oh!"

The slug's impact throwing Jack into the wheel. The horn blaring.

"Ohhh," Jack groaning again, as if all he'd done was turn an ankle.

"Need help with that belt, Jack?"

"Or . . . ? Orlando?"

Sandstrom's first stunned moment then overrun with the instinct to survive. Jack clawing to release his seatbelt. Stretching to find the snubnose holstered at his ankle.

Orlando jammed his own handgun into the agent's backside.

"Not such a hotshot, now, are we, Jack?"

"You don't . . . have to do this."

"Yeah," Orlando smiled. "I do."

He fired again. The slug ripped through the marksman's liver, those steady hands, so skilled, so filled with purpose, jerking uncontrolled for a moment before they were forever still.

"Don't worry, Jack. You got off lucky."

Midge now stirring. Moaning.

Like a fucking calf, Orlando thought. A dying calf, what was it they said? Oh, yeah.

A dying calf in a hailstorm.

Orlando tossed the shotgun to the van's rear seat. Time, then, for the handcuffs, Fuqua cuffing Midge roughly to the van's steering wheel, pulling the diminutive woman on top of her good friend's corpse.

Now to get the key for the padlock that locked the van's reinforced cage.

"Where is it, bitch?"

There. On a ring at her waist. If she'd had anything but dried-up dugs beneath that blouse Orlando might have considered feeling her up, but these were slim pickings.

Besides. He didn't have time.

Didn't take a minute to open the cage and grab the evidence inside.

Orlando smiled to imagine Jack Sandstrom's young family learning that their husband and father had died denying an easy retirement. But the cocaine was not the real point of the exercise.

Where was that rubber?

There it was. The rubber. And now for the fingernails. Orlando stuffed those two transparent bags into the waist of his pants. Only then did he start grabbing bags of coke, a pair of headlights flashing briefly from off the side of the highway giving pause to that labor.

It was a Jeep that rolled languidly into the intersection from the side-road. Eddy DeLeon's driver waddled free of the four-wheeler's open cab.

Strolling up to the van. Just like he had all the goddamn time in the world.

"Evening, Crease. You gonna help? Or just stand there?"

"You got the stuff?"

Orlando tossed him the two evidence bags.

"Plus some retirement."

Fuqua grinning at the other bags on the ground.

"I got it." Crease gathered the cocaine like groceries and walked the drugs and evidence bags back to his vehicle. He tossed the coke onto the floorboard. Deposited the evidence bags carefully in the console. A grind of gears, then, as Eddy's driver backed the Jeep safely distant from the intersection.

When Crease returned to the van Orlando saw a pair of cans in the driver's meaty hands. More like containers, really. Fiberglass. Five gallons apiece. The flexible nozzles were familiar.

Midge Holloway groaning to consciousness. Blood oozing from her skull, her ears.

"—Jack?"

Her voice seemed to come from the bottom of a pool.

Eardrums burst, she realized dimly.

A wave of nausea.

"Jack?"

Midge jerked instinctively. But something sharp and hard snapped her back to the steering wheel.

Handcuffs.

"God!"

She was cuffed to Jack Sandstrom's corpse.

"Oh, God!"

Midge smelling the air from the van's opened rear door. That after-rain smell. She turned deaf and terrified to see Orlando in pantomime with an unfamiliar man. Even in her terror she noted the details. Pale skin. Scarred forearms. Baggy shorts and sandals. A revolver bulging like a tumor through a Hawaiian shirt.

"I could move that white," Orlando was persisting with his plan to retire. "Have that shit on the street in two weeks."

"Too risky," Crease replied.

"No damn riskier than what we're doing."

"Forget it, Orlando."

Midge could not hear what they were saying. But she could see the container that Orlando opened inside the van's opened rear door. She could smell the familiar odor wafted into the van with the wet and heavy air.

"You remember to stick a rag in the tank?"

"Fuck you."

"Just asking."

"Get a move on," Crease frowned. "We don't wanta have some trucker coming through."

Midge kicking. Screaming.

"Noooo! Noooo!"

The fumes of gasoline as potent as any smelling salt.

"Doan!"

Her pleas hoarse. And gargled, too, as if from the mouth of a mute.

Orlando paused from his labor to regard her.

"Got a big kick out of nailing Eddy in front of all those people, didn't you, bitch?"

"Pleeez doan!"

"Shake Eddy down in front of all those people. Cut his dick off and let everybody watch. You loved it. Didn't you?"

"Doan do it!"

Midge turning now to the windshield. Kicking frantically.

"We could just shoot her." Crease touched the revolver in his shorts.

Orlando shook his head.

"Not what the man said."

"Leddem!" Midge gargled.

She could see the gun wadded in the folds of Crease's belly.

"Leddem shood me!"

Orlando sloshing gasoline into the van's interior, tossing in the first can before turning his attention to the second.

"Doan do it! Orlando—!"

Fuqua turning his back on her, the nozzle from the second container trailing gasoline in a volatile stream that led away from the van and toward Eddy's waiting driver.

"Orlando!"

Through the van's opened rear door Orlando could see Midge pulling against her cuffs, a frenzied, savage attempt to sieve her hands through those steel bracelets. Screaming with that effort, that pain. All sense of shame abandoned.

Abandoning that effort. Turning to the steering wheel.

"Lookee here!" Orlando chortling derision.

Midge straddling her driver, her pitiful spine arching back, head splitting over the hump of shoulder, feet planted in penny-loafers to the dash. A ninety-pound cripple straining to rip a steering wheel from its metal roots.

Orlando reached the Jeep with only a splash of high octane remaining.

"Fuqua!"

Midge's scream muffled inside the distant van.

"Fuqua—don't—do—this!"

"Got a way to light this torch?" Crease inquired.

"You got my cash?" Orlando returned.

"You're not done yet."

"Fair enough."

Orlando pulled a Bic from his pocket. A snap of flint. A blue, butane sputter.

"Help! Officer inside—Help me! Heeeelp!"

"See who's King Shit, now," Orlando sneered and dropped the lighter to the asphalt.

A ragged whoosh almost caught the killers unprepared, the road's moisture dispersing the flame, more a creek than a fuse of fire meandering toward the van.

"Not nuthin' like the movies," Orlando groused.

The concussion came with a force not anticipated, two concussions, actually, the torched van's exploding interior igniting the ragged fuse stuffed in the fuel tank's metal mouth. The bruised sky above sucking up a ball of flame. Another *whooooosh*!

The van bucked into the air, a tin box scattering shrapnel of flesh and flame, asphalt splintering like the crust of an oriole beneath. A cartwheel back to earth. Yet another explosion.

"Jesus," Orlando marveled. "Like staring into hell. Ain't it?"

"Just like," Crease agreed and with an icepick stabbed the pale giant through the base of his skull.

Orlando jerked comically erect, on tiptoes practically, before falling facefirst to the blacktop. His arms quivered, then, as if with some electrical encouragement. Another distant flicker of lightning made that seem possible. A Kodak flash followed by thunder. Crease planted his tourist's sandal on the big man's neck. Jerked his pick free.

"Eddy says thanks."

It was late and the skies were clearing through a half bowl of moonlight by the time Barrett Raines got back into his tumble-dried clothes, but things were far from settled as Sharon Fowler walked him from her galley and out onto the polished wood of her deck. She had slipped on a pair of jeans before escorting Barrett outside. A light nylon breaker loose over her T-shirt.

"You mind a personal question, Bear?"

"Does it matter if I mind?"

"What keeps you tied to this Jim Crow coastline? Can't be easy to raise a family here, especially if your skin's a shade darker than chalk."

He rolled a shoulder. "Sometimes the harder a place is, the harder it is to let go."

"Not for me. This time next year I plan to be in New York City."

"And you'll do whatever it takes to get there."

"The truth is what I'm after, Bear. Right now your case against Eddy DeLeon hinges on a used rubber and an ashtray of fingernails. You've got a shaky time line. No motive. And now you're saying Eddy killed Taylor Calhoun?"

"You find me a source can prove differently I'll be glad to take a name."

"I can't betray a source to help you, Bear. But I can *be* a source. I can get Eddy talking, at least. Come on! What have you got to lose?"

"My ass if I'm not careful."

"I'll cover your ass. I'll record every word of every conversation and it won't cost you a thing."

Barrett paused to consider.

"I don't think so, Sharon. You won't name your source, I can't force that, but it really doesn't matter. Roland Reed is ready to go after Eddy with the evidence in hand."

Barrett's decision was answered with the warble of a cellphone.

"Dammit. 'Scuse me." Sharon slipped her hand inside her jeans to find the phone, snapped her wrist as if casting a lure to pop open the display.

"Almond. Sharon, here . . . Matter of fact I am busy, yes . . . No, go ahead . . . A roll-over? Big deal, Almond, you can handle that—what? . . . Wait a minute, is that confirmed? . . . You're sure? . . . Oh, shit."

Barrett felt a crawl along the back of his neck.

"What is it?" he asked.

She pressed a finger to her lips.

"Okay . . . I said, 'Okay', Almond . . . No, I'll take it. Call Dewey; tell him I want to be on-camera in thirty minutes."

"The hell's going on, Sharon?"

"You'd better call Roland, Bear."

She handed him her phone.

"Right away."

14.

Barrett Raines pressed himself into a windbreak framed by the aluminum doors of the Dixie County Courthouse. A Canadian cold front had followed the previous evening's summer storm to plummet temperatures a good thirty degrees and a steady north wind now chilled metal and bone. It wouldn't last, of course, this break from the heat. Just a prick-tease of autumn before a resurgence of summer swelter. But for the moment it was colder than a well digger's ass.

Bear shared his recessed shelter with State Attorney Roland Reed and they both dreaded leaving its protection, though for reasons unrelated to climate. A mercenary of reporters were waiting on the windy street, licking their chops and sharpening their knives behind a cordon of state troopers. Sharon Fowler could see Agent Raines from her news van along the curb. Even at this distance you could see the crease in his khaki slacks and the sheen of a blazer worn daily and dry-cleaned to death.

"Freezing my fucking ass off." Dew Drop stamped his Nikes into the pavement.

"Just make sure the mike's hot." She ignored her tech's misery.

"I got it," he snapped.

"I'm ready."

Dewey bent to his lens. "Three . . . Two . . . One . . ."

Sharon composed an earnest face for the camera.

"Hello, I'm Sharon Fowler bringing you the latest, first. Last night a heavy-duty van protected by armed lawmen and transporting evidence described by State Attorney Roland Reed as, quote, 'crucial to the prosecution of Eddy DeLeon,' was brutally ambushed seven miles south of Perry, Florida.

"Viewers will no doubt recall that Eddy DeLeon was arrested only days ago for the sadistic homicide of Senator Baxter Stanton's only child. The van carrying evidence relevant to Beth Ann Stanton's homicide was dispatched from the FDLE Crime Lab in Tallahassee and was enroute to the Sheriff's Department in Dixie County when it was stopped, attacked, and torched.

"The Highway Patrol has confirmed that FDLE Special Agent Jack Sandstrom and Crime Scene Investigator Midge Holloway were burned to death inside the vehicle. Also dead at the scene was the van's third occupant, plainclothes detective Orlando Fuqua.

"It is not clear what motivated this assault, though the FDLE has confirmed that a cache of cocaine valued at over 8 million dollars is apparently missing. All other evidence was consumed in what FDLE investigators are describing as a massive explosion and fire.

"I see State Attorney Reed, now, approaching the podium with the FDLE's Special Agent Barrett Raines."

Roland Reed's thinning hair lifted off its scalp as he reached a podium anchored with sandbags. He was trying to recover from that loss of dignity when a sudden gust of wind whipped his tie from his vest, the state attorney now grabbing silk as he probed with his free hand to find a windsocked microphone.

"As you know . . ."

Clearing his throat.

"As you know, our staff have assisted Sheriff Rawlings in his efforts to apprehend the person or persons responsible for the murder of Beth Ann Stanton. We were making good progress in that investigation. However, events beyond our control have forced a decision regarding the suspect held in that case . . .

"Earlier this morning I officially notified Sheriff Rawlings that in light of recent developments, specifically a loss of physical evidence crucial to the state's advocacy, charges of homicide against Eduardo José DeLeon will be dropped."

A startled inhalation. Sound booms dipping in unison to receive the news. Cameras clicking.

"Mr. DeLeon has been granted bail for lesser charges of assault and will be released later today from the county jail."

Reed stuffed his one sheet into his pocket.

"No further action is contemplated at this time."

The press exploded like geese breaking into flight. Questions squawked in salvos. A flapping of arms for attention. Sharon slipped her portable Sony into her ever-ready briefcase.

"Okay, Dew Drop, let's pack it in."

Dewey remained rooted to his camera.

"You got to be kidding."

"Pack it. We've got enough, here. I want you to get over to the jail, though. Grab some footage of Eddy's release."

"We're *done,* here? Van gets torched, evidence gets destroyed, no witnesses and 8 million bucks worth of coke floating around, but you don't have any questions for these people?"

"Barrett doesn't know anything. Roland's full of shit. And Eddy's not answering anything for anybody."

"The fuck makes you so sure?"

"Because he's not that stupid."

Sharon Fowler reviewed the morning's footage at her editing bin: Eduardo DeLeon emerging from behind bars without comment. A corruption of reporters assailing the Honduran as he crossed the street to his stretch limousine. The broken phalanx of reporters shouting questions—Did you hijack the van? Did you hire someone to assault the van?

Did you kill Beth Ann?

Eddy eschewing comment as he followed his driver like a halfback behind a pulling guard to reach his Lincoln limousine.

"Not bad," Sharon muttered to herself and was set to cut the footage of Eddy's release with Roland Reed's courthouse statement when Almond Sinclair burst in.

"You're going national!"

She froze at the deck.

"National? You're sure?"

"I just got the call from New York, Sharon. ABC! They're patching you in at six-thirty!"

"Tonight?"

"Tonight! There'll be an intro and Q and A against the van footage. Be a real mix and mash for you, Sharon. Great exposure!"

The tall anchorwoman seemed suddenly unstable on her roll-around chair.

Sinclair beaming. "You don't get chances like this every day, kiddo. Make us proud."

It's easy when fighting alligators to forget you're supposed to be draining the swamp and Barrett Raines was up to his neck in gators the entire day. The entire FDLE was shaken over the hijack of the department's van and furious over the slaughter of its agents. Captain Altmiller was firing emails hourly from Tallahassee. The attorney general was raising hell.

How had the evidence van been fingered? Where had security broken down? How had the hijackers obtained the van's schedule? It's route?

Barrett spent the whole day coordinating state and federal resources in an effort to answer those questions. Whatever minutes remained were spent floundering in frustration at Eddy DeLeon's release from prison.

It was past five o'clock when he got a call from Sharon Fowler.

"I'm sure you're busy. Rough day?"

"It's all right, what's up?"

"It's just I don't think either of us wants to give up on finding out who killed Beth Ann. Or Taylor, for that matter. And I still think I can help."

"I don't see how Sharon. We've got no evidence."

"Makes my proposition the more interesting."

"Makes me look desperate."

"You are desperate. What say we get together around nine? Harvey's place? I'll buy you a drink."

Bear missed Sharon's six-thirty debut, but was home early enough to get in an hour with Ben and Tyndall, if only to supervise schoolwork. The Raines's gifted son was already mastering algebraic expressions while his fraternal twin remained stumped by the division of fractions. Barrett had put in a call to Laura Anne on the drive home, but his wife had not replied.

"She still at the restaurant." Thelma provided that information. "Say she be late gettin' home, not to wait up."

So it was a little before nine when Bear toed open the screen door that was the summer barrier to mosquitoes and flies at Harvey's Cafe & Bar. The gaps between the floorboards of the cafe were so wide you could see fish swimming in the water beneath. Barrett saw a pair of boys dropping scraps of bacon through the floor, hoping without doubt to lure a mullet or carp or crab into view.

The beer joint tagged onto the cafe like an embarrassed relative. A separate entrance made you either walk through the cafe or around it to enter beneath a neon advertisement for Budweiser on the waterside of the marina. Once inside the taproom, you'd find a long counter topped with marine plywood looking over card tables that were never level and fold-up chairs with bent legs. A pool table divoted worse than any fairway swallowed quarters and cue balls at random. The vinyl on the barstools was split, the wool bunting exposed like a wound inside.

There were no windows in the bar at all, just sheetrocked

walls crumbling with humidity and cratered with the fists of fishermen or angry husbands. License tags tacked up by gill nets. Music provided by a faux Wurlitzer. You couldn't find a place much more in contrast with Laura Anne's elegant establishment, Barrett reflected. Harvey kept his windowless bar ice cold with a twelve-ton unit filched off a bankrupt chiropractor in Perry. Harvey bragged that his a/c could put icicles on a hot-plate, but there was no need for that encouragement this evening.

There was always a winter rind of frost on the mugs that Harvey kept in a freezer behind the bar. He was at the upright now, grabbing a pair for his customers.

" 'Lo, Bear."

"Harvey."

"Need a beer?"

"Might take one."

He was trying not to think about Midge Holloway. He had called the ME in Tallahassee not even pretending a professional interest. Everyone knew Midge's fondness for the FDLE's black sheep. He just wanted to know exactly how his friend met her death. The examiner said Midge had been badly burned, but that asphyxiation undoubtedly got her before the flames.

He was trying to soften the picture, but Barrett knew that Holloway was found handcuffed to the steering wheel of the van. He knew she had time to anticipate her ordeal. To see it coming. Barrett took a long swig of brew. Normally on a day like this he'd just talk things over with Laura Anne. Didn't matter what it was—fear or obsession or shame, whatever, Laura Anne would make it better. Even horseplay with Ben and Tyndall was enough in ordinary times to restore some sense of sanity, the routines of bathtimes and bedside reading wiping out the darker parts of the day.

But Laura Anne had not replied to his coded pleas for solace and the boys were way too young to bear such a burden and there was no one, now, apart from a shrink in Tallahassee, before whom Bear could risk airing his real feelings, his real fears.

Harvey appeared with a frosty mug.

"You believe how fuckin' cold it got?"

"Be hot by the weekend," Bear tried to be sociable.

"Be three fifty."

Reaching for his wallet Barrett almost missed the woman who slipped onto the neighboring stool. She was not local. A twenty-something in a mesh top over camouflaged capris. GI boots laced paratrooper-style with white nylon. She was Latin, too, which alone would have made her uncommon in this bar. A Latina with spiked hair. Tattoos on the left breast, and high on the arm of that same side. A filligree of ivy leaves inked around her neck like a collar. Kanji characters, inked deeply, stretched like a sweatband across her forehead.

"A Zuleta," she smiled. "Not some knockoff, the real deal."

Preening her etchings as though they were diamonds from Tiffany's.

"You don't look like a fisherman," she purred.

"Florida Department of Law Enforcement," he replied shortly.

"Oh," she shimmied. "A cop."

"Look, hon, I'm not available."

"You sure?"

The fabric of her pumps stretching tight as she leaned over. Barrett ran his finger around the rim of his bottle. It was chipped at the lip. He could feel an abrasion on his finger deepen with each circuit.

"I come with an invitation," she said.

"From whom?"

And then a voice chuckled at his back.

"Why from me, senor."

Barrett pivoted slowly to find Eddy DeLeon.

"You met my squeeze? Hey, she not coming on to you was she, man? Givin' you a hard time?"

DeLeon leaning past Bear to nibble a pierced ear, the gilded necklace hanging beneath the open collar of his Brooks Brothers shirt. Leering at Bear through a mangle of teeth.

His honey smirking alongside.

"We shouldn't be speaking, Eddy."

"What you gonna do? Throw me out?"

"Will that be necessary?"

"I would not like to be embarrassed again. Especially not in front of my girlfriend."

"If your girl's got shit for brains she'll check out the fate of your last sweetheart and walk out while she still can."

Somebody smacked open a rack of balls at the pool table.

"You still think I killed Beth Ann?"

"Didn't you?"

"But where is your 'evidence' Agent Raines? Hah? Up in fucking smoke."

Don't get baited, Bear warned himself. You have a chance to play him. Take advantage.

"A stroke of luck for you, that van," Barrett saluted with his frosty mug. "Any idea who was behind it?"

"What I hear it was for coke. Some fuckin' dealer. Maybe even some low-life cop."

"Someone like Orlando? I don't think so."

"Who gives a shit what you think? Fuckin' loser. Drinkin' beer all by his lonely self. Where's the wife, anyway, Bear? Cooking shrimp? Washing fucking dishes?"

Their conversation was by now attracting attention. Harvey was suddenly busy polishing glasses beside the baseball bat he kept behind the bar. Barrett saw local fishermen reaching deep into pockets filled with knives, brass knuckles, or the occasional roll of quarters.

About the last thing Bear needed was a brawl in a local bar.

"If you're planning on staying, Eddy, I can take my appointment someplace else."

"Is not necessary." DeLeon wrapped a scarred fist about his girl's meshed waist. "Soon as I top the tanks in my boat this *concita* is coming with me to celebrate my repatriation. Maybe we go fish, hah?"

He cackled laughter.

"Or maybe I just fuck her eyes out. You welcome to join, man."

"Listen, prick," Harvey leaned across his bar. "You don't have any friends here, all right? And I don't need your business."

Eddy smiled.

"Just trying to help the man out. You know, with his problem."

There was a moment when Barrett thought his trigger was pulled. It would be so easy to pick up a cue stick and break it over DeLeon's well-greased skull. Borrow a pair of brass knuckles from one of these shrimpers and go to work on the bastard's ribs.

A white lawman could get away with an attack like that. Smoot Rawlings had gotten away with it, many times.

But a black man with a gun and a badge in this bend of Florida had to be more circumspect than Caesar's wife. Barrett would not be given the benefit of doubt that would automatically accrue to Sheriff Rawlings or any white man.

Harvey intervened.

"Here's how this is going to work, Eddy. I'm about to ask Mr. Raines to step outside and you can try to cut your way through a barful of pissed off crackers. Or you can leave Mr. Raines in peace and go enjoy your senorita anyway you like. Make a fucking decision."

"Drop by Mama's sometime." DeLeon dropped that aside to Barrett as he pushed away from the bar. "I hook you up."

Bear counted to ten, slowly, and by the time he was finished DeLeon was gone.

"You okay, Bear?"

"Sure. Sorry to put you in that position, Harvey."

"No position for me. 'Nother beer?"

He wanted a beer. In fact, for the first time in a long time he wanted a damn case of beers.

"Better make it coffee, Harvey. I'm supposed to be meeting Sharon Fowler and with her it's best to be sober."

"I hear that. You catch her broadcast earlier?"

"If it was about the van, I'd rather not."

"But this was national, Bear. ABC, I taped it."

"All right, then. Sure. Thanks."

Bear was squeezing honey into a fresh cup of coffee as Harvey hiked up a milk crate to reach the recorder cabled to the bar's TV. Took a second or two for the battered player to read the tape but then there she was, Sharon Fowler fielding questions live and red-hot in a high-collared safari shirt buttoned low and tucked into a simple, chino skirt. Tall and athletic and confident.

The feed alternated live give-and-take with footage already compiled in the aftermath of the hijack. Sharon in safari at the studio. Sharon in a white, clinging top before a backdrop of smoke and body bags.

Barrett remembered the stretch of Sharon's back, that bowl of belly, breasts taut. Her commentary was half-drowned in a din of billiards and jukebox but nobody seemed to care. They weren't gathered to listen, these natives of Pepperfish Keys. They just wanted to look.

"Damn woman could coax a maggot off a gut wagon," Harvey declared to wide approval.

Sharon arrived at the bar a little after nine and every man in sight converged to cop a hug or flirt. Locals never before impressed by their local newscaster now begged autographs on receipts fished from worn wallets or on the backs of beer coasters.

Ms. Fowler responded to locals and out-of-towners with the practiced modesty of celebrity. As though she were somebody used to getting attention. Took a while for her to reach the bar.

"Bear. Sorry."

"It's your night, Sharon. Congratulations."

She was tall in a denim jacket. Had her hair pulled back off her face. A smidgeon of midriff showing. Jeans cut below the navel.

"You saw the broadcast?" she asked.

"Harvey taped it. You looked great."

She straddled a barstool beside him.

"Wanted you to know I'm sorry about Midge Holloway, Bear. I really am."

"Thank you. Me, too."

"But you'll find the bastard did it."

"Oh, I know the bastard who did it. He was in here a few minutes ago. With his honey."

"Eddy was here?"

"In the flesh."

"You on anything besides coffee, Bear?"

"Not actively, but I'm considering it."

"Harvey?" she called over to the barkeep. "Got any bourbon?"

"Got somethin' close."

Barrett warmed his mouth with a swig of Folgers.

"So how long's it going to be before you're off to New York?"

She actually blushed.

"I've got a ways to go yet."

"You've got 'a ways'. I'm back to square one."

"Maybe this'll help."

She reached into her denim top, pulled out a rumpled envelope.

"What's that?"

"Five thousand dollars." She dropped the bundle on the table. "Five thousand cash from Eddy DeLeon—to me."

Suddenly, everything in the bar acquired a sharper focus.

"Five thousand dollars to you, okay. For what?"

"Research, ostensibly. I should mention that Eddy made it pretty clear this was an assignment I could not refuse."

"And what was the assignment?"

"To find his girlfriend's killer."

"Are we talking about Beth Ann?"

"We are."

"*He* killed her."

"He gave me five grand to prove he didn't."

Harvey brought over Sharon's drink. A shot of bourbon dark as resin in a plain glass. Barrett waited for Harvey to move on before he gathered Sharon's envelope. He slipped a single bill free of its brothers. Inspected it.

A thousand dollar bill. Recent issue. Very hard to counterfeit. He slipped the currency back into the envelope.

"When exactly did you receive these bills?"

"Day or two before you arrested Eddy. He picked me up at the station, kidnapped me, really, brought me out to some warehouse and predicted you'd be arresting him for murder. Told me he was innocent and gave me this money. Forced it on me, actually."

"Was that what prompted you to see Roland and me in Live Oak? Christ, Sharon, was *Eddy* your source?"

"I can't give up a source," she demurred. "But I will say I really did believe that Eddy DeLeon was not Beth Ann's killer."

"Something change your mind?"

"I'm not sure. But I'm always bothered by coincidence and it does seem like too many people with connections to Eddy wind up with their throats slit. And then this business with the evidence van? Awfully convenient."

"You think Eddy ambushed the van?"

"He's certainly capable. But I'm not interested in that story. Not primarily, anyway."

"Why in God's name not?"

"Field is crowded for one thing; there must be a dozen reporters following the crumbs. But more importantly there's a trail involving the van that goes farther than Highway 19. A lot farther."

"How far?"

"All the way to Pepperfish Keys. All the way, in fact, to Senator Baxter Stanton."

"Ohhhh shit."

"Bear, just hear me out. You need to nail a killer, I need a story big enough to leapfrog a thousand other pretty faces who wanna be a network anchor, and there's a way we can both get what we want."

"All right, let's hear it."

"Until now, I've assumed the senator's story was played out. There is nothing less interesting, after all, than an uncorrupt politician. But I'm beginning to think Baxter Stanton is crooked as a blacksnake."

"I went snake hunting this summer, Sharon. Didn't work out."

"But what if Taylor Calhoun's murder and Beth Ann's involves the senator's business?"

"I can't touch Baxter Stanton," Barrett replied tiredly. "As you damn well know, I'm prevented by court order from investigating anything related to his finances or his campaign. The fruits of that tree are forbidden."

"How about movies? Are movies off-limits?"

Barrett paused over his coffee.

"Who's been talking to you about movies?"

She reached again inside her denim jacket to pull out the type of plastic case familiar to anyone at Blockbuster.

"*Scarlet Moon.* Starring Randall Damone."

"Didn't know it was out on disk, yet."

"It's not even in the theater yet."

She placed the DVD on the bar.

"In fact, the film doesn't premier till sometime next month."

"Where'd you get this, Sharon?"

"At Mama's."

She had his attention and she knew it.

"Funny what you can pick up at a brothel," she smiled. "I was out there doing a story on AIDS, at the time. Risky sex, drug use. That kind of thing. This was weeks before Beth Ann's murder. Taylor Calhoun was working behind the bar. Sort of fell over himself when I sauntered in. I think he was a little starstruck."

"Without doubt."

"Poor Taylor. He was very solicitous. Brought me a beer. Told me everything I didn't want to know about Mama and her whores. The girls wouldn't talk to me at all, though. Mama's got that bunch on a tight leash. Anyway, I was about to decide

I'd drilled a dry hole when Taylor told me to wait up. Said he had something for me. So he brings out this DVD, all packaged and shrinkwrapped and everything. Great artwork, by the way. But when I opened it the little bastard almost shit himself—"

She popped it open. Barrett frowned.

"Where's the DVD?"

"There was no DVD. Poor Taylor, here he thought he was giving me an advance copy of Randall Damone's latest movie and it was a dummy. A plastic case and the jacket to go with it and nothing else. It just seemed like such an odd thing for Taylor to have at all. I figured he stole it."

"Didn't you ask?"

"Sure, and Taylor had a fit. Said he should never have let me see it; begged me to give it back. I left him a twenty and told him not to worry."

She tapped the case's transparent shell.

"Do you have any idea how much money you can make pirating feature films? Worldwide release? Big star? Enough money to buy airplanes. To build mansions. More than enough to finance a campaign for the U.S. Senate."

Barrett inspected the jacket. Randall Damone posing with his latest starlet in exquisite detail beneath a blood-red moon.

"Taylor told me Eddy was involved with the movies," he said finally. "I laughed it off."

"I would have, too. In fact, I did. After all, what can you make of a DVD case with no DVD? I told myself the old coot probably got somebody to download the artwork off the Internet. Faked a jacket, just to impress me. But then ya'll found Taylor hogged down to his parts in the flatwoods and I began to think maybe he really was onto something. Maybe this artwork and this hunk of plastic leads to a bank account with a senator's name on it."

"I can't look at Stanton's books."

"But there's nothing says you can't look at Eddy's books, is there? And isn't Eddy still the prime suspect for Beth Ann's murder? But the weakest link in your case has always been motive. Why would Eddy kill Senator Stanton's daughter? Well, maybe she found out something she shouldn't have. Could it have anything to do with pirating films? Or financing a political campaign with dirty money? I don't pretend to know where all the dots are, Bear, much less how they connect, but if you put me on your team I can damn sure find out."

Barrett helped himself to some of Sharon's bourbon.

"Isn't there something in Journalism 101 about a reporter working undercover for cops?"

"Probably."

"And what would the suits at ABC say if they found out?"

"They won't find out, Bear, unless you tell them. See, I don't give up my sources, not even if they're the scum of the earth."

She took back her amber glass.

"So I guess the real question is: Will you?"

15.

Midge Holloway was cremated in accordance with a will entrusted to Captain Henry Altmiller. Barrett Raines drove ninety miles to the memorial service in Tallahassee. The crematorium seemed incongruous in this bible-belt region, a courtyard of polished marble and running fountains cubbyholed with urns and casks and ashes. The mourners gathered in that yard of death were a grim and small convention. Apart from an aunt institutionalized in Orlando, Midge had no surviving family. The FDLE was her home, her hearth.

Captain Altmiller had assigned Barrett to deliver Dr. Holloway's eulogy.

"She was your friend," Altmiller said.

And so Barrett found himself shuffling a pitiful set of notes jotted down practically at random before a gathering of perhaps a dozen men and one or two women seated stiffly on folding chairs beneath the spreading arms of a water oak.

"Midge would be glad to be remembered by those who knew

her firsthand," Barrett began his hastily scrawled remarks. "Her work, certainly, was meaningful. It will outlast us all. . . ."

Pretty soon it was done. Midge Holloway's life and passion and death adumbrated in less than ten minutes. Captain Altmiller approached Barrett before they were out of hallowed ground.

"Bad day for you, Agent. My condolences."

"Yes, sir. Thank you, sir."

Altmiller smoothed the dark tie inside his gray, wool suit.

"I understand you have a new informant? Somebody close to Eddy DeLeon?"

"Yes, sir."

"Willing to go undercover? Wear a wire?"

"Yes, sir."

"I suppose you'll give me a name."

"If you give us permission for the operation, yes, sir. Of course."

"How's Roland Reed feel about this idea?"

"We're being honest, he likes it too much."

A frown from his captain.

"Okay. See you back at the farm."

The headquarters for the Florida Department of Law Enforcement rises in a polygon of brick and glass on what used to be a cow pasture not far down the road from an insane asylum. Local joke in Tallahassee is that crazy people run both institutions. The conference room reserved for the meeting at the FDLE's monolithic complex looked inward to a quadrangle dominated by a spreading live oak overrun with squirrels. Captain Altmiller sometimes fed the squirrels. But not today. Everyone stood when the FDLE's ranking officer entered the room.

"Seats, gentlemen."

Captain Altmiller bought his suits off the rack, drove a pickup, and got his hair cut military style, tapered, not blocked, at a candypole barbershop in Frenchtown. He was lifelong friends with the governor and Bobby Bowden and absolutely incorruptible. And unforgiving. It was not going to be easy to get Altmiller's approval for another undercover operation, Barrett had no illusions about that. Especially an operation hinging on the loyalty of a TV reporter.

Barrett's boss pulled out a ballpoint pen and legal pad and nodded to a stenographer.

"Everything we say here will be in transcript. No other recordings or records are authorized. Except my own, of course. We clear on that? All right, gentlemen, make your pitch."

Roland Reed led off. "As you know, sir, Eddy DeLeon is now a suspect for five homicides including Beth Ann Stanton's. Problem is, we don't have evidence to make any of those cases. But we do believe we can nail Mr. DeLeon for statutes related to interstate commerce."

"Better not be the kind of commerce that puts this department back into headlines."

"Judge Boatwright said hands-off Senator Stanton and we will conform to that order." Barrett covered his own ass with that opening remark. "I want to state for the record that the informer we are asking permission to recruit will be targeted at Eddy DeLeon, and Eddy alone."

"You on board with that, Mr. Reed?"

"We're after DeLeon," Reed replied flatly. "I have already approached Judge Dickens with requests for warrants and taps. You might recall that Judge Dickens got passed over for Circuit by Judge Boatwright."

"Nice end-around." Altmiller jotted a note. "So, what's the plan? We follow Eddy?"

"We follow the money," Barrett qualified his response. "Specifically we have obtained through our informant a piece of physical evidence giving us probable cause to believe that Eddy is selling or attempting to sell unlicensed copies of feature films."

"Films? You mean movies?"

"Yes, sir. First-release DVDs, probably to a global market."

"Could be millions of dollars in transactions," Roland Reed

declared. "You give us the green light and I will convict Eddy on federal and state charges that will keep him in jail till his dick rots off."

Altmiller frowned.

"Poor substitute for a conviction of murder. Multiple murders."

"It is, Captain," Barrett agreed. "But it's a lot better than what we have at present which, with the loss of our physical evidence, is nothing at all."

"And who knows?" Reed chiming in once again. "If we can nail Eddy for pirating films, some of his crew are bound to wind up in the same net. I'll be dangling jail time in their faces. Situation like that, somebody's going to talk about the evidence van, or Taylor Calhoun. Maybe even Beth Ann. If they do, I'll be glad to cop a plea."

"Is there any circumstance where you would not cop a plea, Roland?"

"I'd cut a deal with the Devil if it strapped Eddy DeLeon to a gurney."

Captain Altmiller turned in his chair to regard the play of squirrels on the long boughs outside.

"Whoever you put next to Eddy DeLeon is going to be in harm's way," Altmiller said, finally. "You saw what happened to Taylor Calhoun."

"Yes, sir, I saw."

"Of course you did. All right, then."

Henry Altmiller pulled himself erect at the head of the table.

"So who have we got volunteering to get next to this son of a bitch? Who's got the balls?"

Barrett took Roland's plated pen from his hand, block-printed a name on the prosecutor's yellow pad.

Displayed it to his captain.

Altmiller leaning over. Scanning the name. Leaning back.

"Well, I'll be damned."

16.

Eddy DeLeon installed himself and his companion before a flat-screen TV and a bottle of Johnny Walker in the seaside condominium that was his official residence on Pepper-fish Keys.

"Sonny Corleone," Eddy was explaining the scene unfolding by DVD. "He's like a loose cannon. So they draw him out, see. They get his brother-in-law to beat Sonny's sister, they know is gonna make him crazy. They know he's gonna come out, man!"

A highly priced architect from Atlanta had been engaged to design DeLeon's Keyside residence, which Eddy soon discovered was no guarantee of practicality or function. The air-conditioning ran either too hot or too cold. The sliding doors allowing access to the condo's metal balcony jammed at any opportunity. Thank God the plumbing was reliable. And Eddy liked the fact that his home turned heads. Boaters inevitably slowed as they tooled below DeLeon's home in their Pathfinders or Chris-Crafts, craning necks from the shifting decks of those pleasurecraft to view his unusual home.

The dwelling swelled above the water like a prop from some Star Trek episode, a squashed egg of cement stilted on thick pillars rising above a skirt of saw grass to shelter the garage and boathouse below. A band of tinted windows divided twin domes into hemispheres from which a balcony protruding over the water to offer a splendid view only occasionally obscured by cat-feet fog.

There was no fog this evening, Sharon Fowler noted as she followed Eddy's loud-shirted driver up the spiral staircase rising from the garage to the shell of Eddy's condominium. She had decided on an evening dress for the occasion. A summer dress, even with the chill, sheer, cut low between her breasts. Dressed as if to turn heads at a cocktail party.

She emerged unacknowledged into the condo's hemispheric parlor to find DeLeon curled on a mama-san with some punker signatured in tattoos.

"Get you a drink?" Crease offered with no hint of hospitality.
"Bourbon'd do."

Crease strolled over to a mahogany bar that looked out to the Keys and water beyond. The sun was setting scarlet into that steaming bowl, its waning light pouring through Sharon's flimsy dress like a flashlight through a butterfly's wings.

Sharon crossed still unremarked to the open balcony looking over Pepperfish Keys. A pair of skiers jumped wakes just offshore. A catamaran rocked as the Mako charged past, spraying water onto the pier of Eddy's boathouse. She could see pelicans making a low pass over the warm waters, the predators active and alert, the prey somnolent, vulnerable. A bill dipped suddenly and next thing you knew a mullet flashed silver in a flying pouch.

Sharon wondered briefly how that omen was to be interpreted.

A pair of ice cubes chattered for attention like dice in a gambler's cup.

"How much?" Crease inquired from the bar.

"A finger, maybe two." She stepped back inside and Eddy smiled as Sonny Corleone was machine-gunned to death.

"How you been?"

This from Eddy, over his shoulder, as if he had just noticed her arrival.

"Busy," Sharon replied.

He took a long look, which she encouraged.

"Come from a party?" he smirked.

"Haven't I found one?"

"Always a possibility. Crease. Seat our guest."

Crease pulled over a zebra-striped chair beside his boss's bamboo accommodation. Eddy leaning far over to plop his drink on a jade vase inverted for the purpose.

"What you got for me?" He was suddenly all business.

"You may have a problem, Eddy." She suppressed a shiver.

"Problem for me?" DeLeon's eyes were cold over a smile that exposed those goddamned teeth. "What the hell kind of problem?"

"You want your girl hearing this, Eddy?"

He darkened then, as if Sharon had violated some unspoken protocol. But then—

"Get downstairs, baby."

"Shit, Eddy, I wanta see the movie!"

He grabbed her spike of hair. Pulled.

"Eddy!"

"Downstairs, *puta*. And lock the doors."

"This is bullshit, Eddy."

"Or maybe I just throw you off the roof."

"This is real bullshit."

Crease herded her downstairs. Eddy waved a remote at the DVD player. The screen surrendered with a "ping."

"Okay." DeLeon seemed finally engaged. "So what the hell have they got on me, now?"

"Roland Reed is still convinced you're in bed with Senator Stanton," Sharon began.

"Thass old news, senorita. You got anything fresh?"

"Barrett Raines is talking to Baxter Stanton. Two meetings that I know of."

"Let him talk. Whass he gonna say?"

"Well, he's pretty well convinced the senator that you killed his daughter. And I get the impression Stanton is willing to do just about anything to make you burn for it."

A scowl tugged at Eddy's habitual smirk. Crease reentered the room and things got very, very still. Sharon could hear blood surge into her ears with every loud thud of her heart. Barrett had warned her to expect that rush, that sudden surge of adrenaline and fear.

Just remember we're backing you up, Barrett had assured her. We'll have people watching. We can be there in no time.

How much time was no time?

"Senator Stanton called the head of the FDLE two days after you were released from jail," she plunged ahead with her prepared script. "He talked to Henry Altmiller, you've heard of Altmiller?"

"He's a suit."

"He's the head of the Florida Department of Law Enforcement. And he's getting calls from Baxter Stanton."

"How you know?"

"It was at Midge Holloway's funeral. The service was over. I got to Altmiller by his car, but before I can get him on-camera he gets a call on his cell. It was from Senator Stanton. Altmiller puts some distance between himself and me, obviously. But the way he reacted I got the impression something new was up."

"What you mean?"

"Well, after the call was concluded, Altmiller gave Bear Raines a thumbs-up. Then I heard him say, 'This gives us a new angle.' "

"Angle? What angle?"

"Something about 'movies'."

"Movies?"

"Or moviemaking. Something along those lines I think."

"I don't give a *fuck* what you *think*!"

Eddy jerked his upturned vase off the wall and hurled it. Shards of jade exploded like shrapnel off the concrete wall. Sharon flinched with a fresh knick next to the scar still healing on her thigh.

"I din' pay you to *think,* bitch. I pay you to *know*!"

"Okay, Eddy," she found her voice. "Okay. Sure."

He withered Crease with a torrent of vituperation. The driver weathering that storm, eyes averted, hands filled with a rag at the bar.

Sharon fighting an urge to retreat.

"Eddy? Eddy! I'm working on Barrett. I am! In fact, I had some drinks with him the same night you were at Harvey's. Not long after you left, in fact."

"After me?"

"You rattled Bear's cage, Eddy. No doubt about it. And I tried to pump him for more information, I did. But I burned Bear badly over the summer; he's not going to open up all at once."

"Motherfucker." That curse rendered almost contemplatively. And then—

"Sharon, you got to find out what he knows about my business, you hear? What's this crap about movies? Whass it got to do with Beth Ann? And *anything* about me and Baxter Stanton! They not suppose to be able to go there. The judge made them give it up!"

"I'll find out what I can."

"Not a matter of 'can', baby. You *will* do, I don' care if you have to follow Raines around like you was his whore. Sleep with him, you have to. Blow his dick, I don' care. I got to know what shit he's running!"

"I understand what you need," she affirmed—

Waiting, just a moment, to sink that hook.

"—but, Eddy, I've got to have a place to start."

" 'Place to start'? Whatchu mean, 'place'?"

Eddy pulling his plated clippers from his pocket. *Snick,* a sliver of fingernail dropping where, Sharon realized, the vase would normally serve as receptacle.

"Eddy, I can't find out what Barrett Raines knows about your connections with Senator Stanton until I know whether you actually have any, or some idea what your business *is*."

"The hell you mean? You a reporter, aren't you?"

"And how do you think reporters get information? Say, Eddy? How do I find out what's going down?"

"Your fucking job, you tell me."

"Here's Rule One: You don't ask a question unless you already know a good damn piece of the answer."

"You already know? Bullshit."

She strolled over as casually as she could. Tall in her sheer gown. Looking down from her height. Just a kiss from the fresh wound visible at her thigh. A talisman of her source's most recent explosion.

"You paying for a kissass, Eddy? Or do you want somebody'll talk to you straight?"

"Convince me."

"Fair enough. Let's make something up. Say, I go to a guy with the FDLE. I catch him at a bar. Warm him up, show sympathy."

"Buy the man a drink," Eddy supplied.

"There you go," Sharon smiled encouragement. "And then I'll say something like, 'I'm running down a story on Sally Shithouse, you know Sally?' "

Eddy retrieved his drink. "He says, 'Maybe. Why?' "

"Very good," Sharon nodded. "And then I say, 'Sally's got a beauty parlor burned to the ground last night. I heard maybe Eddy DeLeon had a piece of the business.' 'I can't confirm that for you, Sharon,' the guy'll say. And then I'll say, 'Of course not, but if DeLeon does have an interest in Sally Shithouse's Salon, and if it was insured for a million bucks, then can you tell me if maybe Eddy's a suspect for arson?' "

Eddy smiled.

"A million bucks. Arson? Could definitely be."

"There, you see?" She settled to the floor, Indian fashion, inviting him to look. "Point of the story is, if I'm going to get anything out the cop I have to already know something about Sally Shithouse and something about Eddy DeLeon. Then I have something to trade."

"Like cards—"

Eddy sucked his ice.

"You can't play 'em if you don' have 'em."

"Precisely." Sharon leaned in closer. "So give me a Sally. Give me a shithouse. I'll grease Bear Raines. Slip it in. He'll never know."

Eddy rose from the plush cushion of the mama-san, palming his plated clippers.

"You hear a lot, don' you, Sharon? For a smalltown reporter?"

"I'm just good at listening."

"You listen, yes, you do. Stand up."

He stood with her, his hands rising to cup her breasts, grazing her nipples briefly, deliberately, traveling then in a rough frisk beneath her arms, down her torso, between her thighs.

"She's clean," Crease grumbled. "I already checked. Hell, you can see right through."

"Never hurts to be sure," Eddy smiling. "Especially with a body like this."

"If you're going to treat me like a whore, Eddy," Sharon withdrew as coldly as she could manage, "you might as well pay me another five thousand."

"You listen good, Sharon, but you also talk, don't you, senorita? You are talking to me tonight. No?"

"Not like you gave me a choice."

She manufactured some heat for that objection.

"Thass so." He bobbed his head. "That is true. Nevertheless, sweetheart, before we take this road together, you need to understand that if anything discussed between you and me, any little thing, leaks out—I'm not gonna ask you how it happened."

"I understand." Sharon hated the catch in her voice.

"No. You don'." Eddy shook his head. "See, if you leak any vinegar from Eddy DeLeon, I slice your fingers off for you a

216

quarter inch at a time. *Comprende?* And that's before I start on the good parts."

"There's no need for threats, Eddy," she replied huskily. "We know each other better than that."

He strolled over to the bar. Considered.

"Okay." He glanced at the hands of his Philip Patek as if extending an appointment.

"So how much you know about movies?"

A half hour later Sharon was edging down Eddy's stairs on legs of jello. It was stifling outside, and warming. An entering fog had settled like a cloud. She could barely see her car even though it was just outside Eddy's gate.

Crease keyed in the four digits releasing the gate; two dolphins carved from sheet metal swung open and Sharon practically lunged through the breach, the invading fog clinging to her sheer gown in silent, suffocating droplets.

"Drive careful," Crease advised and she fought an urge to laugh hysterically. Then came a desperate, humiliating urge to piss.

Slow down, she told herself. Just slow down.

She fumbled her key into the roadster's lock and dropped inside. She keyed the ignition, switched the a/c wide open and a blizzard blew across her dampened gown to ice the sweat beneath.

Sharon lurched her nimble car onto SeaSide Drive shaking like an epileptic. The Rubicon was crossed, but she still couldn't believe she'd gotten away clean. Got away clean.

She wanted to scream, to shout.

Put on the radio, girlfriend! Rock out!

That's when a pair of headlights popped into her rearview mirror. Sharon now breathing shallow and quick. Slow down! Slow it down!

She knew that the Old Town Bridge connected with the county road leading inland. She crossed that other Rubicon and checked her rearview. Still the lights followed. She turned hard south and the headlights behind swept to follow. The blacktop ran behind her like a rip of tar into a well of black ink. The vehicle behind accelerated, lights blinking from highs to dims. Sharon braked hard and slid off the blacktop onto the road's soft shoulder.

Heart hammering in her chest, her long throat.

A panel van skidded to a stop alongside her BMW. The door slid back. Barrett Raines emerged big as a boulder to lean in at her window.

"You did good."

A man and woman whom Sharon had only recently met piled out with weapons drawn to scan the road.

"We need you in the van, please, Ms. Fowler."

An unfamiliar accent beckoning.

Barrett pulled Sharon from her car like a sack of groceries. Another agent anonymous in a Florida State T-shirt slipped in behind the wheel of her BMW.

"Please." Sharon clamped her hand like a vice around Barrett's arm. "Can you find me a restroom?"

The van's toilet was not elegant, but it was welcome. Too bad there wasn't space for a changing room.

"Hold still." The veteran agent retrieving the mike secreted in Sharon's panties was trying hard to provide a modicum of privacy.

"They frisked her *twice*." That accent again, voicing concern to Barrett Raines.

"Take it easy, Cricket."

"Cricket" Bonet was a head taller than Barrett Raines. They had been partners, back in the day, Terese explained when Sharon was introduced to her fair-skinned shadow.

"Cricket Bonet and Bear Raines, yes, ma'am. Had themselves a reputation."

There were other players supporting Sharon's undercover

effort who were nearly entirely anonymous, agents from the feds, deputies from the Sheriff's Department, the Highway Patrol, a SWAT team from Orlando.

A command post for the operation was set up in a warehouse leased by the county. It was a good building, excellent for concealing equipment and personnel. Was a good location as well, not too far from SeaSide Drive but off the hard road and sheltered by a thick stand of slash pine. Signage advertising the "Future Site Of Marion Pest Control" accounted for the comings and goings of various traffic. The random passerby would see county vehicles parked beside panel vans decaled for pest control.

Nothing was more common than roaches.

"Ouch," Sharon sucked in briefly as the matron agent tugged an antenna slender as hair that linked to a transmitter smaller than a matchbook.

"Sorry," Terese apologized.

Terese Banton. Twelve years on the job. Brown hair, not well kept. Big-boned. Unremarkable. She might have sold sweaters at Sears.

"I wanted Terese because she's steady and because she's worn a wire herself," Barrett told Sharon. "The device you'll have is pretty exotic. Not a lot of range, but very small."

"Where'll you put it?" Sharon had asked.

Terese smiled.

"Where the sun don't shine, honey."

Terese would handle everything related to the wire, fortunately.

"There'll be a team of sharpshooters positioned outside the condo," Barrett went on. "You won't see them, but believe me, they'll see you."

Sharon found it hard to believe that anyone could get to Eddy inside his concrete egg, but Cricket assured her that his shooters would have a bead on Eddy's head.

Fog or no fog.

"But I don't want to minimize the risk," Barrett cautioned.

"It's going to be harder to protect you in Pepperfish Keys than it would be in Miami or Tallahassee."

Rural areas did not loan themselves easily to the kind of stings taken for granted in urban settings, Sharon learned. There was no office building or residence or rooftop offering lines of fire into DeLeon's condo. There was no delivery service or maintenance crew to plant surveillance devices and no crib offering quick access to the condo's interior.

There was also no surrounding forest or undergrowth within a hundred yards of Eddy's condominium. Nothing higher than a palmetto behind which to hide. And any vehicle loitering along SeaSide Drive would become immediately suspicious.

The solution?

Cricket put his team on the water. A variety of vessels were to be used. The ski boat Sharon had seen offered cover for Cricket's team, and the idling catamaran. An assault team had their weapons and gear stowed in the bow of the Mako that fishtailed past Eddy's boathouse.

The biggest worry, of course, was that DeLeon would discover the tiny transmitter stuck like a Tampax in Sharon's crotch. Cricket and his team would need to get in quickly in that event, more quickly than a waterborne assault would allow.

The DEA contributed agents to cover that scenario; two extraction teams huddled like mallards in the saw grass that verged onto Eddy's back door, their shaped charges ready to blow his fence. And two teams of snipers roosted like egrets in the limbs of cypress trees, their Belgian rifles steadied forty vertical feet with a perfect line of sight through the generous windows of Eddy's balcony.

"We'll have your houseboat covered, too," Barrett assured her, the Highway Patrol and the marine arm of Florida's Fish and Wildlife Conservation Commission contributing both undercover and uniformed surveillance of Sharon's houseboat.

And finally Sharon would have at least one mobile unit from the FDLE following her day and night, older-model pickups mixing with rentals and SUVs that might belong to any visiting fisherman or tourist.

"You won't have any privacy," Barrett warned.

"How about local cops? Sheriff Rawlings? Does he know what's going on?"

"Absolutely," Barrett confirmed. "And Smoot will have his people looking after you, too. But, Sharon, when it comes to your personal security, Agent Bonet is the MFWIC."

"Muff-Wick?" Sharon had been confused.

"Mother-Fucker-What's-In-Charge," Cricket supplied with a wink.

Sharon had rehearsed for her clandestine role every hour she wasn't at the station. And even now, even after having survived her first encounter in DeLeon's condominium, she felt a pit in her stomach.

"Last one, honey," Terese promised and snatched.

Sharon shivered as if in a meat locker.

"I think I'm gonna be sick," she announced.

"That's natural," Terese clucked. "Natural as can be."

"We can call this off." Barrett sitting on his heels before her. "It's not too late."

"How many more times will I have to wear a wire?"

"I don't know," Barrett shook his head. "I'm sure you noticed Eddy stayed away from specifics. He talked in general terms about how movies were pirated, how you might get an original DVD to copy. 'Possible' sources."

"He said he was partnered with Baxter Stanton, didn't he?"

"But partnered in what?" Bear shook his boulder head. "Eddy's slick. Everything he told you was phrased in ways either too general or too hypothetical to be useful: How somebody *could* steal a digitized linear tape. How you *might* contact buyers to distribute a pirated copy. How a partner *might* get a cut of profits in return for laundering Eddy's cash.

"He gave no names, no dates, no specific amounts of money. The wire you got tonight won't stand up by itself, Sharon. We'll need more."

"I'll get more."

Her hands now steady.

"I know how to play him, now. One way or the other, I'll get him talking. And when he does I'll have it on tape."

"Lady's got balls," Cricket declared and Barrett smiled.

"But right now, you're going to get some rest, okay? Go home, Sharon. Unwind."

Cricket Bonet had Fowler back in her tony houseboat by ten, but it was a quarter to eleven before Bear pulled up to his own modest home. Bear told Laura Anne he'd be late but did not expect her to wait up. Laura Anne had not waited up for him in a while. So Raines was a little surprised to see a long arm reach up to pull the chain on the switch of the light inside his carport.

The naked bulb swaying like a censer to spill cones of light and shadow onto the hood of his Malibu. And there was Laura Anne, waiting, her hair still damp from washing, full and rich and folded like a robe over the swell of her breasts.

"Baby, you all right?"

She wore a simple, white cotton dress. Narrow straps over the shoulders. Cinched just a little at her firm and narrow waist. Hips wide below her torso.

"I left you a message."

Heaving out of the car he saw a pitcher of iced tea on the steps leading into the kitchen. A fruit bowl filled with ice.

Two glasses.

"What's this?"

"I went to Tallahassee today."

She settled on the steps beneath the yellow light. Lemon light on chocolate skin. He plopped alongside.

"Tallahassee? I didn't see you."

"Not Midge's funeral," she shook her head. "I should have been there. For you as much as for her. No, I went to see Dr. Barnes."

Barrett accepted the glass of tea that she gave him.

Scooping ice from the bowl.

"I saw Doctor Barnes and I told her I was tired of being angry," Laura Anne declared. "I told her I wanted to want you again. To laugh when I see my boys."

She shook her head.

"I've hit the wall, Bear."

He reached for her hand. She let him take it.

"And I just finally had to admit I can't get through this on my own. I just can't."

"But you don't have to, baby!"

He pulled her head to his chest. Her hair. That smell of kitchens and boisterous children, of lemon oil and soap and salt and cayenne pepper.

"You've got me." Barrett crushed her in his arms. "You've got the boys. And now you've got Doc Barnes."

"Yes." Her cheeks were wet. "HMO's covering it, too. Isn't that nice?"

He held her a moment.

"Drink your tea," she commanded.

"Yes, ma'am."

"It's sun tea. I made it special."

"Thank you."

"I'm sorry I wasn't with you at Midge's funeral."

"When's Taylor's funeral? We could go together."

"Oh, Bear, there won't be a funeral for Taylor."

"What?"

"County's already buried him."

"Didn't his family claim him?"

She shook her head. "They didn't want anything to do with him."

"That's not right. He should have had somebody. They could have told me."

"I know. I know."

She offered his hand. He took it.

"I'm glad you're getting help, Laura Anne. I want you back. I need you back the way you were. The way we were."

She raised her head from his chest and kissed him.

It had been a long time since they had kissed like that. Warm and slow.

"The ice!" she said after a while.

"Mmhmm?

"It's gonna melt."

"You got that right."

The agents assigned to surveil Sharon's houseboat were discreet. Peeping Toms were not tolerated at the FDLE. The team kept a tight perimeter; they did not go inside their subject's residence. Once a day, usually in the evening, Cricket Bonet walked through the boat's interior before passing the baton for Sharon's protection to agents who mixed seamlessly with the locals and weekenders tying off at Harvey's Marina.

Even Dew Drop did not notice anything out of the ordinary, not at first, and Dewey could be a very observant man. Also a patient man. For example, he'd waited a whole month to pass after Sharon's arrival before arranging to place his modest houseboat in the slip next to hers. He didn't go over right away. He didn't give in to the rash impulse that would have called attention.

Sharon on the other hand invited attention. Dew Drop was running a lead to a new antenna on the roof of his boat one day when he got a view of his boss sweating through her floor exercises. Sometimes after a particularly bitchy day, Dewey would imagine things he could do as she was racked over her medieval ball.

He saw her gutting mullet, once. Off the stern of her houseboat. She had a tank top over a bikini bottom that day. Blood covered her arms and splattered up the washboard belly. Ran down her legs like a period out of control. It was great stuff, but then she retreated inside stripping on the way and Dewey was left frustrated.

It wasn't long afterward that he began to assemble the equipment he would need, the cameras, the video, the software. He would have rules, of course. He would not fake a product, no way. He wanted the real thing, cinema verité. But of course he wanted real money, too. Any plain Jane housewife or anonymous teenager could strip on the Net or jerk off and rake in decent bucks. If people paid for that crap surely they'd jump to see the unguarded moments in a celebrity's life.

Of course, he'd have to delay distribution until Sharon *was* a celebrity. Timing was everything. He'd limit the product, at first. Just a few copies to select customers. Just enough to get the rumors started. He'd wait until Sharon actually turned on that fake smile for some network camera before he put everything on the Web. Talk about sweet. You scheme and scrape and run over everybody around you getting to the desk at ABC and next thing you know your colleagues are laughing behind their desktops as you take a shit or wash your crotch. Not to mention the occasional tourist or cop.

People *paying* to see!

She'd be fired, of course. There would be the usual apologies from network executives, the usual twitter in *The Wall Street Journal* and *Variety,* but no network could afford to have its anchor the object of such voyeurism. They would have to let her go.

Talk about added value.

But for his plan to work Dewey needed a quantity of high-quality material that could not be gained from the roof of his houseboat. He had to get close to his subject.

Fortunately, Sharon was a mooch. She'd be a raving, fucking bitch at work and then come over next day showing off those legs and ass and say, "Dew Drop, can you help me a minute?" He spent a whole Saturday setting up her satellite TV. Her computer. Bitch couldn't even program her own DVD player. But these chores were godsent, a perfect reconnoiter to cover the serious work ahead, and thank God for fish.

The bitch loved to take her open-face rod and reel and head out over the water. She'd be gone for hours at a time, sometimes days. Took a whole week on one occasion to fish off Tampa or

Boca Raton or some damn place. Been nice to have had a camera on *that* boat. A low angle shot of Sharon fighting four hundred pounds of marlin or grouper. Sharon in a sweat-drenched top and cutoffs. Those fast-twitch arms and legs and back stretched to their tensile limit.

Some great footage missed there.

Of course it was one thing to put a camera inside the houseboat and quite another to get footage *out*. As a boy Dewey used to love the Daytona 500, especially those terrific shots over the shoulder, some driver fighting to keep his stock car off the wall. The monitors making those shots possible were basically TV cameras that broadcast a narrow signal to receivers outside.

The equipment secreted inside Sharon's boat was entirely digital and small. Very small. Dewey planted four cameras, the largest of which looked through a lens about the diameter of a tube of lipstick. All four cameras transmitted simultaneously. A Wavecom receiver in Dewey's own bedroom routed the RF to a quad splitter that fed all four signals to his Sony screen. The gear was easy to buy. Dewey got his pinhole cams from a link off I-SPY. The receiver and splitter came from a catalog out of Super Circuits. He mounted a camera above her bed, in her shower. The den's camera was wide-angled and looked down on her inflatable ball. The deck's monitor was easiest to install. He had views of Sharon's living room and john, her bedroom, the sternward deck. Sharon loved to suntan in what she imagined was privacy. Very nice pictures. High resolution.

He loved playing director, switching from one camera to the next as he tracked Sharon from room to room. He assumed initially that the shower would produce the sexiest footage, but it was the den where Sharon really let her hair down. She looked great stretched over that ball. Sweating. Screwing, sometimes. Masturbating. She had some nice toys in that hardwood parlor.

Batteries included.

Not many boyfriends though one night she did bring somebody home. Gave some tourist a ride on her ball. Balled him, you might say. She liked porno tapes; that shouldn't have surprised him. But the biggest surprise for Dewey came when in the middle of that godawful storm he sees Sharon Fowler opening her door for Barrett fucking Raines.

There's Bear dripping water like a field hand. Sharon with all that white, firm skin checking him out. Dewey saw Oscars coming out of that encounter. Bear and Sharon! You're talking Triple X Sex!

But nothing happened! Not a goddamn thing. A real prick-tease, those two turned out to be. Totally. A dud in black & white. 'Course, you could play with the editing and come up with something. If you wanted to. If you needed to.

Dewey had to remind himself of his principles. He wasn't a simple voyeur, he was not! His aim was much more ambitious than porno and he wasn't making fantasy. The idea was to capture his subject au naturel. Doctoring the pixels just wouldn't be *real*.

But then didn't any view of reality require interpretation? Wasn't that where Art came in? Wasn't he already juggling Reality? If a particular view or angle of the camera got stale, he'd just sneak over and move it. He'd experiment with different apertures, different exposures. And of course the material had to be organized, edited.

Sometimes he just wanted to splash it raw all over the Net. Just to see the fallout! But Dewey restrained himself. He wanted Sharon to be seen on national TV, first. Hell, he wanted the woman to be known worldwide so that when she wiped her ass or sucked the occasional dick *everybody* would know who she was. Was that revenge or what?

And to get paid for it!

But there was a problem. Dewey wasn't the only one watching Sharon Fowler in secret. He was certain of this. Monitoring his hidden cameras around four one morning the cameraman was startled to see a redhaired Viking fanning through her home. This was no boyfriend. The bastard was all business and had a gun big as a briefcase.

A cop of some kind, Dewey was sure of that, and not local.

The fuck was he looking for? Drugs, maybe? Dewey had seen Sharon doing lots of things, but never drugs.

One thing for sure, if there was a cop inside you could bet there were cops outside, too. Cops posing as tourists or fishermen.

But why?

Dewey peered cautiously through the blinds of the window behind his television. No obvious sign of sentries. But they were out there somewhere, he was sure of it.

And then the thought occurred—Were they watching *him*?

Dewey felt an added tickle in his balls as he retreated to his computer and activated the cameras next door. It was time to wrap this thing up. Put this puppy in the can. He zoomed in on the shower, first. A towel dripped over the sliding door but that was all. Cameras Two and Three showed the den and deck to be unpopulated. But there was some nice action on Number Four. By the bar, wouldn't you know. On the ball. She was totally naked, tonight, which was not all that common. Looked like she was really letting go, too. Really enjoying herself. Working it.

"Oh, yeahhhh. . . ."

Dew Drop brought his camera in tight. Oh, this was good. Scorcese couldn't do better than this, Dewey assured himself. This would be his final shot, the *piece de resistance*. The final statement. A lonely woman reduced to fucking herself. He was the man, now, the director, the auteur. Also a businessman. People would pay for this kind of product, he knew they would.

And Sharon would, too.

17.

Eddy DeLeon did not believe in omens or karma. He didn't read tea leaves or palms and he did not inspect the entrails of goats. But Eddy did trust instinct and as he ducked inside Mama's back door he balked with the sense that something was out of place. DeLeon paid attention to that sensation. He had smuggled any variety of contraband for years before getting into the movie business; he couldn't have survived those trials without paying attention the tintinnabulation of the bells in his head.

He didn't question where it came from. Whether it was extrasensory or merely a heightened sense of observation. On the drive over from his condo, for instance, Eddy noted a pair of SUVs that traded places behind his limo before breaking off, eventually, on the route from SeaSide Drive to Mama's Place.

A pair of four-wheel-drive vehicles just like dozens of others commonly owned or rented by weekenders visiting the Keys. Except tourists didn't generally get this far off the coastline.

Once you got past the bridge there was nothing to see, that is unless you wanted a piece of ass and a beer at Mama's house of corrugated tin and pleasure.

The locals coming to Mama's to get drunk or get laid drove pickups or vans, mostly. Or ratted-out muscle cars. A few out-of-towners drove expensive off-roaders, but Eddy was familiar with those vehicles.

"Check out the Land Rover and that Tahoe behind us," Eddy alerted his driver.

"One of 'em kept goin', but the Tahoe's turned off the hard road," Crease reported as he nosed the Lincoln down the dirt road that terminated at his boss's brothel.

"He's still behind us."

Crease parked the car out back and let his boss out. From the back porch Eddy watched the Tahoe emerge from the pines to slowly wind through the scattered vehicles of his regular patrons. After making a single tour, the four-wheeler drove away in a roostertail of sand and dust.

"Tags?" Eddy asked.

"Couldn't make 'em. Prob'ly just some dick got turned around."

Could be any number of things, Eddy was thinking. Could be somebody lost, somebody looking for a place to pull over. Could be somebody wanting to pump his girl in the backseat. Nothing to panic about. Normally Eddy might not even be concerned. But Sharon Fowler's revelation that Baxter Stanton was talking to Bear Raines had put Eddy on edge.

Eddy hated uncertainty. He would much rather have hard proof that the senator was prepared to betray him than to be teased with the possibility. Disappointment, after all, was something you could exorcise. But uncertainty—that drew out the demons. And there was more uncertainty waiting inside.

A genuine hellhound had come to Mama's Place. He was inside, now, waiting legs crossed on a high chair at Mama's plywood bar. Eddy noticed five beers untouched on the bar. Mr. Thiet debarked from his utilitarian Cessna attended by four men. A Praetorian guard in tailored silk suits. These were leg-breakers. These were muscle.

Bad enough he orders me out here like I was his fucking houseboy, Eddy kept that thought to himself. Bad enough he spits on my hospitality. But to bring his goons, too?

That was real disrespect.

The string that always looped about Eddy's neck began to itch. Three men, ten men. Fuck it. He'd cut them all! A sudden urge to slaughter threatened his presence of mind.

But this was not the time. This was business.

"Lee, you come to fly my plane?" Eddy smiled through broken teeth. "Tired of that straight and level shit?"

"You owe me money, Eduardo." Thiet's almond eyes were unclouded through the aviator glasses. His hands were brown and slender and folded in repose.

"There is no need for hostilities, my friend." Eddy opened his own hands wide. "I am in the wrong. I admit. I owe you, yes, and I mean to pay in full."

"You are stalling. If I ignore this obvious fact, what will it say to my other partners? Put yourself in my position. You know these kind of men. What will they think?"

Eddy shrugged. "Who's going to tell them? Not me. I like things private."

Lee nodded. "So do I."

Eddy lifted his chin in Mama's direction. It was odd that the largest, most remarkable specimen of humanity in the room, this enormous Earth Mother, the gray emissary in this house of whores, was also the most inconspicuous of Eddy's employees. "How can a three hundred pound whore disappear?" Eddy once asked. And yet she did. Often. As if sucked into the flimsy walls of her house.

But for the moment, Mama was fully present. A fold of flesh swung like a hock of ham beneath a chocolate arm as she flushed the girls out of the bar. One by one the prostitutes sallied off. When Eddy permitted himself a glance around the bar, Mama herself had disappeared.

The room was now cleared for serious conversation.

"You already owe me six hundred thousand dollars, plus three points interest," Lee began without preamble. "I paid you that over and above the first two million invested to guarantee a product that should have been ready a month ago. Over two and one half million dollars I have paid in good faith for fifteen million DVDs and what do I have?"

He pulled a shrink-wrapped display from his suit.

"The package."

"*Si.*"

"So where is my merchandise?"

"Is a week away. Should have been done, like you said, a month ago. I *got* the driver, for Christ's sake! I had a man inside. The hard part was done!"

"Where is your manufacturing facility? *Where?*"

"Mexico."

"So. I have two and half million dollars in Mexico?"

"Not exactly. I ran into a problem with the disc."

"Nonsense. You have millions of discs."

"No. *The* disc. A tape, actually. See, I was supposed to meet the driver, but then I got put in jail. It made the news. My face got splashed over everplace . . ."

"Are you saying you do not have an original copy of *Scarlet Moon*?"

"No, but I can get one. I know where to go. I'll just have to arrange another pick-up, is all."

"Is all? There *is* nothing else!"

"I was in jail. I couldn't go to Los Angeles, you know that."

"I can see that you no longer owe me six hundred thousand dollars."

"I don't?"

"Of course not. I have invested over two and a half million dollars in *Scarlet Moon*. But you do not have the master. You cannot make copies. Therefore, you owe me the entire cost of my investment."

"Thought you people were patient."

"Time to cut my losses.

"What losses? I got a guy inside the studios with a virgin disk—!"

"What you've got," Thiet cut him off, "is a partner prominent in Washington. Senator Stanton is my insurance. He is my bank. Call him. Remind him of our conversation and tell him I intend to collect."

"Is not like he can just pull it out of his pocket!" The string around Eddy's neck by now getting hot as a wire.

Thiet adjusted the glasses over his tortoise eyes.

"Business is business."

"I'm just saying," Eddy backpedaling furiously. "The man's got an election coming. Less than two months to make sure he's back in the U.S. Senate. He can't move shit around right now; people are looking! You follow the news, Mr. Thiet. You know."

"What I know is that you have been accused of slitting his daughter's throat. Which to my mind would strain any partnership."

"So what makes you think I can get dick from Stanton?" Eddy demanded.

"Because if you don't, I will kill you both."

Eddy felt the razor waiting. Waiting inside his shirt.

"I am told you are a cruel man, Mr. DeLeon. I do not in general countenance cruelty."

The moneyman reached across the table to examine the gold-plated bracelet that disguised the twine holding Eddy's razor.

"But sometimes an example is necessary. For a fraction of what this bauble is worth, I can hang you by your ponytail from a hook until tortures you have never conceived are completed upon your body. You will scream, you will shit yourself, you will plead. And between those moments some creature will be up your ass for the sole purpose of his own entertainment.

"You will beg me to take this pitiful razor you are so proud of carrying and cut your cock off so you can bleed to death and I shall say, 'No. There is more.'

"You have a reputation as a hard case in this backward region,

233

don't you, Mr. DeLeon? But I think you will find my associates no less implacable."

Four pairs of eyes regarded him over their boss's shoulder and like Lee they did not blink.

The urge to mayhem was evaporated, now, replaced by something else, something Eduardo remembered from when he was a boy.

A sick, humiliating sensation.

Lee Thiet dropped Eddy's collar back onto his neck.

"We are all afraid. My friend."

Thiet wiped his hands on a bar napkin.

"It only requires a certain set of circumstances to be reminded."

Eddy's visitor pushed away from the bar.

"I am no longer interested in *Scarlet Moon*. Tell Senator Stanton that he is responsible for reimbursement of my investment. And tell him I know he has resources to pay. Tell him, if he must, to sell that ridiculous house, but tell him that in any event I shall expect a transfer of two million six hundred and forty thousand dollars into an account which I will specify within twelve business days."

"And what if he says, 'Suck my dick'?"

Eddy never saw the foot that caught him square in the balls.

"You—! Fuck!"

He cursed from his knees.

Another blow slammed into his kidneys. Eddy writhed on the floor, a rope of electricity burning from his spine to his groin.

He tried to reach his knees. Black stars swimming before his eyes. Nausea.

"Remind the senator of my condolences on behalf of his daughter." Lee replaced his glasses. "Remind him, too, that a failure to meet one's obligation is not politic."

The man from 'Nam nodded to his gallowglass. The four henchmen filed past Eddy to the brothel's rear exit. Their beers remained, untouched.

"Mama!" he croaked.

She appeared from nowhere. Eddy pulled to his knees on the trunk of her arm.

"I got to see somebody," he slurred dizzily.

"Jesus, boss, I'll get Crease!"

"No . . . One of the girls."

"Girls? Right now, boss?"

His feet pedaling for traction on her floor.

"Get me a girl, goddammit!"

Eddy could feel the razor warm beneath his shirt.

"Make sure she's got a car."

A pair of FDLE agents kept their radio handy as they idled on the shoulder of the road maybe a hundred yards past the turnoff leading to Mama's establishment. They were assigned to tail Eddy's limousine, of course. Pretty easy target, you would think, a ponytailed Honduran in a black, stretched Lincoln. A rented Mercury pulled out onto the hardtop in the general direction of the airstrip, its driver hidden behind tinted windows, but the agents paid no special attention. Why should they? The FDLE had no intelligence of Mr. Thiet or his entourage.

The next vehicle to come out barely rated a glance, a '98 Neon with the windows down. A black woman lounged behind the wheel, working the beads in her cornrowed hair like a rosary. Eddy huddled below Mama's whore in the floorboard behind her.

"You see 'em?"

"Yeah. Chu woan me to do?"

"Keep driving."

Eddy waited until the Neon was well down the asphalt before he risked a peek from the backseat.

"Pull over," he said finally. "Gimme the keys."

Two lovers lay in a tangle of silk sheets. But this was not a bordello or a houseboat. Senator Baxter Stanton disengaged from the fine hip cocked next to his groin, Ruby Knowles soughing beside him. Languid and spent on Baxter's king-sized bed.

Woman sleeps like a goddamn rock, Stanton was thinking.

He wished he could.

The senator slid off the bed, threw on a terrycloth robe, and padded barefoot downstairs. The cuckoo clock set beside his wife's armoire had lost its voice long ago. Probably got tired of competing with the missus, an aide used to say. Or, rather—a man who used to be an aide used to say.

Baxter glanced at the time. Three in the fucking morning. He grabbed his stomach. He was already taking antibiotics for the ulcer but it didn't seem to help. Senator Stanton found his kitchen, raided the fridge of a bottle of Maalox and was in the process of chugging that pink chalk down when a razor came to rest cold and silver on his neck.

Eddy DeLeon hovering like a phantom over his shoulder.

"Stomachache? Could be a guilty conscience."

"You going to slit my throat, Eddy? Like you did my daughter! You son of a bitch!"

Baxter trembling violently. Fury fighting fear.

Eddy backed off an arm's length.

"First off, I don't know nothing about Beth Ann. I did not kill her. 'Fact, I got somebody looking to see maybe who did."

"You're a liar!"

Eddy displayed his razor.

"That why you been snitching on me? 'Partner'? That why you pulling down the temple around our heads, hah? For revenge?"

Stanton yanked savagely on the belt of his robe.

"The hell are you talking about?"

"I got a source tells me you and Bear been talking a lot lately, long and hard. An' not jus' about Beth Ann, either. About business, Baxter. Wouldn't have anything to do with my business, would it? *Our* business?"

"Somebody's feeding you a load of crap."

"Don't give me that shit!" Eddy hissed. "I din' bust my balls these last three years so you could rat me out to some fucking prosecutor!"

"Get out of my house. Get out!"

Eddy folded his razor into its inlaid handle.

"The man came for his money tonight."

"What man?"

"Mr. Thiet. Our gook partner? He wants out. He wants back his entire investment. You understand what I mean? All of it."

"You think I give a shit, you son of a bitch? *You killed my daughter.*"

"I fucked your daughter. *Si.* I brought her back and nailed my trophy to her goddamn wall, yes, I did. And then I flushed my condom down your piece of shit toilet. But I did not kill your daughter, senor. What I did do was give you two million dollars out of two million six hundred and forty-fucking-thousand of *my* front money for *your* campaign!"

"I told you it was risky. I told you it was advance payment on the movie, but you said, 'I gotta have it. I need the TV time.' So I give you. I figure, what the hell, the man's done right by me."

"You didn't *give* me a damn thing!" Baxter grated. "You charged me interest! Five points for money that isn't even yours!"

Eddy spread his hands as if on a table.

"I cut in something, sure. A little bite. But through no fault of my own your daughter's murder, no disrespect, has spooked Lee Thiet and now all he cares about is two and a half million fucking dollars."

"That much money, he'll wait."

"He'll waste your ass is what he'll do."

"A United States Senator? What fucking country does he think he's in?"

"The Land of No Fucking Return."

"He wants me that bad, let him come."

"You never see him coming. Now, me, Eddy DeLeon, I got my faults but, hey, we got a disagreement? I come see you face to face. Like tonight, hah? *Mano mano.* But this bastard? He will take you out while you're polishing your Ruby, you know what I mean? Or shining your shoes or taking a shit. With this man you never see nothing."

"I might be able to manage something after the election."

"We got twelve business days."

"Might as well be twelve days of Christmas."

"You can raise it. Borrow on the house, you haf to."

Stanton's shoulders slumped abruptly, as if the tendons in his scrawny neck were suddenly severed. He opened the refrigerator door, leaned in to return the Maalox to its place beside the cottage cheese and Lactinex.

Going in with a bottle of Maalox.

But when he came out, a .45 automatic filled Stanton's hand.

"You killed my daughter."

The heavy barrel leveled squarely in the middle of DeLeon's slender chest.

Eddy spread his arms wide as a priest.

"You wanna shoot me, partner? Then shoot me. But it won't look good in the papers. It won't help you get back to your fucking Senate and it won't get you revenge, neither, *jefe,* because you know why? Because I did *not* kill your daughter. I kill some people, yes. To you I admit. But not Beth Ann. No way. She was my princess, man. My trophy."

Baxter's finger tightening on the trigger.

"What about the van? The deputies? Orlando?"

Eddy crossed himself slowly.

"That was not family."

"My God . . ."

The barrel wavered. Fell.

"Get out."

Stanton released the hammer from single action.

"Whatchu wan' me to tell Thiet?"

"Tell him this ain't Southeast Asia and I'm not about to piss away my life's work just because he's got ants in his pants. And then tell him if he wants anything from *me*—"

The senator shelving his handgun in his cooler.

"—he can come and goddamn get it himself."

18.

Sharon's second meeting with Eddy DeLeon was set up at his seaside bunker on her day off and she was late.

"Any word?" Barrett paced inside the command post.

"Not yet." Cricket shook his head.

"Time is it?"

"Quarter past twelve," Terese Banyon replied from behind the shower curtains cashiered to offer Sharon her only privacy.

A SWAT team inside was already hustling into their gear, other agents huddling over radios, phones, and computer terminals.

"She's not here in ten minutes, I'm pulling the plug," Sheriff Rawlings declared.

"How 'bout we cut the lady some slack?" Barrett suggested loudly to everyone present and Smoot adjusted the fit of his straw hat.

"Two weeks ago you were calling the gal a bitch."

"Two weeks ago she wasn't wearing a wire," Barrett shot back.

"Ten minutes," Smoot repeated himself. "After that I'm pulling the plug."

A minute later Sharon burst through the door making the cause of her delay immediately clear.

"Sorry everybody, I just got off the phone with Eddy. He called me and I had to take it and, Jesus, he wouldn't let me off the line!"

"That's all right, you're here, let's get started."

"Bear—He's changed locations."

Heads turning all over the command post.

"He what?"

"Eddy wants to meet on his sailboat."

"I don't like that worth a shit," Smoot declared.

Raines didn't like it, either.

"What time, for Christ's sake?"

"He said between five thirty and six."

"Where is the boat?"

"The marina. Eddy caught the tiller on an oyster bed. Boat's tied off till he can get it fixed."

Barrett turned to Cricket Bonet.

"What do you think?"

Cricket ran a hand through a straw of hair.

"Well, let's see. We've already got a team in place at the marina, which helps. Would need to relocate our SWAT, and our extraction team. And I'd want a backup CP, something on the water."

"Can you do it?"

Cricket checked his watch.

". . . Yes."

"I don't like it," Smoot announced again. "I say we back off."

"I can't back off, Sheriff." Sharon emerged from behind the curtain. "I already told him I'd be there."

It took more than Sharon's commitment to convince Smoot the meet should take place. Cricket pointed out that canceling the rendezvous would without doubt arouse Eddy's already-paranoid tendency to suspicion.

"Even if we decide not to wire her, she oughta go," was Cricket's assessment.

Sharon's security was the primary concern, of course. It helped greatly that the boat was crippled and that the marina was already saturated with Cricket's people. Bonet told Smoot he would not have to sacrifice Sharon's safety to accommodate the new location and with that Smoot gave the green light.

A test for any agent in the field was how quickly he, or she, adapted to changing situations and Cricket Bonet quickly demonstrated why he was still the best in the business. The Canuck quickly notified all agents in all agencies of Eddy's change in plans and directed the squad leaders in charge of command, communications, security, and extraction to redeploy accordingly.

A shrimp boat redeployed Cricket's team to Harvey's Marina. A pair of runabouts joined that vessel to corral Eddy's boat, giving marksmen lanes of fire from the water and from clandestine locations already established in boats slipped along the pier.

If Eddy's plan was to kidnap Ms. Fowler he'd have to hijack a speedboat and break through the FDLE's cordon, but with the Coast Guard and Drug Enforcement Agency contributing support offshore, Cricket concluded that this was an unlikely and manageable contingency.

"Besides, it's not gonna go that far," Cricket assured Sharon. "We'll be listening and if Eddy tries anything stupid we're coming for you. I'll blow a sting any day before I risk a man inside."

"I can live with that," Barrett affirmed.

"Me, too," Sharon quipped and was rewarded with chuckles from veterans all around.

"We have a description of the vessel?"

This from one of Cricket's marksmen.

"It's a two-master," Sharon answered. "A ketch? Fifty-six foot Formosa with a busted tiller."

"Be sure you coordinate that info with the Coast Guard and DEA," Cricket directed an agent on his team. "Get them the registration, too."

Sharon tucked her feet into a pair of deck shoes.

"Are you sure you're ready to do this?" Barrett asked quietly.

"I'm Sharon Fowler," she replied.

The slightest tremor in her voice.

"Bringing you the latest, first."

At five-thirty on the dot Sharon emerged from her houseboat sexy and self-possessed, a new windbreaker added to her nautical ensemble, along with a canvas carryall. Cricket and his team maintained surveillance as Sharon followed Harvey's pier to Eddy DeLeon's double-masted yacht.

Barrett focused a pair of binoculars on Eddy's vessel from a BayLiner berthed fifty yards away. There was DeLeon, detaching himself from a pair of sunbathing groupies. Sharon stepping onto the gangplank.

"Here she comes." Smoot Rawlings steadied his own glasses as the boat rolled with the wake of a passing jet ski.

Cricket Bonet trained his own glasses in the cockpit.

"Fox is in," Bonet spoke into a field mike.

Barrett saw Eddy take Sharon's offered hand.

Was that a smile? Or something else?

"We reading her wire?" the sheriff inquired.

"Five by," a young agent below confirmed.

"How about the van?"

"They've got her, too, sir."

Barrett lowered his binoculars.

"Make sure they tape everything."

Eddy leered at Sharon from the deck of his ketch.

"You looking good, mama."

"Permission to come aboard, Captain."

" 'Captain.' " He showed his teeth. "I like that."

The gangway swayed beneath Sharon's feet. It was an oddly comforting sensation. She knew her way around boats. And she knew looking over this one that Eddy was not a serious sailor.

"Afternoon, Eddy," she said and extended her hand.

She was surprised how limp his hand felt inside her own.

"Come on." He pulled away. "I show you around."

Lots of chrome and teak on the Formosa's deck. Crease looked unhappy securing a line draped sloppily across a yardarm. Sharon stepped lively past that hazard, following Eddy to reach the guests lounging astern. A pair of locals had replaced Eddy's tattooed paramour; the new girls stretched out topless, soaking up every last opportunity for sun and coconut oil.

"I call them Boom and Rudder. I get a little bent I bring them over."

Eddy gave his crotch a hitch.

"Straightens me out every time."

Sharon answered his fractured smile with a flawless one.

"Why don't we go below, Eddy? I've got things you need to hear."

A speakerphone let Cricket and the other lawmen follow Sharon's exchange with DeLeon.

"Wish she hadn't suggested they go belowdecks," Barrett groused.

"Take it easy, partner," Cricket replied.

The team watched as Sharon swung her canvas bag over her shoulder and followed DeLeon into the sailboat's cockpit. Cricket watching Barrett mash honey into a mug of coffee.

"We've got her five-by, Bear. Everything's tight."

"I just don't like Eddy changing locations on us."

Cricket shrugged. "He's impulsive."

"Thanks for reminding me."

Cricket was about to tell his old partner to lay off the caffeine when the radio squawked.

"Uh oh," the young agent monitoring Sharon's equipment grunted.

"What is it?" Cricket leaned over.

"Problem with her wire." The agent did not seem so young, now.

"Kind of problem?"

"It's not transmitting."

"Shit." Smoot Rawlings spit out his gum.

"It's okay, we've got a backup in the van," Cricket reminded them.

A cell phone warbled. Cricket's man snatched it up.

"Mobile One . . ."

A hurried consultation ensued. The technician turned to his boss.

"Agent Bonet, the van's lost her, too."

Barrett standing by helpless.

"So is it our equipment or hers?" Cricket asked.

"It's on Sharon's end," the younger agent answered directly. "It's not my gear. Not the van's, either."

"We're blind without that wire," Rawlings declared loudly. "She gets in trouble, there's no way you're gonna know."

Barrett nodded. "But if we scrub now we blow her cover. We blow the whole thing."

Then Smoot surprised them all when he turned to Barrett and said, "It's your call."

"My call?"

"You're the one recruited her, you're the one put her in there. It's up to you."

"We need the wire!" Barrett pressed his hands to his temples. "She gets in trouble, how the hell will we know?"

Bear felt the crush of Cricket's hand on his shoulder.

"Let's stay in the here-and-now, all right? You don't know that Sharon's in any danger at all. For all you know, she's got Eddy bragging about every movie he ever pirated. He could be giving up buyers, sources. Could be crowing about every bastard he ever killed."

"And what's to keep him from sharpening his razor on her throat, Cricket?"

"If you can't accept that risk, partner," Cricket's reply was cold as ice, "you should never have accepted her help in the first place."

Cricket turned Barrett aside quietly, privately.

"If you're still blaming yourself for what happened to Laura Anne, now would be a good time to stop. We've got a job to do, buddy. If you can't do your job, you can't help Sharon. You can't help anybody."

"Barrett?"

Sheriff Rawlings breaking that short reverie.

"What do you say, Bear? Are we gonna leave Sharon in? Or pull her?"

"I can make the call if you like." Cricket's offer was wooden and correct and Barrett declined, shaking his head.

"How fast can your people get to Sharon?"

"We can be on board in less than thirty seconds."

A pause, then. Everyone waiting for the decision Barrett knew he could not defer.

"Give her half an hour. Just hold your team in place. Give her thirty minutes more."

Cricket Bonet was smiling as he triggered his radio.

"I'll tell my team."

For the next half hour Bear found himself concocting horrible fates for Sharon Fowler in the hold of Eddy's boat. The parabolic booms that Cricket's agents aimed at the hull easily picked up the inane chatter of Eddy's topside and topless companions, but could not penetrate inside the ketch. So Barrett was stuck with his fears and his watch as Boom and Rudder giggled over beer and coconut oil.

"She'll be all right," Cricket tried to allay his old partner's fears and Bear tried to imagine Sharon kicking back with a beer of her own to the rap of some Honduran gangsta.

Or not.

"How long's it been?" Sheriff Rawlings asked.

"I make it twenty-six minutes," Bear replied and then turned to Cricket Bonet.

"Your team ready?"

"When you are."

"All right, then—"

"Wait. Hold up." Smoot Rawlings was snatching up his binoculars as static broke over the cabin's speaker.

"Point One to Leader. Subject in sight."

"Hot damn, take a look!"

There was Sharon climbing from the hold of Eddy's ketch as casually as she had entered, donning a pair of sunglasses against a lowering sun, bantering conversation on the way to the gangway.

Barrett choked off the flood of emotion triggered by that relief. He remembered how he felt when Laura Anne emerged alive from Strawman's Hammock. Seeing Sharon Fowler unscathed on Eddy's boat did not match that relief. But it was close.

The TV reporter offered a brisk wave over her shoulder as she left DeLeon behind, those long lips and hips in perfect synchrony with the sway of Eddy's catwalk.

"She has got herself a style," Rawlings marveled.

Cricket would hold his team in place until Sharon was off the pier and safely away from the marina. She would drive herself to be debriefed at the FDLE's inland command post, safely distant from Eddy DeLeon.

"Can't wait to hear what she got out of that sumbitch," Smoot Rawlings declared.

Barrett did not reply. He was equally eager to hear what Eddy had to say to Sharon. He just wished to hell they had it on tape.

Sharon Fowler parked her BMW at the loading dock of Marion's Pest Control within twenty minutes of leaving Eddy's sailboat and a platoon of agents converged to usher her inside.

"Are you okay?" were Barrett's first words.

"Fine." She was all business. "But my antenna got yanked off. The antenna for my wire? Did that matter? Could you hear me?"

Barrett's face answered that question.

"Shit!" She threw herself into a chair. "I was going belowdecks and I felt this tug in my crotch—God *damn* it."

"Wasn't your fault," Cricket told her.

"You're safe, that's the main thing." Barrett felt foolish mouthing that nonsense.

Terese Banyon brought over a Gatorade.

Sharon took it.

"Thank you."

"Why don't we go ahead get that wire off?" Terese suggested.

"Okay." Sharon cursed again, and then went on, "But I did get Eddy talking, I really did."

"Good for you," Barrett smiled encouragement. "It's just that if it's not recorded it's pretty much your word against his."

"Need a record, do you? Need it on tape? Well—"

She pulled over her canvas bag.

"Will this do?"

She pulled a cassette from her canvas bag, an ordinary audio cassette.

"The hell is this?" Cricket exclaimed.

"It's mine," Sharon smiled to answer. "Soon as we got below deck Eddy told me he had something special. He sat me down by a boombox. Put in a tape."

"*This* tape?"

"No. His original stayed in the boombox. I just taped a copy with this—"

She unzipped her windbreaker, displayed a vest pocket. The pocket-sized Sony familiar to Bear from a dozen interviews nestled inside.

"My little Sony. Been using it for years."

A stunned silence turned quickly to whoops of elation. High fives all around. The FDLE agents cheered Sharon as though she were a rockstar. Even Smoot Rawlings had a grin going that he couldn't wipe off.

"I'll be dipped in shit."

Barrett tried with only moderate success to silence the troops.

"Can we debrief here, gentlemen? Please! Gentlemen!"

To no effect. Terese joined the other agents to applaud their newest veteran.

"All right, all right." Cricket finally offered Sharon his hand. "Come on. Let's find a room."

Cricket led Sharon and Barrett to his own jerry-rigged office down the hall, Sharon slipping off her windbreaker on the way.

"I was worried the wire wasn't working, and I knew we needed some kind of voice record. Then Eddy tells me he's got this tape he wants me to hear. I figured it was some kind of music, reggae or something, but he said, no, it was some serious shit.

"I always carry the Sony. As you know, Bear—"

Cricket opening a metal door.

Sharon entering.

"So while Eddy's fussing to get his tape in the boombox, I figure, what the hell? I might as well turn on my little recorder. See what I can pick up."

"While Eddy's sitting beside you, you did this?"

"Oh, yeah," she nodded. "He was right there."

"Do you realize how risky that was, Sharon? What a goddamn chance you took?"

"It was worth it," she replied shortly.

"You think so?"

"Definitely."

She paused for a swig of Gatorade.

"And once you hear it, you'll think so too."

19.

Sharon's tape sent *Roland Reed* back to circuit court and Judge Boatwright with requests for multiple warrants. Barrett knotted his double Windsor a half-dozen times in preparation for that audience. Roland Reed was nervous, too, his pen tapping the arm of the wingbacked chair placed beside Bear's. Judge Boatwright had to know that State Attorney Reed went behind his back looking for authority to investigate Eddy DeLeon. The end-around to Judge Dickens was looking less clever now that Roland and Barrett were returned to Boatwright's closed and closeted chambers.

The judge was apparently as averse to sunlight as a vampire. Tall windows that might have flooded the interior were tinted and heavily curtained. A single indirect lamp spilled a yellow cone on His Honor; everything else was subdued. You couldn't make out details on the wainscot or ceiling. Photographs of distinguished Republicans appeared as smudges on shadowed walls. Sharon's audio recorder winked like a miniature lighthouse atop Boatwright's cherrywood desk.

The jurist burst into his chambers tall and erect, long robe flowing like an Oxford don's, arms swinging like Sousa. A nose sharp as a hawk's beak between farsighted eyes. The hair white as snow against the dark linens barring the windows.

"Roland, put that irritating pen away."

So much for pleasantries.

"This had better be good, gentlemen."

Offered as the judge fell into his high-backed throne.

"Yes, Your Honor." Roland cleared his throat. "As directed I've consolidated the warrants and particular instruments . . ."

"Yes, yes," he waved Reed off. "Is this the recording?"

"Yes, Your Honor."

Boatwright took a moment to regard Barrett.

"I hope I am not interrupting my recess for a wild goose chase, Agent Raines."

"No, sir."

"You're quite sure?"

"It's evidence we can't ignore, Your Honor."

"Can't you, now?"

Barrett took that as permission to press "Play." Sharon's boot-legged cassette turned on the wheel of a tape player bought only that morning at Radio Shack.

A few seconds' hiss of leader was enough to make Bear panic. But then a crackle of static broke with the elocution of a Valley Girl.

"Dear Diary. Tonight I made a fuck movie with Eddy and when I got home Daddy came in to tell me if I talked about their business, he'd kill me. . . ."

Barrett could not detect a quiver in the eyes that straddled the judge's stern beak.

". . . He had the razor, Daddy did. It always scares me. Ever since I was little, when he had me alone that first time, and he put that cold blade on my hiney. 'Do it right, or take a bite!' Take a bite—that turned him on. . . ."

The voice of Beth Ann Stanton changing. No longer a Valley Girl. Hard, now. Bitter.

"I hated doing it. I thought maybe if he didn't have the razor, he couldn't make me so I took it. Daddy caught me stealing his razor and said it was going to be more than a bite, this time. That's when Mama came in and found out about me and Daddy and the bathroom and made him put it away.

"I hadn't seen that thing in years, but Daddy sure had it tonight. Took it out of the cookie jar. 'I'm not gonna lose in Washington because of a slut at home! You little whore!'

"Me? A whore? But this little whore can talk. Not about Eddy, though. And not about 'business'! Who cares where the money comes from anyway? But what if people knew about Daddy and me? What if I told the voters about a senator who likes razors and knee pads and little girls? See how *that* goes down! Fucking hypocrite!"

Judge Boatwright reached out with a veined hand to silence the tape. The knot in Barrett's tie suddenly tight as a noose.

"You say that this is a recording of a tape originally composed by Beth Ann Stanton?"

"Yes, Your Honor. Copied by our undercover person in Eddy DeLeon's presence."

"And how did the original come into Mr. DeLeon's possession?"

Barrett cleared the gravel obstructing his throat.

"Your Honor, Eduardo DeLeon was intimately involved with Senator Stanton's daughter over a period of six or seven months. They frequently spent time in his limousine. Mr. DeLeon indicated to our undercover source that his driver while vacuuming the car's interior found Beth Ann's original recording beneath the console that folds down on the rear seat."

"There's no problem with admissibility, Your Honor," Roland chimed in. "We're rock solid this time."

"Mr. Reed," the Judge leaned back, "you have never come before this court rock solid in your life."

Roland flushed beet red. The judge fixing his withering gaze.

"Your Honor?" Roland trying not to stammer.

"Yes, Mr. Reed."

"We weren't looking for accusations against Senator Stanton, Your Honor. Our entire investigation was aimed at Mr. DeLeon's theft of intellectual property."

"*Movies,* Mr. Reed. No need to use a dollar when a dime will do."

"The point is, Your Honor, that Senator Stanton was not the object of our inquiry."

"Is that a fact?"

The judge's gaze now turning to fix on Barrett Raines.

"What do you say to that, Agent Raines?"

Standard procedure called for Barrett to back up his prosecutor. That was the unwritten code. But there was another code, earlier learned, to which Barrett had clung since he was a boy and to which he turned now.

"The truth is, Your Honor, we were hoping to get two birds with one stone."

Roland went purple.

"Your Honor!"

"Hush, Roland. I was speaking with Agent Raines. Well, Agent?"

"Your Honor, we have good cause to believe that Eddy DeLeon is pirating feature films. However, it's also true that we suspected this activity would tie back to Senator Stanton. We even hoped it would. But, Your Honor, we had absolutely no idea that the investigation of DeLeon would implicate Senator Stanton as a suspect for his daughter's murder.

"The tape played in chambers before you this morning is not the fruit of any contaminated tree, Your Honor. We do not bring this tape for the purpose of investigating the senator's campaign finances. We bring it seeking an arrest related to the murder of Beth Ann Stanton. That is the crime on my mind, this morning. That is why I need your warrant to search and seize."

Judge Boatwright turned away from them both, regarding, apparently, the state flag flanking his desk. The state seal was affixed on that flag, Barrett realized. An icon signifying power appropriate for a Pilate.

The judge swiveled abruptly in his high chair.

"I assume your people have authenticated this tape? It's not faked? Not some cut and paste nonsense?"

"No, Your Honor. No forgery. The voice on that tape is Beth Ann Stanton's."

Boatwright paused a long moment.

"I want to see the chain of custody associated with this recording. And you will have before me by three o'clock tomorrow everything you've gathered on Eddy DeLeon. That includes all tapes and transcripts *verbatim* from your man undercover."

"Yes, Your Honor." Barrett did not feel obliged to correct the judge regarding his source's gender.

Roland apparently agreed.

"As for a search warrant for Senator Stanton's domicile—"

The judge who only weeks before placed Baxter Stanton off-limits was grave in his Pilate's chair.

"I am disposed to find probable cause for such instruments. What is it that you need?"

Baxter Stanton's unappreciated plumber and handyman was stuffing bags of garbage into the bin situated to the side of the senator's wide gate when he saw a convoy of vehicles approaching. Clarence Magrue rose stiffly to see Barrett Raines and Sheriff Rawlings leading a pair of cruisers through the senator's iron-wrought gate. Sharon Fowler brought up the rear, riding shotgun in her "live" van. She would get her story, as promised. But Barrett denied Sharon's pointed request to enter Stanton's home.

"We find a razor or anything else, you'll be the first to know, Sharon. If we don't find anything, you'll still have Beth Ann's diary on tape. It's a breaking story, either way."

Miss Wanda met Barrett and Smoot Rawlings at the door.

"Sheriff. Can I do fo' you?"

"We got a search warrant, Miss Wanda. Are the senator and missus home?"

"They at breakfast."

"Then I'll see 'em in the kitchen."

Within moments Baxter Stanton was raging over a cell phone and cursing Bear Raines to the corners of hell.

"Time I get through you won't be able to get a job watching a drunk tank in Jacksonville!"

"It's a legal warrant, Senator." Smoot Rawlings's customary deference was dropped for the occasion.

"It's harassment!"

Barrett was not concerned. The warrant Judge Boatwright granted gave him ample authority to search the home. A pair of crime scene specialists from the department were already assisting Smoot's deputies in a search of the rooms upstairs. Ruby Knowles got flushed from the guest's bedroom without a peep, the senator's mistress apparently unembarrassed by Mrs. Stanton's early return.

"The god*damn* are you looking for?" Baxter's arms extended as slender as wishbones from the sleeves of his terrycloth robe.

Barrett ignored him. Barbara, leaning on her spotless oven, seemed close to a breakdown, but Bear was not here to comfort Caesar's wife.

"Beth Ann said there was a cookie jar," Barrett reminded the sheriff.

"Cookie jar?" Barbara stammered. "My God, Baxter, are these men here for cookies?"

"No, ma'am, we're looking for a razor." Barrett eyed the cabinetwork.

"I don't have a razor!" Stanton protested.

But it seemed to Barrett that the rooster's outrage was suddenly dulled.

"I don't use a razor! I never had a razor!"

"Is that true, Mrs. Stanton? Never had a razor?"

She turned to her husband.

"Just shut up, Barbara. Not a goddamned word."

"There's some jars," a deputy pointed to a shelf recessed above the sink, and, stepping back, Barrett could see a pair of gaudily decorated jars pushed flush to the wall. Finger-painted jars, like a child would give you on the last day of summer camp or Vacation Bible School.

"Is there a step-up?" Cricket inquired.

"Here." The sheriff dragged a two-step over with the toe of his boot.

Barrett mounted the small, folding frame. Reached up to secure one of the containers.

"But they're empty!" Barbara Stanton declared weakly. "They're just for show; there hasn't been anything in those jars for years!"

"Sheriff?" Barrett handed the first jar down.

The sheriff lifted a ceramic lid, peered inside.

"The hell."

Smoot turned the jar upside down and scattered flakes of paint fell to the sink.

"Ain't nuthin' in this one," Rawlings pronounced.

Barrett tried to fight a sense of vertigo as he reached for the second jar. A sudden weight was unexpected.

"Something for sure in here," he grunted and cradled the clay urn as he stepped to the floor.

"It's nothing," Babs protested. "Not for years!"

Barrett set the jar's heavy lid beside the sink.

"See anything?" Rawlings voice was dry as sand.

"It's filled with—" Barrett dampened his finger, touched it to his tongue, "—Salt."

"Salt!" Baxter Stanton crowed. "Salt! Goddamn, I plead guilty to hoarding salt!"

"Wait a minute." Barrett lowered the jar into the sink's stainless basin.

"What're you doing?" Stanton demanded. "Goddammit, I said what are you doing with my salt?"

Barrett dumped the salt from its finger-painted container into the sink. A white and unspoiled cone rose over the drain. A half-gallon of salt poured dry and white and empty of significance.

But with the last briny grains something else spilled from the jar, something ivory-handled and old that slid soundlessly into the waiting mound of preservative.

"Oh, mercy!"

Barbara Stanton's hands fluttered to her mouth.

It was a an old-fashioned straight razor, the kind somebody's grandfather had undoubtedly sharpened on a leather strop. The kind of blade that had slit Beth Ann Stanton's throat.

"How in God's name?"

Stanton blustered.

For a space the width of a gnat's ass no one said anything. But then the sheriff of Dixie County pulled a pair of handcuffs off his belt.

"Baxter Stanton, you are under arrest for the murder of Beth Ann Stanton."

"Beth Ann?" Barbara cringed from her husband. *"Baxter?"*

"This is ridiculous!" the senator looked for a constituency in the crowded room. "I tell you I don't have a razor! I never had a razor!"

"You can't do this!"

Barbara Stanton leaping off the stove.

"You owe him! You owe me! Who do you think got you that badge?"

"Sorry, Barbara."

The teeth of the cuffs ratcheting *snick, snick, snick* about her husband's wrists, and then—

"Agent Raines? Would you read the senator his rights."

Sharon Fowler was ready and waiting "live" with her cameraman as Senator Baxter Stanton was led in steel bracelets through the French doors of his home and onto its spotless veranda. Barbara Stanton followed her husband onto the porch, leaning for support on the arm of her husband's mistress. Miss Wanda and Clarence and other domestics trailed mute and stunned behind.

"Great stuff!" Sharon hissed over Dewey's shoulder. "The mistress with his *wife*! The loyal help! Are you getting this?"

"I got it."

"Sharon," Barrett called out from the porch. "You'd like a word with the senator, this is the time. But make it quick."

Dew Drop framed Sharon from a low angle as she walked up the steps to meet Baxter Stanton on his porch.

"Senator Stanton, can you respond to the charges of homicide made against you, sir?"

"They're untrue, of course." Baxter's ruddy face was paled to the pallor of ash. "The evidence is planted. Had to be! The election . . . My opponent . . . I did *not* kill my daughter!"

Sharon extended her microphone like a wand to the senator's wife.

"Mrs. Stanton? Your response?"

Babs' Tri Delt smile failed as she wrung hands behind her husband.

"I'm sure this is all some dreadful mistake."

"That's enough," Sheriff Rawlings moved in.

"I'm not finished," Sharon retorted. "Bear—?"

"It's the sheriff's call, Sharon."

"You said I'd get an interview! That was our *deal*!"

" 'Deal'?" Baxter Stanton's hands went white in his cuffs as he turned to face Sharon Fowler.

"What goddamn deal? What have you been telling these people anyway? You self-serving bitch!"

"That's enough." The sheriff practically shoved Stanton toward a waiting prowler.

"There's some shit goin' on here!" Stanton fought the deputies who bundled him toward the waiting cruiser. "Some kind of shit, for sure!"

"Some kind is right—I was promised an interview!" Sharon fulminating in turn.

"Take it easy, Sharon," Barrett interceded. "You'll get your interview. Just as soon as Sheriff Rawlings gets the suspect in custody."

"Suspect!"

Barbara Stanton blanching at the word.

"Oh, Lord—'Suspect'?"

Ruby Knowles took her by the arm.

"Don't worry, honey. Baxter'll fix things up."

"Baxter?"

Barbara breaking free, throwing herself onto her husband.

"You can't take him! You can't!"

A pair of deputies joined Ruby Knowles to pry Barbara away.

"Baxter?"

"Go on upstairs, Mother. Ruby, you take her."

Ruby pulled Barbara through the familiar frame of her French doors. Stanton waited for his wife to disappear inside the house before he turned on Barrett Raines.

"You know, boy, this is the second time you've got yourself tangled in my affairs."

"Third, Senator. But I grant you that murder's a more serious affair than campaign finances or pirating movies."

"Think you're clever, don't you, Bear? But it's not gonna turn out, you hear me? You son of a bitch. You *never* gonna be done with me. You hear? Never!"

Smoot Rawlings nodded to his deputies.

"Load him in."

A dozen steps took the prisoner to a waiting prowler. A deputy placed his hand atop Baxter Stanton's regal head as he guided the senator to a bench segregated by a steel cage from the seats up front.

"Looks like you got your man, Bear." Rawlings peeled off a stick of gum.

"He's not convicted, yet. And neither is Eddy DeLeon."

"We'll get DeLeon, even if it's just for stealing movies," Smoot replied. "Sharon's got the little fuck wired."

"About that. I don't want to put another wire on Sharon."

"The hell are you talkin' about?"

"We need to pull her, Sheriff. In fact, we need to get Sharon away from Eddy DeLeon as fast as we can."

"You crazy? She's going to nail the bastard!"

"Not if she's dead. Think about it, Sheriff: Eddy knew Sharon would use the information from Beth Ann's tape to clear him of that girl's murder and you can bet he's happy about that. Happy as a pig in shit.

"But if he ever finds out that Sharon made a copy of Beth Ann's original? For *us*—?

Bear didn't need to spell out the rest.

"If I thought a wire could nail Eddy for Taylor's murder or Midge's or Jack's, it might be worth it. But not for movies. Not so some Hollywood producer can buy himself another Ferrari."

Rawlings worked his gum.

"Sure you're not lettin' other concerns weigh in? Personal concerns?"

"I don't want Sharon winding up like Laura Anne, no. Or Taylor Calhoun. Do you?"

"Shit." Smoot spat whatever juice he'd managed to work up. "All right, then. All goddamn right, we'll pull her."

Bear felt as though a barrel of air left his chest.

"Thank you, Sheriff."

A siren growled briefly.

"We're ready for transport," a deputy informed them and the sheriff nodded his okay.

"Maybe we can turn Stanton on Eddy." Rawlings settled his hand on the gun at his hip. "Baxter could bake Eddy's beans if he had something to gain from it. If we had somethin' to give him."

"We can give him life," Bear pointed out. "A life sentence beats a needle any day."

The siren growled again. Barrett remained with Sheriff Rawlings as the deputies' county-marked car completed the circuit of Stanton's drive beneath a tumble of lights. A black and tan from the Highway Patrol fell in behind the county's vehicle; Dew

Drop panned his camera to follow the convoy as it pulled off toward the gate. Barrett squinted in the bright, bright sun.

"Last time Senator Stanton got this much attention he was in a carriage, remember?"

The sheriff spit.

"Like goddamn Cinderella."

The convoy was maybe thirty yards down the cobbled drive when another vehicle belched into view. A garbage truck. The foul-smelling monster rumbled to a stop over grinding gears beside the plastic trashbin placed just outside Baxter Stanton's wrought-iron gate.

"Pretty early fo' the gahbidge," Clarence remarked.

Two coveralled workers dropped from the stenciled truck. Two white men. Barrett turned his attention from the senator's convoy to observe their activity. Nothing could be more ordinary, two men wheeling a trashcan toward their truck's compactor. The large trashbin fitted to receive the truck's hydraulic arms. An ungloved hand pulled the actuating lever. A pair of steel biceps jerking in response. The plastic bin rising in metal arms toward the mouth that fed the truck's rhinoceros belly.

How much crap could those things hold, anyway?

Sheriff Rawlings's deputies slowed their vehicle to a halt well short of the gate, waiting with their prisoner for the garbage truck to clear. It wouldn't take long. One of the coveralled garbage men was already trundling the plastic bin back to its place near the driveway's entrance. That task completed he whistled once, sharply, to join his buddy already waiting behind the wheel.

The lumbering garbage truck jerked away in black clouds of half-burned diesel; the cruiser carrying Senator Stanton now pulled toward the gate as if drawn in its vacuum.

"Sho' is early," the caretaker again remarked.

The escort by now halfway down the drive.

"Sheriff!" Barrett Raines rose onto the balls of his feet. "Sheriff, stop 'em. Stop that cruiser!"

"The hell, Bear?" Rawlings stared amazed.

"Your phone! Tell them to stop!"

Smoot fumbling, then, to get at his phone.

"Shit."

Barrett shot for the gate in a dead sprint. It had been a long time since he had run like this, spontaneously, without reflection or doubt. Pebbles chimed beneath Barrett's hard-soled feet like coins. But he could feel himself labor. He might for a brief span have been the graceful athlete who glided the length of a hardwood floor in seconds to kiss the ball gently off the glass to score the points that won the game that took his team to its first state final in Cross City. But now—

"Baaaxxterr!"

Barrett bellowed over a hammering heart.

"Baaaxxterr!"

Baxter Stanton turned in his seat, probably not because he heard anything, probably just for a last look at the palace he had raised from muck. He certainly did not expect to see Barrett Raines pounding behind on foot.

"Baaaxxxterrr!"

"What on earth—?"

"Baxter the garbage! The—garbage!"

"Oh, shit!"

The squad car paused in the gap of Stanton's iron gate, a turn signal dutifully signalling intention for a turn onto the blacktop. Barrett could see Stanton animated in his rear seat, imploring Smoot's deputies to gun their vehicle ahead, hands stretched in steel bracelets to finger the olive-green trashcan squatting innocuously at his window.

The concussion came before the sound. Twenty pounds of plastic explosive lifted the squad car on a pillar of flame. It cartwheeled lazily, just once. A second explosion followed the first as the cruiser impacted on the asphalt just outside Senator Stanton's well-wrought gate.

The blast knocked Barrett down like a bowling pin from fifty yards away. Shrapnel ripped the veranda and grounds. There was a pause, an unnatural interim of silence and then a high scream rose from a woman at her upstairs window. Smoot's surviving deputies now shouting imprecations, their curses warring.

Barrett felt something wet on his mouth. Lifting his head he could apprehend nothing but a twisted pyre below a tree of smoke. He remained prone in the rock drive deafened, addled, unsure of his limbs. And then a thought occurred—

"Sharon . . . ? Sharon!"

"I'm here, Bear. I'm okay."

But she was gone in an instant, dragging Dew Drop and his camera to capture the twisted wreckage that burned like a jack o' lantern beyond the framing gate.

Barrett pulled himself to his knees.

A locker's worth of scorched carcass was all that remained of Senator Stanton and his attending deputies, but the microphone in Sharon Fowler's hand never wavered, never hesitated as KEYS's star anchor reported live to a shocked viewing public:

"... *and then only a few moments after Senator Stanton was handcuffed, mere minutes after being Mirandized for the murder of his daughter Beth Ann, justice has taken an ugly and unexpected turn as an explosive device of some kind has taken the life of Senator Stanton and his escort at the very gate of the mansion so well known here in Pepperfish Keys.*"

She stood tall and calm and removed from the carnage. A classic remove, Barrett mulled fuzzily. Like that ice-carved Aphrodite that melted—how long ago was it?—in the Senator's sylvan yard.

Sylvan. Sylvania.

A place of trees, was it? Bear tried to recall.

A light pulsed at the mouth of a tunnel extended before his eyes.

The tunnel closed.

20.

Senator Stanton's assassination threw a bag of shit into a very large fan. The hunt for Stanton's killers quickly took priority at every law enforcement agency in the region and every resource was savaged to support that effort. By the time Barrett was released from the Cross City Emergency Room the murders of Midge Holloway, Jack Sandstrom, and Orlando Fuqua were on the back burner, and Smoot Rawlings formally ended his investigation of Beth Ann Stanton's homicide.

"We know we got Beth Ann's killer," Smoot told his deputies privately. "Or at least we know somebody did."

The effort to nail Eddy DeLeon for any crime was off the map altogether. An unauthorized duplication of Randall Damone's latest movie, no matter how costly to Hollywood, could not compete in time and resources with Senator Stanton's high-profile homicide. All files related to Sharon's undercover role were signed and sealed.

Not that the Keys's rising star seemed concerned for her safety. Sharon was everywhere, it seemed. Taking interviews.

Giving interviews. And you could not see the local news without Sharon's commentary or update. Barrett caught one of Sharon's performances while lunching with Roland Reed at the Dixie Grill.

"*Our top story—the assassination of Senator Baxter Stanton.*"

Sharon looking past the camera to the 'prompter.

"*The week's developments have prompted an explosion of conspiracy theories regarding Senator Stanton's homicide, among them that Barbara Stanton orchestrated the hit on her child-abusing husband, that Ruby Knowles was the jilted lover, or that the driveway bombing was an elaborate suicide organized by Stanton himself to avoid the shame sure to arise from accusations of molestation leveled as if from the grave by Beth Ann herself.*"

"This is journalism?" Roland snorted.

"*In fact,*" Sharon went on earnestly, "*the voice of Beth Ann Stanton was nearly lost forever. I can now reveal that local and state authorities were literally clueless in their pursuit of Beth Ann's killer until this reporter discovered through confidential sources a diary recorded in Beth Ann's own voice, an audiotape which accused her father of sadism and pedophilia and which led the Dixie County Sheriff and FDLE directly to the razor hidden in Senator Stanton's kitchen.*"

Bear felt something go sick in his stomach.

Reed was more demonstrative.

"That bitch!"

Sharon swiveled to her Number Two camera.

"*The FDLE's crime lab has confirmed that traces of blood remaining on the razor found in the cookie jar in the late senator's kitchen matched his daughter's DNA. With the murder weapon in hand, and with the father accused of molesting his daughter, authorities are now willing to admit privately, if not officially, that the most likely candidate for Beth Ann Stanton's grisly murder is her own father.*

"*I'm Sharon Fowler, bringing you the latest, first.*"

Roland flushed beet-red. "Did you *hear* that bitch?"

"What'd you expect?"

"Suppose I just call the networks? Tell them Sharon got her story by ratting out Eddy DeLeon? By going undercover with cops! How'd that play?"

Barrett sipped coffee from a finger-painted mug.

"Roland, the folks who sell advertising don't give a damn how you get a story, as long as you get one. And Sharon's giving it to 'em big-time."

"At our expense?"

"Yes." Barrett gathered the check. "At our expense."

Barrett didn't like seeing his efforts belittled on television and he'd endured much more at Sharon's hand than had Roland Reed. But in spite of that history, Barrett knew he was obligated both legally and ethically to keep Sharon's undercover role secret from Eddy DeLeon.

"We can't rat her out, Roland. We just can't."

Which sucked Barrett into a dispute that involved, ironically enough, the Federal Bureau of Investigation.

It started out with what seemed a simple request. The Bureau wanted to obtain the evidence gained from Sharon Fowler's clandestine work. That would naturally include the tape Sharon copied off Eddy's boombox. No problem there. But the feds also wanted to secure Beth Ann Stanton's original cassette and Barrett adamantly refused.

"First place, we don't have Beth Ann's original," Barrett briefed Captain Altmiller. "Second place, we don't need the original cassette. To what end? There's no trial; Senator Stanton was our suspect and he's dead."

"The Bureau says they need it."

"With respect, sir, they don't. There's not a thing on that poor girl's diary that's going to finger her daddy's killers. But it will finger Sharon Fowler. Sharon is the only person outside Eddy's circle who knows that he's in possession of Beth Ann's original cassette. If the feds come to Eddy looking for that tape, he's going to *know* Sharon's been working both sides of the street."

Altmiller raised a hand to acknowledge.

"So your position is that an attempt to recover the particular evidence requested by federal authorities will put our undercover in danger. That about it?"

"Without a doubt. Yes, sir."

"So convey that concern to the FBI."

Altmiller extended a peanut to a waiting squirrel.

"Work it out."

Initially it appeared as though Bear was going to work things out. He put in a call to the FBI in Tallahassee. A very cordial call. Very professional. Concerns on both sides were adumbrated. A meeting was quickly scheduled at FDLE headquarters and a pair of special agents showed up.

"I'm sure the Bureau does not intend to compromise the identity of our undercover operative," Barrett opened the pow-wow diplomatically. "But I'd be happy to give the FBI unlimited access to the recording our snoop made of Beth Ann's diary."

"Not good enough," Barrett heard his offer bluntly declined. "We want Beth Ann Stanton's original. We want the cassette Eddy claims to have found under the seat of his limousine."

"Let me make this plain." Bear spread his hands to a span of eight octaves. "You cannot obtain the original copy of Beth Ann Stanton's dictated diary, you can't even *look* for it, without putting my snitch in harm's way."

"That's your concern, Agent Raines."

"Then I guess I'll see you gentlemen in court."

Within the week a hearing was convened and Judge Boatwright ruled that federal investigators could not obtain any warrant to search DeLeon's premises if the effect of such search was to violate prior agreements protecting the identity of Sharon Fowler. The FBI, in other words, had to ask Sharon if it was okay for them to put her life at risk. Barrett phoned Sharon to relay the FBI's request for a face-to-face meeting. To his surprise she readily agreed.

It was October by the time Sharon met with Barrett, Roland Reed, and FBI Special Agent Larry Finch at the FDLE's Live Oak office. Sharon came accompanied by an attorney familiar to locals. Thurman Shaw shook hands all around, a small, fireplug of an advocate. The only man in Suwannee County still wearing suspenders.

As Roland Reed made introductions, Barrett was able to look Sharon over. It was the first time he had seen her since the bombing. What a difference a couple of weeks could make. She was no local girl, now. She was hot, her catalog ensembles traded now for more sophisticated labels. Shoes excepted. A pair of Teva sandals that might have come from L.L. Bean offered support for her spine. But the cell phone was snugged inside a Gucci purse. Donna Karran stockings. Everything from the knees up was *Rigeur Lauren*. A charcoal skirt, pleated, summer wool. A wide-collared ivory blouse, button-up.

But the jacket was the thing, slick and leather and shiny. You could imagine a camera slung through those epaulets atop those hefty delts, or a pack of Chesterfields. Not much jewelry, a single bracelet on her wrist. Beaten silver. Might have come from Santa Fe. She was hot, smart, a babe with brains.

She was Diane Sawyer on a six-foot frame.

"We are investigating the assassination of a United States Senator." Finch's apple bobbed in a throat skinny as Roland's pen. A bulbous, barnacled nose. Wire-rimmed glasses. "Any information related to Senator Stanton or his family, any accusation or innuendo, is crucially important."

"Of course it is," Attorney Shaw responded to Finch, pulling a file from his briefcase. "And so is the imperative to protect my client."

"From what I can see, your client has gone public with virtually everything we're requesting."

"Eddy DeLeon doesn't know I made a duplicate tape of Beth Ann's original recording, Agent Finch," Sharon stepped in smoothly. "He doesn't know I was cooperating with the FDLE, the FBI, and God knows who all else. And I can assure you Eddy doesn't want anyone to know he's got Beth Ann's original tape. He sees it as life insurance, and I have been careful to broadcast nothing, nothing! that links his name to that recording."

Finch's reed-thin neck reddened at the collar.

"Look. All I want is a search warrant for DeLeon's boat and residence. But for that, Ms. Fowler, a judge tells me I need your signature."

"Not at present," she refused. "Maybe when things settle down."

"Counselor," the fed now addressing Thurman Shaw, "you should tell your client that if she refuses to cooperate I can compel her to testify in federal court on any matter related to her covert activity."

"You're blowing smoke." Shaw reached for his battered case. "Ms. Fowler has kept her end of the bargain. She delivered."

"She delivered, all right." It was the state attorney's turn to complain, Roland Reed smiling wanly to Sharon. "Problem is—She didn't deliver what anybody expected."

Dew Drop almost missed Sharon's return to her houseboat that afternoon, engaged as he was in his own variety of undercover activity. Cameras One through Four followed Sharon shedding sandals, skirt, and blouse as she padded beneath her mounted trophies on the way to the shower, then the bedroom, then back before the bar where she did her thing on the therapy ball.

She'd got where she could damn near straddle that clumsy thing, toes barely touching the parquet floor as she arched back across the ball's inflated tympanum, reaching to find the hardwood with her fingertips, every tendon, every ligament stretched to the limit as she fought to remain balanced on the ball's capricious moment.

The back must have really been bugging her the last few days, Dewey mused to himself. Lots of stress with success, hah, girlfriend? Lots of kinks to work out before that move to New

York? But Sharon was ready to move, no doubt about it. And when she did Dewey was ready to cash in.

He already had an offer. Five thousand dollars *up front* for the entire archive, that material destined for a website owned by some player in Pennsylvania. Of course Dewey knew he could get more money if he got paid by the hit. And he wasn't sure he wanted to give up the Sharon lode to any single buyer. It was enough to make Dewey consider turning down the easy money, and starting his own site from scratch.

Why not? No telling how many gazillions of hits he could get on Seefowler.com. You could beat five thousand easy. Couldn't you? Even if the site only ran a month? Or maybe he should just take his material and go direct to video. Imagine Sharon Fowler shelved beside Mary Carey in some Triple-X arcade! And he could jump off from there to the real deal.

There were plenty of directors, weren't there, who started out in adult entertainment? And Dewey was already toying with a concept for something independent. The kind of product somebody with a cutting-edge sensibility at Miramax could get off, too. Or one of those players at Sundance, some studio exec in snowshoes.

Or maybe he'd go local. There was one buyer, he knew, who would be particularly interested in a story Dewey had in mind. It wouldn't take much to produce. Nothing at all, really.

Dewey zoomed in on his imperceptive subject. Or maybe he'd just take it an entirely different direction. That time she cleaned her fish inspired a larger vision. The guts displayed on her cutting board. Blood running down those long legs. Dewey could imagine a camera following some improved instrument up that firm valley from her navel to her neck. A little S&M to spice things up.

Or maybe feature Fowler as the dominant player. He could even splice in Barrett Raines for that scenario. Barrett helpless on the ball. Sharon straddling.

Would that be sweet or what?

And it'd be a snap. Splice in a little blood, a few toys. Drop in some audio. CLOSE UP on Bear banging away. Then IN TIGHT for her reaction, Sharon coming on her yellow ball.

Two careers killed for the price of one.

"Turn this way for me, bitch," Dewey urged his distant subject with affection. "Little more . . ."

She was reaching for the vibrator, now. That's when the fun really started, the real floor show.

Sharon was plugged in.

And so was her cameraman.

21. ◼ *A Cuisinart churned briefly beside* the six-inch TV that plugged into the outlet on the Raines's kitchen counter. Barrett ducked in from the carport to find Laura Anne in a T-shirt and shorts dipping a hushpuppy into a blended tartar as she coaxed reception from a set of rabbit ears.

"Hey, babe."

"Hey. Want some 'puppies? Just made the dip."

He dipped a finger into the sauce, tasted it. Then leaned over to her opened mouth.

"How're the boys?" he asked finally.

"They are great."

Her smile lit up their small kitchen.

"I took the day off. We fished off the pier. Couple of tourists came paddling up on kayaks. Kayaks! In Deacon Beach! Think that's something we could afford? Maybe used?"

"I 'magine. Why? Boys interested?"

"Ben especially. You'd think he was part Eskimo."

"I'm glad they're not afraid of the water," he commented gravely. "I'm glad I didn't pass that on."

She took his hand.

"Have another hushpuppy."

He took one. "Any news?"

"Sharon's making hay."

She twisted the small set's antenna and Sharon Fowler buzzed onscreen, installed before the cheap panorama of Pepperfish Keys at KEYS's news desk.

"She's let her hair down," Laura Anne remarked.

The chignon was unknotted to release a pile of hair long and blond on a tailored jacket. Sharon inviting the camera, running an interview with Ruby Knowles.

Laura Anne turned to her husband.

"Seems like she gets a lot of inside information. Know what I mean?"

That observation caught Barrett off guard. There were lots of things on the job that cops did not discuss at home; Bear and Laura Anne had long ago worked out rules of engagement. Typically, if Barrett ignored or evaded a question from Laura Anne, it meant that he could not answer without breaking a confidence.

His wife knew the code. But Laura Anne was just beginning to regain confidence, to trust her instincts—and her husband Bear did not want to shut that off.

"Barrett? How's Sharon know so much?"

"I can only give you a piece of the pie, hon," he responded cautiously. "There are people at risk."

"You don't mean Sharon?"

"I can't answer that. But I can tell you that a lot of what Sharon's taking credit for has come from either our shop or Sheriff Rawlings's."

"Then who's this other 'source' she keeps talking about?"

"I can't go there, Laura Anne. Not even an inch."

"Are you in any danger, Bear?"

"Not unless you drown me in tartar sauce."

She punched him lightly on the arm.

"I don't know why I bother with you."

Almond Sinclair looked over to Dew Drop's camera as he directed the evening's broadcast from the station's archaic booth.

"Off Camera One—"

Almond relayed the command to Dewey as he manned the switcher.

"On Tape One. Go to tape."

Sharon Fowler perched in her anchor's chair as the broadcast segued to a prerecorded interview. Sharon interviewing a very uncomfortable Smoot Rawlings.

"Is it true, Sheriff Rawlings, that you have put the lid on Beth Ann Stanton's homicide?"

"Put a lid on, maybe. Wouldn't say it's nailed shut."

"No? Do you have other leads to pursue?"

"Not really. Between what you've reported and information we have from, ah—other sources, it's pretty clear that the senator had a strong motive, the means, and the opportunity which we think led to his killing his daughter."

"The senator's motive—by that you mean Beth Ann's threat to publicly accuse her father of sexual abuse?"

"Sometime before the election, that is correct. 'Course we don't know for sure that Beth Ann threatened the senator, but the presence of the tape and the threat of scandal, well—it's looking more and more to us like she must have."

"However, we should remind viewers that we don't know this for sure, isn't that right, Sheriff?"

"And we may never know. But, like I said, the case is now closed."

"Great show!"

The news director pulled out the tail of his shirt at the end of the broadcast. Got busy polishing his glasses.

"Great goddamn show."

Sharon left the anchor's desk for the editing bin. The tape engaging her at present was destined for WABC in New York. This would be a composite of her recent broadcasts, a tableau of the Stanton story. It would be her resume for an interview already promised at the Big Apple's ABC affiliate. Sharon knew that this tape was her audition, her chance to impress. It had to be perfect.

A sign outside the bin clearly stated, 'Keep Out—This Means You', but Dewey ignored it.

"Sharon?"

"God damn it, Dewey, can you read?"

"Tell it to Almond. He's out at the van, told me to come get you."

"What's the problem?"

"I dunno. He said right away, though."

"All right. One second."

She stared a half-second at her last edit. Made a decision. " 'Edit'. Okay. Now, nobody better touch this shit. You got that?"

"No problem." Dewey closed the door after her.

Sharon skirted the newsroom, taking the hallway connecting the editing room to what was euphemistically called the engineer's office and a separate room, the junkyard, so named for its racks of cannibalized parts. A rear door opened to the black pool of the parking lot outside. Sharon could see the Live Van idling near the motor pool's gate.

"The hell is Almond?"

"Inside," Dewey answered, hustling to match her long strides across the lighted lot.

"This better be good." Sharon grabbed the van's door, jerking it open.

"Oh, it will be." Eddy DeLeon crouched inside.

Sharon rebounded from the van's door with the instincts of an athlete. But Crease was waiting. A leather sap snapped down. A light went on inside Sharon's head. Then off.

She tried to lift her head.

"Ah!"

A steel wire sliced through the center of her brain. A wave of nausea followed. Stars floating like black asterisks. Sharon shivered uncontrollably. Something cold and hard against her breasts, belly, legs.

It was some kind of belt, she realized. Leather. Metal rivets at the seams burned her skin like cubes of ice. She raised her head painfully and saw an industrial control panel dominated by two large buttons, one red, one green, and in that instant realized she was hogtied on the conveyor that fed Eddy DeLeon's hydraulic cutter.

"Heeeelp!"

She tried to roll over. Couldn't.

Sharon thrashing like a tuna. Nylon straps biting into her wrists and ankles. Her arms were piniomed far out in front. A separate strap trapped her legs above the knee. The sheet metal shop swimming into view, now, a maze of sharp-edged puzzles lit harshly with unshaded lamps. Then, finally, a line of broken teeth.

"Something to wake you up," Eddy smiled and dumped the scalding coffee on her back.

Sharon's scream broke with the arch of her spine. She was jerked short by the straps pinning her to the cowhide rack. Her face collapsed to the belt's harsh pillow. She turned in a puddle of drool to find Eddy. He smiled at the cleavage she presented.

"You need more?"

"No!"

"Then you're awake. Bien."

"Eddy, you . . . You don't need to do this!"

"I hear that all the time."

"Don't you see—?"

Sharon gasping for air like a fish. Like a fish out of water.

"I haven't said a thing! There's nothing I . . . Nobody knows, Eddy? Nobody!"

"Is that a fact, senorita?"

Eddy took her hand. Leaned in to inspect her polished nails.

"I see one needs help."

He pulled the familiar nippers from his linen slacks.

"Eddy, No. Please!"

She tried to close her hand.

"Crease—"

It took both men to trap a finger. But then the silver clippers bit through. Into the quick.

Sharon's scream echoing through tangles of ductwork.

"That's juss one leeetle bite," Eddy informed her. "You want a big one?"

"No! God, no, no, no!"

Eddy pocketed his nail clippers. Reached for the string about his neck.

"Oh, God. Eddy? Eddy!"

The razor gleamed in hard light. Sharon turning away, jamming her head into the leather. He grabbed a handful of hair to wrench her back.

"You think you can snitch on me? Bitch? Hah?"

"Whadda you mean, Eddy, I did what you told me!'

Then she threw up. Vomit spilling with bile on her rack.

"Shit, man."

"I . . . I did what you told me, Eddy! I was . . . Was just playing along!"

" 'Playing'? That's good. That's real good. Matter of fact, I got something here came right out of the playpen."

He jerked her head back once again, his scarred fist holding a rein of hair at the nape of her neck.

"Look," he ordered.

Across from the cutter she could see his flat-screen television. The image on screen was familiar. Too familiar.

"Recognize anybody?"

She saw herself, first, stripped to her pants and splayed over her therapy ball. Reaching for the vibrator.

"Where did you—? How? Eddy?"

"Just watch the show, honey."

Sharon saw the edit. It was sloppy, amateur. But the next cut took you hard to her bathroom where Barrett Raines, in high angle, was shedding his tie and shirt.

"Some renedezvous."

"Eddy . . . Eddy, listen to me, this tape is doctored!"

" 'Doctor and Nurse', maybe?"

"It *wasn't* like that!"

"How was it then?"

His hand traveling the long scar on her back.

"Do you see us screwing, Eddy? Do you ever see Barrett on top of me on this . . . fucking tape?"

"Don' go down that road, mama. Don' try and tell me he din' *do* you."

"Jesus! Well, what . . . What if he did? Eddy, you told me to get close to the man!"

"Not this close. See, I have confided in you, Sharon. Told you things. And now I got these doubts concerning whether you been working for me or for that nigger cop."

She craned her neck to meet his eyes.

"Eddy! Eddy, you're my source. Remember? When did I ever, *ever* betray a source?"

"That is a fair point—"

Eddy turning to watch Sharon on her ball with Barrett on-screen.

"But I need to be reassured."

Crease used both of his hands to trap hers.

"No!"

Sharon clenching her fist into a white-knuckled ball.

"Eddy, don't!"

Eddy popped his razor free of its pearl-cased holster.

"Goddamn you!"

Cursing, now. Trying to keep a shred of dignity. A shred of defiance.

"Crease."

"Goddamn you son of a bitch!"

The doughboy driver helped Eddy pry a single finger free from the ball of Sharon's fist.

"Eddy? Eddy?"

DeLeon placing the blade carefully.

"Jus' remember, baby. The Truth? Will set you free." A rising scream pierced the stagnant air outside DeLeon's metal shed. A heron startled in its roost tumbled into awkward flight. Moments later a second scream bawled into the heavy atmosphere. A third scream rose higher and higher, an awful, agonized soprano.

Then nothing.

22. *Barrett was guiding his sons* through new territory involving their use of the family computer in the moments before he got the sheriff's call.

"No, Tyndall, it doesn't matter that's it's on the Internet; when you download a movie or music without paying for it, you are a thief. Also happens to be a crime."

"But Dad—!"

"There's no 'but.' If you boys want a DVD you're going to have to budget for it, just like everything else."

"But it's already *there*," Ben objected.

"It's stealing."

"Everybody does it!"

"You aren't." Laura Anne's voice, long absent from family discussions, silenced all dissent. "You boys heard your father. You pay for your music and movies or you do without. Now let's eat."

Barrett winked a silent thanks. It was nice to be a team again. Was also nice to see the eroded habits of family life beginning to reform, Laura Anne now calling Bear during the day just to say hello. Taking a break from the restaurant for supper at home. The family was gathered late for their evening meal, but Bear didn't mind. He was looking forward to dipping a hot wedge of cornbread into an ice-cold glass of sweet tea when his cell phone warbled for attention.

"Barrett, here," he took the call cheerfully.

"Barrett, it's Smoot. Sharon Fowler's missing."

Barrett felt his heart stop . . . Start.

"What's the situation?"

It was as if another voice belonging to a disconnected and disinterested mind raced on a separate track to respond.

"Almond Sinclair called it in. He went looking for Sharon in the editing bin around seven. She wasn't there, she wasn't any-place, and her car's still at the station."

Barrett made a quick calculation.

"So she's missing—one? two hours?"

"Somewhere in there," Smoot affirmed.

"Any chance she's with Eddy DeLeon?"

"I swung by Eddy's condo. Place is empty. And I sent a deputy out to Harvey's. Sharon wasn't at her houseboat, but Dewey was. Said the last he saw, she was still in the editing bin."

"Back up. When you say Dewey was there, do you mean in-side Sharon's houseboat?"

"That's right. She's always hitting him up to fix a computer or TV, whatever."

An alarm bell sounded.

"Is Dewey there now?"

"He's back at the station. I can call him if you want."

"I want a look at the houseboat, first."

It was black dark by the time Barrett strode down the pier to Sharon's floating home. Smoot Rawlings was already waiting, attended by a very young, very clean-cut deputy.

"Deputy Folsom's the man checked out the boat." Smoot tucked a flashlight inside his belt.

"I know this man." Barrett extended a hand. "Jody Folsom,

right? How's your dad? Seems like I heard something about an operation?"

"Gall bladder. He's fine, thanks for asking."

"Tell him hello for me. And now can you just walk me through this-here?"

"I took the call from Dispatch, Possible Missing Person. Got to this location little after eight. There was still some daylight."

"Nothing jimmied? Door? Window?"

"Nope." The deputy shook his head.

Smoot swatted at a moth drawn to the doorlight. "No sign of forced entry. No sign of violence."

"Door still open?"

Deputy Folsom displayed a key. "A spare. Dewey showed me."

Barrett ducked through the cabin door and into the familiar den. There were her trophies, stuffed and mounted above the bar. The hardwood floor. The yellow ball shifting with the slow roll of the boat. Barrett exhaled slowly.

"The hell is she, Smoot?"

Rawlings popped in a fresh stick of gum.

"She's either out of pocket or she's in trouble."

"If she's with Eddy, it's trouble."

Barrett glanced out Sharon's living room window to find the silhouette of the boat slipped alongside.

"Jody, where exactly was Dewey when you came aboard?"

"Right here." The deputy spread his hands. "Guess you'd call it a living room or den?"

"Close enough." Barrett turned his attention back inside. "And what was he doing?"

"Couldn't say. Time I got here he was packing his tools."

Smoot snorted. "Problem for that boy living right next door, Sharon's always hitting him up for some damn chore or another."

The little bell in Bear's head was ringing louder.

"Sharon shits on this kid all day long and he leaves work to play handyman?"

"Sharon says 'frog', Dewey looks for a pond," Smoot countered. "Not like he's got a lot of choice in the matter."

"Well, you got that right." Bear separated the slats of a Venetian blind for another look next door.

"I'd like to check out Dewey's boat. Nothing intrusive. Just plain-sight."

"Long as we're here," Smoot shrugged.

The fall of night could not disguise the fact that Dewey's houseboat was a slum compared to Sharon's luxurious craft. Even by flashlight you could see signs of disrepair and corrosion. It was apparent as well that Dewey was a slob. The first thing the lawmen noticed when they boarded was a noxious and overstuffed garbage can begging to be emptied, scoured, and bleached. Beer cans littered the deck. A railing fluttered with underwear tossed carelessly to dry.

"Kind of a floating bachelor's pad," Rawlings observed drily.

"Why don't you lead the way, Sheriff?" Barrett suggested. "What we're looking for is anything that might belong to Sharon Fowler. Article of clothing. A woman's sunglasses. Anything that looks out of place."

Smoot trained his light low and began a clockwise tour of Dewey's sour-smelling digs.

"I see a pair of dishes up top," Smoot's deputy pointed skyward.

Two satellite receivers pale as pearls on a jerry-rigged mast.

"Betchu he gets a hundred channels."

"Couple of hundred, probably," Smoot amended. "Most of 'em running exactly the same crap, and I doubt he pays a dime for any of it."

"Hold up." Barrett froze like a bird dog.

"What you got?" Smoot asked.

"Through the window," Barrett answered tersely. "Kill your light. See that glow? There's a computer inside."

"Yeah." Smoot joined him at the window.

"Check out the screen saver."

"Come on, Bear, people leave their 'savers on all the—what the hell?"

Then Deputy Folsom peered over his boss's shoulder.

"Miss Mary. Kind of shit is *that*?"

A judge in Dixie County gave Smoot a warrant to search Dewey's residence; Harvey supplied the key. The houseboat's interior was about as trashed as the deck outside, tapes and DVDs lying in piles with soiled laundry and magazines.

"Boy likes porn." Smoot indicated a stack of VHS.

"Yes," Barrett acknowledged tightly. "I believe he does."

First thing they saw coming into Dewey's bedroom was the screen saver. A startling image shimmering in pixels as iridescent as snowflakes on a wide, flat screen:

Sharon Fowler balanced topless atop her yellow ball.

Barrett exhaled slowly. "Now we know why Dewey was willing to be Sharon's step and fetch. So he could plant a camera in her boat."

"More than one, I'd say." Smoot flicked a switch and four television monitors buzzed to life beside Dewey's computer. Four cameras for four locations.

"Jesus, Bear, he's all over."

"It's changing." Jody Folsom directed their attention back to the computer's monitor.

The screen saver now dissolving to a new and dynamic display of Sharon and her ball, that yellow sphere now released from its static display and rotating to bring another angle into view. Sharon now stretched naked across her canary globe, her toes and fingertips guiding a precarious balance. A pair of electrically stimulated toys coming into view on the parquet floor.

CUT TO Barrett Raines stripping off his tie, his shirt. Soaked to the bone.

"Bear? The hell?"

The sheriff and his deputy standing stiffly aside.

Bear leaning over to see himself shedding his soggy clothes in Sharon's bathroom.

CUT TO the den. Sharon inviting Barrett to her unstable bed.

"Lord, Lord." Jody Folsom looked like he wanted to hide.

"What's this we're seeing, Bear?" Smoot was grim.

"Fiction," Barrett told his old boss. "Cut and paste."

"You sure?"

Barrett met Smoot square in the eye.

"You know me better than this, Smoot."

Took forever for the next three seconds to pass.

"All right, then. What you want me to do?"

"Call Almond Sinclair. Tell him we're coming. And tell him to make sure Dewey doesn't leave the station."

It was well after nine o'clock by the time Sheriff Rawlings and his deputy escorted Dewey across KEYS's parking lot to Sharon's BMW. A smirk faded visibly when the cameraman saw Barrett Raines waiting.

"Where is she?" Barrett led off without preamble.

"I don't know what the fuck you're talking about."

"Let us, Bear."

The sheriff trapped the brim of his dandy straw hat beneath the Beemer's windshield wiper as his deputy blocked Dewey's escape.

"I want a lawyer."

Smoot leisurely wadded a nice fold of Dew Drop's pusselgut into his fist.

"Son, if you don't tell me where I can find Sharon Fowler, and quick—"

"Aaaaghhhh!"

"—a lawyer ain't gonna do you any good."

Dewey clutching his belly with both hands.

"I said quick."

"She went with Eddy, I don't know where!"

"DeLeon came to the station?"

"He just wanted to see her."

"But he'd already seen Sharon, hadn't he, Dewey?" Barrett leaned in close. "He saw her with me in a movie made for very limited distribution. A fantasy in wide-angle. Except you didn't tell Eddy it was a fantasy, did you, Dewey?"

"I don't know what you're talking about!"

"You seeded cameras all through Sharon's houseboat. There's footage on your hard drive goes back for months. But that little scene featuring Sharon and me was made special, wasn't it? And sold as cinema verité."

"How much did Eddy give you for that trash?" Rawlings growled.

"All he wanted was to see her!" Dewey whimpered. "Just to talk, that's what he said!"

"What'd he *pay* you, fuckhead?"

"A thousand!" Dewey cringed. "Thousand dollars."

Barrett's turn.

"Where did he take her, Dewey? Think. Where?"

"I don't know! God, you think he'd tell me?"

"Settle down. Easy."

Barrett planted his hand on Dewey's chest.

"Okay. So when did Eddy first see the footage that put Sharon and me together?"

"Yesterday. Was yesterday, I brought him a DVD."

"For a private screening. Classy. And where was *that*?"

Eddy's driver plunged a hypo into Sharon's arm. She came to consciousness coughing up the bottom of her lungs, her eyes rolling to find orientation, like a diver with bends. Then she felt the leather belt beneath her, slick with vomit and sweat and a low, animal cry rattled in her chest.

Eddy ran a manicured nail down the length of her spine.

"Parts of you lookin' pretty good, still, Princess. But other parts . . ."

Three knobs of bone tapped on the leather where fingers used to be.

Sharon's scream came out like a gargle of saltwater. She broke into cries, then, imprecations mixed with prayers. Eddy adjusted the video camera to catch it all.

"Oh—God!" Her breath came in jerks. "Oh—God!"

She threw up again. Eddy clucked disapproval from behind his camera.

"Nobody gonna want you now, baby. Not with a flipper like that."

"Kill—!" She gulped for air. "Kill me!"

"If you're good," Eddy promised. "But first, what did you tell Barrett Raines, hah? While you were stroking his balls what did you tell him about me and my fucking business?"

"I told him everything—is that what you want to hear? I told them you eat shit! I told them you eat your mother! Now *kill* me!"

Eddy nodded. "Now, finally, I am reassured. *Gracias.*"

"You . . . welcome." Her head sank to the leather strap.

"But before we part, Sharon, maybe we make a little movie, hah? One time for the camera. You and me. Rockabye, baby. And if you do me right, baby—"

Eddy fingered his razor.

"—I make the end come quick."

The final humiliation. Sharon broke, finally, in long, gut-wrenching sobs.

Barrett Raines gunned a Dixie County cruiser down two ruts of sand at sixty miles an hour. Smoot Rawlings was literally riding shotgun, making damn sure his twelve-gauge was loaded as he worked the radio for backup. Deputy Folsom trailed behind the sheriff and Raines, Jody snugging up to Bear's rear bumper like Dale Earnhardt at Daytona.

"Hang on."

The sheriff thrown against the belts as the cruiser turned

sideways. The deputy recovering behind. Two cars at a mile a minute, at night, rooster-tailing on the remains of a railroad bed.

"Shortcut," Barrett offered.

"Just get us there," Rawlings replied.

Eddy's sheet-metal shop had never been very profitable. A railroad that used to run by the facility's fenced-in yard had been pulled up years earlier, the site given over since that time to the migrations of birds and teenagers. The only reason Barrett knew about the place was because an FDLE audit raised suspicions Eddy was using it to dodge taxes.

Gravel and stone now banged into the heavy plate protecting the cruiser's oil pan. Palmetto pummeled the brushguard shielding the radiator. Barrett and Smoot bouncing inside like BBs in a matchbox.

"How . . . long, Bear?"

"Five, ETA. Backup?"

"I figure . . . ten minutes."

"She may not . . . have ten minutes, Sheriff."

Rawlings pumped a shell into his shotgun.

"I got point."

"You sure, Smoot?"

"Just shoot twice."

Twice, always. Bear knew that rule. You never trusted your life to a single round.

The straps had been loosened to flip Sharon bellyside up. The blood recirculating to her feet and wrists brought a fresh venue for pain. She cried out, legs bicycling feebly, futilely, following a desperate instinct. But then the straps were cinched down again as she was spread-eagled for Eddy's inspection.

He hopped aboard, straddling her belly.

Loosening the rubber band that bound his ponytail.

"Don't worry." He pinched her breasts between his hands. "Eddy DeLeon gonna make you feel good once before you die."

Sharon lost her bladder and Crease hooted behind Eddy's camera.

Didn't people say you should put yourself somewhere else? Or pass out? But the adrenaline still had her heart racing, pounding, and Sharon had an athlete's heart. She would be here for the ordeal to come. She would be present.

There would be no respite.

Eddy traced a meandering line that started on her throat, the clawed nail leaving a pink line as it traveled the valley between her breasts.

"Maybe I even shoot you, hah? End it quick. Enough of this cutting business."

She bucked feebly. Like a sick colt. He pulled down his linen trousers.

That's when four tons of Crown Vic crashed through the fence outside.

"Boss—?"

Eddy's shop split at the seams as Barrett Raines rammed his cop car straight through its sheet-metal wall.

"Take 'em."

Eddy grabbed an Uzi as he slapped the round, green knob that triggered the Cutter's belted conveyor. The blade slicing down.

Waaaah-womp.

Sharon jerking two inches at a time toward an hydraulic guillotine.

"Help meeeee!"

Barrett was already taking cover behind the shield of the cruiser's door. Smoot Rawlings was out the other side, his shotgun across the Crown Vic's crumpled hood.

Both men staring through the steam of a broken radiator to see Sharon Fowler hauled by inches toward a pounding blade.

Waaaaah-womp.

"Sheriff. Cover!"

"Go!"

Barrett made a rush for the Cutter behind an explosion of

Number One Buckshot. But a spray of chattered rounds chewed the floor.

"Automatic weapon!" Jody Folsom sang out that warning from the rear.

"Motherfucker!" Eddy screamed and with a ragged burst tore Smoot's deputy in two.

"Jody!"

Rawlings lurching to save his man.

Eddy and Crease driving him back in a stutter of crossfire.

Sharon lurching forward to meet a death by inches.

Waah-womp.

"Heeelp meeee!"

Bear trapped behind a stack of useless metal.

"Smoot. Shotgun!"

"Here she comes!"

Smoot slid the weapon to Bear over the concrete floor. Barrett fished the weapon in with his foot.

"Cover!"

"Go!"

Bear threw himself once again at Eddy's cutter. Crease's Uzi tinkled brass and something like a baseball bat hit Bear's forearm. He looked down to see blood and splinters and his shotgun clattering uselessly to the floor. Barrett saw Crease's short barrel drop to finish him off.

Two wads of buckshot beat him to the punch. Two rounds from Smoot's shotgun crucified Eddy's driver on a stack of sheet metal and suddenly Crease was out of the fight. But DeLeon was moving to the sheriff's flank.

"Smoot!"

Too late. Eddy pulled the trigger on the ugly lump of metal in his hand. Only a single round left. One nine-millimeter slug.

"Shit!"

Smoot Rawlings grunted as if surprised as he slid to the floor.

Eddy shed the spent clip, grabbed a fresh magazine.

Sharon screaming inches distant from the Cutter.

"Bear!"

"Hang on," Barrett called out but then the unmistakable odor of burnt powder wafted pungent and close to his nostrils.

"You can't help her now, dickhead."

Eddy DeLeon centered the muzzle of his weapon on Barrett's skull.

The blade still falling. Pitiless. Inexorable.

"It's close!" Sharon bucked like a horse in her leather straps. "Bear? Barrett? Oh, Gooood!"

"Let her go, Eddy. Kill me if you want, *I'm* your real snitch."

"And for that you nigger son of a bitch, I am gonna make you *watch*!"

So this was the way it was going to be. This was it. But then two concussions lifted Eddy DeLeon off his feet like a doll of rags and the next thing Barrett knew he was looking at a ponytail pooling in a pond of scarlet.

He jerked around to find Sheriff Rawlings trapping a curl of entrails in one hand as the other handled his .357 magnum.

"You always shoot twice. Prick," Smoot said and passed out.

"Beeear!" Sharon's scream cut through the fog.

How far to reach her? Ten feet? Twenty? Barrett remembered the last time, with Laura Anne, how his legs turned to jelly, and here, now, it was Sharon, and he felt as though he were slugging through a quarter mile of molasses to reach the button red and large as a saucer that glowed alongside the green. Finally it was there.

He slapped the button stenciled STOP.

Woomp—

The blade jerked short.

"Oh! Oh, God!"

Sharon shivering in a pool of sweat and urine and blood.

"Oh, God. Oh, God!"

Her amputated fingers rattling like dice on a crap table.

"Easy, now. Easy."

Barrett pulled himself up on the guillotine's iron frame. A familiar wail rose from outside. Long and low.

Sirens.

"Hear that, Sharon? Hear it?"

He used his good arm to pillow her head.

Her eyes wandering in their sockets.

"Is he . . . gone?"

"He's dead. You're safe. It's over."

23. *Jody Folsom died before the* EMS arrived, a round through the neck killed the young deputy. Sheriff Rawlings was taken in critical condition to Tallahassee Memorial, but survived. His vest saved him. Sharon was transported to Gainesville for reconstructive surgery. Some executive at ABC made a big point of footing the bill.

Barrett's surgery was only partially covered by an HMO, his shattered arm rebuilt in a theater adjoining Sharon's. He was gurneyed post-op to a ward separate from Ms. Fowler's privately financed room. The first person Bear saw as he floated up from anesthesia was Laura Anne.

"Did you have a vest?" First thing she asked.

"Yes," he told her. "Smoot made me put one on."

"Thank God," she said, then repeated, "Thank God."

"How are the boys?"

"They're fine. I just told them you hurt your arm."

"Good. And how's Sharon?"

"I haven't heard."

As soon as he could harangue permission Barrett slung his arm for a visit to Sharon's sequestered room. He found the Key's now nationally famous reporter propped up in bed over a bowl of wobbly Jello and one of those milk cartons you thought you'd seen the last of in elementary school. Dr. Susan Windler lounged in hush puppies to display an X-ray for her patient's benefit.

"The procedure went very well," the surgeon briefed her patient. "You can see the reconstructed phalanges, here . . ."

"You mean my fingers," Sharon said coldly.

"Sure. Sorry. We got the basic structure back in place. Bone and tendons and so on."

"Will I be able to use the hand?"

"I don't know about playing the violin, but for normal activities, I'd say certainly."

"Long as she can fish." Barrett arrived with a fistful of roses in his unslinged hand.

"Hello, Sharon."

"Hullo." Her reply was vacant.

Barrett appropriated a space on the bed.

"Brought these."

Sharon pushed the roses away. "Sorry."

"No, it's okay." He retreated.

"It's just I don't feel much like flowers with—"

She raised a hand swathed in a pharmacy of bandages.

"Doesn't matter to me, Sharon."

"Of course not, it's not your hand."

"I don't think that's what he meant," the doc chided gently and then, to Barrett, "Don't keep her too long."

He waited for the doctor to leave before turning again to Sharon.

"I'm not being a very good victim, am I?"

"Didn't know there were rules for how victims oughta be," Bear smiled. "But you're going to get better."

"I 'spose."

"Suppose, hell. You've got a job waiting, what I hear. In New York?"

A fierce nod confirmed it.

"WABC. Probably start in the spring. I'll miss the November elections, though. Dammit."

"It's not that kind of race, Sharon."

"It is for me."

Barrett shifted his arm in its sling.

"Sheriff Rawlings is still in the hospital."

"Thank him for me."

"Might want to thank him yourself. Hadn't been for Smoot we'd both be dead."

"I guess so."

"I could take him a card. You could just jot something down."

The phone rang at her bedside. Rang again.

"Can you—?"

She waved her bandaged hand.

"Sure," he said and put the phone in her lap.

"Sharon Fowler here," she spoke crisply into the receiver. "Oh, hello! . . . No, this is fine."

Covering the mouthpiece, offering a wan smile.

"My agent."

"Sure, sure. I'll come back."

"Thanks."

"Get out of here we'll go fishing, all right?"

But she was already dragging a pad of paper to the phone, fumbling with her good hand for one of the ballpoints stashed in a glass on her nightstand.

"Okay, I'm ready—"

She did not see Barrett leave.

"Shoot."

The November elections came and went. An unknown Democrat ran in Baxter Stanton's stead to be defeated by a Republican from Fort Lauderdale. A different sort of mandate was given *Scarlet Moon,* Randall Damone's much-touted film opening to mediocre reviews and revenue. Rumors that pristine DVDs of the film were being hawked outside Westwood theaters proved to be untrue, a verdict only slightly reassuring to discombobulated executives.

Closer to home, Smoot Rawlings endured a second surgery that left his intestines a couple of feet shorter than when he went in. First thing the sheriff saw when he woke up was a card that Barrett had fabricated on Sharon's behalf. Smoot's was not an easy recovery, but by February the sheriff was quite literally back in the saddle.

Barrett's arm would take months to mend but his reputation was instantly restored. The same pundits who had raked him over hot coals the previous year now heaped praises on the FDLE's top dog. Florida's attorney general called Barrett personally to insist that his confidence in Agent Raines had never wavered, that the business with Senator Stanton just went to show you.

Exactly what it went to show was not clear.

Altmiller gave Barrett three weeks sick leave which he spent on the beach with the boys and Laura Anne. There was something awfully nice about the Gulf in winter. Wearing a sweater. Watching the tide. The docs told him his arm would atrophy if he didn't put it to use, so Bear bought a kayak second-hand in High Springs and brought it back to the restaurant.

He couldn't paddle worth a damn at first. In fact, the first time he got in the thing he rolled over, which delighted Ben and Tyndall to no end. He started out slowly. No big adventures, just a few minutes daily until he was able to put a steady hour on the water. You could see Bear early in the morning and some days again at dusk, a black boulder in an fiberglass shell bright as a tangerine and not much bigger than a surfboard, the toy-sized paddle working like a windmill.

Took Bear a while to get rid of the side-to-side waddle common to rookies in kayaks, to keep the torso relaxed and stable as he worked the double-spooned oar. Every now and then a powerboat would turtle him, or sometimes he would capsize in the wake of a jet ski. Barrett was surprised to find he looked forward to those unscripted challenges and amazed to discover that we was beginning to actually feel comfortable on the water.

Between sick leave and rehab Agent Raines got more time off from work than he'd ever had in his life. Gave him a chance to relax with Laura Anne, with the boys. He would gladly have given an arm to extend that lazy interval. But it had to end.

Barrett returned to full duty at his Live Oak office with an in-basket stuffed tighter than Dick's hat band. He had about sorted the wheat from the chaff, had responded to the actionable emails and junked the rest, aided by mugs of coffee sopped with honey. He was still henpecking correspondence with one hand, his shattered arm pieced together with screws and plates and propped on a pillow.

He was surprised to find that his plated arm ached worse at the keyboard than it did paddling a kayak in rough water. Amazing how something as apparently innocuous as a computer's mouse could inflict such aggravation. Of course you could always blame the weather. Winters in northern Florida could be bone-cold. This particular day was fairly typical, thirty-eight daytime degrees. Plus it was raining ice cubes. Barrett washed down a junkie's worth of Ibuprofen with a mug of Maxwell House before tackling the final task of the day.

Captain Altmiller had directed the Live Oak office to generate a progress report regarding its investigation of the murders of Midge Holloway, Jack Sandstrom, and Orlando Fuqua. Wasn't much to say. Barrett knew in his gut that Eddy DeLeon was responsible for hijacking the evidence van that became a crematory for Midge and Sandstrom, but it would be a tough case to prove in court. An audit of Orlando Fuqua's holdings did prove that Smoot's detective was depositing large chunks of cash at regular intervals, but there was no way to connect Orlando definitively with Eddy DeLeon or anyone else.

As for Beth Ann's homicide, Roland Reed was happy to tell the one or two reporters who bothered to follow through that the case was now officially closed. There was no new evidence forthcoming, certainly nothing to exonerate Senator Stanton of his daughter's murder. After months and months the in-basket began to slim down and the daily weight of murder and larceny lifted. Barrett kept a routine with his kayak. He'd go fish with the boys, usually off the pier at the restaurant. He looked forward to seeing Laura Anne.

All things close to home.

He did see Sharon Fowler at Harvey's Marina on one occasion. Sharon was just leaving the cafe. Wearing gloves, Bear noticed. He made the attempt at some pleasantry or another but was rebuffed. In fact, Sharon had not initiated any communication since her ordeal, not to Barrett, not to Smoot Rawlings. Barrett reminded himself that he could not interpret that behavior as a personal slight. Sharon had been through a terrible ordeal. Bear had only to look at his own wife to be reminded that the most intractable wounds suffered during an assault lay far beneath the skin.

It would be a long time before Sharon could smell the salt in the air or relish the sun on her skin or look forward to hooking a shark, and that was okay. Barrett was more than willing to let her heal at her own pace.

"But doesn't it piss you off just a little?" Roland challenged him skeptically. "You saved her life, for crying out loud. Isn't that worth a lunch?"

"I've got my meals lined up fine, Roland."

The week before Christmas saw Barrett occupied with new crimes, though there was the occasional blast from the past. Barrett was scrolling his email one morning when he ran across a report that the FBI had video placing a Vietnamese businessman in Senator Stanton's company in Austin, Texas. Probably some fundraiser, Barrett mused, and deleted the text without further inquiry.

He was long past caring about Baxter Stanton. There was a homicide in Madison County that needed immediate attention. Nothing spectacular, just your garden variety shake and bake with a body in a speed lab set up in somebody's tobacco barn. Bear was occupied with that case on the eve of Christmas when

Glenda Starling appeared at his cubicle lugging a U-Haul box on the shelf of her hip.

"Doesn't anyone knock, anymore?" Barrett groused.

"Sorry."

She dumped the box on his desk.

"Roland said you needed to sign off on this stuff."

" 'Stuff'?" Barrett massaged his aching arm.

"Evidence," she replied shortly. "Going to storage. Part of it's from the Stanton case, stuff that Midge sent down early on. And then there's a couple of items related to your sting on Eddy DeLeon."

"Can't we just bury it?"

"Whatever you say. But there's some good stuff."

"Such as?"

Glenda plucked an audio cassette from the litter.

"This is the tape your undercover made on Eddy's boat. Beth Ann's 'Dear Diary'? Could bring a pretty penny."

"Why don't we put it on e-Bay?"

"Here," Glenda offered a ballpoint as she rummaged for a second prize. " 'Nother tape signed to you—'Night Fog.' Is that like hip-hop or something?'

"For sociopaths, maybe." Barrett scrawled his signature again. "Anything else?"

"One more."

Glenda displayed a scrap of paper in a transparent bag.

"It's a receipt," she supplied.

"Lemme see."

When he broke the bag's seal there was just the faintest odor and Barrett felt his stomach turn. He recalled his rush to Beth Ann's commode. That's when he had spotted the scrap of paper now in his hand, the faint aroma of his own bile, still attached, jarring memories off the shelf like the perfume in that O. Henry story.

Beth Ann strapped to her water heater.

Those deep cuts.

That spool of metal in her mouth.

"Oh, right." Barrett smoothed the slip on his desk. "Receipt. For a credit card, I remember."

But then—

"Wait a second . . ."

Barrett took another long look at the water-stained pulp on his desk.

"Bear? Bear can you just sign off the damn thing?"

"Sorry, Glenda, but I need you to call Sharon Fowler."

"Now?"

"Right now."

"She's a pretty busy gal, Bear."

"Tell her I have a story. A big one."

"It's Christmas eve, for God's sake!"

"Just tell her."

Sharon called around noon. Of course, she could drop by. Anything for a story.

"But it probably won't be till after six," Sharon offered as an apology, and Barrett assured her he didn't mind waiting.

As he waited Bear listened to the audio tape that Sharon had given the FDLE. He listened again and closely as Beth Ann cooed her father's sins in that Valley Girl voice. ". . . the senator who likes razors and little girls. See how the voters like that! Fucking hypocrite."

A light fist tapped to interrupt. Barrett killed the tape player and rose to acknowledge the tall woman filling his never-private door.

"Come in."

Sharon stepped inside without acknowledgment. Her hair was back up again in that French knot. Barrett recognized the torquoise set in silver links around her neck. Casual, otherwise, a suede jacket and canvas slacks. She didn't look for a seat.

"Sorry I've been so busy," she opened.

"I understand." His nod directed her to the unoccupied chair.

"So what's this story? Anything I can get on by ten o'clock?"

"Can we just talk a little, first?"

"Sure."

Slipping off her jacket to reveal a short-sleeved workshirt beneath. She kept the injured hand hidden, he noticed. The surgically restored fingers folded beneath the flesh of her uninjured hand.

"Been a while," he opened.

She pulled her chair forward, unexpectedly close, unexpectedly intimate.

"Barrett, I know I've been avoiding you. But I am grateful. And I know I owe you."

"You don't owe me a thing, Sharon."

"Of course, I do. You saved my life, you really did."

"Give Smoot some credit."

"I do, I do." She ran her unscarred hand past her hair. "And I've told myself a dozen times I should call, or write, but it's been . . . hard."

"Laura Anne's gone through something very similar; I got to see it firsthand. It's okay."

"Thanks, Bear. Now—"

Leaning back, offering a smile.

"What's this about a story?"

"Actually, it's more like information. Loose ends, really. Relates to Beth Ann Stanton's murder."

"That's yesterday's news, Bear."

"Might be a new angle to explore." He offered a smile. "Actually, I was hoping you'd be able to contribute."

"Doubt I can do more than I have." She tried to keep the irritation from her voice.

Barrett opened a manila folder. The receipt he had salvaged earlier spread like a butterfly inside.

"I found this in Beth Ann's loo that first day. I was puking in her toilet at the time . . ."

Indicating with delicacy a pink-faded border.

"It's a credit card receipt. Beth Ann signed it. We verified the signature."

"Definitely old news."

"Humor me. The receipt indicates a purchase from a Wal-Mart

in Fort Meyers. A pair of CDs, one by a group called Night Fog. See it? That one there?"

"Is there a point to this, Bear?" she replied coolly.

"Well, as you know, the tape we found stuffed down Beth Ann's throat was also by Night Fog. Looks now like she purchased it with a credit card in Fort Meyers."

"Appears that way. You've got her receipt."

"The receipt, sure. But Beth Ann didn't use her own card."

"No?"

"No. She used yours."

Like a marlin or swordfish used to dangerous waters she refused to rise to his bait.

Barrett read off the receipt, "Master Card. University Credit Union, Tallahassee. I've already verified the card belongs to you, Sharon. Should have clicked with me before, Beth Ann never lived in Tallahassee."

"What is it you want from me, Bear?"

All business, now. All cards on the table.

"I'd like some answers. Like: Did you know that Beth Ann used your card to make this purchase?"

"Yes."

"You never said anything to me about this before, Sharon."

She smiled.

"You never asked me before."

Obviously true. Barrett consulted a scrawl of notes on a pad at his desk.

"Checking your card for the day these CDs were bought, I find a charge at a Fort Meyers marina for diesel fuel. Your signature this time. The boat was rented, wasn't it? Returned later that weekend."

"I was fishing."

"Damn right you were. You were working Beth Ann like a tuna."

"I had her hooked, yes. But I couldn't reel her in."

"So you wine her and dine her and still she wouldn't squeal on Papa?"

"Not to me. Oh, she put out the big tease. Called to say she had an exclusive for me, but was petrified to meet anywhere around Pepperfish Keys. She said she'd be going to a Night Fog concert in Fort Meyers; I arranged to meet her beforehand, in private, so she wouldn't have to worry about Daddy looking over her shoulder.

"But when I got down there the girl totally clanked. Said she couldn't tell me anything about her dad, that if she went public with anything about her father he'd kill her. Which is what he eventually did."

"Why didn't you tell me?" Barrett demanded. "And don't even say it's because I didn't ask you."

She leaned back.

"Barrett, I didn't tell you about Beth Ann because I was trying to develop her as a source. And I don't divulge my sources. Not to you, not to anyone."

"You gave up Eddy DeLeon."

A flicker of anger stirred.

"He tried to buy me off."

"That makes a difference?"

"Yes."

Barrett brushed a speck of lint off his tie.

"Well, there's no point in protecting your source now, is there, Sharon? Because Beth Ann is dead."

"I'm willing to grant that."

"Good. So for the record did Beth Ann give you *any* kind of information regarding her father? Sexual abuse? Criminal activities? Anything I ought to know?"

"Come on, Bear, if she had, I'd have gone on the air with it! I was stuck! I was at a dead end! I had no notion of Stanton's sexual relations with his daughter. All I had was Taylor's allegation that Eddy was pirating films, but I had no way to prove it and I had nothing to connect Eddy's money with Baxter Stanton. Neither did *you,* for Christ's sake."

She crossed her legs.

"When I came to you with the idea of going undercover I was totally up-front about what I knew and what I didn't. I didn't bullshit you. I didn't try to play the saint. Which I have to say at present puts me way ahead of you."

She had a point there, Bear acknowledged privately. "Fair enough, then. Fair enough. One other thing, though, if you don't mind."

Barrett popped the cassette from its player.

"When you recorded this tape, you said that Eddy was right there beside you. He was with you the whole time."

"So?"

"The lab confirms that the tape is definitely a recording of another source, second-generation, probably, and that the background noise is consistent with a boat on the water. But playing it back today I realized that, other than ambiance, there's nothing on this recording except Beth Ann's voice. No comments from Eddy. Nothing from you."

She shifted her jacket and he saw her mangled hand.

"Why would there be? Eddy didn't interrupt because he was gloating over my reaction to the tape. Why wasn't I talking? Well, in the first place I was stunned by what I was hearing—in fact, I couldn't believe what I was hearing—and secondly, I was trying to sneak a recording without getting caught!

"How long are we talking about, anyway, Bear? A minute's lapse in conversation? Less? Considering the circumstance is that so unusual?"

"Thanks for coming, Sharon," Barrett replied, glad to see that her response was sensible, reassuring. "Sometimes I look at things too close."

She offered a smile as she stood from her seat.

"Word from a journalist, Bear. Hardest thing about chasing a story? Especially when it's really juicy? Is knowing when to quit."

Barrett kept that thought all the way home, why he was finding it hard to let go of the Stanton case. He tossed out that problem to Laura Anne, over dinner. One of the things Barrett had missed during his wife's long journey was their restaurant re-caps. It had been habitual for Barrett to eat supper with Laura Anne at Ramona's. It was a blessing to have that ritual restored.

Barrett found his wife at her baby grand. She'd bought a new dress, had Laura Anne, and it was a stunner. Low-backed and wine red. Spaghetti straps over skin colored like cream in cof-fee. Those wide shoulders. Barrett offered her his arm to rise from the piano's bench and heads turned all around, women pausing to see the newly restored owner of Ramona's Restau-rant. Locals and newcomers catching their breath.

"What is it, Bear?"

He realized it had been a year since he'd felt free to burden his wife with any of his own baggage. He had been worried it was too soon to ask Laura Anne for that kind of help. But, as usual, Agent Raines way underestimated his wife.

"Just a case," he threw out offhand.

"You mean the Stanton case," she said. "You said 'a case', but you really mean Beth Ann."

"I'm having trouble letting it go."

"Trouble even naming it," Laura Anne pointed out. "But it's not hard to see why."

"Help me out."

"Let's get a table."

He led her to a booth. Roy brought over a coffee and iced tea and a basket of hushpuppies. Laura Anne made sure they were settled before she reached over to take her husband's hand.

"There is a big difference between Beth Ann's homicide and any other I can think of where you've been involved."

"Which is?"

"You arrested a father for killing his daughter. You had a vi-olent father, Bear. You know firsthand what it's like."

"Yes." Barrett swallowed. "I do."

"But Baxter Stanton was killed before you could put him in front of a jury."

"So there's, what? No closure?"

"None," Laura Anne agreed.

"And I feel cheated?"

"Yes."

"So why can't I walk away? Now that I know it's just a feeling, why can't I let it ride?"

She shrugged. "If that's all there is, you could."

"What do you mean, 'all there is'? What else could there be?"

"Bear, I've seen you work lots of investigations. I've seen you make brilliant calls, stupid calls. But brilliant or stupid you never sat on your first instincts. Even if you turned out to be right, you tried to prove yourself wrong."

"Because I don't want to nail the wrong guy, Laura Anne. For me that's a nightmare—putting an innocent man in prison!"

"Exactly. But in this case did you do that extra work? I realize you've had a million distractions, both at work and at home—"

She stilled his protest with a smile.

"And I know Beth Ann's case is officially dead. But what *isn't* dead . . ."

Laura Anne squeezing his hand.

". . . is in here. So what is it, Bear? What's left to do?"

He hesitated. "It's nothing conclusive."

"I hear somebody saying—'I wish my little voice would go away.' But it's not going to go away, baby. Not unless you do everything in your power to make sure you got it right."

"I don't even know where to start."

"I think you do."

She released his hand, her hair falling heavy as a curtain as she leaned forward. Kissed him gently.

"I think you know exactly what to do."

The competing aromas of stir-fried vegetables and seafood and steak wafted with the ceiling fan's encouragement. Barrett glanced at his watch.

"Is it all right, if I—?"

"Go on, Bear. Go. I can keep a plate warm."

24.

It took half an hour for Barrett to reach the Stanton mansion. Barbara Stanton had abandoned her waterside home within days of her husband's very private funeral and already there were signs of neglect. A riot of kudzu laced the ironwork at the gate in a wreath that strangled the domesticated verge. Barrett could see cancerweed working its way between the cobbles on the driveway. He spotted a patch of rabbit's tobacco in full flower, the telltale heads tiny and white on slender stalks bursting through the carpet of Saint Augustine grass.

Agent Raines eased his unmarked car over what remained of the cattlegap, avoiding the crater where Senator Stanton met his death. Within moments he had pulled up to the house. There was a flashlight in the console. A house key got from the local realtor. Also a pair of latex gloves. Bear stuffed has hands into the gloves. He gathered the key, checked his sidearm, and got out.

The pleasant crunch of pebbles he used to hear when approaching the senator's pine-floored porch was muted now by fireweed. Mounting the steps Bear noted a pair of rocking chairs placed to delay entry through the mansion's delicate French doors. There was no glass remaining in those portals. You could see where shrapnel had grapeshot the walls on either side. Other scars left by the explosion that killed Baxter Stanton remained without repair.

He gathered the key in his hand. There was always something spooky about entering an abandoned home. Added to that archetypal fear was the lore of Barrett's past, childhood superstitions rising from hammocks and graveyards. Stories of dark deeds in dark houses. Old wives' tales, people called them, but Barrett knew only too well that sometimes those tales were true.

The front steps creaked with his weight. He heard a rustle of chains from the porch swing.

A sudden weight thumped to the floor.

"Freeze!"

A rat-tat-tat of claw on pine.

Black shadow striped with white.

Barrett lowered his weapon as the raccoon skittered across the veranda, wide-set eyes sad as an orphan's, a tail matted with sandspurs. Claws scratching for traction. Like the bones of fingers.

"Jesus!"

He pulled a chair aside. The doors gave way with a sudden shudder. Barrett pocketed the house key and stepped inside. Motes of dust hung on rays of light falling through the windows of the twin doors. He tried a light switch.

No electricity.

Barrett climbed the stairs toward Beth Ann's room, his flashlight casting shadow and illumination into phantasmagoria that stalked him on his ascent to that silent chamber.

He stepped into the silent apartment. Heavy-metal posters still leered like gargoyles from the walls of the dead girl's room. The votive candles that Barbara Stanton brought to sanctify the place were long melted into indistinguishable puddles of wax. Barrett revisited Beth Ann's desk briefly. He tossed her chest of drawers, looked again beneath her bed.

Nothing there.

He followed the cone of his light to the bedroom closet. The doors, two of them, slid open on plastic coasters. Her clothes still hung on their hangers. Bear found a couple of blankets on an overhead shelf. A pair of sandals, one of those with a broken strap.

He moved on to the bathroom. Raised the toilet's lid and flushed. Fresh water filling the bowl.

" 'Least the plumbing's fixed," he announced to the empty house.

The linen closet was stacked with towels and linen as if the suite's occupant were at any moment expected to return. Rows and rows of soft brightly striped terry cloth. Barrett could remember hiding in a closet full of soft cloth. The voices outside, the angry voices. The baseball bat in Bear's hand. Waiting for him to come in. To come in.

No time to think about that.

Barrett found the water heater behind the linens, the place where Beth Ann's corpse was discovered. Reaching around that long-cooled cylinder Barrett shivered to remember the other arms that embraced here. He squeezed behind the dead heater, playing his light carefully along the floorboard, then up the wall, to the molding at the ceiling. Not much to see.

"Now, to get out of here."

Barrett grunted and shoved. He couldn't move. He tried sliding off the heater's metal skin. No good. Barrett was stuck, his torso lodged between the water heater and the wall, his legs straddling the contraption. Almost no traction to be gained from the leather soles of his shoes on the tiled floor beneath.

A tight fist that he had not felt in a while began to close inside Barrett's chest.

Don't panic, he chastised himself. You can get out. You just can't be dignified about it.

He jammed his flashlight inside a pocket of his trousers, braced his back into the wall, hands positioned as widely apart as the impotent heater would allow. It was like a bench press, he reminded himself. You didn't do it gradually. You did it fast, hard, recruit everything you could as fast as you could.

"One, two . . ."

Barrett exploded against the eighty-gallon barrel like an Olympic bar. Chest, back, and arms—

The heater rocked forward an inch. Barrett's jacket snagged on a seam of plywood as he yanked free. You could hear the rip of fabric.

"Damn it." Barrett was trying to find the rip with his light when something else got his attention, a panel of plywood popped loose in the crawlspace behind the water heater's pale reservoir.

Barrett was at first only concerned that he had contributed to the further destruction of the house. But as he leaned over to press the panel back flush with the wall he saw woodscrews. Woodscrews. Now, Barrett had done his share of home improvement. On his salary, you had to. So he knew that you didn't need woodscrews to panel a utility closet. This wasn't a place open to view, it wasn't even painted. And you certainly didn't plan on taking the wall apart.

Not normally.

Barrett ran his light over to a neighboring panel, and, sure enough, those plywood sections were secured with nails. In fact, every panel in sight was nailed to its stud except for a small rectangle of plywood screwed into place directly behind the water heater. Barrett took out his knife. A Swiss Army knife. Man could never tell when he'd need a toothpick or awl or stainless steel scissors.

Or a screwdriver.

He was worried that his flatbladed tool would not be sufficient for the Phillip's heads securing the abused panel. But the screws came out easily. Very easily. Barrett steadied his light. There was a niche exposed, now, just large enough to accommodate the overnight bag that waited like a stood-up date inside.

Barrett sucked a jar of air into his chest. He reached in, pulled the bag from its hiding place. Was there anything else? He stuck his flashlight into that hole.

No. Nothing more.

Barrett took the bag away from the crowded confines around the water heater, past the linen closet to the stall of Beth Ann's shower. An unsteady illumination filtered through the skylight overhead; Barrett stuck his flashlight in his mouth as he handled the brass zipper that opened the one-night bag.

A wallet-sized recorder nestled inside, a Sony. Same model as Sharon Fowler's, Bear recognized. A set of headphones coiled alongside the portable player. Barrett plugged in the phones and pressed the eject button to inspect the cassette already loaded inside. It was to all appearances an ordinary audio cassette. No jacket. Unmarked.

Barrett slipped the cassette back into place, making sure its ribbon of tape faced the player's miniature heads. Then he settled the headphones over his ears and punched Play. A hiss of leader held little promise. For a moment Bear thought the tape must be blank and was set to cut it off. But then a Valley Girl voice snapped through:

"Monday, July Fourth, Fort Meyers. Sharon, I made a purchase on your card. Hope that's okay. And lissun, about business, you need to know something. These tapes we're recording? Are gonna cost you a lot more than two thousand dollars.

"I mean let's be fairrr! I'll give you credit for making up the 'Dirt On Daddy,' but I'm the one's got to sell it! I'm the one people have to buh-leeve. So here's the deal:

"I want twenty thousand cash for what I've done so farrr. I can like make more tapes if you need 'em, we can negotiate, but for what I've done alraddy I bag twenty grand or, get this, I'm gunna call those suits intrasted in you in New York and tell 'em when their ace reporter can't, like, find a story, it's no prob, she'll just make the shit up! Like that guy with the memoir.

"Or maybe I'll call *Dateline*, play it up like maybe we're lovers or something, wouldn't be a scur-reeem?

"I've got copies of all our tapes, Sharon. All of 'em. Now, I don't wanna be rude. But you put me up to this gig, remamburr? And now you're cashing in big-time and that's cool. Rully. I just want a piece of the pie."

A hiss of leader returned to bookend the murdered girl's monologue. Barrett sampled the remainder of the cassette. Nothing more to sift from this tape, but there looked to be at least a dozen others, cast like pennies into their canvas keep. Barrett rewound the tape, shed the headset, and placed the lot into Beth Ann's bag. He had his evidence. He had his killer, too.

The flashlight led him downstairs.

The next morning Sharon Fowler received the call from her agent telling her that a five-year contract at six hundred thousand dollars per annum had just been received at his William Morris office from WABC in New York. By nine-thirty she was halfway through her farewell broadcast on KEYS TV.

" . . . *and so the story ends, but does not close. Federal agents continue to investigate the assassination of Baxter Stanton. The senator himself will never face a jury to answer the charge that he killed his own daughter. And as for Eddy DeLeon—? The only thing we know for sure is that the man who courted Beth Ann Stanton was a vicious specimen, and calculating.*

"*What demons drive a sadist like Eduardo DeLeon? What drives a father to take his daughter's life? When does ambition turn to hubris? We may never know. Because the real world, as any honest reporter must admit, rarely concludes as tidily as fiction. But this reporter has tried, at least, to make sense of this chaotic story, and to discern its truth.*

"*I'm Sharon Fowler bringing you the latest, first and for the last time, from Pepperfish Keys.*"

A farewell party followed the broadcast, a non-rummy affair, soft drinks and homebaked pound cake in modest quantity. Almond Sinclair presented Sharon a prepaid ticket, direct to New York, the perfect go-away gift. Sharon accepted the ticket and congratulations from the clerks, techs, and talent eager to participate in the penumbra of her new celebrity. Through the press of those groupies the station's newest engineer, and Dew Drop's replacement, wedged her thin frame shyly between coworkers to reach the rising star's side.

"Great broadcast, Ms. Fowler."

"Thank you. Good job on camera."

"Mr. Sinclair said he'd like to see you, quick as you can. In his office."

"If it's for a raise, he's too late."

An outburst of obligatory laughter rewarding that remark. Sharon smiled to the new hire.

"Tell Almond I'll be right there."

Almond Sinclair's hands fluttered like a gambler's robbed of cards at a desk shoehorned between the station's studio and its newsroom. Modest family photos featured a daughter and a wife with buck teeth smiling before a faux background of "Old Tuscon." The handful of plaques recognizing the news director's two decades of effort propped behind molded folders stacked on top of filing cabinets bulging with things that other men would either discard or display prominently.

But despite that clutter there were only two things that captured Sharon Fowler's attention on entering her boss's cubbyhole, actually one thing and one person to disturb the usual topography. The thing was a small audio recorder propped in the middle of Almond's littered desk. The person, seated and waiting nearby, was Barrett Raines.

"Bear." She ignored Almond's offer of a chair. "You're too late for cake."

"Didn't come for cake, Sharon."

She registered the tone, right away. The set of his jaw, his torso. A straight, military posture.

"Sharon, please." Almond waved hands bereft of a baton. "Take a seat."

"What's this about?" She fished the chair over with her foot.

Her director stilled his hands long enough to start the Sony recorder on his desk.

". . . I mean let's be fairrr! I'll give you credit for making up the 'Dirt On Daddy,' but I'm the one's got to sell it! I'm the one people have to buh-leeve. So here's the deal . . ."

"You know the rest." Barrett reached over to kill the tape.

She didn't give up much, he had to give her that. A flare of nostril. An almost imperceptible shift of posture, no more.

Cold as ice.

"I didn't hear my voice on that tape." Sharon hesitated only a fraction. "In fact, I've never heard that tape until this very moment. And I have no idea where you got it."

"True on both counts," Barrett allowed. "Beth Ann hid this tape behind the water heater. I suppose you didn't notice the woodscrews."

"I don't know what you're talking about." She refused to look at the recorder.

"Always did look to me like Beth Ann's room was ransacked." Barrett shook his boulder head ruefully. "As though somebody were fishing for something."

"It's you fishing now, Bear."

"Here's some bait: Baxter Stanton didn't kill his daughter. Baxter never used a razor in his life. But you did, Sharon."

"This is ridiculous." She glanced briefly in appeal to the news director.

Almond Sinclair perched quiet and pale at his modest desk.

"You needed the Big Story," Barrett went on. "You needed something that would get attention in New York. I couldn't get it for you and you never did find any real dirt on Senator Stanton. So you paid his little girl, his spoiled, angry daughter, to invent a scandal. You gave Beth Ann two thousand dollars to say her daddy was a pedophile, a sadist. Talk about sources, Beth Ann was perfect! At first. Until she got greedy."

"I'm leaving."

"You stay *put*!"

It was Almond Sinclair who broke Sharon's facade.

"Sit," he commanded. And, as if amazed at her own comportment, Sharon complied.

"All Sharon wanted at first was a sensation," Barrett addressed Almond as though his anchor were removed from the room. "Something big enough to kill Stanton's bid for reelection and outrageous enough to put her face on network television."

Barrett turned back to recognize Ms. Fowler.

"But then Beth Ann blackmails your ass. She threatens to rat you out. There goes New York. There goes everything you'd worked for years to accomplish. Shouldn't have come as a surprise, really. You told me yourself Beth Ann was the kind of bitch would drop a match in a room full of gasoline.

"The only way you could protect your source now was to kill her. It's always risky, killing, but there was a bonus to be had with this particular slaughter, wasn't there, Sharon? Because getting rid of Beth Ann gave you the opportunity to break a second scandal. 'U.S. SENATOR MURDERS DAUGHTER.' What an opportunity. A headline to kill for.

"You saw right away how Eddy could be useful. And, of course, you fished me right in and it worked. I arrest Senator Stanton for a crime he did not commit. You take the credit on ABC."

"This is nonsense, I wore a wire to nail Eddy DeLeon!"

Sharon shoved her mutilated hand in his face.

"*This* is what he did to me. If what you're saying is true, what did I have to gain by going on Eddy's boat? Why would I risk it?"

"Because you had to plant Beth Ann's faked diary," Barrett replied calmly. "You had to make it look like Eddy discovered the tape. Eddy was your firewall and you knew I would never compromise it.

"DeLeon didn't change the location for the meeting that day—you did. You took Beth Ann's juicy little lie onto Eddy's boat in your tote-bag. You pulled the antenna on your wire to be sure we couldn't hear whatever actually got discussed belowdecks. It was a nice con.

"And there was a bonus, too. Because the same tape you used to brand Stanton a pedophile could be used to frame him for murder."

"I'm leaving!" Sharon jerked toward the door, but Barrett was on his feet to block her way.

"A good fisherman has patience, doesn't she, Sharon? You had to get rid of Beth Ann, but you waited until the night of Senator Stanton's *uber* party. You made sure you were seen, you finished your broadcast, and went straight back to the station to establish your alibi at the editing bin.

"But you weren't in the bin all night. You knew that sooner or later Beth Ann would come home, she always did. And you made sure you were waiting. Beth Ann always came in by the pool. The back gate. Is that where you hung out, Sharon? I don't think so. More likely upstairs.

"I bet you didn't expect to see Eddy DeLeon. Must have been a bitch, waiting in the shadows for DeLeon to do his business. And then wait some more for Beth Ann to drink her beer and smoke her grass and fall asleep.

"You're strong enough to haul in a marlin, but there was no point in taking chances, was there, Sharon? You waited for Beth Ann to be completely defenseless and when the waiting was done you slit her throat. You dragged Beth Ann to the water heater and took out your frustrations. Then you wiped your prints off the razor and planted it in her daddy's kitchen."

Sharon's smile was grim.

"That's a lot to deduce from a single tape, Barrett."

He reached behind Almond's desk to produce the recovered overnight bag. Shook it. A dozen cassettes rattled like castanets. Sharon's reconstructed hand jerked in a spasm toward her throat.

"Must have been maddening," Barrett prodded. "The one thing to incriminate you beyond question was right there in Beth Ann's room, but you could not find it. You probably knew where she kept everything else—her tapes and DVDs, her dope, her goddamn Tampax. How hard could it be to find a bag full of tapes?

"Is that why you mutilated her corpse, Sharon? Is that why you stuffed a useless cassette down Beth Ann's throat? A fit of pique, was it? Or was it part of the staging? Something else to throw me off?"

Sharon backed away a step.

"That story won't get you past a grand jury, Barrett."

"Maybe not." Barrett opened the bag by its zipper. "But it got me to New York. In fact, it got me all the way to Mr. Reuben Steinberg. Mr. Steinberg, I should mention, is the principal attorney for WABC."

She sucked air between her teeth.

"You son of a bitch!"

"I explained to the gentleman how you came to work undercover for the FDLE, how you snitched on Eddy DeLeon, and framed him, framed the senator, but to be honest Mr. Steinberg was more interested in the tapes you paid Beth Ann to make. I said I'd send copies, if he needed them."

"I've got to go," she said, sweat breaking, finally. "I've got a ticket."

"You won't need it."

Barrett zipped the overnight shut.

"Sheriff Rawlings has your ride."

Perfect Timing

25. *By the time the State* of Florida took Sharon Fowler's life the scene of her crime was reclaimed with a vengeance. Spanish moss clings like a shroud now to the mansion where Beth Ann Stanton was butchered. Tangles of grapevine and kudzu strangle the once-immaculate pleasure dome. A swimming pool glimmers out back, its once-fresh waters now fetid, the Mexican tile once polished and smooth now rough with weather and algae. No one swims here anymore. The pool is a home for frogs. A hunting ground for water moccasins.

A plain of saw grass still marks the boundary between the grounds and Pepperfish Keys. The sun settles blood red into that wide bowl, chasing a flight of pelicans off open water to seek an evening's roost. In a cedar tree, perhaps, or perhaps in one of the beetle-ravaged pines that rise as solitary sentinels from the saw grass's damp pasture.

The private dock that once received Senator Stanton's supplicants and guests extends now like a broken finger, its pilings jammed into the rising silt at odd angles. Like forks tossed carelessly into a kitchen drain. The sun's fiery plunge seems to cut short as it reaches those pointed timbers, as if impaled on the tines of massive silverware, molten and bilious. And below that angry and failing sun, teetering on the pier's unstable extremity is a vision from a fairy tale.

It's Cinderella's coach.

The coach remains as ever a hoax, a fiberglass pumpkin on a rusted chassis. Party streamers long faded hang like dishrags in the carriage's uncensored windows. And it is from that cast-off and artificial vantage that a cop in khaki slacks and a navy blazer holds vigil with a cassette recorder and a gun.

Barrett had been invited, if that was the word, to witness Sharon Fowler's execution, but had declined. Instead, Agent Raines spent the day sorting the desiderata attending the crimes of other liars, thieves, and killers. A small light winks to assure Agent Raines that he's on *record*.

The cassette turning on its tiny axle.

"You get attached to a place, it's hard to let go, but dreams? They'll flat kill you. . . ."

He slips the device inside his blazer.

"A dream tempts you, makes you believe you can have it all. Baxter Stanton had a dream and he used every thing and everybody to make it come true. He used Sharon Fowler at least as much as she used him. He used Eddy DeLeon. He used his wife, his daughter. He used Roland Reed, for sure. He used me.

"And we used him right back. Different reasons, different motivations. Everybody chasing his dream."

A pause. Barrett checks the safety on his Smith & Wesson. Chambers a slug.

"Problem with dreamers is that their grab nearly always exceeds their grasp. You can get away with that now and then. You can kid yourself that you can get away with it forever. But sooner or later. . . ."

He checks his Timex.

"Five," he counts down the seconds aloud, "four, three, two, one . . ."

Barrett displays his cheap watch and his weapon to the man newly arrived at the fiberglass carriage.

"Been waiting for you, Roland. Come in."

State Attorney Reed slaps combs of dog fennel off the cuffs of his woolen slacks. He has left his suit coat in his car but a Mont Blanc pen peeks its cap above the pocket of his catalog shirt and white socks sneak as usual above the tongues of wing-tipped shoes.

"Is that a gun, Bear?"

"Take a seat."

The prosecutor hesitates a fraction before edging into the plastic coach.

"Sharon Fowler was executed just now." Barrett taps the face of his watch for emphasis. "Matter of fact, she took the needle just as you arrived. Guess you could say it's perfect timing."

Reed squirms on the carriage's Naugahyde bench. "That why you brought me out here? To worry over an execution?"

"No, no. Not that."

Barrett holsters his handgun. To Roland's obvious relief.

"Dammit, Bear, you said you had something important."

Roland puffing up, now. Regaining his sense of superiority.

Barrett extends a leg thick as an oak to the prosecutor's bench.

"See, Roland, I never got over that feeling that somebody was ratting out our investigation into Senator Stanton's business. I'm talking early on, before Beth Ann was killed."

"Jesus Christ, that's ancient history."

"Is it?"

"Look, Bear—clearly, there was a leak. I take responsibility for that. Prob'ly some reporter got one of the clerks spouting off. Could have been Sharon Fowler, probably *was* Sharon."

"Bullshit."

"You know as well as I do the woman could talk an Eskimo into buying ice!"

"What about the wiretaps? We never got a tap in place that wasn't tipped off as soon as the warrant was signed. The clerks didn't have that information. Neither did Sharon."

"Who did, then?"

"I did, Roland. The judge did. And then there's you."

"Don't think I like where this is headed."

"It was you tipped off Senator Stanton about the wiretaps, Roland. My guess is you handed him pretty much everything else. You were Baxter's boy."

"That's—! That's preposterous!"

Roland slides toward the carriage's doorless exit. Barrett flexes his trunk of leg to block the way.

"It started out a promising case, didn't it, buddy? A U.S. senator getting dirty money in the middle of a national election. High crimes and high visibility. Perfect for a prosecutor looking to get attention.

"But then Stanton turned up the heat and you panicked, didn't you, classmate? What kind of dirt did he get on you, Roland? Some girl knocked up somewhere? Some cash under the table? Whatever he got, it was big enough to put your ass in jail.

"Of course, you could have fought it. You could have recused yourself and come clean. Or you could have told Baxter to go to hell. But, no. I'm guessing even the hint of jail time was all it took. You've sent too many low-lifes to prison to risk being on the other side of the aisle. Plus, like most prosecutors, Roland, you are convinced that anybody accused deserves conviction.

"So you sabotaged the investigation. You gave Senator Stanton the farm and for that service Baxter agreed to leave your office largely blameless, turning his lawyers instead onto the FDLE. Onto me."

"That's nonsense!" Roland's face is bright orange in the carriage. "That's total conjecture."

"And that's not a denial, is it, Counselor?"

"You want an apology, dammit, I apologize!"

Barrett leans across the already cramped interior.

"And how about Taylor Calhoun? How you plan to apologize to him?"

"The hell did I do to Taylor?"

"You killed him."

"I *what*?"

"You told Senator Stanton I had a snitch working at Mama's. Probably didn't take Stanton ten minutes to pass that information along to Eddy DeLeon, and you knew what Eddy would do. Would have been more honorable if you'd slit Taylor's throat yourself."

Roland presses himself to the wall of the carriage.

"A judge would throw this tale out of court in twenty minutes, Barrett."

"Not going to a judge, Roland."

Barrett reaches into his blazer's vest pocket.

"This once belonged to Sharon Fowler."

He shows Roland the Sony Executive, that compact recorder quietly spooling its cassette on brand-new batteries. The green light shining.

"Thing's been sitting in our evidence room," Barrett commented. "Glenda made me sign for it."

"You son of a bitch! You son of a fucking bitch!"

Fury and fear in Roland's pale face.

Barrett switches off the recorder. Pops out the tape.

"If your resignation is not in the hands of the attorney general by sunset Monday, you're going to be hearing this conversation on the ten o'clock news."

"You think you can bully *me*? *Extort* me?"

Roland's chin wattles like a turkey's.

"This ain't basketball you black son of a bitch! I'm not some second stringer on your goddamn team!"

"Been a long time since we were on the same team, Roland."

Barrett pulls back the leg barring escape.

"Close of business. Monday. Or this black man will bench your ass for good."

Barrett took his time driving from Pepperfish Keys to Deacon Beach, arriving an hour after sunset at his wife's fine restaurant. A gentle breeze redolent with brine pushed in from the Gulf.

Some evening sailor was tacking up-channel against that gentle resistance as a shrimper pushed in from a day's hard labor. You could see the ticklers hanging off the shrimper's nets, the running lights bright and red and green as the working man's boat ran the buoys off Laura Anne's lanterned pier.

There were cars and trucks stacked three deep outside the restaurant. It was heartening to see the return of familiar patrons, the moms and dads and mechanics and fishermen and schoolteachers who were Barrett's neighbors and sometimes even his friends climbing out of their rusted Fords and Chevrolets and Toyota pickups.

And there were newcomers, too. Bear spotted a posse of youngsters spilling like loose change from an SUV decaled with the Seminoles' fierce insignia. A carefree bunch in T-shirts and baggy shorts and low-riding jeans. Barrett remembered Laura Anne mentioning some choral group from Florida State. That must be it. College kids happy to ride ninety miles for a free meal.

A measure of "Moonlight Sonata" escaped from the diner's cedar interior to disperse beneath amber stars. Somebody at the baby grand, for sure, but it was not Laura Anne. Barrett's wife stood at the ornate and sea-salvaged door of her restaurant, greeting out-of-towners and natives alike with a regained and easy familiarity.

She was dressed as if for a summer in Burma. A cotton sarong cinched below a sexy navel. A strapless top. That long scoop of belly in between. Approaching his wife Barrett inhaled an ambrosia of aromas, cinnamon and cumin and cayenne pepper and beer all mixed up and caught in that African hair. All seeped into that remarkable skin.

"How'd it go?" she asked him.

"It's done," he answered.

She smiled.

"You hungry?"

"Ravenous."

"And are you familiar with our menu, Mr. Raines?"

"Remind me."

"Fresh mullet daily. Crab cakes and flounder. Roy has grilled some terrific snapper this evening, and somebody said there was a mess of pepperfish, too, but as you well know that dish has to be taken with a grain of salt."

Her waist warm and firm on his arm.

"It's salty, then? The pepperfish?"

"Oh, it can be, but never you mind. . . ."

She guided him inside.

"I've got something to wash it down."